6 CHAMBERS, 1 BULLET

6 CHAMBERS, 1 BULLET

SONNY BARGER

» with Keith and Kent Zimmerman «

WILLIAM MORROW

An Imprint of HarperCollins *Publishers*

6 CHAMBERS, 1 BULLET. Copyright © 2006 by Sonny Barger Productions. All rights reserved. Printed in the United States of America. No part of this book may be used or reproduced in any manner whatsoever without written permission except in the case of brief quotations embodied in critical articles and reviews. For information address HarperCollins Publishers, 10 East 53rd Street, New York, NY 10022.

HarperCollins books may be purchased for educational, business, or sales promotional use. For information please write: Special Markets Department, HarperCollins Publishers, 10 East 53rd Street, New York, NY 10022.

FIRST EDITION

Designed by Daniel Lagin

Printed on acid-free paper

Library of Congress Cataloging-in-Publication Data

Barger, Ralph.
    6 chambers, 1 bullet / Ralph "Sonny" Barger ; with Keith and Kent Zimmerman.—1st ed.
        p. cm.
    ISBN-13: 978-0-06-074531-8
    ISBN-10: 0-06-074531-2 (alk. paper)
    1. Motorcycle gangs—Fiction. I. Title: Six chambers, one bullet. II. Zimmerman, Keith. III. Zimmerman, Kent, 1953– IV. Title.

PS3602.A833A134 2006
813'.6—dc22   2006041902

06 07 08 09 10 WBC/QWF 10 9 8 7 6 5 4 3 2 1

For Zorana

6 CHAMBERS, 1 BULLET

The bedroom was dark as a tomb, just a beaten-up mattress and some empty bookshelves. Bob Dylan howled "Tombstone Blues" on the box. Loud. Drifting in and out of sleep, Patch Kinkade could barely hear the ring of the telephone above Dylan's nasal litany of the outlaw ghost of Belle Starr, Jezebel, Jack the Ripper, and John the Baptist.

Patch stopped the CD blaster at the foot of the mattress by hitting the pause button with his big toe. He fumbled for the receiver nearby on the floor and knocked over a half-full shot glass of amber, which seeped into a stained, creaky wooden floor.

Hung over a metal dinette chair was Patch's patch. Infidelz MC. Motorcycle Club. All Harley. All men (of course). Closing in on a quarter century as a member. The toughest club on the Left Coast—a challenging distinction the Delz were vigilant about and always defending.

A gruff voice on the other end of the blower was unmistakable. It was Rancid. Not the smell, but a real person named Rancid, a longtime member and current president of the Palm Desert chapter of the Infidelz Motorcycle Club. A handful of old-guard MC members called him Henry. Some Hank. He had a small but serious emergency on his hands.

"Henry. Jesus Christ, it's after three. What the hell?" Patch loathed middle-of-the-night phone calls, a loathing that came with age, relationships, and responsibility. Who was in trouble now? Who'd gotten themselves fucked up with John Law?

Three A.M. didn't used to matter. Back when Patch was an Infidelz MC officer, his phone rang at all hours—calls to party, calls to put out fires or to spring members from stir. Raising bail was bleeding the Infidelz MC treasury dry. The younger officers handled such tasks now, so early-morning phone calls usually meant dire emergencies. Henry ringing this early (or late) meant urgency. He wasn't one for drama, nor was he prone to panic.

"Patch. I'm afraid we gots us a shitstorm here, Chief."

Patch shook the fog out of his head. He was glad he'd spent the day riding in the sun, washing and wrenching on his bike after a long dusty ride, working out instead of drinking himself shitfaced.

"Where you calling from, Henry?"

" 'Cross town, a few miles away from the Palm Desert clubhouse. Did I wake the missus?"

"There ain't no missus, she's long gone." A heavy breath into the receiver. "It's just me and the boy."

Hollister Timmons was the surviving son of the late Oakland Infidelz rider Angelo Timmons, whom Patch brought with him when he'd transferred from California to Arizona.

Palm Desert. About a five-hour ride.

"Clue me in, Hank. What's shakin' on your end?" Three A.M. was no time for social chitchat.

By now Hollister was wide-awake, the boy standing in the doorway of Patch's bedroom.

"What's wrong? Everyone okay?" Hollister asked.

Jeez, the kid's such a pessimist. Patch covered the phone with his palm. "Everything's cool. Something's up out in Palm Desert. I'll handle it. You go back to sleep. You got school."

Hollister shrugged and staggered "walking Spanish" toward his bedroom. Patch was amazed at how the weedy boy had grown and filled out. He was buff and tall—just like his father had been—and judging from the intermittent nightly phone calls from giggling adolescents, it was something the girls had already noticed.

"Patch? You there, brother?" asked the raspy voice on the phone.

"Yeah, yeah, I'm here. What's shakin'?"

"It's Wrangler again." The kickboxer champ, the NoCal Infidelz member, one of Patch's loyal colleagues back when he rode with the club in Oakland.

"What's he doing in the desert? He hates the dry heat."

"He's got that girlie on the side down here, so he splits his time between north and south. In fact, she's the one who called us out."

"Yeah, I know her. Lacy. Sweet, sweet thing."

"Wrangler's been a tad off the rails lately. Don't know how she puts up with it."

"Who, Wrangler? What else is new? You call me at three A.M. to tell me Wrangler's tweakin' again? Well, stop the fuckin' presses."

3 «

"Seriously, last week he got done in for possession of crank and ephedrine with intent to cook."

Bummer. In earlier days, Wrangler had been a walking, talking human laboratory experiment on the prolonged use of controlled substances. Acid. Weed. Dust. Over the last ten years, he'd cleaned up. Or more precisely, it was either clean up or die. Lately, though, just when it seemed like he was home free, Wrangler renewed his romance with home-cooked speed.

"What Wrangler does on his own dime on his own time is no crime. And none of my concern. Although I wish to hell he'd lay off that cookin' crystal shit."

"Well, it ain't that, exactly. He's free on bail."

"I'm failing to see the problem here, Henry. How much was bail set for?"

"Eleven thousand five hundred, NoCal handled that. That's not the crisis."

"Then what the fuck *is* the problem?" Henry had trouble getting to the point.

"Well, he's tweaked out of his tree right now is what, and he's got the pretty little missus holed up with him. I suspect we got us a classic combo domestic-dispute-slash-hostage situation. So far we've managed to keep it low-key. Don't ask me how."

Patch stood up from his mattress and felt another twinge of pain in his lower back. *One day I'm actually going to buy a decent bed.*

"So why me?"

"According to Lacy, he's been asking for you. In fact, he's *demanding* your presence. Like I said, he's spinning out of his gourd, and he's got Lacy inside, God knows—"

"Shit."

"In a nutshell. What we got is Wrangler and Lacy and a virtual arsenal and a huge cache of drugs, holed up in this here house."

» 4   "I mean shit, Henry. Why call me? Do you think the neighbors might have called the cops?"

"Don't think so. Number one, no shots were fired yet. Two, we can't just head out and leave Wrangler. There's no tellin' what he might do."

"No cops involved? You sure?"

"Fuck, no! This here's a Mexican neighborhood. Nobody calls the cops, and they won't come out here anyways on a domestic dispute. Not unless there's gunplay or somebody gets . . ." Henry's voice trailed off.

"Good. Whose house is he at?"

"Not real sure. I'm out front now with a couple of our best club guys." Henry shouted out to them: "Who lives here? Never mind, Patch. Nobody knows. Doesn't matter anyway."

"Shit, Henry, I'm hours away. Are you gonna be able to stave him off that long? It's gonna take me a few minutes to gather my shit, then another five hours on the fuckin' road, man."

"Jeez, Patch. He's askin' for you. Don't shoot the messenger."

"Okay, okay. Keep things as even-keeled as you can till I roll in."

"He's been up for four days as it is. Don't see how another five hours is going to make a damn bit of difference. If anything serious happens while you're en route, I have your cell. Worse-case scenario, we'll throw you a helluva party when you get here. Or else a funeral. Remember that redhead with the tits out to here?"

"I'm leaving now," Patch said.

While Patch didn't relish a five-hour megaputt from Arizona to the SoCal desert, what was his alternative? He didn't want the freaking law poking around. Patch would crawl across broken glass before calling the cops in to clean up any club mess. Besides, Mean Machine was gassed up, all shiny, ready, willing, and tweaked. Obviously, so was Wrangler.

There had been a few changes in Patch's life since he switched bottom rockers from California to Arizona. As much as he'd liked living in Phoenix proper, after eighteen months in the city, he had the unmistakable urge to kick it farther into the desert. He was acting out on a new mantra, which was, simply stated, "Just fuckin' move."

Patch had needed to move. And move he did. He packed up the few boxes that comprised his worldly possessions and landed a modest three-bedroom ranch-style compound fifty kliks (or thirty miles) outside Phoenix on the road to Flagstaff. It was a "distressed property" that had been put up on the auction block. Patch submitted a ridiculous lowball cash bid for the fixer-upper on a decent parcel of land and was shocked when he emerged as lord of the manor. Well, not exactly *shocked*, considering that a pack of desert-rat Infidelz rode up to the auction site and mean-stared anybody else who'd dared to show an interest in entering a competing bid.

Patch's exodus deeper into the balmy Arizona desert had been precipitated by a further need to gather more open space around him, separate himself from people, safely ensconced away from budding housing developments and calorie-laden burger franchises. For the second time in three years, Patch had stood up and requested a transfer within the Infidelz MC. The first time was from NoCal to Phoenix. Not as an officer, but as a foot soldier. Patch's tendency to shed skin from leader to loner shadowed him again. Patch had chosen to widen his retreat and hooked up with a small misfit chapter of Infidelz Nomads, ten other younger riders scattered around various points of Arizona. Like Patch, the Nomads Ten were in no mood to be hog-tied to one dot on the map, except to hook up at least once a week for "church." One member lived as far away as Tombstone. The rest of the guys, mostly loners like Patch, occupied the outlying rural areas and tiny desert outposts, living in trailers and hovels.

There were no hard feelings surrounding Patch's transfer request to the boonies. Besides, it was a feather in the cap for the Arizona Infidelz in general to have inherited Patch from California in the first place. Although he hadn't been a club officer since he served prison time back in the 1980s, Patch was a good man to have around to iron out various problems, resolve conflicts, or arrange sit-downs between different chapters whenever the inevitable frictions arose. Patch was diplomatic; the unofficial point guy to have on hand at the monthly OMs (officers meetings) in order to clarify chapter rules and arrange compromises. Some members called him a conciliator, a role Patch would neither confirm nor deny. The way the club figured it, as long as he was semireachable by phone, he could live and ride wherever he damn well chose. Lately Patch had chosen more solitude.

Good news, bad news. The bad news: Patch hit the highway to Palm Desert at about half past three in the morning. The good news: Patch hit the highway at about half past three in the morning. Perfect time to be traveling light and hauling ass. For two hours he'd race the sun over the mesas before watching the orb rise around Quartzsite. He'd cross state lines in another hour or so after that, then cruise into the arid Palm Desert by breakfast time, meet up with the guys, slam down some black coffee, and come up with a battle plan to crash-land the tweaker. He'd talk Wrangler down before he got himself into deeper shit with felony assault and a trafficking beef. That was the mission. Within minutes, Patch was packed up and rolling thunder.

Nobody on the road but us truckers and deviants. The fast lane was a clear shot for a hundred miles. The Mean Machine thrived on the opportunity to run balls-out and blow out some carbon. It was a green 1997 Road King, hard driven with nearly 140K miles, designed more for long-distance travel than sheer speed off the line.

After a couple of hours of good road vibrations, Patch's travel calculations proved dead on. By Quartzsite, the sun *had* risen up over the dry horizon and it was as good a time as any to gas up. In the old days, Quartzsite had been a fort, a watering hole, a stage-line stop that served as a brief respite from Indian attacks. After Patch gassed up his bike, he pulled over on the side of the road and took a couple of quick hits off a tight pinner joint he'd rolled to groove to the dull hypnotic routine of the remaining desert highway.

After a few hits, Patch dialed up Henry on his cell, hoping that the situation was now under control, had resolved itself, false alarm, and Patch could one-eighty back around, head for home, and call it a ride. No such luck. The situation was a tense stalemate. Wrangler's rants could be heard in the street. Henry and the guys were barely keeping things from boiling over enough to attract the cops.

"Hold on," Patch said, starting up his bike. "I'm a-comin'. Cavalry's on the way."

It was back onto Highway 10, roaring through Blythe with a pleasant buzz before hanging the huge right turn up toward California and Twenty-nine Palms. That's when it started getting hot on the road.

Patch rolled into Palm Desert on a brand-new stretch of freeway. *Shit.* More new freeways sprouted here than on any other region Patch could recall. That's because all roads lead to L.A. On the plus side, he'd made excellent time. It was a little past 8 A.M. Patch dug the cell out of his inside jacket pocket and thumbed the send button, since Henry had been his most recent call.

"I'm rollin' in, buddy. Where'm I headed?"

Henry gave Patch specific directions past the herd of windmills to a part of town that had seen its day, to a dead-end street with only a few shacks with cars, bikes, and trailers parked on the lawns. That was good. Mostly Mexicans and shade-tree mechanics who minded their own business. In minutes, Patch stood in front of a small brown tract house with dark trim while a half-dozen Infidelz roamed the front yard, sitting on a dried-out weeded lawn, trying to be as low-pro and discreet as six giant guys with sparkling motorcycles and wearing garish black-and-orange patches could possibly be.

After going through a combination handshake-and-hug routine, Rancid Henry gave Patch the download. He spat a dribble of tobacco juice onto the dirt.

"He's still up, I take it," Patch said out of the box. He was hoping Wrangler had conked out. That way the party with the redhead with the big tits could soon commence.

"Ooooh yeah, bro, he's up all right."

"That's what I figured."

Crystal meth was a slippery slope that a lot of Patch's pals had slid down over the years, or were still tumbling down. He'd tried it a few times, but he didn't quite understand its appeal. Patch preferred to approach his life—riding, fucking, and fighting—analytically and methodically, with a clear head and an even disposition. Living day to day was enough of a headache. Tweakers were in a mad-dash rush, while Patch didn't feel the need to pile-drive through life at record speed. What's the fucking hurry anyway? That's why Patch preferred pot. Good ol' Mary Jane. She gave him the luxury to step back, slow shit down, and gaze at the big picture ahead. Patch had a mind that worked more like Sam Spade than an Easy Rider, which is why he got calls in the middle of the night to help out.

Meth was a huge bummer for the club, a broad brush that painted many club riders because, well, a lot of them got caught up on its wicked treadmill. Not many could handle its sheer power, and Wrangler was no exception. He'd taken the fast track from low-intensity user to binger to high-intensity tweaker with relative ease.

It didn't help matters that Wrangler was a big motherfucker with a propensity toward violence. Already naturally hyper, being a crystal freak only intensified his shortcomings. He was a hasty guy, known for making bad snap decisions. Throw in the fact that he was tough and built like a house; it took large doses to affect him. As a result, he partook voraciously, snorting mostly, since the club had a strict "no-needle rule," allowing Wrangler to test the thin line of his standing in the club as far as possible. Over time, as each crank rush became less and less euphoric, Patch watched his friends on meth flush each and every opportunity that came their way, from women to gigs. Wrangler, sober and straight, was a patient, talented wood cabinet finisher and a master bike builder and car mechanic. The Infidelz had tried to keep him focused and off the dust, short of the final ultimatum—expulsion. But lately, Wrangler had strayed from his own sobriety program and was now selling the shit, too. If he lived through this episode, Patch and the club would have to put the hammer down.

Enter Lacy. When Wrangler met Lacy, she was the best thing

11 «

that ever happened to him. She was a prime reason why Patch hadn't just hung up the phone when Henry called. She was a sexy, curvy woman (if only she didn't belong to a brother) with a boundless supply of energy, pride, patience, and love for both Wrangler and the club. Patch couldn't count the times that Lacy had kept Wrangler out of jail or the morgue. Lacy, the perfect old lady. It made Patch wonder why her physical and spiritual beauty wasn't enough of an incentive for Wrangler to keep his shit together.

"Gotta know exactly what I'm walking into here." Patch asked Henry as he checked out the front doorway. "Specifically, what's inside that I need to know about?"

"A shitload of contraband. Beyond that, I can't tell ya."

According to Lacy, this was the home of Wrangler's dealer and drug partner. It was filled with an incriminating inventory—drugs, guns, and money.

"Jeez Louise," Patch said. "You guys keep a watch for the law or anybody else. Give me some room and don't come barreling in unless you hear a gunshot or worse." *What could be worse than a gunshot?* Patch shuddered to think what he might find inside. He hated it when corpses were involved. It created a removal problem.

The screen door was unlocked, so Patch opened the squeaky door and crept inside. Wrangler would hear Patch's boots hitting the hardwood. The living room was covered with cocked firearms, loaded pistols and rifles, while the dining table was a pile of clips, money, bullets, and traces of powder, paraphernalia, and rolled-up currency used to snort. Not a comfy home-sweet-home sight.

As Patch rounded the hallway, his first sight of Wrangler standing in a doorway took him aback. He was bare-chested, like a crazed Tarzan meets Rambo, drenched with sweat, thinner than when Patch had last seen him almost a year before, but a solid motherfucker with arms like fireplugs.

"Wrangler?"

"Patch, you made it, dude!" Tears filled Wrangler's jittery eyes.

"You asked me to come, so here I am, brother. So let's talk. Otherwise I rode all this fucking way for nothin'."

With that first exchange, Patch took a quiet but significant step closer.

"You drinkin', sport?" he asked, taking a second careful step.

Alcohol and speed was a bad, bad mix and Patch needed to get closer to survey the situation. Unfortunately alcohol is what Wrangler habitually used to drench and offset his discomfort while tweaking. *He doesn't seem to be hallucinating, one good sign.* Wrangler was valiantly fighting off the inevitable crash, which was the whole point of taking this shit continuously. The crash hangs over the user's head like a bad Monday morning. After a week awake, the crash becomes more and more unavoidable, while the battle to avoid it becomes more and more desperate. Even Wrangler knew he couldn't hold out much longer. Hence the standoff.

13 «

The present situation was tricky and called for extreme caution. Patch figured he was confronting Wrangler at the worst possible moment. He would soon explode into a million jagged pieces. He hoped that his pal was coherent enough to recognize him as a longtime comrade with good intentions, as opposed to a threat to his high. Already long past the depression and lethargy stage, Wrangler's mind was racing like a Thoroughbred. Then Patch noticed the gun Wrangler held in his right hand, a brushed-silver Smith & Wesson revolver Patch had given him as a Christmas present a few years back. Talk about bad karma.

After spotting the gun, rather than retreat, Patch inched a few steps closer.

"I'm here for you, partner." Patch spoke reassuringly, offering his hand.

"It's so good to see you, Patch, so good to see you, so good to see you, Patch . . ."

Wrangler rambled on and trailed off like an endless tape loop. His eyes were alert enough considering the lack of sleep. His speech was sharp and staccato. But then he waved the pistol furiously in a circular motion over his head like a demented bandito. Shit. Patch feared it might go off. On closer inspection, Wrangler's beady eyes were moving rapidly, rolling like a slot machine. Patch slowly took off his colors, hoping to distract him, shaking them in front of Wrangler: Patch as Manolete; Wrangler, snorting and slobbering strings of spit, the crazed bull unaware of its own brutish strength.

"Where are your colors, Wrangler?"

"Colors? Colors? What colors? What color are you?"

Shit. He's well out of it.

Patch prayed a police car wouldn't pull up. A cop's uniform would really set Wrangler off and get them killed.

"I asked you, are you drinkin', partner?"

Wrangler was a mean drunk, meaning he would be much harder to talk down. Or take down. Then Patch saw the near-empty Jim Beam bottle upright on the carpet while another dead soldier lay on its side not far away. *Double damn.* Patch took another step forward. After killing two bottles of Beam, Wrangler was acting far from drunk. Amazing. Patch couldn't get a read on the guy.

"W, put the gun down, okeydokey? I didn't give it to you to wave in my face." On the floor was another piece in its holster, a snub-nosed .38, which Wrangler must have worn earlier but had thrown onto the floor once his skin began itching and twitching with drug bugs. As a last resort, Patch could dive for the piece and neutralize the situation. But that had to be the final straw. Patch was unarmed. Except for his blade, Sharpfinger, riding the back of his hip.

Sharpfinger was Patch's blade of choice. A leather-sheathed fixed blade, three and a half inches sharp, one had hung on Patch's belt for years. He now owned a drawerful of them ever since Schrade, the company that forged the knives, frequently dubbed "Old-Timers," went under in 2003. Sharpfingers were indestructible but getting rare.

Patch gazed past the doorway where Wrangler was standing and into the room. Lacy was tied to a wooden chair, wrapped up with gaffer's tape, extending from her mouth to her neck and dark shoulder-length hair. Her eyes were wide open; she could barely breathe through her nose and control the sobbing.

"You gonna talk to me or not? I mean, shit, I've come all this way, W."

Wrangler grabbed his own head and wept, then pistol-whipped himself with the wooden grips of the S&W. He was hearing voices and trying desperately to bludgeon them silent. Blood streamed down the right side of his head. Then, holding the gun, Wrangler snapped. He spun around toward Lacy and began screaming.

"Bitch. Cocksuckin' slut. Cunt. I'll blow your fucking brains out, you fuckin' sleaze-whorin', cop-callin'—"

» 16   Then Wrangler spun back around toward Patch. Delirious.

"Who the fuck are you?"

Oh, shit. Here we go.

When Wrangler frantically turned around again toward Lacy, Patch dropped his colors and made his move. He dived toward the hulk, jumped on Wrangler's back, grabbing him from behind, encircling his arms around Wrangler's broad chest and gargantuan arms, riding him down like a scared calf. The move infuriated Wrangler, who went even more ballistic. Patch knew no other way than to hold on for his life.

Wrangler spun Patch around the room, his legs flying around like a kewpie doll's, knocking over furniture. After just a few seconds, Patch lost his grip. Centrifugal force took over and Patch flew against the wall and onto the floor. Wrangler jumped on top of him, and the two wrestled, rolling around on the hardwood floor. With superhuman, drug-crazed strength, Wrangler got up and lifted Patch off the floor and threw him headlong into a hutch, shattering the glass doors, the shelves, and the bone china stored inside the upscale piece of furniture. Patch felt his shoulders painfully smash the structure to bits as glass and broken ceramics dug into his scalp and skin.

Patch lay on his back rubbing his eyes. He watched Wrangler aim the gun toward him. Lacy's muffled screams penetrated the gaffer-tape gag. The discharge of a .357 hollow-point rang through the room and the hallway. Fortunately speed freaks are notoriously bad shots, and the bullet went wide of Patch. Then a second bullet shattered the living-room mirror into seven years of dreaded bad luck. Moments after the second shot, Patch saw the room fill up with Infidelz patches.

Five Infidelz tackled Wrangler and wrestled him to the ground, while a sixth, Henry, brought a rope and a Taser. Soon Wrangler was zapped and tied up, drooling and convulsing. Then another member, a youngster whom Patch didn't know, rammed a hypodermic needle into Wrangler's jugular and squeezed the plunger. In less than a minute, he was crashed out, facedown on the floor, out of commission.

Nice work," Patch said as he got up slowly and carefully brushed the broken shards of glass out of his hair. "What'd you stick him with?"

"Fuck if I know, but it sure did the trick. I got it from my brother. He's an epileptic."

"Don't you know this club has a no-needle rule, son?"

"Chief, I didn't . . ."

"Never mind." Patch laughed, clapping the kid on the back. "I'm joshin' ya. You guys saved my bacon."

After a member freed Lacy, she ran over to tend to Patch.

"Patch, did he hurt you bad?" she asked.

"I'm okay, but someone musta heard the shots and the cops gotta be on their way. I say we sweep this place for any club stuff, most of the money, and then get the fuck outta here," Patch said. "You guys throw Wrangler in the truck."

In minutes, Patch, packing Lacy on the back of Mean Machine, headed north for Berdoo. He veered off into the mountains, up toward Lake Arrowhead, just as the rest of the Inland Empire had begun their zombie morning commute into the Los Angeles basin. Rather than join that throng, Patch headed the opposite way to a little breakfast joint he remembered from years back. Hopefully it was still there. A ride into the mountains for a pile of eggs, bacon, hash, and a righteous stack of pancakes with a babe on the back of his bike sounded like just the ticket after a mad wrestling match with a drug-crazed behemoth as immense as Wrangler.

Patch felt the firm squeeze Lacy had on him as she laid her head on his shoulder while the two glided through the open and windy uphill mountain road. A tinge of loneliness ran through his body. Someday he'd find himself another old lady that he could call *his* own. Then he remembered the redhead he'd be seeing tonight. Someday might be tomorrow night.

At sundown, on the south end of Phoenix, near a factory district, three Infidelz Nomads on bikes congregated in a secluded area behind a small abandoned industrial park. An Infidelz Nomad van pulled up. One of the bike riders motioned the driver to park the vehicle a few dozen feet away from the bikes. The van's driver, Wheeze, an Infidelz Nomad uncomfortable off his motorcycle and behind the wheel of a rented van, shut off the engine and waited. A few minutes later, another van pulled up toward the three waiting Nomads bike riders and van. One of the Nomads went by the name of Baldy Boris Badenov. He did the talking, while his two brawny cohorts, Sanchez and Tito, stood sternly as taciturn bodyguards. Wheeze, parked nearby, listened in.

"How we doin' here today?" Boris asked the driver of the second van cheerfully, offsetting the seriousness of his two partners.

The driver of the second van jumped out of the vehicle. He twitched his shoulders and shuffled his feet nervously. He looked around behind him, causing Sanchez and Tito, both wearing mirrored wraparound glasses, to scowl and tighten their neck muscles.

"So far, we're under control," said the van driver, lighting up a smoke. He had dark spiky hair. "I'm a little wiped out, and to tell you the truth, I shoulda taken a leak before I left," he continued, blowing smoke out of his nose. "Can I get your two guys here to help load up my wagon while you and I settle up? I got the cash in the back of the van. You plan on counting it?"

Boris nodded slightly. "I'll know it when I see it."

"Don't worry. It's all there."

"Better be," Boris said, his smile evaporating into concern.

With the back doors of both vans wide open, a black canvas gym bag filled with $100,000 in tightly packed twenties and fifties was handed over to Boris, who took it over to Tito's ride, rested it on top of the bike's seat, and unzipped the grip. Boris rustled through its contents without taking any of the tightly wrapped stacks of crisp new bills out of the bag.

As for the cargo, whoever was buying this haul was getting a real steal. A belt-fed machine gun, new in the box. A couple of Barrett .50-caliber rifles. Winchester shotguns. A cache of pistols—semiautos, single- and double-action revolvers. Assorted ammo.

21 «

Several long wooden crates and square ammo boxes were slid out of the back of the Infidelz's van and were hastily stacked into the spiky-haired guy's van. The exchange went down quickly, after which Sanchez slammed the other van's back doors shut. The spiky-haired driver jumped back inside his ride and gunned his engine. Sanchez walked over to where Boris and Tito were standing over the canvas bag.

"We happy?" he asked Tito.

"Yeah," answered Tito coldly. "We a hundred-grand happy." Sanchez gave the thumbs-up sign to Wheeze in the van.

"Can I get outta here now?" the spiky-haired driver asked nervously.

"You're loaded up and free to go, brother. Enjoy your haul," muttered Boris as he scooped up the bag and jogged briskly toward the back of the Nomads' van. He tossed the booty inside and watched the gym bag slide up and hit the back of the driver's seat. Wheeze turned around and placed the bag on the front bucket seat next to him. Boris slammed the van doors, making sure both were securely locked. Then he walked around the van to his wheelman. Wheeze rolled down the driver's-side window and started the van's ignition as the two spoke quietly.

"You know where to meet," Boris said.

"Roger," Wheeze answered.

Both trucks slipped into gear then rolled out of the back driveway of the industrial park. The van now loaded with weapons made a right turn onto a frontage road while the Nomad van made a left toward the freeway. Both vans were out of sight in a matter of seconds. After that, the three remaining Infidelz bike riders retreated back to their Harleys, threw one another loose salutes, fired up their engines, and scattered in separate directions, with Boris following in the general direction of the Infidelz van.

The deal was done in less than a quarter of an hour.

After the gun deal went down smoothly, Baldy Boris and Sanchez putted on their bikes directly over to the Delz's "middlemen," a shady pair of Baldy Boris's buds who located the gun suppliers and bought the weapons with the front money Boris had given them. The two Infidelz pulled up to an anonymous industrial loft space to deliver the last installment of dough. Baldy Boris pushed the intercom button down for one long and two short buzzes then jumped back onto his ride. Within minutes the large metal security door was raised as both Infidelz scooted their bikes into the ground-floor workshop. There were no signs outside the building. This was where the two arms peddlers lived: a place where they also built special-ordered customized bikes and choppers, selling them off to jaded and wealthy RUBs. Rich Urban Bikers.

As the garage's door slid back down into the locked position, the two Delz riders approached a pair of white heavyset guys wearing matching navy-blue mechanic's coveralls. They were eating fat deli sandwiches and drinking coffee, seated at a large rectangular workbench in the middle of the workspace. A boom box blasted vintage Black Flag. Sanchez threw the small dark canvas grip full of money onto the tabletop and shoved it toward the two men. Boris reached over and turned down the music.

Romanowski, nicknamed Ski, and his partner, Kemp, were friends of Boris's since childhood. Boris, an Arizona native raised by Russian immigrant parents, was strictly working-class stock, as were Ski and Kemp. Together they'd started an early association shoplifting candy bars and baseball cards, graduating to small burglaries. Since they had a history, Boris saw them as the perfect middlemen he could trust and lean on. Ski and Kemp weren't exactly hardened thugs; they were just opportunists and scammers.

"Here's your final cut," said Boris, "another twenty-five grand, which I assume is all yours. Sweet pay for just a couple of phone calls, huh?"

Ski unzipped the money bag and dropped a few bundles onto the table. The transaction was paid out in bundled twenty- and fifty-dollar notes. He flipped through a couple stacks, stuck one pack up to his nose, and took a strong whiff—mmm, inhaling that unmistakable scent of fresh currency.

He gave a hearty thumbs-up to Boris and Sanchez. "That's magic, guys. Can we get you fellas something? A Pepsi or some coffee? "

"We're cool," said Boris, speaking for both riders.

Kemp stood up and walked into the other room. While the Infidelz small-talked further with Ski, Kemp returned with a money-counting device tucked under his arm. He set it down on the workbench top, unrolled the power cord, plugged it into a nearby electric socket, and pressed the on switch. He reached over and dumped the bag's entire contents onto the table, then sorted out the bundles in two high stacks of twenties and fifties.

"No Benjamins. Just twenties and fifties," Kemp observed.

"Hey, it's legal tender. In God we trust."

"This shouldn't take too long. Who delivered you the dough?" asked Ski.

"The guys who fronted the deal on the other end, and that's all you guys need to know," said Boris.

Kemp slipped the bands off a few random bundles of twenties and loaded up the counter. He grinned as he heard the rapid fluttering noise.

"Don't you dig that sound? I sure do." Kemp was a currency connoisseur.

The digital readout amount was right on the mark. Kemp readjusted the denomination setting on the counter and opened up two packs of fifties and placed them into the machine. Then he took out an individual bill and tugged at both ends of the crisp unused note a few times, making a flapping sound. He nodded again with approval and brought the fifty up to a low-hanging fluorescent light hovering over the workbench. Kemp stared through the bill carefully. Then he grabbed another fifty out of the counter tray and held it up closer to the light.

The good-natured expression on Kemp's face turned somber. He knocked over the stack of bundled bills, opened another random package, and pulled out a single bill from the middle of the stack. He held it up to the light.

Kemp looked over at Ski and frowned. Kemp flashed a nervous stare at Boris and Sanchez.

"Anything wrong?" Ski remarked worriedly to Kemp in a low voice. "Problemo?"

Boris and Sanchez moved in closer.

"Dunno," said Kemp, staring intently through U. S. Grant's face with the glare of the fluorescent tube shining through. "There's a subtle lack of sharpness. Something's not right."

"What's not right?" demanded Boris. He stood next to Kemp and peered closely at the lighted bill. "I don't see anything wrong."

Kemp took the currency from the light and checked the printing. "This bill is dated 2005. It feels right, the texture seems cool, but something looks wrong. Lemme go get the manual for this machine from the other room."

"You don't think this money is—" Ski couldn't utter the C-word as his partner disappeared into the back room and returned a minute later.

Kemp flipped through the book then took another virgin fifty and held it up to the light.

"What's going on here?" asked Sanchez.

"Give me a minute," said Kemp. "It says here that on Grant's collar just under his beard is supposed to be tiny script that says 'The United States of America.' " Kemp scrutinized another fifty in the light. "Shit, it's not here. This is weird."

Kemp studied the manual again. "New fifties are supposed to have the word *fifty* in all caps repeated on both side borders. I don't see that. Damn."

Kemp snapped his fingers at Ski. "Gimme a couple of those twenties."

Kemp referred back to the book while Ski handed him two Andrew Jackson'd notes.

Kemp grimaced as he examined the twenty-dollar bills. "Fuck!"

"What's up?" asked Boris.

"These may be phony, too. If you look at the lower right-hand corner of a new twenty, there's supposed to be a faded watermark image of Jackson's face. There's none here. See for yourself."

Ski pulled out a twenty from his own pocket. "Check it against this one."

"Yeah," said Kemp, "there's the watermark on your bill, but I don't see it on the ones you guys brought in. Check it out, Boris." He held up Ski's bill.

"You see it there?"

"Yup."

Then he held up the bill from the new stack. "Look. No water-mark."

"Fuck this," hissed Boris.

Ski flicked on a small ultraviolet lamp located inside the

money-counter contraption. He stuck another twenty-dollar bill underneath the beam.

"According to this," said Kemp, reading from the manual, "there's supposed to be a watermark to the right of Jackson's face that says 'twenty' spelled out and 'USA' in all caps right underneath. Then to the right of that, it's inverted to say 'USA' and 'twenty' underneath."

"I don't see either one," said Ski.

"Lemme see," insisted Boris. While he couldn't locate the watermark on the fresh note, he spotted it easily on the twenty from Ski's pocket. "Damn, the paper feels real to me. Maybe these are just brand-new bills and they're changing them all the time."

"This cash looks counterfeit to me," said Kemp gravely.

"Sounds like we got us a big problem here," said Ski firmly. "To the tune of twenty-five grand. These bills are bogus. We're not taking this money. You guys must have gotten fucked over on your deal."

"Jesus." Boris put his hands to his forehead and started hyperventilating with rage. This couldn't be happening. He had never seen a counterfeit bill, much less a whole bag of them. "Shit, I can't fucking believe this!" he muttered to himself, and then stomped his steel-toed boot on the concrete floor.

"Well, Boris, you better believe it. I've handled enough cash in my day. We've been burned."

"What the fuck?" said Sanchez to Boris, heart pounding.

"Look, you guys," said Ski to the beleaguered Infidelz Nomads. "We've been doing biz together for, what, a couple years? You gotta sort this thing out right now. We need to get paid. You know our terms. Forty-eight hours. That twenty-five thousand was our profit, man. What the fuck?"

"Those goddamned motherfuckers burned us!" said an enraged Boris to his cohort. "This is fucking unreal."

"You need to get to the bottom of this right now," Kemp repeated.

"Look, Boris, you're family, and we respect the club," added Ski, "but you got to see things from our side. I don't have to tell you—"

"I know, I know," said Boris irritably. "Just give us a little more time to sort this whole thing out and get you your twenty-five grand."

Kemp shook his head anxiously. "You need to take care of it *today* and get us our cash. Either that or get us back the guns."

Sanchez stepped away and phoned the Nomads clubhouse. As the call went through, he looked back over at his middlemen. "Don't worry, we'll deal with this."

"This is highly fucked up," Sanchez said under his breath.

Sanchez waved his hand as he spoke into his cell phone. "Hello? It's Sanchez. No, everything is not okay. You need to call Tito. We got problems. Right. I'll explain later. Okay. Fine. Okay. Listen, just get Tito down there. Boris and I are on our way back."

Ski picked up the bogus currency, stuck it back inside the grip, zipped it closed, and handed it back over to Boris. Kemp raised the metal garage door.

"Look," said Boris as his rage kindled with each succeeding minute. "Nobody's going to fucking burn the Infidelz. This will be dealt with."

"You guys go do what you gotta do to get the hardware back."

Boris and Sanchez revved up their Harleys out front.

"Somebody's in for some heavy shit," Boris said. "Nobody, and I mean nobody, pulls this crap on us and lives to brag about it."

"A hard rain is gonna fall." Sanchez sneered.

The two veered off and roared into the traffic.

The next morning, a Spanish-speaking dude dialed 911. He sounded plenty freaked out. It was the start of another workday when Sheriff's Deputy Tom Howe got the call. Now he had four dead bodies to go with his doughnuts and coffee. The call came in from Angel's Meat Packing, a Latin outfit that had been operating in an unincorporated part of Phoenix for four generations.

Howe sent ahead a small army of deputies, a forensic expert, and crime-scene people to cordon off the packing plant. As he arrived on-site, Howe recognized FBI Inspector Rance Kelly's car already in the lot. Another telltale government-issued vehicle was parked next to his.

Howe turned to one of his cohorts. "I want you to run a check on this meatpacking outfit to see if they have any ties to criminal enterprises or street gangs. See if they hire cons to work there. And don't forget the Mexican Mafia."

Not a lot of the employees spoke English, and many of the illegals ducked out the back. There was tension in the air as local and federal cops secured the premises. Tagging along with Inspector Kelly was another federal agent called Lockwood.

"Say hello to Ed Lockwood, Tom." Howe and Lockwood shook hands.

"I'm with the Secret Service," Lockwood replied.

"Secret Service?" Howe seemed confused. "Where you head-quartered, Ed?"

"Straight outta D.C.," Lockwood answered.

Howe scratched his head. This was shaping up to be a real unique case.

Howe had never met Lockwood before, but he knew and liked Rance Kelly. Feds were promoted and reassigned in and out of Arizona all the time. The state had become a federal law enforcement minor-league farm system. But Kelly had stayed long enough to make friends across the law enforcement spectrum.

"Wait'll you see this one," Kelly said, approaching Howe. All three men donned rubber gloves and nylon jackets, uncommon pieces of apparel for Phoenix in the hundred-plus-degree summertime. Howe slipped the freezer jacket on. It was a few sizes too small, which caused his ample belly to protrude. Not a good photo op. So Howe left the garment on the chair and entered the freezer in his shirtsleeves.

Technically it was a walk-in meat warehouse. A gargantuan cooler where huge sides of beef could be cooled down and frozen in a matter of hours. The cops entered the freezer through a large electric garage-style sliding door, one of several entrances that made it plausible, even easy, to wheel in deliveries of massive cow and pig carcasses. One of the meat plant's senior employees who spoke decent English led the trio of LE through dangling cattle carcasses, half sides of beef, slaughtered hogs, and mile-long links of sausage hanging from foreboding meat hooks. The temperature inside was a brisk thirty-four degrees, relief from the relentless Phoenix sun outside.

The crime scene took Howe aback. He hadn't ever seen anything like it. Not so much grisly as artistic. Four human beings were posed impressively, frozen stiff astride motorcycles, all

Harleys, all beautiful mechanical specimens, side by side. Four frosty snowmen, big men, straddling four frosty "motorsicles." Had one tipped in the right direction, the others surely would have toppled like dominoes. But they'd remained upright, and the stiffs looked clean, calm and serene.

The only other mark, aside from small gunshot wounds to their heads, was an odd set of lacerations carved on a bald bike rider's right forearm. On the outside of his arm, the detectives could see four parallel cuts, each perhaps an inch in length. None of the cops had any idea what kind of wounds they were. They weren't severe enough to be considered a major injury. More like a signature. A calling card.

"Unfuckingbelievable," said Howe. "These men died with their boots on. How'd they get in here?"

The company guide shrugged. "Beats the hell outta me. Morning shift found 'em about eight-thirty."

"Isn't there a graveyard shift?"

"Not since the cutbacks and layoffs."

From a distance there was no sight of blood. Up close, that wasn't quite the case. Three of the victims had shoulder-length hair that was now taut and iced, as if they'd been caught in a blizzard for hours. The backs of their heads were caked with small circles of frozen blood. The fourth rider had a shaved head with more obvious head wounds. Upon closer inspection, these were small-caliber holes through the left side of each of their heads, with matching exit wounds coming out the back of their skulls. Again, there was very little blood, as if they'd been wiped clean. The baldy was bearded, with tiny icicles hanging from his eyelashes, brows, facial hair, and mustache.

All four victims wore the same patch from the same club, their colors black and orange.

Howe turned to Kelly.

"Jesus Christ. Infidelz."

"I *thought* that might interest you," said Kelly.

"Can I ask you a question, Kelly?" Howe asked, motioning him toward one of the hanging meat carcasses. "In private?"

"Sure, Tom."

"What's with having this guy Lockwood around?" Howe inquired.

"Secret Service is part of the Treasury Department," answered Kelly, citing Law Enforcement 101.

"Yeah, I know that, but where's all this goin'?"

"I'll show you," Kelly said, leading Howe back to the bizarre row of bodies straddling bikes. Walking over to the bald bearded biker, he reached his rubber-gloved hand into the inside pocket of the rider's vest. He pulled out an inch-thick pack of fifty-dollar bills.

"Counterfeit?" Howe asked.

"That's right. All four of these guys had phony dollar bills stuffed in their mouths. Among the four of these corpses, we've sifted through what looks like a hundred grand worth of phony greenbacks in twenties and fifties. Maybe more."

» 32

"Jesus," said Howe, stuck on the word. "You're sure they're bogus?"

"Positive. So, what do you think?" Kelly asked Howe.

"Isn't it obvious? Biker-gang retaliation. Only I'm surprised these guys, the victims, are Infidelz. They usually dish out the punishment. The bald guy was beat up the worst. His nose looks freshly broken. The rest have visible scars, but that looks like ancient history. We'll find out more once we slab 'em. I'd say we got a street war on our hands. I've seen it before. We'll see it again. No big mystery," Howe replied.

"Can we get outta here already?" Kelly asked. "I'm freezin' my tits off."

"Yeah, sure," said the shirtsleeved Howe, who hadn't shivered once.

"Isn't the work a little clean for rival biker murders?" FBI

Inspector Kelly asked, taking off his parka in the hundred-degree weather. "Didn't you notice the precise small-caliber entry and exit wounds? And those weird scratches?"

Howe cleared his throat with a cough. "Believe me, these fuckin' bikers are capable of almost anything. They're a ruthless pack of bastards. Lately they've recruited some technicians, professional killers. Then somebody encroaches on somebody's turf or business interests, probably from out of state. We've had trouble with the Infidelz for years, especially the last couple. One thing bothers me, though. I hate to think that the Infidelz are passing bad money on the streets. If so, that's a new one on me. We've got the gang squad investigating them, but they've never mentioned anything about counterfeiting. But these guys live in their own world. They operate by their own rules. Personally, I say we keep this low profile for as long as we can. It serves nothing to call a press conference. And don't be surprised if we find another fresh batch of corpses. Hell, if bikers wanna kill each other, shit, that's fine by me, not speaking officially for the sheriff's department of course, but you get my drift."

Kelly scratched his head with uncertainty. "I hear ya. Makes my job easier, too. But I don't know how long we can keep this mum. Tom, I got Homeland Security to answer to nowadays for this stuff. Jesus, this could get a lotta play in the press once it hits. Let's talk later and get our stories straight."

"There's nothing to discuss." Howe chuckled. "Resort to the usual. 'No comment. Investigation pending.'"

The two men headed out of the freezer, pulling off their rubber gloves, leaving the Secret Service agent behind to conduct further tests on the bills.

"Early lunch?" Kelly asked.

"Hmmm," Howe answered.

"I'm buyin' at the diner."

"Best offer I've had so far."

Later that afternoon, Tom Howe had the bodies ID'd from county criminal records and resources before they thawed.

The longhairs:

Donald "Tito" Woods
Chester "Wheeze" Raymond
Miguel Ernesto Sanchez, a.k.a. "Sanchez"

The baldy:

Alexander "Alex" Yeshenko, a.k.a. "Baldy Boris Badenov"

No next of kin listed for any of them. All were patched members of the Infidelz Nomads.

Since Wrangler didn't die, there was no funeral. So when Rancid Henry talked about throwing a party for Patch (instead of a wake for Wrangler), he wasn't fucking around. At the Palm Desert Infidelz clubhouse, the chapter rolled out the barrel: a major bash with Patch Kinkade as the attending guest of honor. Besides the West Coast Delz chapters, brother clubs made the scene, young and old, from the Bushido Blades on Jap bikes to original members of the King Snakes on vintage knuckleheads. There were more than enough ladies to go around.

The NoCal Delz led by Prez Ahab, riding front right, made a slow-roll entrance of pomp and torque. It was a Delz reunion of sorts. Streeter, Eight Ball, Mitch from Sonoma, Frisco Paul, Red, Richmond Pete, and a few youngsters, new members Patch didn't know. It was a welcome sign that the northerners were in-fusing new blood. Patch, already a little stoned and a little drunk, hugged and sloppy-kissed them all.

Patch and Ahab exchanged a few good-natured punches. Ahab whipped out his commemorative pistol, a proud trophy, a Colt .45 six-shooter.

"Very nice," said Patch. "Just don't shoot out any streetlights tonight, okay? Remember what happened last time? You dark-ened the whole block."

"We'll see, we'll see." Ahab smiled, nodding his head. Just then, a young eighteen-year-old biker college girl dragged him away with very little resistance.

"Patch Kinkade," boomed a deep basso voice from behind.

Patch replied even before turning around. "What are you doing down here, partyin' on a school night? Didn't your mama raise you proper?"

"You leave my mama outta this." Rollie George stood smiling with his arms folded, a wide grin on his black-as-night face. He looked like ebony Mr. Clean, red kerchief tied around his bald dome. Toned and in solid shape, Rollie was no small fry, but the two black sergeants-at-arms who surrounded him made him look like a peewee.

"We happened to be nearby for a black biker Roundup meeting and heard you were the subject of some serious partying. So here we are, the only black dudes here."

Patch introduced Rollie around, though most already knew him as the longtime founding president of the foremost black bike club, Soul Sacrifice MC out of Oakland.

"What brings you to the California desert, Patch?"

"One of our guys, Wrangler, needed a little straightening out. He's sleeping it off."

"How's Arizona treatin' you?"

"Hot and cold. Hot, the weather, which you know I like. Cold, the cops, which you know never stops. They don't let up."

Just then Rancid Henry bounded out of the clubhouse door, addressing the riders who were outside with a bullhorn. The crowd had grown, men clutching their beers, out for a little fresh night air or a quick smoke or toke. Inside, the clubhouse was packed with revelers. With Rancid Henry's announcement, it would now get tighter inside.

"Dancing-girls time! Dancing-girls time!"

Henry grabbed Patch, who saluted Rollie as he was forcibly ushered inside to an empty chair that was taped off and reserved, sat him down, and pushed a fresh cold longneck into his hand. Patch was front and center and before him was a huge steel cage with a large swinging door, held open by Big Bird, one of Rancid Henry's lieutenants. After a pair of dancing girls stepped into the cage, Big Bird shut and locked the cage door.

MC Rancid Henry grabbed the mike. "All right, you guys, I'd like to introduce two lovely sisters just down from Reno. Let's hear it for Layla and Leila!"

Up went the music. "The Rover" by Led Zeppelin. Down went the lights. Layla and Leila undulated their bodies to roaring approval from the men in the room. The cheers were deafening, especially when the dancers shed their glittery costumes. All that lay between the two girls and the ravenous pack of sex-crazed coyotes tossing greenbacks inside the cage was that one locked cage door.

Patch closed his eyes. This was the right place to be at precisely the right time, kicking back as the beer he was holding quickly rose to room temperature. Amid the exhilaration, Patch felt a light and persistent rub on his shoulders. He turned around slowly to the sight of a long cascade of curly red hair, huge green eyes, and curvy breasts. Seconds later, she was straddling his chair, face-to-face, her back to the dancing-girls cage, obstructing his front-row view of Layla and Leila. Patch didn't mind in the least.

"I'm supposed to take you out back."

"You lead, I follow."

"And Rancid instructed me to pay strict attention to your every need tonight. Remember me?"

Patch scanned his long-term memory. Cloudy.

"Yeah. Susan, no Suzi, no Samantha, help me out here, babe."

"You remembered!" The redhead's green eyes lit up and her full lips puckered. "Since you remembered me, you get the royal treatment." Trouble was, Susan/Suzi/Samantha didn't designate which was the winning name, but it didn't seem to matter. She pulled Patch to his feet and led him to a back bedroom, part of the clubhouse. As they entered the small room, Patch latched the door and turned around just as Miss S pushed his back to the closed door. She planted a kiss on Patch's lips, and as her hands made their way mischievously down his shirt, she fumbled with his belt buckle. Patch reciprocated by unbuttoning the girl's soft lavender blouse, revealing a pair of softer thirty-eights and a pair of enormous pink nipples that drove him crazy.

After a few deep kisses and a ceremonial unbuckling, the redhead fell to her knees, her shirt open, and went to work. Patch closed his eyes as his heart pounded. He could feel her lips and then her mouth and then her throat devour his cock as she eagerly worked it to strict attention. Patch looked down and saw her eyes smiling coyly with the pleasure she was giving. Her oral skills were making his knees buckle and his legs weaken. Patch slightly shivered and shook while the redhead remained on her knees, moving her lips and mouth faster over his erect unit. Patch wasn't sure he could remain standing much longer, let alone savor this experience and delay his orgasm. He tried holding back, summoning up a few Roberto Clemente batting averages, but the divine Miss S sure wasn't holding back as she kept up the pace, not too brisk, with just the right cadence and speed and sounds, making his climax inevitable. Patch felt the works inside his body begin to quiver and crescendo. An eruption was imminent. As she brought him closer and closer, Patch could feel a layer of anticipatory sweat forming on the redhead's shoulders, where he held on for dear life, her head and breasts bobbing rhythmically. It would only be a matter of seconds before he lost it.

Just then, Patch felt a vibration buzz at his heart. It startled him at first until he realized it was his cell phone. *Fucking thing. Don't answer.* The vibrations continued for four more buzzes, then stopped. It wasn't fair. This lovely, ample-breasted redhead was supposed to take precedence tonight. But the intrusive vibrations started up again, and while the redhead persisted on her mission, unaware of the rude interruption, unfortunately the cell phone persisted as well, and at an increasingly annoying rate.

"Shit! Fuck!"

Patch stopped the girl, reached into his breast shirt pocket, and flashed her an embarrassed half smile with a raised forefinger, as if to say, "Give me just one minute, darlin'," and he took the phone call. *Shit.*

"This is Patch and this better be good. No, strike that. This better be excellent fucking great."

It wasn't good, especially since it was Hollister's voice calling in. He'd been trained to phone only in dire emergencies.

"Patch. I've been trying to reach you. I'm sorry to bother you, but, well, we've got a problem. A big problem."

A rush of sobriety suddenly flew through Patch's body, bringing him down hard, crashing from his sexual high.

"Can't it wait?"

"Four Infidelz Nomads. Dead. Murdered. Frozen."

Patch sobered immediately.

"Slow down, slow down. What murder? Frozen?"

At the sound of the word *murder,* the redhead stopped what 39 **«** she was doing and looked up in alarm.

"The Nomads. Frozen dead bodies," huffed Hollister. "It's fucked up. We need you here now. The chapter is out looking for you. The phone is ringing off the hook here. There's an emergency meeting set for tomorrow morning. Didn't you check your messages?"

"Me and the boys were riding all day, dirt-biking in the desert. Out of range. Hollister, listen carefully. Who got killed? Do you have any names?"

"Uh-uh, I'm not sure, Patch. It's on TV. But no names. Club guys here are scrambling for facts."

Hollister was a head case on a good day. In a panic, he got his facts completely messed up. There was no use trying to get the full story now, judging from the alarm and confusion on Hollister's part.

"Listen, Hollister. Do me a big favor. Calm down, get your

facts straight, and I'll call you back from the road. When's this fucking meeting supposed to be?"

"Eight-thirty tomorrow morning."

Great. It's a little past 1 A.M. West Coast time. That means it's past two in Arizona. To comfortably make an eight-thirty meeting, I needed to be on the road an hour ago.

"I'll call you from the highway. Stay by the phone."

Patch punched out of the call. He felt nauseous and dizzy. Four Nomads dead. He wanted to vomit on the spot. The anger had not yet replaced the shock. He felt a gaping hole in the part of his chest where physical passion had so recently filled him. The last thing he wanted now was sex, an individual act, when the group, those around him, needed help. While death and motorcycles were frequently intertwined, he had never become used to the calls alerting him to the loss of yet another brother and family member, no matter the circumstances, no matter who or what was to blame. With all due respect to the beautiful and willing girl in the room, getting his nut was now rock bottom on his priority pile. Patch needed to speed home and tend to the home fires. Now.

» 40

The redhead was now sitting on the edge of the bed, buttoning up her blouse, shaking her head in disbelief. Misinterpreting Patch's lack of attention, she was no longer enthusiastic about taking him over the finish line. Patch was hardly in the mood to explain the circumstances. Time would not permit.

"Par for the fucking course." Patch cursed himself out loud as he tucked in his shirt with a shrug. Bad news traveled hand in hand with good fortune. And this girl had definitely been Patch's good fortune. A bona fide beauty.

"Bad news on the line. Sorry about that."

"Your loss. I hope for *your* sake that phone call was superimportant." She smiled weakly. "We were just getting to the good part."

"Tell me about it. I wish I could stay, but I gotta go, babe. Maybe next time."

"That's what you said the last time. You know, Patch, I'm starting to take it personal. Plus you're missing the best part, where Leila and Layla join us for a triple feature."

"Please, you don't have to rub it in," Patch said, kissing her forehead, then gazing into her green eyes. She was young. Late twenties.

On his way out, Patch passed Layla and Leila bouncing down the hallway, skimpy costumes in hand, on their way to the back bedroom. He cursed his balance of good and bad luck again. As he strode outside the clubhouse, Patch looked over at Mean Machine. If it had a voice, it would be goading him.

"C'mon, Kinkade. Let's blow this pop stand. You can get laid anywhere, anytime. We gotta book. Let's go. Your brothers need you."

Word of the catastrophe had not yet reached the party. For some strange reason, out of pride, and a little shame, Patch kept matters to himself. The information would drop. Besides, he had only the sketchiest of details himself. His grip containing a few articles of clothes and a toothbrush was already tucked inside the saddlebag. The tank was three-quarters full. He cursed his devotion to duty and responsibility to the club and the way it encroached on his pleasure. After a few quick good-bye bear hugs to Henry and the NoCal boys, Patch was on the road, burnin' it back to Arizona.

On the trip back, Patch had consumed only a fast-
food breakfast sandwich, a cup of lukewarm bad
coffee, and vague snippets of information to stitch together. Hollister phoned him with the details, including names of the dead.
Each one felt like a punch to Patch's solar plexus. Baldy Boris.
Tito. Wheeze. Sanchez. All gone. Fucking dead. They were found
murdered, frozen stiff in an arrogant show of defiant violence
against the club, but by who? Who'd had the balls, not to mention
the resources, to take down four Infidelz in one swoop, and then
pop them in the freezer like they were so many Popsicles? Was
the club at war? Not to Patch's knowledge. This execution made
no sense. Patch could fathom one or two guys fallen on the highway or being shot in a card game, or exchanging gunfire with the
cops, or a shoot-out inside a casino, an attack by a jealous husband, or some out-of-state intruders, that much he could understand, but the annihilation of the four young members at once,
the act of someone thumbing their nose so blatantly at the club's
standing and reputation? Four guys down, four guys versed in
the art of street fighting and sticking together till the very last
drop of blood? What kind of force was at work? An army? Aliens
from outer space? As absurd as that sounded, it was as plausible
as four burly Infidelz going down without any sign of struggle,

which is what the early physical evidence seemed to suggest.

Patch didn't exactly receive a hero's welcome when he pulled up to the front of the Nomads clubhouse forty-five minutes late for the meeting after a bleary-eyed nighttime/early-morning glide back across the desert. He sensed he was being watched. He turned around and saw a variety of vans and trucks, any one of which could be housing cops.

He felt a frigid wind blowing throughout the clubhouse the second he walked through the door, like the deep freeze where they'd found four frozen stiffs of his compadres. The remaining Nomad brotherhood was gathered in the back, chairs in a circle, arms folded, solemn and quiet, so quiet Patch could hear a screw drop. There were five empty seats, one each in Boris, Tito, Wheeze, and Sanchez's honor. Patch took the last empty chair and sat down. The Nomads were now down to six.

"Brothers." A sandy-haired young rider dressed in motorcycle boots, baggy surfer shorts, and a Delz tank top addressed the other five.

Big Head, a junior member of the Nomads, was one of the club's lieutenants whom Sanchez had been grooming for big things. He stood up to call the meeting to order since Sanchez was now the chapter's late prez.

"I don't know what to fucking say." He spoke with uncharacteristic softness, gazing down at the floor. "We lost four of our strongest, most respected members. Why? We don't know. How? We don't know that. Guys, we don't have a fucking clue."

Just then all five pairs of eyes—Big Head, Greek, Tommy, Gorgeous George, and Caesar—turned toward Patch.

"Patch, you got any thoughts you wish to share?" Big Head asked.

"Yeah," George chimed in. His long, curly blond locks and muscle-bound physique had earned him the nickname of the famed wrestler. "Or does the shit have to fly for your brothers in California before you got something to do or say about all this?"

Patch felt the cold sting of George's barb. *Motherfucker.* Looking at the rest of the members, he sensed that George wasn't alone in his disdain for Patch's ill-timed absence. On any other occasion, he'd have walked over and clocked George for such a disrespectful comment. But these guys were young and scattered and shell-shocked. Losing four brothers in such a sudden and bizarre fashion, four key members of a young charter that, at its best, had struggled in the shadow of the other, larger Infidelz chapters, had rattled their judgment and confidence. A punch-out would accomplish nothing. Patch swallowed hard before answering, determined to keep his cool.

"What's that supposed to mean?" Patch asked George, leveling a cold gaze at him and the others.

"It means, where the fuck were you?" George fired back, raising his voice.

"Where the fuck was I? Helping a friend. A brother. They called. I answered."

"At the expense of your brothers here?"

"That's fuckin' unfair. I'll pretend for your sake and safety I didn't hear that."

"Don't bother, Patch. In fact, you pretend enough." Caesar picked up the ball, a burly Italian with his dark black hair slicked back like Antonio Banderas. "Sooner or later, you've got to stop pretending and decide just who is worthy of your loyalty and attention. Is it California? Phoenix? The Nomads? You've been hopping around from one charter to another for years. Shit, brother, you lack focus and commitment in my book."

"Your fucking book? Are you questioning a twenty-five-year member's dedication to this club? Is that what I'm hearing? If so, then just fucking say it."

"I'm saying it and that's exactly what you're hearing," Greek chimed in. At fifty, he was the only member who was older than Patch, although Patch had him as far as years in the club.

Patch got up and strode a few feet toward where Greek was

sitting. Greek, a head taller and about twenty pounds heavier, rose from his chair to meet him. Big Head jumped between the two as Patch tried to reach over and grab Greek by the neck. All the Nomads joined in separating the two.

"Lemme go!" Patch yelled to Big Head, who had Patch restrained with the help of Gorgeous George.

"No swinging fists. Promise," insisted Big Head.

"I fucking promise," Patch said. The two Delz released him.

"Lemme turn the tables here, guys," Patch answered, catching his breath and wagging his finger at the Nomad brothers. "Big Head. You were closest to Sanchez and Baldy Boris. What were these guys up to? Who did they do business with? Who did they hang with—outside of the club, that is. Any idea?"

Big Head cleared his throat uncomfortably. "Patch, I don't need to tell you that what our members do on their own time is their own business."

"As opposed to hanging out like brothers, all as one, sticking together in times of crisis? IAAI?" Infidelz Always, Always Infidelz. "Whatever happened to that? Just a bunch of words now? Minding your business doesn't excuse you from not watching a brother's back. Shit, Big Head, at least I was out there trying to help a brother from drowning in a sea of crank and sweat. And I've got the bruises and welts to prove it." Patch stood up and pulled his shirt up, revealing a flat stomach and a collection of recent bruises and cuts from the ride that Wrangler had given him around the dining room.

"Fuck you, Kinkade," Big Head challenged.

"Fuck me?"

"Yeah. You're just as guilty as anybody here. At meetings, you're a ghost. A million miles away. Running from one charter to the next. To think I respected you, dude. Now all I see is a hollow shell of a man. Yeah, Kinkade, fuck you. You don't give a shit about the Nomads. Never did. For all you fucking care, it coulda been all of us in that freezer."

Patch stood up, and with his steel-toed boot kicked the folding chair he was sitting on well across the room. Greek and George got up, fists clenched at the ready, faces flushed with anger. Patch thought about jumping them both and teaching them a hard lesson. But he came to his senses before he acted and calmly turned and headed for the door.

Before walking out, though, he turned around and pointed his finger at Big Head. "How dare any of you motherfuckers question my dedication to this organization. All gave some, some gave all. I fuckin' gave till it hurts. But that's neither here nor fucking there. I don't expect a medal from you or nobody. I make my own choices and I live with them. You motherfuckers are acting exactly how the cops want us to act. How whoever killed our boys want us to respond. With fear. And doubt. Disunity. Go ahead and sit around, bickering and pointing fingers, feelin' sorry for yourselves. 'Woe is fucking me. Boo-hoo-hoo.' Guess what? People die. Yeah, club motherfuckers fuckin' die. As for me, I'm outta here."

Patch slammed the clubhouse door behind him so hard that the plaque on the door bearing his name, one of the ten names forged on it, fell to the ground. He looked around at the trucks and vans still parked out front. *Okay, which one of you is loaded to the gills with cops?* Then he gazed at Mean Machine, which seemed to be speaking out.

"Nice move, buckaroo. You told them a thing or two, all right, didn't ya sport? Now who do you got besides me? Nobody."

Shut the fuck up and get me to the Iron Horse Bar & Grill, pronto. I could use a few words with my friend Jack Daniel's.

Patch fired up his green monster Harley and pulled up to the Iron Horse in record time. The nearly empty Tuesday-morning parking lot at the bar—just one other bike and nary a car in sight—was a welcome relief. Patch was in no mood to deal with people or to address nosy speculation or answer stupid questions. He had a serious hard morning of drinkin' and thinkin' ahead of him.

» CHAPTER «

11

The IH was always there for the hardcores, mad bikers who, after a night of partying, bypassed a night's sleep for a morning round before heading off to work. Patch pulled open the creaking door, which was badly in need of a blast of WD-40. The bar was chilled inside, like a cold-filtered bottle of beer, as if the A/C stayed on since the previous closing time.

Patch slid up to the bar and sat on an upholstered stool. Petey was behind the plank opening the register while a young Mexican pushed a wide dust mop across the dance floor, finishing up the janitorial duties.

"Patch," Petey shouted over from the register. "I'm so sorry to hear about Boris and Sanchez and the boys. Hope you guys catch them dudes."

Shit. The word spreads.

"Whattaya know, Patch?"

Patch put his hands up, and Petey knew from the body language to back off.

"Perhaps a better question, chief. Whattaya drinkin'?"

"That's more like it." Patch looked up with a half grin. *No use taking it out on Petey.*

"Beer. Sidecar of Jack. Keep 'em comin'. Maybe an order of hush puppies if the kitchen's open yet."

"Comin' atcha, sport," Petey said, counting out the last of his opening dollar bills. "I'll check up on the kitchen."

Patch palmed his cell and dialed home. He had a few minutes to catch Hollister before the boy rode off to school. Hollister picked up on the third ring.

"Hello."

"Hollister. Patch."

"Patch. How'd it go? The meeting."

"Not so good. We'll talk later. I'm running a few errands. You go to school."

"But, Patch—"

"You heard me. No discussion."

Patch punched out the call then yelled out to the barkeep.

Patch bypassed the beer and tipped the shot of Jack Daniel's back and banged the empty glass on the bar.

"Didja hear what I asked?"

"Keep 'em comin'. Yes, sir."

» 48   After a second shot burned its way down, Patch slammed down a long pull of Dos Equis.

"Kitchen'll be up in a flash," Petey reported, sliding a third shot of Jack down to Patch.

Patch didn't notice the only other customer in the bar until he'd slammed down his third shot. Then his eye met the stranger's. Though it was already a hundred degrees outside, the guy wore a heavy black leather vest, dusty black jeans, and some heavy steel-toed black engineer boots. He had on a tattered white long-sleeved T-shirt under his vest. He looked about Patch's age, old enough to know better, young enough not to give a shit and to keep ridin'. Patch couldn't see any chains or hardware, though the man jingled as he walked over, hand outstretched.

"Mr. Patch," he said in a slow drawl, eyeing the Infidelz colors on Patch's back.

"Do I know you?" Patch asked, angling his head and squinting his eyes at the tall drink of water.

"Nah. Folks call me Redbeard."

Peculiar, because this Redbeard had dark hair and dark eyes and a graying dark beard.

"I don't get it," Patch slurred, rubbing his fingers on his chin, the alcohol kicking in. "You don't have red—"

"Long story." Redbeard motioned toward the stool next to Patch. "You mind?"

Patch slapped the bar stool's leather cushion. The Jack was doing a number on his swirling head and empty stomach. This morning, he was a friendly drunk. "Sure, why not? One for my friend here, Petey."

"Much obliged."

Patch looked at himself in the adjacent mirror, didn't like what he saw, and then he turned to the stranger, this Redbeard.

Redbeard broke the awkward silence. "What do you know about those four Infidelz they found in the freezer?" he asked.

49 «

Patch slapped the bar and broke into a sinister laugh. "What do I know? That's an excellent question, Mr."—he paused—"Mr. Redbeard. I know absolutely zero. Jackshit. Nothin'! Like who did it? Why they did it? Better yet, how? I know absolutely zippo. And I don't give a fuck anymore. Okay?"

"Have you been down to ID the bodies? Contacted next of kin? Any of that?"

Patch looked cross-eyed at Redbeard. "You some kinda cop or something? You're not a reporter or one of those Court TV idiots?"

Redbeard shook his head in resignation. "Far from it. Tito is, or he was, my brother, the baby of the clan."

"Goddamn, partner," said Patch, genuinely sorry. "What can I say? I'm sorry. I didn't really mean to trivialize your brother's, uh . . . listen, where you from, stranger? Lemme spot you another round."

"I rode in from Tucson to try to get to the bottom of all this. I used to be a lawyer. Sometimes I do PI insurance work to make ends meet, but I gave up the law for the open road," he said, lifting his vest to expose an empty shoulder holster, a gaggle of keys clipped to his belt, a knife, and a biker wallet shoved into his back pocket.

"You ridin' for a club in Arizona?" Patch asked, slumped at the bar, not bothering to look over and check the back of the stranger's vest.

"Naw, I guess I'm one of the last of the true independents. I ride alone. For myself. By myself. I haven't practiced law, officially that is, for a few years now."

"Ain't no crime in ridin' alone," Patch said. "Lately I been thinking seriously of cutting the same path."

"It has its advantages and its downside. The road gets awful lonesome."

Petey approached the pair from behind the bar.

"Another one, Patch?"

"He's had enough, amigo," Redbeard said, reaching over.

Patch looked over at Redbeard, arching his eyebrows in disbelief. "What are you, my fuckin' mother? Bring me another."

"Look, partner. I need you to follow me. I want to show you something and you'll need your wits about you."

Patch threw his hands in the air. *What-the-fuck-ever, man. How much weirder could things get?* He eyeballed the stranger from head to toe. Didn't seem like a cop, but what's a cop these days? A different breed of outlaw. Four Delz just got killed. Was this guy secretly lookin' for trouble or was he legit? Better yet, did he have information? *What the fuck. I can take care of myself.* "Okay, buddy, let's ride, partner. Show me what you wanna show me," Patch said. "Why the hell not? C'mon, let's go. You lead, I follow."

Redbeard laid down a small stack of cash. "This is for the drinks and the kitchen."

"Don't worry about it, stranger," said Petey, shoving the bills back. "You guys go and do what you gotta do. Just so you catch those bastards. And take care of my friend Patch."

"Will do," said Redbeard. Patch, staggering slightly, followed him out the squeaky door.

Redbeard walked out to the parking lot, over to a jet-black knucklehead rigid, while Patch fired up Mean Machine, the trusted Road King. Patch followed and blasted out of the parking lot, shaking off the Jack Daniel's haze, sharpening his boulevard gaze, instantly sobering up. This motherfucker Redbeard rode fast. Patch kept up. *Where we headed?* Patch grew a little apprehensive when the two pulled up in front of the cop shop, near a building next to the jailhouse.

"Where we going?" he asked suspiciously.

"You'll see," Redbeard answered cryptically.

After the pair passed through security, no small feat considering the amount of metal hanging off both of them, they snaked through the back hallways with Patch keeping up with Redbeard's long stride, just as he'd had to keep up with him on the road, until the two got to a couple of large oak doors, one marked CORONER and the other, MARICOPA COUNTY MORGUE.

"What's this about?" Patch asked, grabbing Redbeard by the arm and jerking him back.

Redbeard was smooth, Patch would give him that. After flashing ID and some fast-talking banter with a couple of the staff, the pair found themselves inside the morgue with a county employee with a nameplate—PABLO—all of a hundred and twenty pounds.

"Lemme see, boys, yeah, here they are. Woods, Raymond, Sanchez, Yeshenko, We grouped them together. No next of kin has come forward. You are the first to claim them."

"That's what I figured," said Redbeard sadly.

Pablo pulled out four enormous drawers. It was just like the movies, giant hulking dead men covered in sheets with tags on their toes. Boris was sewn up like a football, with coarse thick stitching running up and down his neck and torso. His skin had a sickening gray pallor.

"Who the fuck did this?" Patch asked.

"Oh, that, that's the coroner's work. To determine the cause of death. Part of the criminal investigation."

The rest of the crew—Sanchez, Wheeze, and Redbeard's brother, Tito—were also slashed and stitched. The sight of these lifeless members lying unclaimed on a county-morgue slab first saddened, then angered, Patch. He looked over at Redbeard, who was staring impassively at his brother, laid out on the slab drawer. Except for one tear Redbeard had sniffed back at the Iron Horse, the man showed little or no emotion. He stood over his brother stone-faced.

53 «

A few memories came flooding back to Patch. He remembered horsing around with Boris at the Iron Horse. Who could down the most vodka shots the fastest? Patch had won but paid the next day, nursing the mother of hangovers. Tito helped Patch move into his new home, and enlisted a friend to landscape Patch's front yard, no charge. Wheeze—Patch was ashamed to admit he didn't know the guy that well, neither his virtues nor his faults. But he did know that Wheeze left behind an old lady and three kids and a job as a union pipe fitter.

Pablo, sensing Patch's outrage, took two slow steps backward before leaving the room.

"I'll give you guys some space. Ten minutes?"

Redbeard looked over at Patch. "Still don't give a fuck?"

Patch balled both his fists in fury. "I'm gonna find out who did this, and then I'm gonna kill the motherfuckers. Shit, I imagine you should be way more fired up than me, seein' that's your blood there."

Redbeard looked askance. "Trust me, Kinkade. I am. I am."

A moment of silence passed as Patch took a long last look at his four fellow Nomads, then he turned away, shaking his head in disgust.

"Excuse me," Redbeard said, sidestepping Patch. "I'm just curious. Give me a minute to have a more thorough look-see."

Redbeard bent over closer to the slabs and closely scrutinized the entry wounds on Baldy Boris, then Wheeze and Sanchez. Then he leaned over Tito's desecrated body. With a gloved hand, he wisped his youngest brother's hair. Then he leaned farther in and whispered into Tito's lifeless ear. Patch was curious what, but didn't dare ask.

Redbeard took a small black leather-bound notebook out of his vest pocket and scribbled down some notes to preserve his observations. It was a task Patch didn't have the stomach for. Finally, with a quick and unexpected jerk, Redbeard tore off the tag that was dangling from Boris's lifeless big toe. He did the same thing to Tito's tag, this time carefully untwisting the wire attached to it. After he finished checking the bodies one last time, Redbeard pulled the sheets back over the four just as Pablo came back into the room.

With the coldest expression in his eyes, Redbeard said to Patch, "You're right, Kinkade. We are gonna find the motherfuckers who did this. And I'm gonna help you."

"If you don't mind me askin'," Patch asked, "when was the last time you saw your brother alive?"

"A couple of months ago he was smilin' and up on two wheels in Tucson catching the wind on the highway. The kid always had something goin'. I wish I could say we were closer."

Patch clapped Redbeard on the back.

"Look, man." Redbeard turned to Patch. "We need to stick

together. It's a matter of self-preservation. From the cops. From the government. We're the last of the Mohicans, Kinkade. We have to keep the roads open and free, otherwise Arizona becomes another California. Three strikes and helmet laws. You and me are cut from the same cloth. A dyin' breed. Old school. We need our freedom, otherwise we both get to feelin' restless and itchy."

The guy was right about that. Patch was old school. And he *was* feeling restless. And itchy.

"Look," Redbeard said. "Let's sit down and see if we can't get to the bottom of this quickly. If *we* don't, who the fuck else is gonna? Otherwise, just say the word, Kinkade, and I'm on my way down the road, goin' back to bein' bored and retired."

"Retired from what?"

"I told you. Lawyerin', and tryin' to figure out if there's still room in the US of A for two guys like us who really know what true law and order means."

"Listen," Patch said. "Let's get one thing straight. If we're gonna work together, all due respect to your brother, this is my town. I lead. You follow. Understand?"

"*Comprende.* Fully."

On the way out, Redbeard handed Patch the tag he had ripped from Baldy Boris's toe.

"Souvenir. I'll be in touch. We'll meet in a few days. Give me time to sniff around."

Patch took the tag and stuffed it in his jacket pocket. Outside in the parking lot, he watched Redbeard twist Tito's toe tag onto the handlebars of his coal-black Harley. Patch mounted Mean Machine, waved in Redbeard's general direction, and headed homeward with a head full of questions. Judging from the cold look in Redbeard's eyes, whoever killed those boys, they were sure as hell dead meat.

Patch returned to an empty house. He grabbed the newspaper. The headline below the fold made him cringe.

FOUR FOUND DEAD IN BIKER WARS. A lame story quoted mostly federal LE officials. Nothing substantial. Nothing helpful. It was nothing more than inaccurate speculation from gang-squad "authorities."

Patch dusted off his pants, threw down his jacket, dropped his keys in the bowl by the doorway, sank into the couch, and let out a long exhausted sigh of relief and exasperation. His body disappeared into the cushions. He'd gotten the couch because his last old lady, Ramona, insisted that he buy at least one or two pieces of furniture, a few chairs, and a long huge sturdy coffee table that held up his and Hollister's booted feet. It was the most furniture Patch had owned in his life, and it barely put a dent in the vast front room where he and Hollister spent most of their time shootin' the shit (Patch and the kid had no trouble communicating), sippin' whiskey or beer, smokin' a little now and again, or silently watching the box. Patch bit for the longer couch because it was soft, something he could pass out on, and it had a Western, Native American, hunting-lodge motif stitched into it. Undeniably the most male piece in the store.

Patch reached for the cordless phone on the coffee table and dialed an Oakland number tattooed in his brain. His phone number for over three decades. Now it was hers.

Two rings. Pick up.

"Eve."

"John."

Patch wasn't sure why he was calling, or what he would talk about or reveal. First on the agenda, their divorce. Eight weeks ago, it had become final.

"So, babe, how's it feel to be free?"

"Don't give me that. I've always felt free. Maybe too free. That mighta been our problem. So, how are you?"

"Mas o menos. Been a lot better. Been worse."

"Christ, John. You called me. Now talk to me. Not this middle-of-the-road noncommittal chitchat."

"Okay, I'm on a bit of a downswing lately, satisfied? Been reading the papers?"

"Not really. What happened now?"

"A few of our guys bit the dust."

"Whattaya mean bit the dust? Wait, I think I heard about this. Those weren't the guys they found in the freezer? Tell me those weren't your people."

"I wish I could."

"Oh, John. Dear God. What happened?"

"I wish I knew. It's fucking bizarre. We haven't a clue. But I'm working on it."

"Oh, John. I'm so sorry. Anything I can do? Send flowers?"

"Naw. You know how I feel about flowers. We're undecided about the final arrangements. In fact, my next call is Wheeze's old lady. Between the four of these guys, only one of them had kids and a family per se."

"I guess that leaves it to you."

"Guess so. It always does."

"So, maybe I'm a little out of line to tell you what's happening with me, considering what you're going through."

"Go ahead, Eve. Shoot. I could use some uplifting news from any front."

Eve took a long breath, which Patch could hear on the other end of the line. "Well, here goes. John, I'm getting remarried."

Eve's good news felt more like a kick in the head. Of course Patch wouldn't show his reaction.

"Hello?" Eve asked.

"Yeah, I'm here. I guess I should say congratulations. Who's the lucky fella, and do I have to have a prenuptial conference with him to make sure he treats you special? You know, I will."

"Congratulations will do, John. He's a wonderful man. A widower. Two young girls and a teenage son. We met at a Starbucks."

Tell me you didn't say fucking Starbucks. "Eve, I'm happy for you. Guess that officially gets me off the alimony hook."

"Like I ever asked you for a nickel."

"So, do I get the house back? Just kidding."

"He's a wonderful guy. I'll admit I was about ready to give up the ghost and become a nun or a lesbian. But this guy just fell out of the sky. I'm so happy. He's an investment counselor for large industrial accounts. Works at one of the big brokerage firms."

"Like I said, Eve, I'm happy for you. You deserve this." Patch felt a strange sting of jealousy shoot through his belly. *A fucking suit grabs my ex on the rebound. Better that than some blue-collar asshole knocking her around. That would only give me one more worry to throw on the fire.* Even though the state of California had granted their divorce, Patch would feel responsible for Eve until the bitter end, till one of them was lowered into the ground.

"So, who you seeing?" Eve asked. "Last one was that Ramona girl, living at the house. She was dark, beautiful, and mysterious."

"She's mysteriously gone back to California. But yeah, she was a beauty. Part Indian, I mean Native American, and part Mexican."

"They always are, John. Beautiful, that is. Now if only you could match up inner beauty with the outer."

Yeah, right, and if the queen had balls, she'd be king. "Easier said than done, Eve. Listen, I gotta jump. I just wanted to call and say hey."

"John?"

"Yeah?"

"You okay? Don't forget, baby, I know you better than anyone. You're incapable of hiding things from me."

"Yeah, I'm fine. You know me, I'm all right. I'll pull through. You just make sure this guy, what's his name?"

"Amos, Amos Foster."

Amos like in Amos 'n' Andy? *Jeez.* "Whatever, you tell him, if he steps out of line just a little, I'm on him. And I mean that."

Eve laughed softly. "And I appreciate that. You're my guardian angel. And I'll always love you for that. Please be careful."

Rather than respond, on that note, Patch put the phone down, shook off the call, and prepared for the next one, which wasn't going to be much better. Worse, actually.

Three rings. Pick up. It was the voice of a tiny child, a boy. Patch could hear the squall of a baby and a television in the background.

"Hello? Is your mama there?"

"She's here, but my daddy isn't. He's dead."

Kids. So honest to a fault.

"Yeah, I know. That's what I'm calling your mama about."

"My mama says he's not coming back because he's dead."

Patch doubted the kid understood the concept of death, though he'd seen thousands of TV kills by now. *God, how I hate making these calls.*

"Lemme speak to your mama, okay, kiddo?"

Lots of noise and clatter as the kid handed over the telephone.

"Yes, this is Jenny."

"Jenny. I don't know if we've met. This is Patch Kinkade from the club."

"Yes, we've met. Hold on." Patch could hear the woman shouting out to the kids. "Excuse me. I'm sorry."

"No, Jenny, I'm sorry. So sorry about Wheeze."

"Chester."

"Yeah, right, Chester. I know he worked hard and loved his family."

Long silence. "Yes, he did."

"Look, I know it's of little consolation, but if there's anything we can do to help out, the club would be happy to provide in any way we can." *Yeah, like food, shoes for the kids, credit-card bills, rent, electric bills, college educations?* Patch's offer was paltry compared with the true reality this woman now faced. That's why he hated these calls. What was he offering? A few invites to the clubhouse for Thanksgiving. A lousy few hundred bucks. Help around the house fixing this or that. Small consolation after losing the man of the house with a couple of tiny kids. But Jenny let Patch off easy.

"I appreciate that, Patch. Thank you so much. You're kind to call and I know Chester thought a lot of you . . . His bike. I don't know what to do with his bike."

"Look, I understand this isn't the best time to ask this, but is there anything you can possibly tell me that might shed some light as to who did this to him and why?"

"Chester kept that part of his life secret, apart from me and the kids. At first I thought it was for the best; now I wish I knew more about exactly who he was. I'm sorry. If I think of anything, I'll call. But I seriously doubt it. I mean, he loved his children, but outside of them and his job, we didn't talk about much else. I assumed he was with you guys at night. You know more about that part of his life than I do."

That part of his life. Patch honestly didn't know much more than that he rode a turquoise Road King, was a two-year member of good standing, paid his dues on time, didn't swear too often, and was building stuff for the clubhouse.

"I understand. But if you—"

"Listen, I have to go. I've got the kids, it's dinnertime. We were just getting ready to sit down."

"Once again, I'm sorry. Let me know if there's anything we can do. Or if you can think of anything."

"I will." Jenny hung up the phone quickly.

61 «

Ouch. The bum's rush. Maybe Patch and the club deserved it. Maybe they didn't. Wheeze was a grown man and he made his own choices. *We have to live with our choices. I live with mine.*

Unfortunately none of that logic made things any easier, so Patch smashed the phone down. He got up, opened the fridge and extracted a cold Corona, and grabbed a piece of jerky off the kitchen counter. He flicked on the TV set and spent the next hour glaring through the picture tube, practically unaware of the images dancing and flickering on the screen.

Patch walked outside, slamming the screen door behind him. He jumped back on his Road King and fishtailed toward the roadway, leaving behind a sheet of gravel pelting the front of the house. As he throttled away at full speed, Hollister, just home from school, ran out after him from the garage.

"Patch! Where the hell you goin'? I got food for tonight." His voice trailed off as he watched Patch disappear into the horizon.

Patch stopped outside the central Phoenix Infidelz clubhouse. He stomped inside the clubhouse and found Prez Rotten Rick nursing a cold one at the mahogany bar. He eyed Patch and shook his head.

"Don't start on me," Patch said before Rick opened his mouth.

"Grab a brew from the fridge and sit down, will ya?" Rick slapped the bar stool next to him.

Patch plopped down on the seat.

"I got a call from Gorgeous George and the Greek, Patch. The Nomads are pissed at you."

"Hey, Rick. I'm tore up about Boris, Tito, Wheeze, and Sanchez, too. I was the one down at the morgue identifying their bodies. Members die. It's a fact of life when you wear the patch."

"I know, I know. Give 'em time. Things are chaotic right now. There's a big West Coast officers meeting planned at the end of the week so we can deal with this stuff head-on. We don't know what the downside of all this is gonna be later on. Do you?"

"I think the cops are on my tail. I've been on the horn with a few club presidents up and down the coast. Nobody sees this as revenge from another club. After the problems we had in the past with the Two Wheelers and the Gun Runners were resolved, things had been quiet on the one-percenter MC front."

"Look," said Rick, "you're in the shithouse with the Nomads, and I'm not taking sides. But I want you to dig into this thing and see what you find. If you wanna work it out on your own, that's cool. I'll trust your instincts on this one, and cover for you at the OM, but just check in with me. Promise?"

"I promise. Thanks, Rick," Patch said as he headed for the door. "If I need the cavalry, I'll be callin'."

"And we'll be there. Rest assured. Later, Patch."

We got company," said Hollister, tromping through the kitchen in his coveralls and dusty work boots. The boy was a tall son of a bitch. He wore his hair unfashionably long, tied in a ponytail in the back. Dusty blond. Quarterback physique. Shy and strong. Sensitive and responsible. Honestly, Patch admitted, the kid lacked the reckless abandon, and the ambition, to one day prospect for the Infidelz. *But the kid could develop into a helluva fighter.* Hollister was starry-eyed, frequently wore a wide smile, and took life in stride, especially when he was horizontal in front of the TV watching Formula One racing with a baked frozen pizza and a liter of Mountain Dew. He pulled down high marks in school when he wasn't distracted riding his yellow Harley chopper, which he and Patch built together in the garage. Hadn't applied to any colleges, though a few were already calling on account of his wrestling reputation at school. College was a subject he and Patch would have to wrestle with soon. A new ride was more important to Hollister than a full ride to some hotshot university.

It was a little shy of high noon. The tube was on, sound down, hooked up to a pirate satellite black box. Patch was hunched over his cereal, spooning shredded wheat into his pie hole, checking on the TV how badly the A's had slaughtered the D'backs the night before. *Fuck interleague baseball.* A Ray Wylie Hubbard CD played on the box, country rock and roll, musical common ground for Patch and Hollister. "Screw you, I'm from Texas," was a household sing-along favorite.

"We got company, Patch," Hollister repeated, and pointed out the big picture window that framed a wide and wild expanse of desert, technically Patch's front yard.

"So I hear and now I see."

A cloud of dust and the distant sound of a chopper was nearing the house. Patch listened harder to the approaching rumble of the engine bounding up a long dusty trail that served as his snaky driveway. Patch checked his watch. *Already noon and ninety-nine degrees on the rusted Pepsi-Cola thermometer outside.* Not many riders got this close to Patch's spread unannounced or uninvited. But Patch knew who was coming. He and Redbeard had set up a meeting.

» 66   Patch had woken up in a bad mood. Right now the whole situation with these murders stank, a jumbled mess without a solid lead or clue. Patch was antsy. The meeting with this bike-riding former legal eagle had better be productive because Patch wasn't going to rest easy until he had some investigation up and rolling. That was exactly what he wanted to get started with Redbeard, who seemed sharp and on top of his game.

"Who's at the door?" Hollister asked Patch.

"Guy named Redbeard. Turns out he's Tito's older brother."

"Aw, jeez," said Hollister.

"Yeah, I know. But, hey, he's part lawyer, part gumshoe, and a bike rider, as you can see." That meant he "got it" and Patch wouldn't have to waste hours explaining a lot of motorcycle history and legacy. "I'm hopin' he's more resourceful than those monkey-suit-and-tie attorneys we've had to use at three hundred bucks an hour."

A loud knock echoed through the house.

"Get the door and let's get this thing moving." That antsy vibe was hanging over Patch like a bad cold.

Hollister led the tall dark-haired visitor to the table, where Patch had just finished his breakfast.

"Thanks for stoppin' by. Any trouble finding the place?"

"Not really." Redbeard spoke in a drawl. "I'm an early riser, so I gave myself ample time to get rat-fuckin' lost. But I didn't. Ended up I was early, so I stopped off at that snappy little diner near the off-ramp."

"Luke's?"

"That's the ticket. Got to talking to the waitress there. Cute skinny girl."

"You mean the spacey Winona Ryder waifish-looking chick?" Hollister smiled with fondness.

"That's her."

"She's good people," said Patch. "Hollister here digs her the most."

Patch gazed out the picture window past Redbeard's hog parked outside, preoccupied with the thought of four dead Nomad brothers and the undetected hows and whys that lay out there to be discovered. Then he snapped out of his dazed look.

"Oh yeah, this here's Hollister Timmons. He's my godson from Oakland."

"Nice ride," Hollister said, pointing outside at the black knucklehead. "And I'm sorry about your brother."

"Thanks," said Redbeard, anxious to switch subjects. He pointed to his bike outside. "Gets me where I need to be, quick like. Time is more valuable than money."

"I hear you. How about a beer? Hollister, get the man something to drink."

"Beer will be fine." Redbeard looked different. Younger. He was now clean-shaven, which prompted Patch to ask the obvious question again.

"Before we go any farther here," Patch asked, "why the hell *do* they call you Redbeard? You aren't redheaded and now you don't wear a beard."

"Long story, actually."

"The suspense is already killing me," Patch deadpanned, then pulled out a chair and called over to Hollister, who was lugging two beers and a Dew.

"Sit down, Hollister. I want you in on this. Got anything for me, Mr. Beard? So far I'm cranky and coming up dry. Stumped."

Hollister took a seat at the head of the table. If he shut up and listened, he'd learn quicker and get up to speed with what was happening.

"I was up earlier doing a little more research," Redbeard began, "and I logged in a few phone calls these past few days." He pulled out his typed notes from the leather satchel he was toting.

"There's something about these executions that doesn't quite ring right. According to the papers, four dead riders were found in a row and carefully staged. Now, I know bike riders are no pack of angels, but I suspect none of our kind are apt to work this professionally as executioners in taking guys down with a single pistol shot to the head. Our guys are more adept with their fists and blunt instruments and higher-caliber weapons. You know, come out blasting, ask questions later. Yet since I got a long hard gruesome look at those boys the other day, what I'm seeing wasn't your standard shoot-'em-up ambush by any stretch. Four Infidelz were put down professionally and efficiently, but I'm having trouble getting a fix on any organized-crime people around here that could do a job as first-rate as these guys did. Little sign of a struggle, and we're talking about big hulkin' dudes evenly lined up, bikes all staged. And those weird four scratch marks on Boris. Somebody sure is trying to make a strong statement. They had to be hauled into the freezer, or else trucked in."

"Meaning?"

"Union guys like Reese Brothers Trucking or Big Benny Fratello, for instance, might know about that level of talent from Vegas or back east. I figured you guys are amigos down here. Maybe they'll open the kimono if you reach out."

"Good idea. I know Boris drove for Big Benny. Maybe Tito, too. The club and those Teamster guys go way back. Our guys drive for them. We work their sites and bounce for their events and dances."

"Why would they off four Infidelz?" Redbeard asked. "As a rule, you guys keep your business separate, but you work together and stay out of each other's hair. Maybe they know something."

"That's why this thing is so damned strange," said Patch. "I can't get my head around it."

"Even the Mexican mobsters," Redbeard continued. "These murders hardly bear their signatures. Bikers can't shoot that straight and clean. I think the cops know this. Believe me, they're as stumped as we are."

Patch nodded at Hollister then looked over at Redbeard. This guy had his shit together. Patch felt inspired to kick the investigation into high gear.

"Man, you've done your homework. So, if you were me, where would you start?"

Redbeard took a swill of his beer.

"We need to know if there's been any recent Mob activity sprouting up in the Southwest. Something we don't know about, but maybe your four friends did. First off, the money found on the bodies was funny, we know that."

"And that's what confuses me the most. This whole counterfeit-money angle. Now we got the cops calling in the FBI and the Secret Service," Patch said. "They're looking for motive. So now they've got us pegged as counterfeiters or else they think we're moving money on the streets. If we are, it's news to me, 'cause I could use cash, real or fake."

"You and I both know the Infidelz are not printmakers," said Redbeard. "Nobody in the club has the steady hands to crank out bogus twenties and fifties. That's bullshit. There's no evidence of that. No presses. No surveillance to lead the cops to any equipment or organized operation. It's not going to be easy, but I have a feeling that if we sniff around hard enough, we'll come up with something. Hardest thing is jumping in and getting wet."

Patch shrugged. "So what about the executions?"

"A thing of beauty."

"I'm not sure I share your taste in beauty."

"Check it out." Redbeard threw down a two-inch pile of grisly crime-scene eight-by-tens and corresponding paperwork. "I was able to get these through a friend at the sheriff's office."

"A friend?"

"Don't ask. Let's just say I've got connections, a mole who happens to be a pretty little señorita, a fan of yours truly and my special skills. Unfortunately she's not a redhead. Check out these photos. There was very little blood, only a small splash, some leakage to the back of the heads. When the coroner's office examined closer, according to the cops' own medical reports here, they noticed that on each cadaver, the blood vessels in one eye had burst, filling it with a single drop of blood. The victims each had been shot once, execution style, at close range above the right ear at the hairline with a twenty-five-caliber handgun. The bullet went from the entry wound to the back of the head. Handsome work. Very clean, and because of the small caliber, very little bleeding. Even the cops know it's an extraordinary work of art. They're in awe of whoever did this because they had talent. The cops must know bikers are not—how would you put it?—that subtle. I think law enforcement is in a massive state of denial. They must be freaking out right now at the prospect that their Southwestern paradise is beginning to bear the strange fruit of a new Mob presence, which is what we need to confirm first. For now, it's easier for the cops to just blame you guys, blame a biker war, like things are out of control when they're really not."

"A series of hits carried out with a twenty-five-caliber handgun? Get serious."

"You tell me, how many bike riders bother packing a popgun like that? Hell, we don't pick our teeth with nothing less than a thirty-eight."

"Who do you s'pose—"

"Look, we both been around clubs long enough, and I've ridden with a few in my day, to expect anything. We're capable of a lot of bullshit behavior outside the organization. But I honestly don't believe bike guys did this."

Patch scratched his chin in bewilderment. This was the sunny Southwest, not New Jersey or Philly or the Bronx. Outside of a few scattered wiseguys and Mexican mobsters, there couldn't be that much cooking down here. Or could there?

Redbeard added, "Maybe the cops have nothing else to spend their federal subsidies on other than bikers and Mexicans. What time you got?"

"Just past two."

"Good," said Redbeard. "We're done here. I made you copies so you can study them. Now it's time to get some riding in. Let's tear up a corner of your desert paradise. I think better when I'm riding."

"I'm game for that."

"Me three," said Hollister. "Lemme grab my lid."

I t wasn't like Patch to be up so early. He was more of a
nighttime guy. But there he sat at home in the extreme
A.M., slumped in a stuffed chair in his front room with his hand
wrapped around a lukewarm cup of black. The sun popped up
over the horizon, bringing in the day's first rays of sunlight.
Patch gazed blankly out the window, ignoring a local wake-up
show on the tube with the sound down. Bright-eyed, prepro-
grammed, good-morning zombies grinning on camera in stuffed
suits with too much hairspray and way too much makeup on the
ladies. It wasn't Patch's world; he couldn't relate to the happy
talk, traffic-jam reports, and bad news.

Hollister shuffled in.

"You sleep okay, Patch?"

"A little." Patch shrugged.

"Are the Nomads going to be okay?"

"Dunno. I wish I could say for sure, Hollister." Patch shook his
head in disgust. "They're pissed off. Maybe they got a right. If I
had been here for *them* instead of riding up to Palm Desert—"

"But Wrangler and the guys needed you. And you were there
for them. I don't know how you do it. Sometimes you get tugged
at from so many different directions with the club."

"It's what we do, bein' brothers." Patch pointed over at the television screen. "And I see less and less of it in the everyday world."

The Infidelz and Hollister were pretty much Patch's whole family. Technically, his twelve-year relationship/marriage with Eve had gone kaput two years before and she would soon belong to another. He wouldn't be talking to her anytime soon. Patch lost track of any blood family, like brothers and sisters. Patch and his ex-wife, Eve, had no kids, none that he knew of anyway. He grinned wearily at Hollister and recalled the old days on Oakland family runs with Hollister and his dad, Angelo. Back in the boy's younger and more innocent times. The secret of the kid's dad and *his* death tugged occasionally at Patch's gut during times like these.

"You know, you're a lot like me, kid. We don't have a lot of kin left. So we go with who and what we got."

He shifted his stare over at Hollister. Here was a kid a year away from graduating high school. What chance did he have in life? Even odds, maybe better, *if* the kid hustled. God, what he'd been through, so short on breaks. Plus Patch owed the kid, since Patch was responsible for the death of his father, who turned rat. An informant. A cop caller. The guy had had to go. Someday Patch would have to broach the subject with the kid. He wasn't looking forward to that conversation. No way. It was now Patch's responsibility to help mold Hollister into a man and not some addled, scatterbrained perpetual adolescent like his late dad, Angelo Timmons.

Patch decided this time he would be straight up with his godson about what was going down with the Nomads and bring him up to speed. Take him in, confide in him, and let him help out. This was no time to hide things; it was time to throw him into a front-row seat on the real world. Who knew? He might contribute.

"Get dressed, Hollister. I need you to come with me. We're going into the city. We got somebody to see, and I need you to help me sort this stuff out. Be ready in a half hour."

Patch rustled through the contents of a half-empty cardboard box sitting near the chair. He pulled out his bound address book and looked up a name and number. When the clock struck eight he made a call. A live voice answered.

"Benny Fratello, please . . . When's he due in? . . . Eight-thirty? . . . Sure, fine . . . Could you please leave him a message? . . . Tell him Patch Kinkade is coming into town for a visit . . . That sounds good . . . Let him know that I'll stop in around nine."

That morning, Patch and Hollister motored up to Big Benny's dispatcher's office and backed both bikes into a couple of car parking spaces out in front. Big Benny Fratello ran a trucking company down by the Southwest Railroad train-yard facility. The guy employed Infidelz as lumpers and drivers. That had recently included Boris and Tito.

"So what do you need me to do, Patch?" asked Hollister.

"I need you to sit back and watch. You can be my reality check. See if my friend Benny is on the level with me. Otherwise, just stay focused. Benny's in tight with the union fellas, the trucking people around Phoenix, and he knows more than a few 'made' guys, too."

"You mean, like Mafia guys?"

"Kid, keep your voice down. Remember, I need you to play it cool. Let me give you some advice: smart guys know things, but wise guys don't let on what they know or where they get their information from." Patch put a hand on Hollister's shoulder. "Look, we're dealing with some strange shit here. I need you to be my extra pair of eyes and ears. If you can't handle—"

"Don't worry. Count me in. I swear."

"Good. It's down to you, me, and Redbeard to untangle this mess. Besides, three heads are better than one."

The two strolled inside the main dispatch unit at Benny Fratello's, where a small crowd of truckers were reporting in to begin their delivery routes. A hefty, older, balding fellow with broad shoulders, about six-five, with bifocal glasses, stood by the Mr. Coffee, topping off a steaming cup of mud.

"Patch! Gail said you were comin' in to see me."

The two shook hands and smiled.

"Benny, this is my godson, Hollister Timmons. Hollister? Benny Fratello."

"Pleasure to meet you, sir," said the youngster respectfully.

Benny pointed toward the open door of his office. "Come on in. Let's talk."

Big Benny headed behind his desk, put his coffee down, and settled in to a squeaky reclining antique walnut desk chair.

"What's on your mind, Patch? Club life treating you okay?"

"I won't mince words, Benny. These are shitty times. Four guys killed. The cops are sitting on their asses on this one, but I'll take that as a positive. We don't need 'em."

"Yeah, it's terrible. I had two of those guys on my payroll. Boris and Tito. Straight-up dudes. RIP."

"And we appreciate that, Benny. But I need info. The papers

and the cops are cryin' bike wars, but we suspect some slicker dudes."

"Oh, Jesus." Benny's brow furrowed up. He shook his head and frowned.

"The feds have jumped in, too. There's Secret Service involved."

"Secret Service?" Benny's eyes darted over to Patch's. "What's up with that? They think you're out to kill the prez?"

"Crazier than that. They got us tripped up on some bullshit counterfeiting charge. That's why I'm here. I gotta ask you about what's going on around these parts. My members aren't into funny money. They're workin' guys."

Benny tilted back in his chair and rolled his eyes. "This sounds pretty serious. Can I bring Gus Hatch in here?" He picked up his phone and buzzed his secretary. "Gail. Can you please tell Gus to step into my office? I know he just got here. Tell him it's important."

Within a few minutes, an Italian man in his late fifties tapped on the door then let himself in. Hollister got up and surrendered his chair.

"Sit down, Gus. You know Patch Kinkade. He rides with the motorcycle group the Infidelz." Benny turned to Patch. "Gus is a partner of mine. He does a little bit of PI work with the company when we have problems like, well, you know . . ."

Gus glared over at Hollister, who stood by the door with his arms crossed. "The kid—"

"He's with me, Gus," said Patch. "It's okay. I was just telling Benny that we suspect that the club has become underworld targets." He made eye contact with both men then continued. "I gotta ask you this: Either of you two guys heard anything about any strange new Mob shit goin' down in the area?"

Both men stared back, at a loss for words. They shook their heads. Patch continued his query.

"We suspect the whole thing involves some counterfeiting

that's operating here in Arizona. Now my guys aren't that clever. But I need to know who is. Just between us four, who's capable of passing funny money around the Southwest?"

"To tell you the truth, Patch," said Benny, "I only saw bits of it happening, but around here, not so recently. Maybe action left over from Vegas and the East Coast or some amateur shit floating around the barrio. I know more than a few wiseguys around these parts, but it's not their thing. Too expensive. Too risky. Like you said, Secret Service. Who needs that shit? Gus?"

"Well, if you ask me, and I guess you are asking"—Gus snickered cautiously and paused nervously—"I'd have to say it could be Eastern European Mobs. They're the only guys with the balls to come into this area and pull stuff like that. They're into stolen cars and breaking them down and selling parts. That and smuggling. Cigarettes. Fucking around with federal subsidies. Welfare checks. Medicare fraud. All kinds of shit."

"That's right!" said Benny. His eyes lit up. "I did hear about somebody getting burned on some stolen auto parts and getting paid with phony bills. To the tune of twenty grand. That was a few months ago. It might have had to do with some foreign types."

"Who is this guy dealing stolen parts?"

"Some fella named Wilbur. He runs a junkyard out toward where you live."

"Wilbur Gallagher? I've been to his place. You remember, Hollister. We got the fenders for your bike there."

Hollister nodded.

"Listen, Patch, are you familiar with the Rachkov brothers?"

"No, Benny," Patch answered.

Gus jumped in without hesitation. "Tough guys, but strictly legit business guys. Couple of ex-boxers. Crazy motherfuckers. Got a bar in town with an escort service, girls doing in call and out call. A little dicey. Liquor distribution. Even got a boxing gym. It's down on lower Bell. Can't think of the name of the bar. It might not have a name. You boys been down there lately?"

"Lower Bell you say?" Patch asked. "I gotta check it out."

"It's a whole new world down there. Check it out. I know Boris hung out there a lot, both in the bar and with the girls. Ran up a big tab, I understand. They were putting together something. I know because Boris came around looking for capital."

"Did he say what it was he was doing with those guys?"

"It never got that far. I told him I wasn't interested. I've my own troubles. Lately the cash flow around here hasn't been what it should be."

"Sounds like I need to meet these Rachkov guys."

"They're okay fellas. Like I said, they own a liquor distribution business. I understand they can come on heavy with the local tavern owners. They do all right. Our trucks do some deliveries for them, which is how Boris mighta first met them, him bein' Russian, too. They might be able to help you. It's worth a try. I can put in a call." Benny was a big help.

"Nowadays," Benny broke in, "things are so—how do you say it?—global, that the Southwest is home to all kinds of groups. The days of just blaming us Italians, wiseguys—"

"Or the bike riders," Patch interjected.

"Right," Benny continued. "That shit's over. It's old school. Nowadays it's fucking worldwide; you got your Eastern Europeans, Mexicans, South Americans, Chinese, Asian cartels up to different activities everywhere. Man it's a big ol' crazy world. Any of those, er, organizations could be moving counterfeit bills, who knows? A lot of these groups keep to themselves. What's an old wiseguy like me to do?"

"If I were you, Patch, I'd check in with the Rachkovs," advised Gus. "Find out what's going on. They must know something. I guarantee you, they'll already know about your troubles, knowing Boris and with the Infidelz getting whacked. Sorry, I mean, killed, uh, murdered."

Patch got up and reached over Benny's desk and shook his hand. He turned to Gus. "Here's my number. Next time you're at one of our parties, I'll introduce you around to meet the guys, make you feel at home. Thanks, gentlemen. I'd appreciate it if you hear about anything that might help me out here, I'm all ears. If you can hook up with the Rachkov brothers and put in a word for me, that would be great. Call me or leave a message through the Nomads clubhouse. They'll know how to reach me."

Outside, Patch and Hollister rolled out their Harleys toward the intersection.

"Well, gut feeling, what did you think, kiddo?"

"Those two looked pretty solid to me, but nothing at first. Then they let the info flow. That was funny. Once they trust you—"

"Remember what I said about telling what you know? Those old-schoolers are no fools. Do they know more? Hell, yeah. A lot more. They're not ones to talk much. I knew that goin' in. But they threw us a bone, they gave us a break, and it's a start."

Patch started up Mean Machine, still warm from the ride in. Hollister's ride joined in on the rumble.

"I think it's time to pay a visit to these Rachkovs. I'm sure Benny's on the horn right now blabbing. Besides, we need a little crash course on the lay of the land, these Russian types especially. The club intersects a little with these union Mob guys, but it's a whole different world. I'll call Redbeard. Maybe he can ask around and we can track these guys down. Shouldn't be difficult."

79 **«**

Patch was breathing easier. With a break, no matter how small, it was at least something to chase down. Patch needed a lead right now. Like Redbeard said, it's a matter of jumping in and getting wet. *Yeah. It feels good getting wet again.*

Next day around noontime, Patch and Redbeard took a ride down to the mysterious side of Bell Avenue. Gus Hatch was right: there was a brave new world situated there that Patch hadn't noticed. No more than a few blocks. A small Russian empire. Shops. A specialized grocery. Video store. Electronics shop. A limo company. A car mechanic with a slew of beat-up foreign cars parked out front waiting to be wrenched and repaired. Some storefront "social clubs" with no signage; just blanked-out picture windows and double-locked doors. Bail-bond offices. In the center of this new community was a gym crowned with a pair of flashing neon boxing gloves. Next door to the gym was the Caspian Deli. Next to that, a no-name bar with a fleet of late-model Mercedes-Benzes, Lexuses, and Escalades with dark tinted windows parked outside.

There were a handful of gents hanging around the no-name bar, mustached and carefully coiffed double-breasted-suited men in their twenties and thirties, young for wiseguys, engrossed in heated debate over college games and point spreads. Patch noted their thick guttural accents. It was as if a small foreign country had sprouted up out of the cracks on the sidewalks. Patch and Redbeard, American as apple pie by comparison, wheeled their bikes up between one of the parked Benzes and the no-name entrance. A hefty bearded driver with a silver toothpick sat behind the wheel. He eyed the pair of bike riders closely.

"New world order. You been down here before?" Patch asked Redbeard.

"On and off, but I didn't notice the—whattaya call it?—change of culture. I remember when these parts were wall-to-wall car and truck mechanics and a mass transit graveyard. Dead buses everywhere. Times have changed."

"Let's step inside and get our bearings straight," suggested Patch.

"Good idea."

The two entered the barroom to the sounds of late eighties music. The size of the place was deceptive, much bigger on the inside than it appeared on the outside, with mirrored walls and a large central empty dance floor. "Love Will Lead You Back" by Taylor Dayne played softly over the sound system. *Always hated that song.*

"What'll it be?" the young bartender asked, twitching his butt slightly to the music.

81 **«**

"Two beers for two steers," Patch said. "Say, doesn't this here place have a name? I guess I musta missed it on my way in."

"Sure does. Brighton Beach West. But the owner never got around to putting up the sign. So we call it the No Name."

"You're a ways from the beach, partner." Redbeard laughed to the bartender.

"Tell me about it," the bartender said, flipping his hair back behind an ear that sported half a dozen piercings along its rim. "I'm way behind on my tan, boys. Two beers right up."

The crowd over in the corner by the pool table sharply contrasted with the bartender's flitty demeanor. There was a loud table-slapping session of dominoes going on with laughing, clapping, the thunk of shot glasses, and the rude chorus of cell-phone rings. Everybody was talking at once. Patch spotted a shoulder holster cradling a .38 dangling from one of the pool shooters wearing a dark sport coat and tan dress slacks. These were tough customers, and not cops.

"Nice place," Redbeard said, eyeing the framed pictures of athletes and music divas over the bar, mostly boxers, with the photographs signed. "What would you call this, a sports bar?" he asked the fey bartender.

"Schizophrenic, if you ask me. By day, we get a lot of Eastern Europeans in here, spillover action from the deli and the gym. At night it's more of a disco, a club. DJs. The works." He pointed over at the domino game. "Most of that group is in here every day. The owner should charge them rent. Fucking pain in the ass and they tip like shit, if at all."

"Who's your boss?" Patch asked the bartender.

"The owner?"

"Who's the owner?"

"You mean owners? Those guys up there," the bartender said, pointing dutifully to the wall, leaning in closer toward Patch. The picture showed two victoriously grinning twentysomething brothers, both wearing matching red boxing gloves. Nicholai and Vladimir Rachkov had dark hair, capped smiles, noses straight and intact, faces handsomely unscathed, with chiseled features. Hair tossed in sweat. Chests and arms bulging with baby-oiled muscles. Both men's biceps were decorated with tattoos.

"Where can I find 'those guys'?" Patch asked, pointing to the picture, leaning in closer.

"That's easy. You can find them next door. In the gym. Knocking each other silly. Why? You into that sort of thing?"

"Maybe."

Redbeard coughed as he downed his bottled beer and turned to Patch. "Shall we bolt?"

"Yeah, let's book," Patch said, throwing a ten spot on the bar. "Keep the change."

Outside the No Name, Patch turned to Redbeard.

"You ever boxed?"

"Can't say I have. I've been in plenty of fights, but not for sport."

"Well, it's the most physically exerting activity I can think of. Two minutes in the ring and you're suckin' wind, exhausted. Ever been to a boxing match?"

"Not since I was a youngster. Golden Gloves."

"You're in for a treat."

The smell of the Brighton Beach West Training Center was exactly what Patch had braced himself for—a mixture of sweat, Pine-Sol, and stale cigar smoke. There weren't a lot of people inside working out, compared with the size of the place anyway. It was massive. And noisy as hell. The sound of a couple of moving speed bags mixed with an unusually loud fan and rattling ventilation system, giving the place a superloud ricocheting ambience. Even with not much of a crowd working out, you needed to practically yell to communicate. Patch and Redbeard kept quiet.

Distributed evenly throughout the gymnasium were three raised full-size regulation boxing rings and a dozen heavy bags. Along the far wall were weight-training stations with free weights and benches. The equipment looked brand-new. In the center ring were a couple of muscular dark-haired men, thirties, the same guys in the picture, slightly thicker, but svelte nonetheless, sitting in opposite corners, both drenched with sweat, water, and Vaseline, each being tended to by diligent bucket men. Another cigar-chomping comrade was down below, circling the perimeter of the ring, barking out orders in another tongue. Patch assumed it was Russian. The two fighters looked like brothers. Upon closer inspection, they were twins. Identical.

"Looks like we've found our guys," Patch said to Redbeard.

Each boxer slipped on red padded headgear, covering most of his face and ears. A bell rang and the two brothers jumped up and emerged from their opposite corners. Patch and Redbeard walked over to get a closer look, staying well out of the way of the cigar man stalking the ring's exterior.

The twin boxers tangled. Patch could barely make out who was who. Both wore dark trunks with silver striping and ruby-red eight-ounce gloves. Both exchanged punches with a fisted fury that made Patch wince. One of the fighters had an extremely vicious left, the other an equally fatal right. Redbeard caught the same detail.

"Mirror twins," Redbeard said to Patch.

"One of these motherfuckers is left-handed while the other is right. This is gonna be hard to watch. They're so equally matched, these guys might kill each other."

One of the bucket men served as the ref. He kept the two intermittently apart. As the spar wore on, it was hard to pick out the tougher of the two. Just when Lefty appeared to be dominant, Righty came back. They had astonishingly similar styles. Light jabs, then boom boom to the face. These guys weren't much on body blows. They mainly went straight for the kisser. They had long torsos and tremendous reach. The grunts and groans came in alternating pairs and filled the gym above the noise of the ventilation system and the speed bags. These guys weren't sparring. They were going at it full throttle. Righty tired just as Lefty jumped in for the kill. Then, as if he'd been momentarily distracted by overconfidence, Righty seized the moment and delivered a sharp body blow to Lefty's liver.

Down went Lefty.

At about what would have been the seven count, the victorious right-hander laughed and reached down and scooped up his twin brother before the counter made it to ten.

"Vlad, Vlad. You okay, brother?"

Lefty was dazed, bleeding slightly from his nose. "I tink so."

Patch turned to Redbeard. "I've seen enough. Let's see if we can gather any info on the street about these guys before we approach them. I want my ducks lined up before talking to these two, that's for sure."

Patch and Redbeard made it out to the parking lot and hopped on their bikes and split up. Redbeard headed back into town as Patch rolled north toward home.

On his way home, Patch made a pit stop. He needed a crash course on boxing. Kenny's Sports Central had televisions scattered around the barroom. Patch remembered Boris talking about the place. In addition to being a glitzy sports bar, it was a local betting parlor, a place where Boris had brought his "locks" each week during football season. Sports Central. Actually, Sports Overkill. Sports Church. Baseball games, basketball play-offs, classic sports matches, ESPN news, and live events piped in from numerous time zones, pulled in from out of the sky by a massive satellite dish system installed on the roof. The room was predictably decorated with memorabilia, jerseys, pennants, NASCAR and FSN logos, Arizona Sun Devils helmets, tennis rackets, an electric guitar, signed head shots, framed magazine covers and articles, and signed posters of bare-midriff Arizona Cardinal cheerleaders. It was late afternoon and empty. The after-work crowd hadn't yet materialized.

Patch's Infidelz patch broadcast his affiliation with the club to the two sports-bar guys, one behind the bar, the second finishing a club soda. Upon entering, Patch noticed the Infidelz support sticker on the door, a sign that Boris, notoriously sticker happy, had visited. The "assistant manager" approached Patch right away. He was a round humongous guy and, if Patch had to guess, tipped the scales at about three hundred pounds. His wrinkled suit fit him like a tent and he wore a gray fedora.

"Patch Kinkade, we know you. I'm Damien Daniels. And this is Toby." Damien motioned to his partner behind the plank. "Toby, a drink on the house for this man. We support the Infidelz. We're sorry about what went down. Boris was a friend."

"Much obliged."

"Are the cops gonna catch the bastards who killed your guys?"

"Fuck the cops." Patch grabbed a seat at the bar and shook his head. "We're working on it. Actually, I got a question for you two. What do you guys know about the boxing scene?"

"I'm no Bert Sugar, but I know my way around the ring."

"I mean locally. There are these two Russian guys that run a gym—"

"You mean the Rachkovs?"

"Yeah."

"Vladimir and Nicholai. A couple of palookas, but they're cool guys. As fighters, nothing special. I think Vlad got on a few light-heavyweight cards, but no great shakes. West Coast mainly. They're businessmen now. They own a bar down on the north side and some other stuff."

"Yeah, I was just there. Nice place."

"Sure is," said Toby. "I catered a grand-opening party for them. We had a great time. Man, the girls they had on hand, beautiful, man, splendido."

"No shit," added Damien. "Total knockouts, but not a single one of them spoke much English. They just kept coming out of the back room in waves."

"They took care of biz that night," Toby quipped.

"What else do these Rachkovs do besides sell booze and work out?"

"I suspect they're into a lot of things," said Damien. "They started out running a titty bar out on Victory Road with a massage parlor upstairs. Now they're down on Bell running a big nightclub. I understand most of the buildings are theirs. They're rubbing shoulders with the local politicians. They're tight with a lot of the city-council people, state politicians; I saw a picture of them with McCain."

"They throw parties for the politicians, raise money for their campaigns. AIDS fashion shows—stuff like that gets them close to the beautiful people," said Toby. "I don't know if it's true, but I heard that Putin's daughter showed up at one of their benefits with a couple of armed bodyguards."

"Really? Did Boris hang out with the Rachkovs much?"

"Yeah. I've seen the three of them here together a few times."

"When was the last time you saw Boris?" Patch asked.

Damien scratched his head. "Last week? With the Rachkovs, actually."

Patch swallowed his draft beer and wiped his mouth with the back of his hand. He noticed another signed picture of the boxing twins on the wall behind Damien and Toby. What was it about bars and restaurants that hang signed photos of mediocre celebs and over-the-hill athletes on their walls? The unanswerable question. In this shot the Rachkovs stood back-to-back, shirtless and mugging for the camera, wearing matching burgundy boxing trunks. The same tattoo decorated their arms. Napoléon Bonaparte.

89 **«**

"I need to sit down with these guys."

"Another beer, Mr. Kinkade?"

"Fellas, you've been more than kind, but I'm headed home."

"So listen," said Damien, serious, voice low. "We feel bad about Boris and your guys getting hit. Lemme know if I can do anything to help out."

Getting hit? Ouch. Patch hated hearing citizens talk like that. He hid his annoyance.

"You've helped out already."

Patch headed back out to the parking lot. The radical jolt from the refrigerated sports bar out into the blazing heat was something he hadn't gotten used to since he moved to the Southwest. He screeched and laid down a long, black skid mark. He took off and sped open-throttled and lidless down the freeway on the Mean Machine, with the force of the wind battering his face.

Redbeard rolled up to Kinkade Kompound right after the afternoon rush hour. "Ding dong," he shouted through the screen door.

"Be right out." Hollister and Patch bounded down the front steps. Redbeard was already on his bike, ready to bolt.

"Where we headed, Patch?" he asked.

"To the wrecking yard not far down the interstate. A guy named Wilbur Gallagher runs the place. Benny said he recently got stuck with a fistful of bogus bills."

"Lead the way." Redbeard turned the key on his ride.

Patch, Redbeard, and Hollister rolled loudly into Wilbur's junkyard like Three Horsemen of the Apocalypse. *Wilbur's monster truck and tow.* Patch could hang around and rummage through a place like Wilbur's all day long, happy as the proverbial pig in shit.

Two men, a short Mexican and a tall, slim older white dude, came out to greet the rumble of the bikes. Patch remembered the white guy as Wilbur. Wilbur remembered Patch as that scary guy who rode with the Infidelz.

"Can we help you fellas?" Wilbur asked, not waiting for the trio to dismount from their Harleys. "Looking for bike parts?

Educated guess." He smiled to show a silver tooth in the center of his mouth.

"Bike parts? Not exactly. More like auto parts." Patch stuck out his hand. "The name's Kinkade. You Wilbur Gallagher?"

Wilbur spied Patch's colors and nodded. "I remember you." He pointed to the fenders on Hollister's yellow chop. "That's some of my hardware there."

"Is there a place we can all talk?"

Wilbur spoke Spanish to his assistant, who dashed off. Then he pointed to a barred-window shack. "The office. Follow me."

Inside, Wilbur pulled out four mismatched chairs.

"This'll do fine," Redbeard said, scanning Wilbur's decades-old hubcap and side-rearview-mirror collection panoramically arranged around the room. "Sorry to outnumber you here, uh, Mr. Gallagher."

"Call me Wilbur." He was anxious not to piss off the visiting contingent.

"Wilbur, we're gonna cut to the chase." In spite of his road-warrior look, Redbeard had a graceful, lawyerly tone to his voice. "We're here about something that went down a while back."

Wilbur's eyes darted nervously. Redbeard anticipated hesitation.

"Listen, Wilbur, what's said here stays here. We're not cops. We mean no trouble. We just got questions. Can we keep this conversation on the down-low?"

"Sure, sure. What's this about?"

"A while ago," explained Patch, "you were paid off for a shipment of auto parts. The money turned out to be counterfeit."

Wilbur hung his head and searched for the right response. He shuddered and breathed hard. "Yeah, that's right. I got burned." His face stiffened. "How'd you know about that?"

"I hear things from some people. How much did they stick you for?" Patch asked.

"About twenty grand."

"You know," Patch continued, "Infidelz aren't cop callers, either. Did you call them?"

"No fuckin' way," said Wilbur. "I had no choice. So I had to eat it. I can't have the cops snoopin' around here checkin' up on my suppliers. But, listen, I swear to you guys, honest to God, I don't deal in no stolen bike parts. Believe me, I'd rather be chased by the Green Berets than have the Infidelz on my ass for stolen bikes."

"We're not here about stolen bikes," assured Hollister. "We just want to know more about the guys who passed you the funny money."

Wilbur looked more at ease.

"We're lookin' for information," said Redbeard. "Just tell us what you remember about the guys who burned you on that parts shipment. Were they regular good ol' boys? Foreigners? Mexicans? What?"

"Actually"—Wilbur scratched his head—"they had foreign accents. Four white guys. Russian, I think. Young, in their twenties, I'd say. I remember one guy had a tattoo of a cat. Never dealt with 'em before. And I didn't small-talk with 'em. I wanted to keep everything off the books. They were okay with that. No names. No receipts. They loaded up the, uh, inventory and paid me in cash. Well, I thought it was cash."

"What denominations?"

"Twenties and fifties."

"No hundreds?"

"Nope."

"What did you do with the dough?"

"Eventually burned it. I tried to track them down on my own, but they vanished as quick as they appeared on the yard."

"How long ago did this happen?" Patch asked.

" 'Bout three months. It's over and done with now."

Patch stood up and shook Wilbur's hand again. "And we're done, too. Thanks for your time."

The three riders gathered by Wilbur's gate.

"I think our buddy here got burned out of twenty grand by some Eastern European types," surmised Redbeard.

"Yeah. Just like Benny and Gus said, looks like we have a case of Russian criminals passing phony bills. If this kind of stuff is happening on our turf under our noses, we need to know about it and nip it in the bud. I think we should check in with those boxers, the Rachkovs, next and see what's up with them, if only to protect our turf. After all, this is our town."

23

Back at the Kompound, the phone rang. Redbeard on the horn. After sniffing around asking a few acquaintances, pumping some Phoenix politicos, consulting a couple of boxing experts as well as a local-beat sportswriter, he had assembled a partial sketch of the Rachkovs.

"Here's what I got so far. Their father raised them in the city of Kishinev, south of Kiev, in a part of the former Soviet Union now called Moldova, an independent state since '91. They never knew their mother. She was part Jewish, died in childbirth having them. Not a lot of Jews in Kishinev. A dozen years ago they came to this country with a few hundred American bucks they'd saved and what little cash their father scraped up on the black market. This was when the United States of America opened its arms to persecuted Russian Jews looking for new opportunities. Their dream was to bring their father over to taste the fruits of American prosperity. They landed first in Brooklyn in the Brighton Beach area, stayed there awhile, but found it—how do you say?—occupied territory. Too much competition from too many Russians who beat them to the punch, pardon the pun.

"They got jobs as nightclub bouncers, then started boxing professionally. It was a natural transition, bouncing and boxing. A novelty act. At first, the promoters wanted them to fight each other, a real carnival act. But they had promised their poor old papa they would never fight each other for money. They'd trained hard in Kishinev as boxers when they were teenagers."

"These guys have a real story, don't they?" Patch asked.

"Typical immigrant success story," Redbeard said. "Once their father died, they decided to leave the East Coast. According to one article, they picked a place on the United States map by throwing a dart and decided to make a new life in the Arizona desert. They borrowed two grand and headed out west. Not the religious types at all. Just a couple of self-made men who started out with nothing and built a small empire from the dust. I don't see them as mobsters at all."

"Nice work," Patch said. "You really are a PI."

"If it paid more, I'd probably still be doin' it," Redbeard answered.

After Patch had heard Redbeard's findings, it was inevitable that the two of them pay a little visit to the No Name bar, if only

to spar a few rounds with a couple of Russians.

Big Benny and Gus must have put the word out on the street, because Patch and Redbeard didn't get ten feet past the bouncers into the No Name on a Thursday night before they were intercepted. Just as the day bartender had warned, the No Name was a different place at night. It was jammed. Darkened with loud nonstop bumpin' and thumpin' house music shaking the walls. Patch recognized their "interceptor." He was the burly bearded fellow with the silver toothpick who'd been staked out front, sitting in the Benz when he and Redbeard first rolled up to the No Name.

"We've been expecting you," he muttered to Patch. "Come with me."

The dance-floor crowd was dressed in the latest streetwear. Clingy skintight outfits on the girls. Athletic floppy hip-hop gear on the guys. All shapes and sizes, from whirling foxy Latin mamas to upscale too-cool white boys leaning at the bar, occupying the sidelines, eyeing the ladies while nursing a lust-filled booze buzz. Redbeard spied the quick-change bartenders selling E pills along with their nonstop drink orders. Unlike most nightspots, where the studs outnumbered the fillies, Patch noticed an inordinate amount of beautiful women prowling the premises. You could hardly swing a cat without decking a nine or a ten as girls crammed the dance floor in waves and circulated throughout the crowd.

Over in the farthest roped-off corner, seated in and around half a dozen plush red leather booths, was a different crowd of partyers from those at the bar or on the dance floor. They resembled the wiseguys who had circulated out front the other day, whom Patch and Redbeard had watched shoot pool. Their scarred, etched faces were already familiar. A pussy patrol of beautiful cocktail waitresses scampered at their beck and call, hovering over the men in the booths in low-cut necklines, balancing trays crammed with colorful umbrella drinks for the women and whiskey and vodka shots for the men. The most beautiful of the waitresses, a statuesque blonde with a slit gown, buzzed from booth to booth pouring from an enormous bottle of Stoli vodka entombed in a block of ice.

This was no hangout for the biker-bar crowd. Patch and Redbeard were in the minority, way underdressed in T-shirts and black jeans, clomping in their dark motorcycle boots. Patch was the only patron sporting a three-piece MC patch. He and Redbeard were conspicuous as they threaded their way through the crowd, following Silver Toothpick Man to the back of the club. Patch hadn't realized how gargantuan the place was until now, as they navigated their way through the cavorting beautiful people and Mob guys.

The Rachkovs' private domain was up another few stairs in the back. The guy with the silver toothpick knocked three times on a brushed-metal door then slipped a key in the lock and opened the door wide. Patch and Redbeard walked in first. It was clear that the Rachkovs had spared no expense furnishing the office they shared. The walls were neatly decorated with more framed photographs, pictures of the twins with President Bill Clinton, and then a variety of sports figures and fighters, movie stars, politicians, American heroes, and past presidential candidates whose names Patch had already forgotten, both

Democrats and Republicans. *These guys are players, schmoozing both sides of the political aisle.* There were grip-and-grin photos of local and state politicians whom neither Patch nor Redbeard recognized. There was an assortment of shots with the chief of police, the sheriff, and a few superior-court judges, one of whom Patch vaguely remembered giving one of his members stiff time. (His Honor looked more relaxed in a white tennis outfit than in his customary black robe.) The Rachkovs were connected, and like most moneyed immigrants Patch had met, they craved respectability and acceptance from America's power elite.

Sitting behind two adjacent matching desks were the same two guys, Palooka Left and Palooka Right, whom Patch and Redbeard had watched spar it out in the boxing ring across the street.

"Gentlemen." Lefty was the first to venture from behind his desk. "Mr. Patch Kinkade. Vladimir Rachkov. I understand we have a mutual friend in Mr. Benny Fratello. I spoke with him the other day."

The Rachkov twins were dressed casually, in jeans and shirtsleeves. Patch recognized the matching Bonaparte tattoos on their arms from their old fight-card portraits. Both were tall and solidly built. Their long faces were triangular, their chins coming to a near point, with dark deep-set eyes and thick, dyed jet-black hair. Perfect teeth. No sign of a scar or a broken nose on either of them. Both smelled strongly of identical cologne. Patch immediately looked down at their shoes, a habit he'd picked up as an ex-con. The brothers wore expensive black cowboy boots with a reflective military shine that made Patch recall his army days. If he hadn't seen them in action, he might not have pegged these two as pugilists.

Patch shook the boxer's hand. His grip was viselike and extended an extra second.

"How'd you peg us so fast at the door?"

Vladimir laughed. "Mr. Patch—can I call you Patch?—it wasn't that difficult. This is my brother, Nicholai. Please call him Nicky. And call me Vlad."

Nicky, the boxer formerly known as Righty, stepped from behind his desk and nodded without speaking. Vlad continued.

"We were very good friends of Boris, a member of your organization, who we are very truly sorry to hear is now dead. Believe me, Mr. Patch, we know what it feels like to be targeted by the authorities in power, larger-than-life forces."

"I don't follow. What 'larger-than-life forces' are we talking about?"

"Never mind." Vlad waved off the odd comment. "More on that later."

Okay.

"Quite the crowd out there tonight." Patch picked up the conversation. "Especially the fun bunch in the corner booths."

"*Brodyagi,* we call them."

"Meaning?"

"How would you say it here?" Vlad said, looking over at Nicky for linguistic support. "My English is not so good sometimes translating Russian words. Wiseguys, on the rise. On the way up?"

"Precisely," Nicky acknowledged.

"They keep the neighborhood safe," said Vlad, "and us businessmen honest."

"Ahem," grunted Redbeard, clearing his throat to call attention to himself.

"Oh, sorry, pal. This is my friend Redbeard. He's my partner in crime. I hope you don't mind—"

"Why, no," Vlad said, shaking his head and running his hand over his chin, confused by Redbeard's lack of orange or red facial hair. "Mr. Redbeard? Why, if you don't mind me asking—"

"Don't ask," advised Patch.

Nicky picked up the conversational slack. "Why don't you have a seat at our table? We've taken the liberty of putting together a light spread."

Vlad nodded to Silver Toothpick, who was stationed stalwartly in the corner, arms folded. He exited out the door and back down the stairs as Nicky led Patch and Redbeard to a conference table crammed with a strange delicatessen-like food spread, along with red and white wines and a large bottle of vodka.

"Come this way," Nicky said.

"We hope you arrived hungry." Vlad laughed.

"Actually, we ate," said Patch. "But thanks anyway. We're mainly here to talk and ask a few questions, if you don't mind."

"Nonsense. You eat anyway," Vlad commanded. "We eat, we talk, we drink a little bit, too. Where we come from, how you say, our humble beginnings back home, it's an insult to us for you not to partake of this," said Vlad, pointing to the food.

"Very humble beginnings," confirmed Nicky, shaking his head sadly. "So of course we are very proud of this." He waved a hand at the twins' wall of fame. "America, we so love America."

"Don't we all?" Patch responded drily and rhetorically.

"Not all, Mr. Patch, not all," said Nicky, with a serious tone in his voice. The look in his eyes grew somber. Sizing up the two, Patch decided Nicky was darker and moodier, while his brother, Vlad, was more upbeat and diplomatic.

"How long you boys been in the US of A, if you don't mind me prying?" Redbeard asked, reading Patch's mind with his question.

"Not at all," Nicky answered. "It's been over a dozen years; we left when we were twenty-four."

"So you guys, uh, brothers, operate quite a few businesses in this part of town?"

Nicky smiled broadly. "Mainly this nightclub and our gym, among a few other things."

Patch looked around the room. He already admired the Rachkov brothers' drive and ambition.

Nicky and Vlad turned their attention to the food-and-booze spread that remained untouched on the conference table.

"Allow me," said Nicky, giving Patch and Redbeard a rundown of the deli spread. "Smoked salmon, sturgeon, pickled mushrooms. Fresh fruit. A variety of meat pies and cold meats. Cheesecake. Dig in, gentlemen." He clapped his hands. "Please."

The centerpiece was a frosted bottle of vodka.

"We can start with that," Redbeard said, pointing at the frigid magnum-size vessel. "And hold the OJ."

"Absolutely." Nicky's huge hands gripped the bottle as he poured the contents across a lineup of four short but stout stemmed glasses, splashing a stream of Stoli onto the satin-finished tabletop. Then it was Moldovan wine, from the Rachkovs' homeland. Situated around the table, the four men then toasted the USA, Mother Russia, and the Infidelz MC. The food went down fast, including the sturgeon, a gigantic, butt-ugly variety of fish/sea monster that Patch remembered once helping bludgeon to death on a bizarre fishing trip up north with a couple of drunken and crazed Alaskan members. Speaking not a word of business, the four men gorged themselves, saying little, eating a lot, putting an impressive dent into Vlad and Nicky's sumptuous spread. Where Patch's renewed appetite came from, he didn't know.

After three-quarters of the vodka had been poured, Vlad walked over to his huge oak desk, opened one of the top drawers, and pulled out a fistful of Cuban Cohiba contraband.

"Cigar?" he offered, passing a cutter and a torch. Soon the four were puffing smooth but robust Cuban tobacco.

"Please," Vlad urged Patch and Redbeard. "Sit back and relax yourselves. You are our guests."

"Yes," Nicky said, pressing his hands together. "Now, what can we do for you?"

Relaxation had been the last thing on Patch's mind before the influx of vodka. Now, kicking back didn't sound like such a bad idea. But instead, he cleared his throat and took a long draw off his stogie before setting it irreverently on his food plate. He leaned forward on the couch. Patch had dealt with Mob types before. Show respect. Kiss the ring. Break bread. Throw back a couple of pops. Smoke 'em peace pipe. But now it was time to stop the glad-handing and fucking around and start asking the tough questions.

"You knew Boris."

"That's right."

"And I know that you guys were seen with Boris before he died."

"Is that right?" Vlad asked in an offhand manner.

"Trust me," Patch said. "It's true. I got four guys from my club slain execution style, small-caliber gunshot wounds to the head, as clean and efficient as we've seen. Now here's the big question: What the fuck went down with you guys and Boris before my boys got killed?"

"Don't you know?" Vlad asked, his voice turning sour.

"Enlighten me."

"What kind of leader do you call yourself, Mr. Patch? Shouldn't you know what your minions are up to?"

"First off, the Infidelz don't have minions. We have club brothers. Second, what our members do on their off time is their own business. But I'm askin' you, what went down?"

"Boris came to me. We had set up a little under-the-table deal. Your boys blew it. Badly. Absolute imbeciles."

Imbeciles? That one comment raised Patch's temperature a few degrees.

"Specifics, Vladimir. What deal?"

"Like you said, Mr. Patch, what your members do on their own time is none of your concern. Nor is our business any of your concern. Beyond that, I have nothing to say."

Patch's vision fluttered as he felt a rush of blood flow to his brain. He wasn't used to being spoken to in an arrogant manner, even by Mob guys. Acting purely on instinct, he leaned across the table and grabbed the impudent Vladimir Rachkov by the throat. Just as Nicky jumped up in defense, fists clenched, Redbeard responded likewise and pulled his knife.

"You guys need to install a metal detector out front, brother," Redbeard said. "Now just answer the fucking question."

Vlad, struggling in Patch's grasp, silently turned several shades of red. As the veins popped out of his neck and forehead, Patch's grip tightened. And tightened. And tightened. Vlad began turning a purplish shade of blue.

Then the office door burst open. It was Silver Toothpick with a trio of bouncers, the same bunch Patch had seen standing around the front door, joking, checking IDs, and keeping a watch out for trouble—and now looking like they just found some.

All four bodyguards could have doubled for the Arizona Cardinals' front line, but instead of rushing some poor quarterback, they blitzed Patch and Redbeard. Silver Toothpick grabbed Patch by the wrist and gave it a savage twist, breaking Vlad free. Patch felt an excruciating jolt of pain. Like high voltage, a sharp buzz shot through his throttling hand. The next thing he remembered was flying heels over head over the couch, into and against the wall, his back pulverizing a set of framed pictures that came crashing down around him on the floor. Next came a swarm of kicks to his ribs. Patch felt the oxygen immediately explode out of his lungs, leaving him breathless and groaning. Then came solid blows to his face. Spitting blood, his face throbbed, his eyesight blurred.

Through the one eye Patch could barely see out of, it looked as if Redbeard wasn't faring much better. Vlad and Nicky's boys were all over him, giving him a sound beating. But it was a sweeping kickboxer shot to the side of the head that brought Redbeard down with a loud—*timber!*—thud as well. Patch could hear and feel the thumping of the house music downstairs through the floorboards. Then the lights went out.

25

Patch lost his sense of time. Out cold for minutes or possibly hours, he woke up to the sight of Vlad and Nicky's faces dancing in his slim field of vision.

Patch stirred. He wasn't tied up. Nor was he taped, cuffed, or chained. He was free to stand up, rattle his brain back and forth, and survey the physical damage. Patch got up then looked down at his swollen wrist. He didn't like how it was sorta bending the wrong way. Plus, it hurt like hell.

"You need to work on your people skills, Mr. Patch," Vlad said.

"Where the hell am I?"

"You're in heaven, Mr. Patch. We are your guardian angels," said Vlad.

"How come I'm not fresh out of a trash compactor on my way to the municipal dump in one of Benny Fratello's garbage trucks?"

"Because we like you, Mr. Patch, and we're not mobsters. We have no beef with you."

Patch looked over at Redbeard, out cold, half his face bloodied.

"How's he doing?"

"Still alive at least, and breathing."

"Jesus Christ." Patch groaned rubbing his bruised ribs. "I gotta hand it to you fellas. You gave me one old-fashioned Louisiana ass-whoopin'. And if I can speak for old Redbeard over there, ditto for him. Seriously, why are we still alive?"

"I told you. We have no beef with you, Mr. Patch."

"I guess I'm not following you, Vladimir. Rewind."

"We know who killed your comrades."

"Wait a minute," Patch said. "Freeze right there, Vlad. Explain."

"Boris came to me with a deal, a proposition. He said he had a transaction of some sort, and he was twelve thousand five hundred short and needed financing for a haul of guns and ammo."

"Guns? What fucking gun deal?" asked Patch.

"He needed twelve grand more for up-front money. His middlemen needed cold cash to buy the guns, for which Boris had already found a customer willing to pay a hundred. If we spotted him the twelve-five, Boris promised we'd double our money. It was small potatoes for us. We did it as a favor to Boris. But then things got screwed up, your guys ended up dead and in the papers. We laid low. It's not enough that we lost our investment. Now the cops, the feds, and the Secret Service are snooping around. Murder. Counterfeit money. Not good for two legit Russian immigrants."

"How do I know you guys didn't just knock my guys off for pissing away your money?"

"You think much too small, Mr. Patch. What do you take us for? Thugs? Do you think that we'd kill four men for twelve grand and then go to the trouble of putting them in a freezer to make the front pages? I paid more for my couch. I can assure you, Mr. Patch, we like publicity, but not of that variety."

"We're trying to run a business," Nicky continued, "not start wars with motorcycle gangs."

"Clubs," Patch huffed, though talking made his rib cage ache profusely.

"Clubs?"

"Yeah, clubs. We're a club, not a fucking gang."

"Whatever, Mr. Patch. Club, gang, how ever you wish to say it," Vlad said.

At the risk of another provocation, even though the Russians' henchmen were no longer by their sides, Patch stubbornly asked the question again: "Who the fuck killed my guys?"

"We know who killed your comrades, Mr. Patch," said Nicky. "If you hadn't been so rude the first time around, we would have told you then."

"Then tell me now, dammit." Patch felt another jolt of pain shoot through his rib cage and wrist.

Nicky continued.

"Well, Mr. Patch Kinkade. Some people come to this country with their eyes on the easy money, the quick buck."

"Spare me the lecture. Who killed my guys?" Patch was sick of talking. Nicky ignored Patch's comment and prattled on.

"Did you know, Patch Kinkade, that the former Soviet Union now has the largest amount of billionaires in the world? The streets of Moscow are filled with Rolls-Royces and Bentleys."

Though he was racked, literally, from head to toe, Patch's patience was tested . . . again.

"What does a bunch of Rolls and Bentleys have to do with my boys getting snuffed and thrown in the deep freeze?"

"There are many crews here now," said Vlad. "They deal in drugs, smuggling, counterfeiting. Believe it."

Counterfeiting. That got Patch's attention. *Maybe we're getting somewhere.*

Nicky finished Vlad's thought.

"Here in the Southwest, believe it or don't, we now have brand-new Eastern European crime families taking root—back home my father called them *tieps*—who rival your Italian and Mexican wiseguys. Only much meaner and more merciless. One group on the rise here is called the Cartel . . ." Nicky's voice trailed off.

"The Cartel? You mean like an oil cartel? Arabs?" asked Patch.

"No, no, much worse. We believe they are the murderers. These animals killed your friends."

"A cartel killed my guys?" asked Patch.

"We believe so. It was only a matter of time before your organization ran into them," replied Nicky, nodding his head.

"They move counterfeit cash?"

"Yes, we believe so," repeated Nicky. "And buy guns."

"And they give honest men like us bad name," Vlad said.

Honest? Patch had now met the latest version of "honor among thieves." The Rachkovs were a lot of things, but honest? The last thing Patch needed was a convoluted line of Russian bullshit; in any case, Patch feared another dead end where he would have to start again from scratch. So, right now, Vlad and Nicky's cartel theory was as valid as the next one. Except there was no next one.

"The Cartel murdered your guys," Nicky repeated, agitated and waving his hands, "and the cops will do nothing. It's easier to single out motorcycle people than root out the real scum. It fucks us all."

"A cartel killed my guys," Patch repeated. "Shit, I need a solution."

"Unfortunately, Mr. Patch, we don't have a solution. Like terrorists, these guys are invisible. Run by a spineless coward who is already in prison."

"Wait a minute. What guy in what prison?"

"A guy. In federal prison. Colorado?" Vlad half asked, looking over at Nicky, who shrugged.

"This so-called Cartel. Can we see them?" asked Patch. "Are they out on the street, or are they just a spook story like Bin Laden and his Al Qaeda boys? Not really there, but everywhere. Omnipresent."

"Mark my words, they will strike. Something big will happen. And you will know it when you see it. The Cartel is part Al Qaeda, part IRA. They bomb buses and they rob banks. Big scores. They rob big and they rob small, in the thousands and the millions. Just like the IRA did in London, robbing all those millions. Like an earthquake, they are due to shake things up while the police and the government won't have a fucking clue. I can't say how or when, but we'll be hearing from them. You can be sure. And you'll know it was them. They usually leave a calling card—a claw mark. Four scratches if you give an identity to terror, a myth, it makes it more real to people. Terror is right under our noses. What happened to your guys is merely—how you say?—the tip of the icicle."

"Icicle? You mean iceberg."

"Iceberg?"

"Yeah, tip of the iceberg."

"Whatever."

With that, Vlad leaned over and poured a final round from the vodka bottle. Redbeard came to, perplexed as Patch that he was alive to taste another hit of the juice. Patch gave him the all-clear signal and then knocked his vodka back, leaving behind a trace of bloody saliva in the glass, feeling the burn of the alcohol as it traveled down the hatch.

109 «

Vlad glanced at his watch, an expensive Rolex. "We must go, as must you. Perhaps we'll meet again. If not, have a nice life, Mr. Patch. You, too, Mr. Redbeard."

Outside the No Name, Patch brought Redbeard up to speed. The question remained for the two of them: Who was the Cartel that had killed the Nomads? Who was this mysterious kingpin running the Cartel out of a prison? What about these four scratches? Patch and Redbeard limped toward their Harleys. It was way past closing time, nearly sunup. They both must have been lights-out for a few hours. Their bikes remained untouched in the parking lot.

"Whattaya figure?" Patch asked.

"Hard to say." Redbeard scratched his swollen, clean-shaven chin. "I need to go home and clean up."

Despite the beating he and Redbeard had endured, Patch felt the apprehension he'd felt toward the Rachkovs melting away. The Infidelz had always been on the shitty end of the stick in terms of political influence and judicial power. Constantly spied on and persecuted. But these Rachkovs had low friends in high places, potentially working for them if the Delz played their cards right.

"Reckon you should call out the cavalry and go after these cartel guys for payback, Patch?"

Patch rubbed his aching wrist and remembered Nomad George's disdainful sneer. "Not if we can't see or touch an invisible enemy. Believe it or not, Redbeard, I'm gonna back off and find out exactly what Baldy Boris Badenov got himself into. There's more than meets the eye with these Russians."

If we can't follow the money, maybe we need to follow the guns," Patch told Redbeard as the two dismounted their motorcycles in front of the Nomads clubhouse. He had called an emergency meeting, and despite the frosty response his desire to assemble the troops had received from Big Head, the members were concerned to find out if Patch had any updates regarding who'd whacked Boris, Tito, Sanchez, and Wheeze.

As Patch opened the front door of the clubhouse, the light went on. He led Redbeard to the back of the place, where Big Head, Greek, Gorgeous George, Caesar, and Tommy were already waiting.

"This here is Redbeard, Tito's older brother. He's been assisting me in my investigation."

Big Head stood up and reluctantly shook Redbeard's hand, introducing the rest of the crew.

Patch dispensed with the pleasantries, opting to give the guys a quick update.

"Unfortunately we still have a lot more questions than answers. Any facts you guys can help us with will put us further down the road toward finding out who killed our guys."

Patch looked around. The Nomads were with him, attentive.

"Here's what we know so far. Some kind of gun deal went down with Boris."

The Nomads exchanged furtive glances, nodding. No one was surprised.

"Apparently what happened was, someone fronted the guns and Boris and the boys did the deal. The final payment was in counterfeit currency. Then four of our guys are dead. What I need to know is this: Who would buy the guns for Boris in the first place? Any ideas?"

Big Head scratched his goateed chin. "My guess would be two guys, Romanowski and Kemp. Boris and those guys have been buddies since they were kids. Ski and Kemp were once featured on one of those bike-building TV shows. But they're into running scams. Whatever you need, these guys can get it for you, so you don't have to go out on the street. I know Boris was close to them. They used to buy, sell, and trade together, if you know what I mean."

"Anybody interested in paying Ski and Kemp a little visit?" Patch asked the Nomads.

The response was unanimous. "Hell yeah. Let's see what those motherfuckers know."

A loud beating on the sliding steel door of their shop startled Ski, causing him to drop hot coffee on the lap of his coveralls.

"Goddammit!" Ski muttered angrily, reaching for a rag, then the shotgun lying underneath the front counter. He jacked a round and then walked over to the front sliding door.

"Who's there?" he shouted back, clutching the shotgun.

"It's not the police," said a gruff voice. "Open up."

Confidently armed, Ski hit the red "open" button on the wall. As the steel door gradually lifted, the sunlight hit a *Wild Bunch* lineup of seven backlit bikers. Ski gulped out loud, gripping the shotgun tighter. A real Sam Peckinpah nightmare come true.

"G-g-gentlemen," Ski stammered. "What can I do for you today?"

Patch and Redbeard moved a step forward from the rest of the crew.

"We got a few questions and we're here for answers," Patch said.

"Try me."

Kemp came out from the back of the shop, wiping his hands of oil and grease.

"What's going on here?" he asked.

"We got visitors," Ski replied.

"I see that," Kemp answered back.

"We can make this as quick and easy as you want," said Patch. "Boris Badenov and three of our other guys had a deal going down with you. We need to know the particulars."

Ski spoke up first. "It just so happens we're a little short on particulars. You see, Boris fucked things up and we're out twenty-five grand. The last time we saw Boris, he was supposed to clear things up. Then he ended up dead, and like I said, we're out twenty-five grand."

"So *you* fronted the guns?" Redbeard asked.

Kemp interjected: "Boris gave us twenty-five grand down, which we used to buy the weapons. He promised us another twenty-five K, which was to be our profit."

"How much did Boris move the shipment for?"

"A hundred grand," said Kemp. "Relatively small-time."

"But enough to get my guys killed," replied Patch.

"Like we said," Ski said, cradling the shotgun, "we got fucked, too. Once Boris got murdered, we had to lay low."

"Any idea who Boris sold the guns to?"

"No idea. Boris arranged a blind drop," Kemp said. "He figured the guns would change hands a few more times anyway, that there would be others taking a taste along the way. None of us cared, as long as we got paid."

Patch looked over at Redbeard. Ski and Kemp were losers, too, fucked out of a twenty-five-thousand-dollar commission.

"You guys hear anything about a Cartel? Russian dudes? Does any of this ring a bell?" Patch asked them.

Ski and Kemp looked at each other and shrugged.

"We don't know nothin' about no cartels, no Russians, no anything. We just wanted our money. Or else get the guns back. Boris wasn't able to retrieve any of it before he died."

Patch turned around and scanned the lineup of Infidelz darkening the doorway. He nodded and shrugged.

"We'll live with that for now."

Ski put the shotgun back under the counter, picked up a rag, and wiped the sweat off his face. Patch nodded to the Nomads as they walked outside to their bikes, started them up one by one, adding layer after layer of thunder to Ski and Kemp's reverberating workshop.

"We'll be in touch. Bank on it," Patch said.

Ski hit the button. As the steel door hit the concrete floor with a loud crunch, both Ski and Kemp let out long gasping sighs.

115 «

The funeral of Boris, Tito, Sanchez, and Wheeze—or "the Frozen Four," as the newscasts called them—kept the club at the top of the newscasts and above the fold on the front page of the newspaper. *Not a good thing. Plus, there's no such thing as a low-key bike funeral,* Patch thought. The spectacle, the rumble, and the torque-busting decibels alone attracted more attention to, never mind more curiosity over, the mysterious circumstances surrounding the Four's grisly deaths.

Patch glanced over at a nearby strip mall where a trio of guys were snapping photographs with cameras mounted on tripods. Gang squad. Goon squad. They see patches, and they do what cops do. Playing Big Brother. As Patch, Redbeard, and Hollister strolled toward the chapel, Patch waved at the contingent of rooftop cameramen atop the Craven Auto Parts store across the street.

Cheese. Patch smiled wide and pretty. Sweet surveillance.

The atmosphere was a near carnival when Patch arrived at the funeral home with Hollister and Redbeard. The publicity surrounding the Four's demise drew sympathetic bike riders from around the Southwest, the West Coast, and as far east as New Jersey, Florida, and the Carolinas. The Four had become a symbol of biker mortality, and attending the service was many riders' way of showing two-wheeled solidarity against the rash of recent FBI crackdowns against motorcycle clubs across the country. The interstate on the way to the cemetery out of town was jammed with Harleys revving and lane splitting. The glimmer of the chrome. The smell of the oil and the burning of three-bucks-a-gallon gasoline. Raised fists in the air. Freak flags vigorously flying high amid the whooping and hollering.

The Infidelz's West Coast brotherhood was present in strength, showing their support. The most welcome face appeared outside the chapel, where the services had already started. Henry Rancid. Patch and Hank hugged warmly.

"Patch, what the fuck happened to you?" Rancid asked, seeing the bumps and bruises across Patch's face and arms. "Which locomotive ran over your sorry ass?"

"Don't ask," answered Patch. "It ain't nothing I'm not gonna settle down the line, believe me."

"Listen, bro," Rancid continued. "I heard you caught a mountain of shit from your Nomads chapter. I'm sorry about that because I know you were there for us in Palm Desert. Answering our call. So sorry it's cost you, brother."

"No regrets. I'd do it again, especially the redhead part." Patch winked, shifting the subject. "How's Wrangler?"

"Behaving himself. I told him if he steps outta line, I'm sending you back to avenge the beating he gave you. Jesus, Patch, you do look pretty banged up."

"It hasn't been easy bein' me the past few days. Henry, say hello to my partner Redbeard and my godson, Hollister."

"Redbeard, how do you do? Hollister, it's an honor. So, you guys have any idea who did this? The rumor mill is buzzin' with everything from an FBI kick squad to rival MCs. I hear the cops ain't got shit."

"Fuck the rumors, Henry. If it don't come directly from me, then don't believe it."

"Whatcha got so far, Patch?"

117 «

"Not much. I got a lead a couple of days ago. You heard of an underworld outfit called the Cartel?"

"Doesn't ring a bell."

"Some Eastern European outfit, supposedly run out of a pen in Colorado by some kingpin?"

"A prison gang?"

"Doesn't sound like it. Their capo is supposedly in the pen callin' the shots. That's all I know. I'm comin' up empty down here. All I get are tight lips and shrugs."

"A pen in Colorado? If it's federal, that would be Englewood. Actually, one of our guys on the Big Pen List, named Wolf, he's housed in Englewood. Patch, you remember Wolf from Berdoo?"

"The name rings a bell," said Patch, flexing his sore throttle hand.

"He got tangled up in some interstate-trucking hijacker beef last year. He's got about twenty-two months left on a four-year stretch in Colorado before he's out. We got a visit set up with him next week. Why don't I have him put the word out. Wolf's got juice inside. He's bound to dig up something."

Patch nodded at Redbeard and Hollister.

"That would be sterling, brother, a real help. Even if you come up dry."

"We roll into Denver around Sunday. We'll see Wolf on Monday. I'll shoot you a call after that."

"Would ya?"

"You bet I would. Anything for you, Patch. I owe you bigtime."

Outside the chapel, Patch could hear the final strains of the closing music inside. Willie's version of "Amazing Grace" into Dire Straits' "Brothers in Arms." The doors flew open and soon the street was filled with riders of every affiliation, starting up their bikes for the slow roll to the cemetery. Redbeard and Hollister got separated from Patch and they rode on ahead. Patch found himself more and more shuffled in the maze, farther and farther back, toward the rear of the miles-long pack. He tried following the crowd for a half mile or so, until he felt a restless tug, besides the sore ribs twinging inside his chest. When the entire pack turned right, Patch hung a hard left.

Something contrary, unexplainable, beckoned him to break off and just ride. The combination of the Four's deaths and his own dark but restless mood. Free from the speed constraints and the stilted tradition of yet another gigantic slow-rolling funeral pack, Patch hit the open road fast. He revved Mean Machine for all she was worth and hit the empty highway hard until he was, according to his gauges, just shy of 95 mph. His tank full, Patch rode until he rolled into Flagstaff, where he stopped off at Macy's coffeehouse. Sitting on the stoop, nursing a cup of black coffee in the chill, he was tempted to keep on riding until he hit the Grand Canyon or some pit stop like Tuba City. Or else he could head on east, toward Texas or Oklahoma, and points beyond. And never fucking come back. As he sipped his brew, a coal-black mixed-breed Lab loped over and sat next to him. As Patch petted the dog, he wondered what exactly the canine was thinking. A rain dog who lost his way, his scent back home. *Kind of reminds me of me. Happy to be lost and unaccounted for.* The dog was restless. So was Patch. Alone. So was Patch. Content to have roamed far from home, free from the crowd. So was Patch. Could this be one of those times when Patch merely took off, with only the clothes on his back, no gear, very little money, no plans, taking a cross-country jaunt on his loyal Road King? How could a mangy black dog inspire such a grand spontaneous gesture?

Patch's thirst for revenge for the murder of his brothers created polar-opposite sensations inside him. Distilled to its essence, his feeling was one of wanting to kick ass while at the same time needing to run away. He was at a crossroads: between the extremes of wanting to enter the fray of battle while the next minute, fuck it, he was tempted to leave it behind.

Patch thought about the five years he'd spent in prison. As

hellish an environment as it could be—the boredom, the bureaucracy, the noise, the violence, and the petty bullshit of prison-yard politics—at the same time it had been *The Great Escape*. It was the total opposite of Steve McQueen jumping his motorcycle to freedom. When Patch was "inside," the problems that arose on the outside had to be dealt with by other people in the club.

Ultimately, responsibility had gotten the better of him. Instead of running farther to points east, Patch jerked his ride, reversed course, and headed back, taking in the red dusty beauty of Sedona on a side-road detour back. The red dust and red rocks and shale of Sedona were the closest he'd come to communing with the splendor of nature. Heading east two thousand miles away *was* a tempting proposition. There was a safe-house Infidelz club-house in Greenwich Village in New York. But his sense of duty to the Four and to Hollister and Redbeard exerted a stronger tug.

A couple of days later the phone rang. Henry.

"Brother Hank."

"Dude. I may have somethin' for ya."

"Speak."

"Wolf, the brother locked up in the Englewood, Colorado, pen. Says there's some Russian dude inside and that there was a shitstorm of feds and government guys prowling the yard last week or so. Everybody's been in lockdown. Something's going down. He thinks it might have to do with your Cartel stuff. According to one of the snitch trusties, there's a guy they keep moving around. Sometimes he's in solitary, in SHU"—security housing unit. "Other times he's on the yard, in the general population as a shot caller for a bunch of Russki gangsters. Sometimes he's in the hole for disciplinary reasons. Being disobedient. Refusing to eat. Stuff like that. Wolf said this Cartel thing rings a bell. Say, Patch, is your phone clean?"

"Think so, but call me on the pay phone just in case. You have the number. Give me ten minutes to get down there."

Patch rode MM to a nearby convenience store. A few seconds later, the pay phone rang.

"Henry."

"What I was gonna tell ya is, Wolf said, hey, if you trace this bullshit back to anybody on his yard, he'd be glad to arrange a strike for you, on the yard or in the hole. Could be easily done and nobody would be the wiser. Wolf assured me it would be done quiet and efficiently. Why not let your fingers do the walkin' on this one, whattaya think?"

"Lemme think on it. It's tempting. If I can push the remote button on this, I just might. But I wanna be sure. No use doin' it if I don't find a real connection. Or what if the guy is innocent? Sounds like a golden opportunity, though. Call me when you hear more from Wolf."

"He's got a phone call scheduled for tomorrow evening, about eight o'clock, so I should have more for you tomorrow or the next day."

"That's cool, Henry. To think I could end this all so easily in the joint is a relief. You're a prince."

"Brothers till the end, over and out."

Patch put the phone down. *Progress.* It might not be so hard to close the book on this one after all. What he needed was a definite connection between this Cartel and the murder of the Four. Or else for the Cartel to send out a message or a sign of some sort that they were out there. Visible. Vulnerable.

Patch didn't have to wait too long until the next perfect storm rolled in . . . and the Cartel would step from the shadows as subtle as a nine-hundred-pound gorilla.

It was a few minutes past eleven o'clock on a sleepy Thursday night at a serene suburban residence on the outskirts of Phoenix. The Taggert family—a father, his wife, and two teenage sons—prepared for bed. Dad had already turned the television off and was in the kitchen, timing tomorrow morning's coffeemaker, when he heard a loud rustling noise in the side yard of his house. He switched the outside lights back on, and when he opened the front door to investigate the racket, three men wearing ski masks and waving pistols overtook him.

Gunman Number One stuck his piece in the frightened man's face. With brute strength he threw the man to the floor and kicked him forcefully in the direction of the living room.

"Get up on your knees and put your hands behind your head." The gunman slipped a pair of handcuffs firmly on his wrists.

In the background, the father heard screaming and struggles in the vicinity of the bedrooms of the single-level dwelling. The rest of his family was soon herded into the living room. Gunman Number Two ran into the kitchen and threw three chairs into the living room. Gunman Number Three bellowed to the mother and her two sons.

"Each of you grab a chair and sit down," he commanded in a

strange throaty accent. "And don't make a sound! Otherwise you're dead." The assailants used absolutely no profanity.

None of the gunmen told another what to do. They had their routine down pat. The husband watched in horror as his wife and two kids were bound and gagged to their chairs with gray gaffer's tape, then blindfolded. Their arms were secured behind them with nylon zip ties. Nobody was going anywhere, and a long night lay ahead. A shock wave of panic and uncertainty coursed through each captive family member. There was nothing they could do but pray they'd see the light of the next morning. It was a well-executed home invasion. How would it end? With assault? Burglary? Murder?

None of the above. Instead, the gunmen methodically sat and waited until sunup. They helped themselves to food and drink and calmly watched over their prisoners for what seemed, to the bewildered middle-class family under siege, an eternity. By six-thirty that morning, the next phase of the operation was set to begin. They had explained to the father what he was expected to accomplish that day.

"Okay," said Gunman Number One with an eerie tranquillity to his voice. "You know what you've got to do to save your family. Go to work like normal this morning and do exactly what we told you. This nightmare will be over in twenty-four hours. That is, unless you screw up. Then the nightmare just begins."

The troubled father tried to suppress his darkest fears as he drove his car into the hub of Phoenix, where he worked as an officer at the Bank of Arizona, supervising the cash-disbursement center located in the basement of the main downtown branch. If he did not cooperate fully or if he called the police, he had been duly assured that his family members would be killed.

After putting in a full day's work, by four o'clock that afternoon, Taggert the bank officer walked out of the complex with a canvas Diamondbacks holdall bag filled with nearly a million dollars in cash. He slipped around the corner and handed off the bag to a waiting stranger, who then made a call on his cell phone as he evacuated the area. Taggert had done as he'd been instructed. It was only a taste of what would happen next. Taggert had one more money drop to organize to satisfy the captors who still held his family hostage.

An hour later, five o'clock, just before closing, a white-paneled van drove down to the basement premises and backed into a shipment bay located on the eastern side of the bank's cash-disbursement center. Three crates of used bills (another $11 million) were stacked and waiting to be loaded into the van. After the pickup, it took off in a northerly direction, toward the vicinity of Esplanade Avenue, and made a routine exit out of town.

But it still wasn't over.

Twenty miles northeast, in Scottsdale, a charcoal-colored SUV with tinted windows was parked, motor running. Same bank. Different branch. Friendlier. And full of Scottsdale riches, land of wealthy suburbanites and golf addicts. A new team of bank robbers, three men wearing loose-fitting lightwear jackets, donning baseball caps and dark sunglasses, jumped out of the SUV and walked a few yards into the branch. Being payday Friday, the building was filled with customers.

It was not a typical note robbery, where tellers are simply handed a slip of paper and instructed to empty out their cash drawers.

"Ladies and gentlemen," announced Scottsdale Bank Robber One with a clear, booming, authoritative, but guttural-accented voice that bounced and echoed around the high-ceilinged marble interior. "This is a robbery. Do what we say and nobody gets shot."

He drew an automatic rifle and waved it toward the crowd in line. His two accomplices pulled their rifles out.

Like its downtown counterpart, the Scottsdale branch of the Bank of Arizona was FDIC insured, which "insured" that if the bank robbers were apprehended, they would be looking at federal charges and automatic twenty-year prison sentences, minimum.

Bank Robber Two disarmed the pudgy black security guard standing by the main entrance and knocked him onto the floor.

Bank Robber One pointed his rifle toward the patrons flocking nervously in the roped-off teller line.

"Everybody. Facedown on the floor."

Bank Robber Three was stationed over at the administrative area. "I want you people," he ordered sternly, "to line up, faceup against that far wall. Hands up. Mouths shut."

The next few unlucky bank patrons to walk in during the robbery were instructed to join the others facedown on the cold granite floor. According to most of the criminals that Patch knew, robbing banks ranked as the most addictive and exhilarating crime out there. It's relatively safe, since bank tellers and employees are strictly instructed, at the risk of getting fired, to cooperate and hand over their cash without resistance.

While Bank Robber One provided armed cover, Robbers Two and Three ran over and hopped up onto the main teller counter. They hurriedly and efficiently stuffed their shoulder bags with currency. They plundered each cash drawer to the tune of eight to ten thousand dollars (the usual capacity of an end-of-the-day cash drawer). The ready cart, which services the tellers, was fully stocked with bundled greenbacks. That accounted for another eighty grand in loot.

So far, no casualties. An elderly man propped up against the wall began to feel dizzy. Fearing he might suffer a heart attack, the robbers permitted him to sit on the floor and place his head between his knees.

Amid the commotion surrounding the old man, a bank manager tried to slip a "dye pack" of bills into one of the cash drawers. Once the robbers had left the premises, the activated stash would have detonated an explosion of red dye and tear gas, disabling them and dousing and blinding them in indelible red coloring.

6 CHAMBERS, 1 BULLET

Unfortunately for that bank associate, the gunman spotted the sleight of hand. To the loud gasps of the hostages in the bank, the offending employee was shot dead. There would be no more dye packs or homing-device-activated "bait money" slipped into these robbers' kick that day.

Once the branch had been cleaned out of nearly all its money, one of the robbers ran his fingers down the side of one of the walls, leaving four short scratch marks. Then the three gunmen walked briskly outside, jumped back into the waiting dark SUV, and disappeared north on old 101, a full two minutes before the area was overrun with sirens and patrol cars. From start to finish, the heist lasted thirteen minutes. By the time the Scottsdale police arrived, the bank robbers had scored a couple hundred Gs. Grand total of all three robberies, over $12 million.

Patch was chewing on a roast-beef sandwich and staring at the tube when he turned up the volume on the six o'clock news. A "hat-trick robbery" graphic appeared behind the well-coiffed local TV newsman. Patch yelled for Hollister, who darted into the living room.

"We have a bulletin just in," alerted the plastic man on the screen, reading "just-in" copy off his teleprompter.

"Around three o'clock this afternoon, the central downtown Bank of Arizona was robbed of several million dollars at their cash disbursement center. Nobody was hurt or killed there. No shots were fired. Police believe the money was taken in two separate heists, one for a million, the other nearly eleven million, from inside the downtown cash center.

"Then at five o'clock this afternoon, a third robbery took place. Three gunmen, armed with automatic rifles, robbed a Scottsdale branch of the Bank of Arizona on North Boulevard. One employee was killed. One elderly patron was sent to the hospital for a heart condition. Police believe all three robberies were connected."

"Hollister," said Patch, chewing and pointing at the talking head. "Why am I not surprised this is goin' down?"

The broadcast continued.

"It's been called the 'hat-trick score' at the Bank of Arizona in the heart of downtown and in Scottsdale. Police and eyewitnesses report it was carried out with remarkable precision. There is speculation about organized-crime involvement, though law enforcement officials are perplexed."

"Holy fuckin' shit," exclaimed Patch. "I can't believe the cops are spilling this much information to the press on the airwaves. The clones on the TV are comparing these robberies to the IRA, just like the Rachkovs, when they predicted 'something big.' Fucking unbelievable!"

Just then the newscast showed video surveillance footage of the three gunmen in the Scottsdale robbery. Gunman Number One looked up directly at the security camera, his face obscured by shades and a ball cap pulled low over his forehead. Using his remote, Patch froze the gunman's face on his TV screen.

"This must be the Cartel." Patch snarled at the television screen, eyeballing the disguised robber, and pounded on the coffee table as the news broadcast concluded the story of the daring daytime theft.

"Authorities say this is the first triple bank robbery in Bank of Arizona history."

Patch watched as the newscast concluded with an update. There were more stunning developments.

"And now these related stories just in. A woman and her two teenage sons were found wandering near a Highway 17 roadside rest stop just outside Phoenix. Preliminary reports say that the three have been identified as the wife and children of James Taggert, the downtown Bank of Arizona bank manager, whose family may have been abducted by gunmen in connection with the hat-trick robberies. No injuries were reported. Nearby, in the Sycamore desert park area, where the freed hostages were found, a white panel van was found blown up and set on fire. We'll have more information on our eleven o'clock report tonight."

Patch shook his head in amazement. "Fucking millions, gone

without a trace, along with the guys who did it, no evidence left behind.

"These guys know how to rock-and-roll," continued Patch. "Big scores. Counterfeit dough. Russian mobsters. And now this. They cleaned the whole bank out. I need to talk to Redbeard, and fast. These gotta be the guys the Rachkovs said killed our Nomads."

Rancid Henry's follow-up call came the day after the triple bank heist. Like the day before, Patch was in a rage.

"Patch, just got off the phone with Wolf. You might find this interesting."

"Hit me."

"Just yesterday the feds came in and swept this Russian guy off the yard. Again. The scuttlebutt is that he's been subpoenaed by a federal grand jury to testify. Guess where?"

"Phoenix?"

"Yep. Guess for what?"

"How the hell should I know, Henry? What's this, twenty questions?"

"Don't you watch the fucking news? That robbery, that bank heist, the one that went down in broad daylight."

"What about it?"

"There's a massive grand-jury investigation. Indictments are going to be handed down."

Suddenly the fog lifted.

Charges. Indictments. Bank robbery. Twelve million dollars up in smoke. Four Infidelz dead. Russian Mobs. Grand jury. Federal investigation. The feds were putting it together. Why not beat them to the punch?

A flash of clarity lit up Patch's brain, lifting the weeklong haze. *Yes! Of course! Grand-jury investigation!*

"Hello? Hello?" Henry's voice screeched through the phone lines.

"Yeah, yeah. I'm here." Patch was smiling for the first time in days. "Listen. That's news I can use. Gimme a few days to roll things around in my head. Gotta run, Henry."

Patch hung up the phone and called in Hollister. The boy was parked in front of the damned computer. *Someday that fucking Internet is gonna suck that boy's brains into the eternal void.*

"Hollister, get your ass in here."

Silence.

"Now."

Hollister hupped to. "What's shakin', boss?"

"I need you to get Redbeard on the speaker," Patch said pointing to the phone parked on the dining-room table.

"I got him on speed dial. Press nine."

With the push of one button Hollister had Redbeard's drawl wheezing through the speakerphone.

" 'Ello." At all hours Redbeard sounded half-asleep.

"Redbeard. Patch."

"Chief."

"I need you to set up a meeting with the Rachkovs. Tomorrow. First thing."

"I don't understand. The last time we saw those guys, they whooped our sorry asses. You sure?"

"Just fucking do it."

"As soon as I drop this call, I'm on it."

"Breakfast on me. Tomorrow morn. We meet in town. Nine A.M."

"Sounds like a plan. Over and out."

Patch had his devious smile plastered on his face. Hollister eyed him suspiciously.

"What's up with you, Patch? You ain't smiled in weeks, now you're grinnin' ear to ear, and I don't like it. You gonna tell me what this is about?"

"In due time, kid, due time. Tomorrow I might have a research project for you. Meantime keep your powder dry over the next coupla days, even if you gotta call in sick for school. I might need you on a moment's notice, so be on call."

No school. That got Hollister's attention quickly.

"Yes, sir. Three bags full, sir." He smiled and saluted.

"Now get the fuck outta here. Dismissed," Patch said to the boy. Hollister resumed the position. Back in front of the flat-screen computer monitor.

Even before his customary two cups, Patch was wound up, channeling his exhilaration into hunger, ready to devour his huevos rancheros the second the waitress let go of the plate. He doused and attacked his eggs with a Tabasco bottle in one hand and a corn tortilla in the other.

"So, are we set up with the twins?" Patch asked Redbeard.

"Ten A.M. at their bar, previous scene of the crime." Redbeard looked at his watch. "That's T minus fifty-five minutes. So what's this about?"

"Got a call yesterday from Rancid Henry."

"And?"

"He said that according to one of our guys in the Colorado pen, there was a Russian dude on the yard that the feds are moving around. Now he's being extradited to Phoenix, probably because of that bank heist. Counterfeit money and gangland murders, too, I'm thinkin'. And I'll bet the grand-jury suspects that the murder of the Infidelz Nomads are related to all this."

"Uh-huh."

"Here's the hookup. We once had a guy, Filthy Fred. Twenty-year member. A real nose for the law. Cops hated him. There was a huge federal grand-jury investigation over some club members' involvement with an interstate stolen-motorcycle scheme. They had already arrested about a dozen of our guys. Fred had nothing to do with it. But they called him in to testify anyway. Fred resolutely refused to testify, which royally pissed off the government. They immediately threw *his* ass in the same can. Pronto. Contempt of a federal grand jury. Fred didn't pass go. He went straight to jail. The federal stir."

The wheels continued to turn inside Patch's head.

Redbeard looked lost.

"Don't you get it?" Patch asked impatiently.

"Not so sure I do."

"There's speculation that this bank heist has Mob links. But everyone we talk to, from Big Benny on down, they're in the dark about it. Remember the Rachkovs' rap about the Cartel and the big scores? Maybe that's our link."

"Link?"

"Yeah, between the bank heist and the murder of our guys. Then there's our guys and the counterfeit money. The execution-style killings."

"I don't get it."

"That puts the capo of the Cartel right in our backyard. The guy pulling strings from the federal pen in Colorado running his Mob, now he's coming to a theater near us. He's on our turf now."

"I don't exactly call the federal lockdown in Phoenix our turf. Besides, what's this got to do with Filthy Fred?"

"Filthy Fred refused to testify. They threw him in the federal jail, where he was able to meet inside with our guys and help plan and organize their defense. Subsequently they beat the charges. Then Fred walked out with them. Free as a bird."

"You wanna go inside and chase this guy around a federal penitentiary?"

"If we already had one of our guys inside, he could take care of it. But we don't. He's here now. So somebody's gotta go inside. Might as well be me."

"You're gonna voluntarily check yourself into a federal lock-down facility? Are you nuts?"

"Why not? It's where they hold you in contempt of a federal grand jury. And they leave you inside there until you decide to be a good boy and cooperate. I'll be in the same place as the Cartel's kingpin. I could be inside for as long as it takes to accomplish what I have to accomplish. I hit pay dirt, knock him out, and come back out."

"First off, Patch. Infidelz don't cooperate with grand juries. Second, you can get yourself an automatic eighteen-month sentence by not playing ball with a grand jury."

"Sometimes you get more accomplished inside than out. Besides, I can do the time."

"That's fucking ridiculous, Patch. Doin' time now compared to back in the eighties is a whole different trip. I can't let you do it. I *won't* let you do it. What's Hollister say about this?"

"He doesn't know yet. But I say it's worth a try, and that's that. I want to meet with those Rachkov twins. I got an idea how they can help us."

"Care to put me in the loop?"

"Sure. Lemme finish my breakfast and I'll fill you in. I'm so fucking hungry, I could eat a mule."

As he rode Mean Machine to the meeting at the No Name with Vlad and Nicky Rachkov, Patch's head was spinning at high velocity.

This will put this Cartel motherfucker within striking distance.

But how would Patch get close enough to whack him? A better question: Just who was this guy? Patch didn't have a name. Or a description. What the fuck did the guy look like? This guy was a virtual fucking Casper the Unfriendly Ghost.

Outside, Patch only hit walls; it was dead-end city. Maybe the answers lay on the inside. Somebody needed to light the fuse to force an explosion. The first domino had to fall, and with their connections and influence, he hoped the Rachkovs could provide the first push to set off a huge chain reaction.

The No Name was dark and empty when Patch and Redbeard pushed the unlocked door open. The place reeked of stale beer and smoke. Vlad and Nicky were seated at their own bar, speaking to each other in English. At the sight of Patch and Redbeard, they switched to Russian. Patch hoped this time their meeting wouldn't end so painfully. He still ached in places.

Vlad got up from his bar stool while Nicky remained seated with a hardened look of suspicion on his face. Vlad was noticeably bubbly. Nicky was not.

"Mr. Patch. I honestly didn't think we'd meet again."

"So, you come back for more?" Nicky replied sarcastically. "How's that wrist?"

Patch shook his wrist with a wry smile.

"You mind?" Patch asked, grabbing and pulling out the stool next to Vladimir.

"Please, sit down. What's on your mind? Please sit, too, Mr. Redbeard. Can I get you something to drink?"

"We'll drink what you're drinkin'."

Vlad gave Nicky a nod. Nicky got up and walked around behind the bar. Bending down, he disappeared momentarily before surfacing with two cold ones, Michelobs.

"I wanna talk about the Cartel," said Patch.

"Yes, we knew you would. Didn't we tell you? Did we or did we not warn you?" asked Vlad, pounding the bar.

"I take it you're referring to that bank job," Patch said. "Yeah, okay, we'll give you that one. I gotta admit, you guys called that one. Just like Babe Ruth pointing to the bleachers and parking one in the seats. Which gave me an idea."

Patch continued his pitch, choosing to lay down his cards honestly.

"We have it on good authority that the guy you mentioned doing time in Colorado, heading up this Cartel, what's his name?"

"I never mentioned his name. Nobody knows his name. His aliases—he has many. Even the United States government is in on keeping the guy in the closet."

"The dark."

"The dark?"

"Yeah, the dark. You said closet."

"Whatever."

"Let's call him Casper the Friendly Ghost," Patch said. "What if I told you that Casper is being extradited here to testify before a grand jury? What would you say to that?"

Vladimir's eyes widened while Nicky turned away, seemingly bored.

"How do you know this?"

"Trade secret, fellas. A man's gotta keep some mystique."

Vlad continued: "Suppose what you say is true. What does that have to do with us?"

"Yes," Nicky interrupted his twin. "What's in it for us to become involved with low-life, the Invisibles, motorcycle gangsters."

"Hey, motherfucker! We're called the Infidelz," Patch reminded him.

"Brothers, please," Vlad shouted. "Let's at least hear what each other has to say. Start over, Mr. Patch. How can we assist you?"

"I was thinkin' about those pictures on your wall. The politicians, city fathers. I was thinkin' about how you could drop a tip, anonymously, to the grand jury. Just drop my name, sayin' I might have something to contribute to their investigation, related to the murders or the bank heist that will get me inside their federal facility, next to this character."

139 **«**

"This is insane, brother," Nicky said to Vlad as he lit a cigarette, got up off his bar stool, and paced in a circle, like a tiger in a cage. "Why should we risk our standing in the community getting involved with the likes of Infidelz? I forbid this. This discussion is over."

But Vlad was just beginning to envision the merits of Patch's preposterous plan.

"Not so fast, brother," he cautioned Nicky. "Tell me more, Mr. Patch."

"It's simple. If this guy murdered my brothers—and it's beginning to smell like he had a hand in it—then this is my chance to even the score."

"But the risks, Mr. Patch," Vlad said, "they are considerable. First, isn't it a crime not to cooperate with a federal grand jury? And if you get next to this jackal, whatever you're planning to do, you could end up in prison for the rest of your life."

"First off, Vlad, if my suppositions don't wash, I'll simply cooperate with the grand jury, tell them nothing special because I know nothing special, and I'm outta there. If I end up doing more time than I'd planned, say eighteen months, let's just say I've been inside before, and there are worse places to bide time. Prison is much better than ending up in an old folks' home. At least in prison the youngsters listen to your stories and buy you ice cream. Prison doesn't scare me. I've done enough time to know my way around that world. I'm willing to take the risk if it means getting this bastard."

"And what do we gain from this?"

"To kill the snake, you must first remove his head. You eliminate those who are making it harder for you and your friends to do legitimate business down here. Surely that doesn't sound so terrible, does it?"

"Mr. Redbeard. What are your thoughts on this?" Vlad asked.

"I think it's a fucking crazy idea, but once Patch gets something in his head, I support him fully."

"Like I said . . ." Nicky stubbed out his cigarette impatiently. "This sounds like crazy talk. Good day, gentlemen. You take care of this, Vlad." With that, he stalked off and raced up the stairs to his and his brother's office.

But Vladimir tipped back his bottle of beer in interest. "You know, we can make a phone call or two to our city-hall people about the grand jury. But I think something else needs to happen—something much more dramatic—to get their full, undivided attention. Do you understand what I'm saying, gentlemen?"

"We have to grab the grand jury's attention," Patch said. "That gives the illusion that the Infidelz are indeed the targets of a faceless Cartel Mob."

The next afternoon, in front of the Infidelz Nomad clubhouse, a powder-blue Harley-Davidson AMF-era Sportster sat next to a Dumpster. It had been a cool enough ride in its day, but now it was slightly beat up, its paint cracked and oxidized. The mileage showed a mere 12,800 miles, proof that the odometer had flipped over at least once, as had a few of its previous riders. The Sportster had been sitting unattended next to the Dumpster since after midnight the previous night. Maybe it had broken down. Nobody but an AMF Sportster enthusiast would have given the beater a second look.

A length of wire ran to the gas tank. On the other end of the wire was a clump of greenish clay, connected to a remote detonating device. As the clock struck four past four in the afternoon, something inside the AMF stirred. The old blue Sportster fizzled in a puff of flame, then exploded and shattered into a thousand pieces. Motorcycle shrapnel, shards of fender, cracked pipe, flying parts, and flaming bits of tire sprayed the area within a thirty-yard radius. The explosion was loud. The fiery Harley frame shot twelve feet up in the air and flipped end over end into the middle of the street. The impact of the blast fractured one side of the Dumpster and blew the lid off, sending its contents everywhere, creating a putrid black smoke.

Gorgeous George and Patch ran outside to check out the commotion. As they did, a van full of surveillance cops already parked across the street emptied out and revealed themselves. More sirens sounded. A fleet of police cars raced toward the charred ruins of the detonated motorcycle to inspect the damage and possible casualties. The fire department and the bomb squad arrived to investigate and clear the debris. Nobody was hurt.

FBI Inspector Rance Kelly arrived at the blast scene a few minutes later. He wiped his brow, relieved that the errant explosion had claimed no victims. Kelly scribbled a couple of pages of notes on a small pad. He approached Patch, who was standing nearby, and flashed his FBI ID. Neither Gorgeous George nor Patch showed any interest in cooperating.

"Any idea who might have done this?" Kelly asked Patch, fully expecting the cold shoulder.

"Hell if we know, Officer." Nomad Gorgeous George shrugged. "You're the guys with the stinking badges."

"Well, it seems more like a threat of some sort than anything else, wouldn't you say?"

"Who knows?" Patch said.

Agent Kelly looked Patch in the eye. "Look. Don't bullshit a bullshitter. You know much more about this than you're letting on."

Kelly's cell phone rang. It was Sheriff's Deputy Howe.

"Excuse me." Kelly walked away from Patch. "Kelly here."

"What's going on down there?" Howe asked. "Something about a bomb blast in front of the Infidelz place?"

"Yeah, but save yourself the trip. I just spoke to Kinkade. He's not saying shit. We have the bomb guys already down here determining what kind of explosives were used. From early indications, it's a Semtex-type material, the same stuff that blew up that white van out in Sycamore Park after that big bank robbery."

"Not only that," said Howe, "we know that Kinkade was seen visiting somebody down by the Caspian Deli."

"I'm starting to think there might be some kind of blood feud going between these bikers and some other group," said Kelly.

"You reckon a turf battle?"

"Looks that way to me. Forensics was going over the bike that was targeted, and it's a mess, but they also found that it had been keyed or slashed with something. Four parallel scratch lines, claw marks, carved into the gas tank, what's left of it. Like what we found on one of the victims. And now the bank. These bikes are important to these guys, and desecrating one would be a pretty bold insult. Might be something. Listen, I'm on my way back to the bureau, I'll call you when I get in."

In a futile gesture, Kelly handed Patch his card. "You *will* call me if you find out anything."

"Certainly, Agent Kelly," Patch scoffed, reading the card. "Anything to help out the good ol' FBI."

Patch walked inside Hollister's bedroom and clapped his hands like a drill sergeant. "Close those books. Off your ass and on your feet! Let's go grab a burger. We gotta talk. Let's ride."

The two walked into Luke's Diner, along the desert highway. Although the place was nearly empty, Patch headed toward a booth in the very back. After the two gave their orders, Patch broke the news over a couple of iced teas.

"Listen, kid. There's been a break."

Hollister's eyes widened. He kept his voice low. "You guys find out who did it?"

"In time."

"What does that mean?"

"I mean we have some pretty sturdy clues as to who is involved."

"So you can patch things up with the Nomads and we can get back to normal, right?"

"Not for a while. I have to take off for a spell and you're gonna have to spend some time around the house without me until we get this straightened out."

Hollister lost his smile. Patch fiddled with the paper on his straw, stirred in some sugar in his tea, then took a drink off the giant tea tumbler.

"Patch, what is this about?"

"It's about a plan I cooked up."

"What plan?"

"Well, uh," Patch stammered, then he leaned in with a low whisper, "the less I tell you the bet—"

"That ain't our agreement, Patch." This time the kid was getting tough with his godfather, which Patch didn't hesitate to do when the shoe was on the other foot. "I'm gonna ask you again, what is this about?"

"Well, ahem, like I said, it's a plan that I came up with." Patch shifted in his seat. "I'm going to spend some time in a federal detention center, the FDC," he whispered cautiously.

Hollister leaned across the table? "A federal what? You're going back to prison? Are you crazy? What the hell—"

"You're right, Hollister, it is crazy. But I promise. It won't be for that long."

"Meaning?"

Patch paused, and then looked up. "Meaning I'll be away for a month or two . . ."

"A month or two? Jeez!" Hollister tried to keep his voice down.

"Or three or four. Eighteen at the worst."

"WHAT!? You're putting *yourself* in jail for eighteen months?"

"Yeah, I got this idea to piss off the grand jury. Look, kid. It's a harebrained scheme, but I'm convinced it will work. I need to hook up inside a federal facility to find somebody."

"And it's one of those fucking goons that knocked over that bank? Patch, are you fucking insane?"

"Keep your voice down," Patch warned. "This is serious. Listen, my mind is already made up. You won't have to be alone at our place. I've already made arrangements for Redbeard to come out and stay there. You two need to work together."

"And what does Redbeard think about this so-called plan, Patch?"

"He's okay with it. He supports me," replied Patch.

"Oh, that's just great." Hollister grimaced, folding his arms and rolling his eyes.

The waitress brought two large platters of cheeseburgers and fries. Hollister looked down at his food with a stern face. He was in no hurry to dig in.

"I'm not happy about this. What happens if you don't make it back out? Then I lose another—" He couldn't finish the words.

Patch reached over and grabbed the boy's arm and shook it gently. He tried a smile. "Look, kiddo. I'm just gonna play a few mind-fuck games with the grand jury. That's it. They'll put me away for a little while. I'll figure some shit out, and then you guys spring me. No more than that. I promise you. Plus I'll need you and Redbeard to visit, keep me up-to-date, and I'll do the same."

"Bullshit, Patch."

"Look, Hollister. I need you on this. I know what I'm doing. You need to set up home base for Redbeard when he comes to stay. And just like we talked about, I need you to help me out. The two of you will have plenty to track down for me on the outside while I'm inside. I'm just a phone call away from getting sprung, honest to God." Patch tugged at Hollister's shirt. "I need you to be on my side."

Hollister picked up his burger, but before he bit into it, he blurted, "Just promise me that you're not gonna fuck up my life."

Patch reached for his burger and smiled. "Of course I'm gonna fuck up your life. I'm practically your father. Roll with me on this one, and when it's over, we'll start work on Mean Machine Two."

The landline rang at Kinkade Kompound. Hollister picked up. A man with a Russian accent was on the other end.

"Vladimir Rachkov for Mr. Patch Kinkade."

Hollister slid the cordless phone across the table toward Patch and Redbeard.

"Patch. A guy named Vladimir?" said Hollister.

"How the fuck did you get *this* number?" asked Patch.

"Never mind that, Mr. Patch. Are you ready to rumble?"

"I'm ready once you guys set the table and confirm my reservations."

"Things are proceeding nicely." Vlad cleared his throat. "And speaking of reservations, I'm calling to invite you and your friends to a party my brother and I are throwing at the nightclub for a local boxer my brother and I are managing. We want you to drop by. Show you there's no bad blood between us all."

A night of partying, courtesy of Patch's new Russian buddies. "Sounds cool. Provided we don't get beat up."

"Good. Fun starts at eleven. And please pass on a personal invitation to Mr. Redbeard."

"Will do. He's sitting right here. I'll let him know."

Patch put the phone down and guffawed. "It looks like Vlad

and Nicky are playing ball and have invited us to their club. To-morrow night."

"Hollister," Patch shouted out with a grin. "Tell you what, champ, tomorrow night you're comin' out with us. A little field trip with Mr. Beard and myself."

"So this is your idea of progressive parenting?" Redbeard pointed over at Hollister and laughed loudly. "Put a big hat on him, throw on some shades, an overcoat, nobody'll know he's a kid. Once you're inside, son, you're on your own."

oly Bada Bing," exclaimed Hollister as the three rode up to the No Name entrance. The place was already jammed. Vlad was outside puffing on a massive Cohiba Churchill, glad-handing and welcoming every guest who strolled inside. The place was already filled beyond capacity. Searchlights were illuminating the sky. Politicos and socialites everywhere.

"Gentlemen, welcome," Vlad said between cigar puffs, snapping his fingers and dragging Patch, Redbeard, and Hollister past the towering bouncers. "Champagne!" The Rachkovs' version of a prospect came running with a bottle of Cristal and four glasses.

"Drink up, drink up!" Vlad shouted above the music blasting from inside.

The room was dark and smoky, with brass poles fastened from the long wooden bar to the top of the ultrahigh ceilings. Dancing on the bar were shapely topless babes, some with large bolt-ons, dressed in satin lingerie. The gorgeous statuesque looker dressed in a purple camisole led Patch, Redbeard, and Hollister to a booth in the gangster ghetto and took their drink orders. The same group of hoods Patch had seen here before babbled on in what he presumed was their typical Russian or East European dialects. A few of the gangsters nodded respectfully in Patch's direction. Patch looked up at the towering waitress, model, dancer, or whatever other occupational talents she possessed.

"Beer."

"Beer," said Redbeard.

"Beer," chimed in Hollister.

"Make that two beers and a ginger ale," Patch told the waitress as Hollister slunk down in the booth, mortified.

As the drinks arrived, Vlad Rachkov approached the booth.

"Mr. Redbeard, Mr. Patch. Can we take some time to talk together before it gets too lively and festive?"

"Too lively and festive? Whaddaya call this?" Patch pointed to the bar dancers. "Slide on in."

"We might better talk upstairs?"

"Suit yourself."

Patch and Redbeard scooted out of the booth and followed the broad-shouldered ex-boxer upstairs toward the "Staff Only" locked metal door. Patch turned around and shouted back to Hollister.

"Why don't you take a little stroll? Check out the lay of the land. We won't be long."

Hollister wormed his way out of the Mob booth and back toward the crowded bar, where he grabbed a vacant stool. He set his soda down and gazed longingly up at a blonde bumping to a four-on-the-floor blues standard. She had a Harlow eighties porn-star look right down to the pouffy platinum moussed hair and Wonder Woman implants. She flashed Hollister a sexed-up smile. It was the first time the boy had been so close to such a feminine wonder of the world. Yet the crazy thing was that she was, at the most, only a few years older than he. Hollister had watched enough movies to know what to do next. He pulled a couple of crinkled dollar bills out of his pocket, straightened them on the bar, and reached up and tucked them into the hem of her stocking. The platinum girl smiled, bent down, and planted a long wet kiss on the youngster's lips. He smelled her perfume and tasted whiskey. After the kiss, Wonder Woman grabbed Hollister's hand and ran it slowly across her bare but firm thirty-six Double Ds. Then she danced her way farther down the bar.

A couple of dapper-dressed male patrons seated next to the boy hooted loudly. Hollister's heart rate shot up instantly. He had just been deep French-kissed by a bombshell. The incident left him flushed in the face. He bolted from the bar and made his way toward the back exit that led out to an open parking area behind the club. The wave of fresh air felt good on his sweaty reddened face.

As Hollister leaned up against the wall to catch his breath, he relived the kiss one last time. A voice interrupted his solitude. A dark-haired young woman. He wasn't alone behind the club.

"Excuse me."

"Huh?" Hollister was taken by surprise.

"First time here?" She had a pronounced Eastern European accent, while her command of English was barely proficient. Out of the shadows stepped a thin, lithe, barely legal brunette dressed in a gilded teddy. Though she was dressed sexy, something about her was girl-like, nothing like the cosmetically reconstructed pole dancer on the bar who had planted her collagen lips on Hollister a few minutes earlier. Whereas that girl was vavoom Pam Anderson, this one was innocent and doe-eyed, with a crooked smile and young girlish features. She repeated her question, like it was a suave setup line borrowed from an old Bogey film.

151 «

"First time here?"

"Ah, yeah, actually," Hollister stammered, avoiding her eyes. "But I have my own reserved booth inside."

"You live around here?"

"We—we got a place outside Phoenix. In the desert. Me and my da—I mean, my guardian."

The young girl stepped closer and extended her hand.

"I'm Valentina."

Hollister adjusted his leather jacket, took her outstretched hand, and lightly shook it. She wore no rings. No expensive jewelry hung around her neck.

"They call me Hollister. You're new to these parts?"

"I arrived about a month ago," she replied.

"Me, too, I mean, sorta new. I've only been in Arizona for, hmm"—Hollister paused to count the time—"well, eighteen months." He nervously studied the girl's face, trying to ascertain her true age. Seventeen, eighteen max. "I take it you're working here tonight. You know, uh, dressed like that."

Valentina changed the subject. "I saw you ride in, on a motorbike, I think."

"Yes. I rode in all right, but not a bike. A chopper," replied Hollister proudly.

"My father, back home, he had old police bike. Rode it everywhere."

"Harley-Davidson?"

Valentina wrinkled her nose as she tried to recall the make of the bike.

"I think it was . . ."

Hollister moved in closer to better hear her soft voice. Valentina played with her dark hair like the innocent teen she had been a few months before.

". . . A Norton?"

She had a different inflection in her voice, Slavic. Russian. Hollister couldn't figure out which.

"Yes, I believe it was Norton or a Triumph, like the sports car, no?"

"Did he let you ride it?"

"Oh, no." She laughed, waving off the idea. "I was too much young. Never rode. My father, he is dead now."

"Sorry to hear that." Hollister's voice cracked. "So's mine."

"I'm sorry, too." She put a hand on his shoulder. Hollister felt a tingling surge through his innards.

"So, how's about a ride? On my bike, I mean. A short spin. It's a monster."

"A bike ride?"

"It's right around the front. You'll die when you see it."

Hollister took off his jacket and wrapped her thin frame inside it, took her hand, and headed around toward the front parking lot where his bike was parked.

"So, Valentina, where's home?"

"Hmm." She paused and ruefully replied, "A place far, far away from here."

Patch and Redbeard sat huddled with the Rachkov brothers in the office upstairs while the sound system thumped and shook below them.

"I believe we've planted the right seeds and lit the correct fuse," said Vlad, mixing his metaphors. "Mr. Patch, you should expect a subpoena in next day or so requiring your testimony."

Vlad continued: "Our lawyer emissaries have passed on the info, and from what we've heard, the feds are quite interested that you might know about the counterfeit money and the robberies and the murders."

"You'll be inside jail walls in no time." Nicky scowled in a deadpan manner.

"I hope you're ready to rock, sport," said Redbeard. "Enjoy your last few days of freedom."

"Ready, willing, and able. I'm anxious to do my time and get this shit behind us," Patch said as he got up from his chair, uneasy and tense as he gazed out the window. Down below, he could see Hollister and a young girl talking. *I'm gonna miss the kid.*

Vlad rose from his chair and clapped his hands. "Well, I say we go downstairs and get sociable. Let's not let these lovely girls go to waste a moment longer."

"I'm with you on that," Redbeard said. With that, the four stormed out the door, following the music downstairs toward Action Central.

Patch, Redbeard, and Hollister sat on hard stone-cold benches in the otherwise empty federal marble hallway, outside the deliberation room where a federal grand jury was investigating Mob and biker activities in the states of Arizona, New Mexico, and Colorado. Patch's invitation to the party had come directly from the Office of the United States Attorney thanks to a few well-placed calls by Vladimir Rachkov and friends and the bombing in front of the Nomads clubhouse. Presiding over the affair was a United States magistrate. This drill was far different from Patch's past dealings with the criminal-court system.

The activities of the Cartel, heated up by the recent dramatic bank heist and the quadruple murders of the Delz, had blipped clearly onto the grand jury's radar screen. In Patch's estimation, whoever this dude was who led the Cartel, once Patch tracked him down, he would be one sorry desperado.

"I guess I just go in and tell 'em to get fucked," said Patch, getting up to pace the hallway, waiting for his summons. "That'll get me inside for sure."

"You might wanna be a little more diplomatic than that," suggested Redbeard.

"I can't take the Fifth. I have no lawyer present. Are we in America?"

"This is not America," said Redbeard. "This is the United States federal government."

In the past, when Patch had played defendant, he had a lawyer by his side. It wasn't until the last minute that he realized the gravity of his current situation—that he would soon be facing a grand jury alone. He'd been prepped for court appearances in the past. Coached and questioned ad nauseam. This time he was flying blind.

"Once you get inside, be extra careful," cautioned Redbeard. "If you answer one question, you're required to answer them all. Better not to answer any questions. None."

Patch paced the hallway, seemingly oblivious.

"Did you hear what I said?" Redbeard asked. "No answers. Patch, I'm serious."

"I heard you twice the first time."

The cloak of secrecy surrounding the hearings didn't mean that grand-jury testimony didn't sometimes leak out prior to a returned indictment. It did mean, though, that in between questions, if Patch got stuck, he could venture outside and ask for legal advice from his peanut gallery.

Just then one of the magistrate's bailiffs opened the door.

"Mr. Everett John Kinkade?"

Redbeard, hearing Patch's real name, sniffed back a laugh.

"Watch it now." Patch pointed his finger accusingly and followed the bailiff inside. He was dressed indifferently, an Infidelz T-shirt, black Frisco jeans, and the same exact funky pair of black motorcycle boots he'd worn for going on three decades.

Seated inside were rows and rows of what were supposed to be ordinary John Q. and Joan Q. Public citizens serving on the federal grand jury. One woman, an attractive brunette, well dressed, wearing a hefty diamond ring on her left hand, had the faintest hint of a smile on her face when Patch entered the room. The majority of the jurors blanched at the sight of Patch's strut and his overly casual attire.

Don't tell me this is the first time you've laid eyes on a criminal.

The U.S. attorney for the district of Arizona sat on one side of the table. There was no other side. Patch sat alone. A grand jury is supposed to be a nonadversarial investigation. Theoretically, an indictment is simply the method by which a person is charged with criminal activity. Consequently there is supposed to be no implication of guilt or innocence in the questioning. But after Patch was sworn in, the interrogation began.

"Mr. Kinkade," began the U.S. attorney. "For the record, can you please state your full name and occupation?"

"Excuse me, Your Honor. Just a minute," Patch said. He calmly got up from his chair, walked back out into the hallway. Both the U.S. attorney and the magistrate were stunned.

"They want to know my name and occupation."

"Well, Jesus Christ," Redbeard hissed, "don't give it to them."

"Didn't think so. Just checking." Patch laughed.

Patch walked back into the courtroom, sat down, cleared his
throat, and hunched over toward the mike.

"You know my name; otherwise why ask me to come down here?"

A slight ripple of laughter moved through the courtroom.

"Are you a member of the Infidelz motorcycle gang?"

There it was, the G-word. Patch was tempted to go on a tirade about being labeled a gang member. Then he remembered Redbeard's strict instructions. Don't answer a single question; otherwise you'll be required to answer them all.

"I refuse to answer."

"Okay," said the U.S. attorney, surprised. "What can you tell us about the murder of four men found frozen in a Phoenix meat locker?"

"I've got nothing to say."

"Mr. Kinkade, was the explosion of a motorcycle in front of your clubhouse related in any way to Mob retaliation that has to do with a vendetta going on as a result of the murder of four of your members?"

That's a loaded question, and quite a mouthful. Patch fought the urge to comment. "I've got nothing to say."

"You don't know, or you refuse to answer the question?"

"I refuse to answer any of your questions. These proceedings are a joke, and I refuse to be a party to them."

"Your Honor," the U.S. attorney said to the magistrate, "in calling this witness, I was under the impression Mr. Kinkade was going to be more cooperative in supplying information. If you could please order the witness to merely answer the questions."

"Mr. Kinkade," said the magistrate, "we are not here to determine anyone's guilt or innocence."

"You must be; otherwise why am *I* here?"

"Please answer the question or I'll find you in contempt of a federal grand-jury investigation. That, Mr. Kinkade, is no joke."

"I never said it was a joke. I just refuse to answer your questions."

"Maybe you're not understanding me, Mr. Kinkade. You have no right to refuse. Refusal is not an option. Not cooperating with the grand jury can result in automatic jail time."

"Then bring it on."

"You are hereby ordered to answer any and all questions put to you by the U.S. attorney; otherwise you will be found in contempt of these proceedings and will be immediately incarcerated at a federal detention center until you decide to cooperate with this federal grand-jury. Do you understand, Mr. Kinkade?"

"Your Honor, I understand that you are hereby welcome to kiss my flat white motorcycle-ridin' ass."

Patch noticed the attractive brunette woman with the Hope Diamond on her finger holding back a snicker. But the magistrate was far from amused.

"Mr. Kinkade, I'll give you one final opportunity before I have you hauled into federal lockdown for contempt. Answer the question."

"Since I can't, don't want to, nor can I, nor do I need to take the Fifth, I refuse."

"Suit yourself, Mr. Kinkade. I find you in contempt."

The magistrate motioned and in a matter of seconds, two stocky United States marshals cuffed Patch and led him out the front door, which surprised him. He'd expected the back way. The hallway was still empty except for Redbeard and Hollister. As Patch was paraded by his friends, he stole a glance at Redbeard. Hollister was stunned. But Patch took it as a joke.

"Somebody call my poor mother. Oh, the shame of it!" Patch yelled over to Redbeard, quoting his idol, Chino, from *The Wild One*. The marshals, who remained silent, responded by jerking him harder by the cuffs. The cold metal dug into his wrists. Then the marshals stepped up the pace, leading Patch quickly down a back hallway. Next, he was stuffed into the backseat of a waiting federal prowl car, which sped off in the direction of county jail.

"Sweet home county jail," Patch sang low to the tune of his favorite Lynyrd Skynyrd song, his hands cuffed behind his back. After a few interim days in County, he figured he would be transferred to the federal detention center, FDC, where he would begin his manhunt. *Finally.*

The U.S. attorney took Patch's disdain for the grand jury as seriously as Patch had hoped. The proof was in the leg irons and the handcuffs (attached to a waist-high body chain) that he now wore. Patch spent his first night of "contempt" in the bowels of the Maricopa County jail system, stuck in bureaucratic limbo, shuffled back and forth from holding tank to holding cell, bouncing around so much he felt like an incarcerated Ping-Pong ball. All the hardware and moving around was the system's way of making it difficult (1) to scratch your nose and (2) for anyone on the outside to keep tabs or make contact. Years back, in the joint, they'd called it "bus therapy," moving you around so much that family and legal counsel briefly lost track of your whereabouts.

Patch figured he'd officially go through "intake," the long, laborious process of being processed once he reached the federal detention center by bus. Good thing Redbeard and Hollister were in on the plan; otherwise they'd be on the outside playing a hopeless game of Catch Patch.

"Kinkade?" a voice asked from behind the holding-cell door that had just opened. *Finally.* Patch would be glad to get out of this stuffy puke-green room, even for a stinky, stifling gray bus. The voice belonged to a bespectacled marshal holding a clipboard, checking off his name. "Ready to take a little ride, Everett John Kinkade?"

"Ready, Teddy." Patch held out his cuffed and chained wrists, hoping that at least some of this pig iron might fall by the wayside. But no go. The marshal ignored his gesture. Patch shook his head and his chains. Walking down the long hall, he sounded like Jacob Marley's ghost. *Looks like these sons-of-bitchin' chains are staying put for the ride.*

The hazy memories of being processed into "the system" came flooding back in Technicolor as Patch was prodded onto the bus. Judging from the sheer fatigue he was feeling, abetted by the hours he'd spent under artificial lights, Patch guessed it to be around four in the morning, yet he wasn't sure since they'd taken his watch along with his street clothes. The FDC was located on the southern tip of Maricopa County, which meant an interminable long-assed bus ride. Patch wasn't surprised. A detention-center bus ride to the joint was supposed to take hours, especially since the bus always made multiple long stops at different facilities. Incarcerated bus rides could be grueling, spirit-breaking, all-day and all-night, mind-numbing, exhausting affairs with nothing to read or occupy your mind, save for a vivid imagination or schizophrenic conversations with yourself. There were stories of seemingly eternal two- to three-hundred-mile bus odysseys that sometimes took weeks. It was part of the game to disorient and break you.

Bus therapy was an emotional mind breaker for the mentally weak. No wonder some prisoners smuggled dope in with them and stayed high throughout the journey.

Patch hadn't spoken to a single soul for hours. And he wouldn't, not for the next several hours, until he was officially led off the bus. Where his property might be, his clothes and personal effects, was anybody's guess. Theoretically, they were supposed to catch up with him at the FDC. But this was no airline. This was government custody, "con-air" on wheels. Your baggage wasn't lost, it was merely rerouted and searched, and if it took weeks (or months) for it to catch up to your sorry ass, then tough fuckin' shit.

Instead of his street clothes, Patch now wore a jumpsuit made of disposable blue nylon cloth that, in a past life, had been a bunch of recycled plastic Diet Coke bottles from Wal-Mart. Naked as he was underneath, the dry morning (or whatever time it was) breeze wafted through the sheer fabric.

"No talking," a guard ordered loudly as Patch bounded up the steps of the bus. The Grey Goose. That's what Patch and his friends called the buses that delivered them to prison. The coach was half-empty, but that would surely change after only a few more stops. Then it would be sardine city, with each inmate chained to the person next to him. Patch took one of the remaining empty green plastic seats and tried to spread out, but to no avail. No legroom. His knees were painfully wedged into the cramped seat space. (Thankfully, Patch wasn't a tall dude.) Above his seat was a tiny loudspeaker playing a fuzzy semi-tuned-in Arizona AM country station. Patch was barely able to pick out Tim McGraw singing about his dead father. The Goose's thick shatter-proof windows were darkly tinted, latticed sheets of metal, and bars were welded to the outside of the bus, obscuring any hope not only of escaping, but of sneaking a view of the mesas and desert on the way. Patch already missed Mean Machine. Badly.

163 «

Since Patch was the very last passenger on his particular stop, once he found his seat, the bus coughed once and started up with a belch of black smoke and chunky diesel fume. Patch caught a glimpse outside through a slim crack in the reinforcement. It was actually a beautiful morning. Funny how each and every time he had been sent off to jail or prison, it was a beautiful day. God's reminder of the wonderful world he was about to leave behind for who knew how long.

The passengers on the Grey Goose weren't your usual collection of losers and hard-lucksters. These were federal prisoners, a cut above the common thug, which didn't make them any prettier to look at. Most, like Patch, were in transition, some on their way back and forth from court, or a grand jury, some awaiting transfer to yet another uncertain federal facility, wherever the feds chose at the last minute to ship their sad convicted asses. Until Patch was ready to testify, his life belonged to Uncle Sam.

A growing contingent of Mexicans, a couple of blacks, one Vietnamese dude, and a mostly Caucasian crew were en route to the Phoenix FDC. Patch scoured the bus for a Russian face, but what the fuck did a Russian face look like? No talking meant no telltale accents to hear. Patch looked around at the wretched crop of detainees. These were his people, his peers. Society's castoffs: smart men, but criminals nonetheless, stupid enough to get caught.

The Grey Goose riders wore long scowls and days of itchy growth on their faces. Their hair was dandruffed, greasy, and uncombed. Patch felt unkempt and oily from the heat, the sweat, and the hours spent chained and waiting. At full capacity, after an hour's ride, the bus stank from a combination of dried sweat, unwiped ass, and toe rot.

As Patch tried to readjust his numbed, needles-and-pins, tingly knees around the hard plastic seat, he thought about the bank job the Cartel had pulled off only a few days before. Those millions and millions of bucks vanishing into thin air, circulated by now into a worldwide network of money laundering. Whoever led this Cartel, in addition to being a cold-blooded murderer, was one smart cookie. But soon he would be one *dead* smart cookie.

The heist *was* a work of patient planned genius, precision timing, and paramilitary perfection. If only Patch's crew had been clever enough to pull off such a seamless coup, he wouldn't be sitting on the overheated Grey Goose milk-stop run chasing some elusive Russki ghost. He and Hollister could be in Costa Rica soaking up sun, downing *muchas cervezas*, and chasing scantily clad sun-kissed señoritas on the white sand beaches. His cramped legs and aching joints pinched by lack of circulation caused by the rigid chains and cuffs made Patch all the more eager to resettle himself inside a cell and make the necessary friends and alliances to track this bastard down. That's what jail was about. Surviving through alliances based on race, religion, area code, or whether you rode a motorcycle or robbed banks. A series of small "cars" and prison subsects, united by a common hatred of authority and the criminal-justice industry. Once acclimated to the inside, Patch would start putting things together, and then he would find this Cartel leader, neutralize him, and make him suffer. After that, he would duck out the legal back door and return to "civilized society." At least that was the plan.

Patch had been dead right about the bus ride. It did go on forever. Seemingly. The longer it took the Grey Goose to trundle through its appointed rounds along the Arizona outback, the more its ragtag cargo of castoffs grew. While Patch had no way of knowing what beef each passenger had his ticket punched for, he imagined these guys could be anything from right-wing militiamen to tax cheats to interstate identity thieves to dealers pushing dope across state lines to wiseguys and top earners doing straight time away from their Mobs. The hard-ass criminal element was offset by what Patch presumed to be newly incarcerated *ilegales* with visa problems, and not necessarily just border jumpers, but tax-paying workingmen dragnetted by Homeland Security (formerly INS) after years of living under the pre-9/11 federal radar.

Patch had the cramped green plastic seat to himself. Until the very last stop. At one stop a fairly large dude with a gray Howie Long crew cut, buff with a solid chest, barely six foot, early forties, chained and cuffed like Patch, walked onto the bus and took the seat next to him. After he was escorted to Patch's seat by the federale—"Comfy, gentlemen?" the marshal chortled—he was manacled and chained just tight enough to his new partner to make it a little too cozy between the two.

Gray Crew Cut grunted a nonreply to the marshal's quip. He wasn't clad in a blue nylon jumpsuit. He wore standard prison dress-down blues. Baggy in the butt, denim pants so ill fitting, they resembled hip-hop jeans. Blue chambray shirt open at the collar. White trainer sneakers. Thick gold chain around his neck. Elaborate athletic watch. The two men exchanged swift glances, then the don't-cross-him-don't-boss-him gray-headed stranger threw Patch a quick nod.

Just as the roasting heat inside the bus was bordering on the unbearable, the vehicle approached a stone-cold fortress. Patch figured he was at least twenty-five miles outside of downtown and at last headed for the federal lockdown. The lifeless edifice looked to be about five stories high. No glamour slammer here. It had no character or aesthetic, as if the feds had somehow figured out that a bland gray slab of concrete breaks a man's spirit quicker. As the bus drove through the front gate in low gear, it disappeared into the bowels of the building's basement labyrinth, weaving through broad sally ports, a testament to how huge—wide enough for a fucking bus—the interior of this structure actually was. The cool temperature of the basement chilled the bus as the marshals, clammy and equally tired of the stench, cracked open a few windows. Once the bus stopped, they quickly pulled open the doors.

The dispensing of the human chattel was swift and regimented as Patch, chained to his beefy crew-cut neighbor, was shuffled through double-reinforced doors and enormous hallways with twenty-foot-high ceilings. Then the group was led into a large room identified by a single sheet-metal sign that read IRC, IN-MATE RECEPTION CENTER.

Otherwise known as intake.

The first line to stand in removed their prisoners' chains and cuffs. Patch detested standing in lines, but here was one he didn't mind. Both of his wrists were scraped and bruised from the cuffs digging into his flesh for nearly twenty-four hours. He was relieved to have them removed. He almost felt free. Almost.

Next, the men were stripped of their clothing and ushered down yet another long and seemingly endless hallway. Gray Crew Cut, butt naked like the rest, sported his gold chain, which put him on top of the FDC best-dressed list.

"Follow the yellow stripe, men, follow the yellow stripe," the marshals barked sporadically as the bus passengers marched in ominous step, following yellow as opposed to the blue, red, or white painted lines. What followed was the day's most inane, and if it had not been so humiliating, most hilarious dance.

The FDC Hokeypokey.

"Hands out."

"Wiggle your fingers."

"Run your fingers through your hair."

"Bend your ears."

"Open your mouth wide."

"Now lift your tongue."

"Lift that nut sack."

"Turn around."

"Face the wall."

"Lift each foot."

"Wiggle your toes."

"Bend over."

"Grab your ass cheeks."

"Spread 'em."

"Get back up."

"Give me two good coughs."

End of USDA inspection. No dope up the butt. No weapons hidden. Just your run-of-the-mill degradation and humiliation. The men's response to the inspection ranged from defiance to unfazed acceptance. *It's amazing what you can get used to.*

Next, Patch and the naked inmate procession were herded into a small holding tank filled with fifty or more guys. Gone was the relief of the hallway space and the welcome feel of cold concrete floor on bare feet. Unlike the hallway, this room was sizzling, nearly as bad as the bus and just as smelly as sweat dripped from one man's body onto the next poor sap. Every man in the room sat naked, crammed shoulder to shoulder, skin to skin, on benches that took up the better part of the small holding tank. After about a half-hour wait, Patch and his cohorts were shuffled into a huge shower room for a shower that, while lasting about fifteen minutes, furnished no soap.

Shower time ended suddenly as the water was cut to a pisslike dribble. Yet another line formed as trusties—inmates who serve as clerks and sometimes are rats—randomly handed out bundles. Inside each bundle were white socks, white boxers (too bad Patch was a briefs man), a white T-shirt, black slip-on Jap Flaps, and a blue jumpsuit that was heavier and more conventional than the nylon one Patch had previously been given. Then Patch carried his bundle to another holding tank with one toilet and hard metal benches that ran along the walls. This time there were far more men than seats. As everyone dressed in their T-shirts, boxers, and jumpsuits, it was almost as if the feds had intentionally handed out the smallest jumpsuits to the biggest guys and vice versa. Up to now, no one had spoken to anyone. Suddenly the small room erupted in verbose banter as the horse trading began. Smaller men bartered with larger men for the closest correct size of underwear and jumpsuit. Names, area codes, and affiliations were bandied around. Mexicans hooked up with Mexicans. Blacks with blacks. Whites with whites. The few "others" (Native Americans, Islanders, Asians)—well, they were on their own till they hit the yard. Patch watched the old prison social dance unfold: stick with your own kind, be loyal to your own race, and if possible associate with your own area code.

Patch recalled an unwritten rule, an unexpected one, in jail. The people you arrived with, no matter what race, shared an unspoken bond. Seeing them later in the dayroom or on the rooftop yard, you knew that you'd survived an ordeal together. The endless bus ride. Intake. Reception. The FDC Hokeypokey USDA

169 **«**

Inspection. The no-soap shower and the sweltering holding cells. The bundles containing clothing that didn't fit. It was enough to transform a group of disparate criminals and hustlers into a tight band of brothers. That is, until prison-yard politics would later set in.

Hours passed in the final holding tank as the alliances fell into place. A standard sack lunch containing a sandwich of questionable meat with the letters *LOF* on the package was passed out. Patch cautiously opened the sandwich, checking out the mystery meat in disgust.

Just then a marshal came in, calling names and forming small groups that were led to yet another line and taken into a large room that was divided up into stations. First was fingerprint-and-picture time. In the old days, fingerprints had been taken with an ink blotter. While it's usually done electronically nowadays, this FDC had reverted back to the old and most efficient method. *Hurrah for tradition.* Roll each finger, roll each thumb, roll each palm, side of hand, the other four fingers. Welcome, Everett John Kinkade, to the permanent federal government fingerprint database.

Then came the photo. The process took Patch back to his days as a schoolkid. Picture day, his first childhood mug shot. Making the school photographer's job a living hell by pulling ugly faces. No such insolence here. The last thing Patch felt like doing was having his picture taken. *No wonder convicts look mean when their mug shots are shown on television or in the newspaper.* Most pictures were taken directly after that hellish smelly bus ride to prison. As Patch's picture was snapped, his number was placed underneath his mug electronically. *Shit.* He missed the old method, where you held up the card under your mug. *Progress.*

Patch's next stop in the large room, once his picture had come out intact, was to receive an abrasive hard plastic wristband with his picture imprinted, tightly affixed to his wrist. Patch immediately hated the thing, which scraped his skin worse than the cuffs and instantly made his sore wrist sorer. *This thing's gotta go, if it means gnawing my own fucking hand coyote-ugly style.*

Then came the interview process conducted by a bored and detached intake officer checking off a form asking basic questions like:

"Are you in a gang?"

"No." *The Infidelz are a club, not a gang.*

"Are you a homosexual?"

"No."

"Do you hear voices?"

"Fortunately, just yours."

"Ever been suicidal?"

"Who hasn't, especially after this?"

"Are you disabled?"

"Only when cuffed and chained."

"Ever been in PC"—protective custody.

"Fuck, no."

"Do you have any enemies?"

"Gimme a few hours and I'll run 'em down for ya."

"Are you trying to be a smart-ass?"

"Yes, sir."

Patch's answers to the staccato quiz would decide the level of his security and housing needs, whether he was to be isolated or whether he would dwell in GP (general population). Next, Patch walked over to the medical station. Check his vitals. Blood pressure. Heart rate. Allergy questions. TB jab. An eye exam. A quick look at his teefers. Piss in a bottle. Blood draw (a.k.a. drug/AIDS test).

Fingerprints. Photo. Psych. Medical. It resembled a sick cattle call and suggested some permanence, like he'd be sticking around for a while. The feds weren't fucking around. They took Patch's noncompliance with the grand jury dead serious. And as long as he withheld his cooperation, they were more than willing to incarcerate him.

As he was ushered back into the crowded holding-tank benches, Patch noticed some of the men had been left standing. Then he felt a hand grab him by the back of his jumpsuit, pulling him down onto a tiny portion of the bench. His first instinct was to turn around and clock whoever had grabbed him until (1) he remembered he was in jail, no sense spending the first night in the hole, and (2) he realized it was the buffed-out Gray Crew Cut who grabbed him. As a result, the two now shared about twenty-five and a half precious inches of bench.

"McAllister. Nate McAllister. Call me Big Nate." He held out his hand.

"Patch. Kinkade. I go by both."

McAllister's handshake was firm, like a robot grip. "Sorry to jar you, but we're gonna be here awhile, so you might as well take a seat. Trust me, this could go on awhile."

"Much obliged." Then silence.

A minute later, Big Nate tapped Patch on the shoulder. " 'Scuse me, partner, but you're a bike rider. You've got the tell-tale tats."

"Maybe."

"Shit, my Harley's part of the reason I'm here. The wife gave the ultimatum: the bike and my friends or her. I chose the bike and got arrested a few months later. That was eight years ago in Jersey and I ain't ridden since."

"What kind of Harley?"

"FXRT. I understand they don't make 'em anymore."

"That's right. In fact, I rode an FXRT for a while. It was the best fucking bike Harley ever made."

"I knew there was something I liked about you, Kinkade. You got good taste."

The room filled up as more guys returned from the medical stations. Time passed. Patch valued his meager inches of bench space more and more. At first, the guys relegated to standing stood like they preferred to stand. But after a few hours, they soon lost their coolness and weren't ashamed to curl up on the floor amid the garbage and take a snooze. After a while it was time to be assigned to a cell. Big Nate was called first.

"I'll be seeing you around, amigo," Big Nate said to Patch.

"Stay cool, brother," Patch answered as he moved his ass over to luxuriate in the extra inches of bench Big Nate left behind.

After almost thirty-six hours since being held in contempt, Patch was allocated to a cell and handed a blanket roll-up consisting of a change of whites, a towel, and a "fish kit," which contained toothpaste (jailhouse glue), a motel-size bar of soap, a razor incapable of shaving the hair off a monkey's ass, and a stub-handled toothbrush. Patch grimaced, remembering when one guy got stabbed by a sharpened toothbrush. No more.

As Patch was led to his cell, he was surprised by its cleanliness. While it was a small and confined space, here was a half-empty two-man cell with a stainless-steel sink and a toilet. A two-man pod (with only two men) was considered the Ritz, and Patch was more surprised when he discovered the bottom bed of his bunk already occupied by a familiar face.

Big Nate McAllister.

"Welcome aboard, bud. I left the upper for ya. I'm afraid of heights, whether it's five feet or five thousand feet."

"Thanks. I appreciate that. I prefer upper," Patch said tersely. He was bushed, but he'd survived what many believe is the hardest part of doing time. Dreaded intake.

Despite the long exhausting ordeal, Patch was tense and jumpy, eager to start his investigation. He had plans, but first he needed to adjust his body clock to the slow stroll of jail life. *Be Patient. You're not going anywhere.* Next he needed partners. Just like on the outside, he would surround himself with smart people, extra sets of eyes and ears. There was little doubt as to who his first recruit would be.

"So, Big Nate, mind if I ask you a quick question?"

Big Nate didn't readily respond. Instead, Patch heard the sound of a blubbering snore. He looked down from his upper bunk. Big Nate was already dead to the world. Patch's questions would have to wait until morning.

Sleeping didn't come so easy for Patch. He had trouble dozing off, as years and years' worth of prison ghosts, long dormant, revisited the cell. Maybe he should call that doc back because he sure as hell heard voices now. They were the spirits of lockdowns past, his memory flooded with names and faces of club members and legendary bike riders who had gotten their freewheeling wings clipped behind bars: former cellies, some alive, most dead, some kicked out of the club and forgotten. Patch wondered how Redbeard was holding up. How was he progressing on the outside? And Hollister. How was he taking this, knowing as Patch did how skittish he was since his dad had died? A few minutes later, Patch dozed off to the nonstop loony-bin-type jailhouse chatter. In this case, the inmates were not running the asylum.

On his first morning inside the FDC, Patch woke up
to the sound of the daily "court pull."

With an abundance of federal prisoners in the midst of their
trials, the god-awful predawn ritual was one that most inmates
thankfully slept through—that is, unless it was *your* day to face the
judge. If you were headed to court, the morning-shift sergeants
pulled your deadbeat ass out of your bunk at 4 A.M. At least you
sneaked ahead of the pack with shower privileges. You then
scored a virgin razor to drag over your stubbly face and got a
fresh change of duds to look spiffy for the judge, jury, and pros-
ecutor.

Patch's first night in his cell became the first decent doze he'd
had in weeks. Something he'd forgotten: he was one of those rare
creatures who slept comfortably inside a two-man jail cell. A little after five in the morning, Patch felt the stir of his cellie down
below. Then he heard a voice.

"Kinkade. You conscious?"

"Yep."

"How'd you sleep, pal?"

"Like a baby," Patch said. "Every fifteen minutes, I woke up
screamin' and cryin'."

"Yer kiddin'."

"Yeah, I am. Seriously, I slept pretty fuckin' well. Best in weeks. I sleep okay in jail."

The two men laughed. Patch felt lucky in the cellie department. Nothing was worse than a cellmate with a screw loose, jabbering nonstop, pawing your property, and jerking off.

"So, Big Nate, what were you doing on the bus?" Patch asked.

"Out for a little ride. They had me testifying in court on a drug case. I was no help. I told 'em zip 'cause I knew zip. So they put me through intake again as punishment, I guess. They do that sometimes. How long you here for, Kinkade?"

"Indefinitely."

"I'm on month thirteen servin' a three-year stretch." Big Nate exhaled. "I keep thinking they're gonna ship my ass out, but here I stay. You're my ninth cellie in a year, the first able to string four words together in English. That's why I used my pull and grabbed you. Hope you don't mind."

"Hell no. I've had bad cellies and good cellies. I know the pain."

Patch jumped down and took his first 360-degree look around at the Arizona FDC, surveying his brand-new digs.

"You know, this place ain't half fuckin' bad. I expected far worse."

"*I've* done time in worse," Big Nate said, stretching on his bottom bunk, rubbing his eyes and wiggling his toes.

Patch slipped on his Jap Flaps and looked down at the floor of his cell. Clean and spotless. Compared to county, man, this place *was* the fucking Ritz. Leave it to the feds to have access to the slickest lockdowns. But that also meant the slickest security. Something Patch would suss out immediately.

Looking around the cell, Patch found his property at the foot of the bunk, his stuff present and accounted for in a clear plastic sack. Wasn't much. Just another fish kit with the shampoo, soap, razor, deodorant, toothbrush and paste, along with his ID card, paperwork, and docs.

Patch was especially relieved that his athletic shoes and his wristwatch had made it through the maze without being pinched. He quickly kicked off his Jap Flaps and happily laced up his Reebok kicks, shoes that carried the dust from home. He was tempted to sniff the dirt, as if that would give him a taste or smell of home. While he missed his bed a little and his bike a lot, and Hollister, he was just as happy to be inside feeling useful, glad he had a purpose in life, a task in front of him, hunting down this character who, for all he knew, he mighta shared a smelly bus ride with the day before.

According to Patch's watch, it was approaching quarter past five. *Pretty fuckin' early.*

"An hour to chow," Big Nate announced as he tumbled out of the bottom bunk and rolled out a woven mat from under his bunk and onto the floor. Then he began a series of bizarre body stretches.

"What the—" Patch asked.

"Yoga," Big Nate explained. "I picked it up while I was in Quentin. Keeps the body limber and the mind clear. I ain't rotting inside here, buddy, no fuckin' way. I plan to stay alert and clear. That's the key to keepin' it real."

As Big Nate did his pretzel poses, Patch eyeballed the spartan cell. McAllister kept his home free of clutter and bullshit. One book, *The Art of War.* More for show than for reading. A few fish-and-game and fitness mags. Nothing on the walls, no family snapshots, only a pocket baseball schedule dutifully updated with *W*s and *L*s. San Francisco Giants.

"My team." Big Nate grinned proudly. "Fuck the Dodgers."

There was a small silver metal writing table and stool across from the bunk. Toward the back of the cell was a sink and the shitter, over which Nate had rigged a towel as a privacy curtain, something that was technically illegal and could be ripped down by the COs (correctional officers).

After Nate finished his morning stretches, he dusted off his fanny, more a force of habit than a necessity since there was little or no dust on the floor to speak of. *The trusties keep this fuckin' place spick-and-span.*

"Lemme give you the nickel tour. Since this place is self-enclosed, we can pretty much move around here unescorted. I'm sure you'll find it"—Big Nate paused as he searched the air for the correct adjective—"accommodating. At breakfast I'll introduce you to my homeys."

"You lead, I follow." The two men walked.

This was a contemporary lockdown with all the Mod Cons (modern conveniences), no pun intended.

"Okay, Big Nate, fill me in on the lay of the land real quick. What's the capacity here?"

"This whole overall FDC houses six interior tower units. Each tower has four pods on two separate levels, two up, two down. Each pod contains fifteen two-man cells." Big Nate calculated. "Let's see, thirty guys per pod, with four pods per tower, that's a hundred and twenty inmates per tower times six towers . . . hmmm, that makes a capacity of seven hundred and twenty inmates. And we're just about at max capacity, too. This hotel is booked up, bubba. And that's not counting protective custody and High-Power."

"You some kinda math wiz, McAllister?"

"Used to be."

As they walked across the main line, Big Nate had the place figured out as he nodded to the approaching correctional officers and inmates of all races—blacks, Mexicans, a pair of huge Usos (the Samoan term for "bro" or "homey"), and the tattooed whites.

"I get along with everyone here. Let's just say I've earned my stripes." Big Nate was tough enough to hold his mud yet old enough to command respect among the youngsters, and smart enough to stay one step ahead of the cops, the correctional officers, the COs, guards, bulls, whatever you called them. They weren't to be messed with. They were tough.

FDC was like its own biodome, a small town, and Big Nate was the perfect Original Gangster/Olde Guard to have in your corner. The Mayor of Dogpatch. He had this place mapped and figured out.

"How's security inside this place?" Patch asked.

"Tight as a twelve-year-old. Fuckin' place is lousy with cameras. But there are blind spots where the cameras don't overlap. We got those figured out. But you can't wipe your ass around here without sayin' cheese. Except for church. That's where they hafta draw the line. It's the only place to get any solitude."

There was an odor of disinfectant and ammonia as Patch and McAllister walked toward the chow area. McAllister pointed out more and more landmarks in different directions.

"Over there's the kitchen. Over there is admin, where Francine works."

"Francine?"

"Yeah, Francine's a fox. We need to hook you up. Next to admin is the law library. Inmate laundry. The visitation area is next to the chapel. Twenty-four-hour medical clinic next to that."

"Where's the yard?"

"We have three recreation yards, one large, two small. Each yard has a backboard, rim, net, and one fucking ball. High-Power is upstairs, fourth floor. They exercise on the rooftop. All workout areas and ball courts segregate themselves. Blacks, whites, and Mexicans stay separate. The large yard has a volleyball setup that doesn't get used much. And since they banned weights, we keep in shape doin' burpees and isometrics."

"I hate burpees," Patch said. They were the devil's mix between a push-up and a squat. They killed his back, but kept many a con in tip-top shape without access to a gym, free weights, or exercise programs. Lots of guys did burpees to drop fat and to increase strength.

"It's indoors, dude. You won't see the sunshine till they haul your ass to court or if they send you upstairs to High-Power to walk the roof. Never fear. I've got the hookup so's we can roam around anywhere. Outside of the rooftop, that is."

"Anything else I need to know about?"

"You don't come off to me as the religious type, but on Fridays, when there's no visitation allowed, there's just chapel. That's where anybody can go, no matter what race or security classification. You're free to commune with the man upstairs. It's un-PC for the cops to mess with our religious freedoms, so that's one place where you can get away from the noise. They conduct all kinds of services. Like I said, I might go there just for a little serenity and downtime. It's an unwritten rule that you don't abuse the sanctuary. How 'bout you, Kinkade? You a praying man?"

"Nah. Ain't one for church," said Patch, looking around at the immense indoor structure. "Not yet, anyway."

Patch noticed the noise level rising as the men made their way closer to the massive chow area.

"What level of security is this place?" Patch asked.

"FDCs are rated different, depending . . . this is what you call your multiclassification security detention center. Lotsa open space but not a lot of nooks and corners. When you hear the alarm, drop to your knees. It's a tough place to shank someone. But that doesn't mean shit don't happen. This joint was originally built in '92 for medium- and maximum-security inmates awaiting trial. Slowly, it became almost exclusively medium security. But today we see a shitload of classifications. A large chunk of unsentenced transients—"

"That's me, unsentenced transient in contempt."

"Most of the guys here are medium security, some fully sentenced and ready to be shipped out to God knows where."

"No maximum security?" Patch asked.

"Fuck yeah; we got a few 'no work status' guys, so-called disciplinary cases or dudes with mental problems. Head cases. J-cats."

"Does this place have a nuthouse or shrinks for the guys who lose it?" A J-cat cellie, or a verbose prison crazy, could make insanity a contagious disease.

"The shrinks were the first casualties of the first budget cuts," Big Nate said. "The best way to ward off insanity is a job or taking classes. But jobs are scarce and school in here is nonexistent."

"Maybe I can get the trash-hauling gig. That's what I did through the last part of the eighties. When I was outdoors, I rode shotgun on the trash truck. Cherry gig," Patch recalled.

"At first I worked for six months for something to do, putting together small electrical parts for some hospital equipment, then I said fuck it, so I spend most of my time in my bunk. Sometimes I don't go out into the yard for a week, outside of chow. We have breakfast in the chow area. Bag lunch to the cell. Supper back at the chow hall. Yard closes at nine P.M."

"Could be a lot worse."

"A helluva lot worse!"

"So, what's the pecking order around here, dude?"

181 «

"The usual. GP, your general population. PC, protective custody for the rat motherfuckers and snitches on the third floor, and then there's HP."

"High-Power is upstairs you said?"

"Fourth floor. Guys with serious affiliations, gang members, or bail over a mil. Media stars. Once in a blue moon. Male Martha Stewart types and convicted Enron and WorldCom white-collar thieves. High-profile dudes shipped in from everywhere. They don't stay long. That ain't you, is it, Kinkade? You some kind of star?"

"Maybe. Where do they house these so-called media-star guys anyway?"

"HP is way upstairs, another world. I hardly see any of them dudes except in the medical hallways, some lining up for hot meds, or in chapel. Right now it's chow time. Don't wanna get there after they run out of oatmeal surprise. Plus, I wanna introduce you to my car, my group. You might find someone you know, or a friend of a friend at the very least."

"Highly probable, my man. I'm startin' to feel at home already."

The chow hall was already packed and noisy as voices carried, bouncing and echoing off the high concrete walls and ceiling. The room was filled with large hexagonal stainless-steel tables, each with six protruding seating stools attached to it. Patch and Nate joined the chow line and snaked their way through the food selection. Pretty standard fare. A thunk of oatmeal with a few raisins poking through. *Fingers crossed they're raisins.* A tiny box of cold cereal, a small milk container, a slab of mystery meat, presumably ham, and two slices of white bread.

Patch eyed the white bread suspiciously. No fuckin' butter.

"You know what I'd give my left nut for?" Big Nate asked. "A fuckin' stack of toast. That's the one thing I miss when I'm in the joint and the first thing I'll order outside. Wheat-ass motherfucking toast."

"Big Nate." A loud voice shrilled from a table in the dead center of the chow hall. Seated around the steel table were three white guys with three empty seats.

"Okay, listen up, fellas," said Big Nate, approaching the table. "I'm only gonna say this once. This here's Patch. Patch Kinkade. He came in yesterday. We're cellies now."

Big Nate pointed around the table, first at a dark-haired,

muscular fellow about Patch's size. Hair swept back. Giant guns for arms. Sleeveless sweatshirt. Arms and shoulders covered in tats.

"Say hello to Rhino."

Next was a tall, gangly redheaded guy. Looked a little like Ronald McDonald.

"Smoke. Pleasure to meet ya," he introduced himself.

The last guy easily tipped the scales at three hundred, perhaps more.

"One Ton," said Big Nate.

"Cal," the man corrected Big Nate. "Calvin Simon."

One Ton was one of those fat guys inside of whom you could see the thin man he'd once been. Calvin Simon had grown up inside the prison system of New Mexico, starting with Youth Authority. Decades of living on starchy prison grub had taken its toll on his body and on his desire to live a long healthy life. He'd taken to eating snack foods as a form of slow suicide. To One Ton, the worst thing about prison life was no butter.

"What brings you inside, Kinkade?" Rhino asked out of the box.

All eyes were riveted on Patch.

"Let's just say I had a little run-in with a grand jury. A little gang and Mob investigation and I didn't feel like talking. So they held me in contempt. Here I am."

"That's an automatic eighteen-month sentence, Kinkade," said Smoke.

"They haven't thrown that one at me officially—not yet, anyway," said Patch. "My sentence so far is indeterminate. That is, as long as I clam up, I stay. If I testify, then theoretically I can leave. Tell you the truth, I'm here to rest my dogs. In the meantime—"

"What gang activity they investigating?" asked Smoke.

"I ride with the Infidelz."

"Jesus Christ, I thought you looked familiar," said Rhino, standing up and slapping his palm on the steel tabletop, attracting the attention of one of the nearby correctional officers. Rhino meekly sat down. "I'll be goddamned," he whispered loudly across the table. "My brother-in-law hangs around your Flagstaff chapter. He's aimin' to join. Good kid. A hella tough fighter, too. His name's Scooter. Wait'll I tell him. Patch Kinkade. Shit."

"I can put a word in for your boy if he's near as good as you say."

"So, what's the grand jury asking you about that's got their hackles up and bent outta shape, if you don't mind me askin'?" Nate queried.

"I'll tell you," Rhino butted in. "Them cats they found in the freezer, throats cut, counterfeit cash. I read it in the papers. Your boys. That's some serious fuckin' shit. Who did that?"

"Beats me," said Patch. "And that's what I told the grand jury, too. So, what's the common beef among you guys?"

The four exchanged knowing glances, then they burst into laughter.

"All right already. Lemme in on the joke," said Patch, taking a hit of milk. Fuck the cold cereal.

"No joke," said Big Nate. " 'Cept the thread that runs through this table is that we're all bank robbers."

"Oh, yeah? What do you experts think about that triple bank robbery in downtown Phoenix that got pulled about a week or so ago?"

"That heist was a fuckin' masterpiece," said Nate. "I'd love to meet whoever pulled that shit off just to shake his fuckin' hand. They not only knew their shit, but they had the brass fuckin' balls to do it three times. In one day! I honestly think the whole deal was politically motivated. I can't think of anyone who would risk pullin' such a crazy move in broad daylight for that big a haul unless they were some driven motherfuckers, pushed by something way beyond cash. It hadda be more than greed motivatin' that crew."

Exactly, thought Patch. *On the right track.* He looked around

185 «

the chow hall. "So, what's the inside? Give me the skinny on the groups here."

"Pretty straightforward. Everybody here sticks to themselves. Except we like to think we've got a higher grade of criminal here. No fucking around with that stupid tiny shit. The card games are high fucking stakes. Stay away from those unless you got money to lose. Drugwise, you can pretty much get anything. The lockdowns are minimal. Even if someone gets stabbed or the place goes apeshit, hours later, maximum one day, we're back on the main line. Not like those joints in California where they lock the Mexicans or the whites or whoever down for weeks and months at a time. None of that shit here."

"So gimme the eyeball tour, McAllister," said Patch.

"Over there you got your blue bandannas. On the opposite end way over there, the red bandannas. They can't stand each other. Push comes to shove, the reds align with the browns, while the blues, they might side with the whites. That's a general-ization. We got a few centrals from California, in the middle. Then you got the border brothers."

"BB?" Patch asked.

"They're the first-generation Mexicans from Mexico. Old-school drug running as opposed to your second- or third-generation street gangs, grand theft auto, and gangbangin'. Then you got your basic groups, your cars. There's the white car, the black car. Then you got your more isolated pockets. Italians. Russians."

"Russians?" asked Patch.

"A growing community. Young and mean. They stick to them-selves, and talk to nobody. You can tell them by their tats."

"Who else?"

"You got your bikers. Sooner or later they'll be shouting out once the word spreads you're here. Bikers are cool in that they tend to stick together, with a few exceptions. Unlike the other races, the bikers leave their affiliations at the gate. They watch out for each other inside. You got your Christians. With them, it's

about praise Jesus and let me convert your ass. They pick up the Bible when they get here and leave the Bible when they run out, back to the same old shit. Then there's your peter puffers, the gay car. There's not a lot of sex on the yard with those guys. It's on the down-low and hidden. That's not to say the odd dick won't get sucked, but if you're gay, you gotta check in with your race and not make waves or generate unnecessary heat. So the gays are pretty low-pro, cool about it. Consensual stuff, not much rape. That punkin' shit goes down in county and not just among the homos. Otherwise, it's the usual drill, Kinkade. You know it. Don't share a smoke or eats with a homosexual. Same thing with a cat from another race. A guy got stabbed a couple weeks back because he drank out of a black guy's coffee cup while they were jammin' on guitars in the band room. It upsets the applecart. I know it's stupid bullshit, but if I'm a faggot, before I let you take a hit off my cigarette, I'm gonna let you know I'm homosexual. But you don't have to worry about that. Smokin' is banned. Thanks to the legislature, there's a brisk tobacco black market
brewin'.'"

Big Nate lowered his voice. "That's my stock-in-trade. Tobacco futures. And the football pool. That's mine, too. Steady trade in stamps, tobacco pouches, soups, shoes, jewelry, that's about it. Since the smoking ban, biz is boomin'. Unexpected revenue during the off-season."

"I'll smoke my own, thank you. Besides, I ain't here to join no car or share smokes or get laid," Patch said.

"Sooner or later, Kinkade, you gotta choose sides and run with your kind."

"Granted, but I don't need no fucking car. I have no time for area-code or state politics. It's how I did time before. I took care of my friends. Period. I'll ride solo, thanks very much. I'm a lone wolf. I prefer to roam alone. Kick me at the curb."

"That's an admirable position, but hardly practical. You're welcome to run with us bank robbers."

"Yes, sir," chimed in Rhino. "I'll gladly watch the back of Patch Kinkade."

"I appreciate that." Patch looked over and spotted a huge CO, about six-six, 260 pounds, carrying a two-foot flashlight. His utility belt was crammed with keys and cuffs and a long-ass donkey-dick billy club. *Guys keep their distance from this guy.*

"What's the deal with the cops?"

"A pretty mean squad, but sometimes they turn a blind eye to smoking—tobacco, that is. The trusties run the joint, shuffle the papers and clean the place up and shit. They're the guys dressed in green coveralls. As for the cops, we got three lieutenants, seven sergeants, eighty detention officers, and one administrative assistant. That's Francine, who I told you about. You'll know her when you see her. She's an oasis flower in a fucking desert."

"Very poetic, Nate. So who's the big guy with the flashlight?"

"That's Bartkowski. I'd steer clear of him if I were you. He's bad fucking news. Ain't afraid of givin' out a little flashlight therapy."

"Flashlight therapy?" Patch asked.

"Yeah," said Smoke, the Ronald McDonald redhead. "As in one of those fuckin' lamps upside yo skull, bro. You'll wake up in the infirmary."

"I'll remember that."

Breakfast was over, and the roar of the crowd moved outside the chow hall. It was just shy of 7 A.M., time for a little more shut-eye back at the cell and a little daytime TV outside the pod. Or a shower. Or a phone call. Patch needed to set up some visitation, to keep Redbeard and Hollister in the loop and vice versa. But it had been a productive chow. Patch was booking good time. He'd learn the factions. He needed to stay on course with his mission. It would be easy enough to slip into just doin' time, but that wasn't what he was here for. Patch would find this Russian dude if it killed him, or better yet, when *he*, Patch, killed *him*.

46

The noise in the big house took some getting used to. By noon, the sound of the FDC was deafening, practically unbearable. Prison's nostalgic charm was beginning to wear off. Clanging, hooting, shouting, whistling, mixed with the smell of old socks and rancid food. It was hot and humid. Patch closed his eyes. *Sounds and smells like the WWF in here.* Big Nate and the rest of his crew were hanging around the living area outside the pod, oblivious to the high-volume raucous. Smoke, Big Nate, Rhino, and One Ton were locked in mortal pinochle combat. Patch, never a card shark, looked on and wondered which day would come first, becoming acclimated to the noise and the stench or going batshit? He kept his yap shut. No complaints. No bitching.

Patch looked up at the TV. Stupid morning sitcom rerun. A quorum of muscular black dudes had laid claim to the TV. That's what jail is. Fiefdoms and power trips. Who controls what, TV, phones, etc. Nobody gave a squat what was on the fuckin' box anyway, unless it was NFL season or NASCAR and somebody had a few too many tobacco pouches riding on the weekend matches. During baseball season, the betting died down, interrupted by spurts of interest in the NBA play-offs. Big Nate handled most of the gambling action. Each week he passed out tiny betting slips he managed to get photocopied through one of the trusties on the COs' own copy machine. The cops knew the score. Some got in on the action. Each slip listed a full week's NFL rundown with the early Vegas line. Big Nate took all the action he could get his hands on. By following the Vegas line, he rarely came out behind the eight ball. He made most of his "money" running not only the gambling action but trading in postage stamps. To place a bet, it was cash—or more accurately, stash—on the barrelhead. Last week, Big Nate scored the mother lode. One of the ink slingers lost a bottle of ink to a round of lousy football "locks." Ink on the yard, food for fresh tats, was premium merchandise.

Big Nate's gambling racket dealt in cash, stamps, and tobacco pouches. If dudes got too far behind in their gambling debts, it would then fall on his shoulders to collect or beat up the guy; otherwise he'd be pegged as a pushover. So he never branched out into the credit-and-lending business, not Big Nate's style. Cash no credit was his creed. He also dealt in soups and stingers

(devices that heat water), cookies, sodas, ramen, and other non-perishables, including ink. No drugs. Drugs were especially synonymous with debt. Big Nate was a businessman, not a dealer, smuggler, or enforcer.

Only rarely would something major, a big-ticket item like a wedding ring, watch, jewelry, or a new pair of sneakers, surface onto the recreation yard from a newbie who had just checked in with no money on his books, his canteen account bare, and scared shitless. Inside Patch's cell was the Bank of Nate, a foot-lock stash of tobacco products, snacks, guitar strings, and shampoo and soap supplies, which he was generous with anyway. By not hoarding his stash, he instantly became a popular inmate and a peacemaker. Not a charitable institution, but not a money-grabber. He was the "go-to" guy when there was tension or questions by the inmates or the cops. Big Nate tried his best to serve the interests of himself and his homeys first, keeping the cops in the dark as best as he could.

Smoke was the nerd of the bunch. Freckly red face with long thin arms and horn-rim glasses. Skinny as hell. He looked more like a gangly schoolkid than a federal con. He was inside on an investment scam. He'd come in speaking like a banker; now he jived like a hip-hopper. Smoke was real vague about his past, dosed daily on various experimental psychotropics, a.k.a. "hot meds," that the medical clinic dispensed to a long steady line of inmates like clockwork, 6 P.M. daily. What made Smoke interesting was the way the meds spun his head out into multiple personalities. The meds—such as Seroquel—were supposed to neutralize irritability, rapid speech, racing thoughts, insomnia, poor attention span, inflated sense of power and self-worth, and poor judgment as a result of bipolar disorders.

In other words, better incarceration through chemistry. Sometimes they helped.

But sometimes they didn't. Sometimes they only made matters worse for everyone. Guys who got hooked were sometimes paroled with a large sack of meds designed to tide them over for a few months while roaming the streets, disoriented, frightened, and/or confused. According to Big Nate, the stuff they fed Smoke split his mind in two and brought on severe but opposite effects. Original Smoke had started out as a cagey white-collar criminal, then morphed into Smoke-1, a sullen character who couldn't sleep, missed his family (who disowned him after he was convicted), and boasted of an encyclopedic knowledge of sports. Then there was Smoke-2. He was a demon card shark who took to fighting and to the dark side of being a convict like a duck to water. Temperamental, argumentative, and illogical. That side of him was a real drag to be around.

Big Nate laid his pinochle cards down—a hundred and fifty points on the button, which caused Smoke, Rhino, and One Ton to groan aloud in unison.

"C'mon, Kinkade. Let's get away from these losers."

Patch and Big Nate lived in Tower Five lower level. On their way walking, a white kid was sitting in lotus position, strumming an acoustic guitar and blowing a harmonica lodged in a metal brace that hung around his neck. Sounded and looked like Bob Dylan circa 1962, wearing shades and a Huck Finn corduroy cap. His strumming and blowing was a welcome sound as it poked through the incessant clanging and chatter. The kid sounded great. Reminded Patch remotely of Hollister, near the same age, not too far north of eighteen. If Patch had planned on staying long, he'd keep an eye out for the kid, make sure he didn't get picked on or fucked with.

"There is a house in New Orleans, they call the Risin' Sun," the kid sang in a pinched, nasal voice. In between verses, while strumming, he wheezed in and out of the harmonica like a human accordion.

Shit, Patch missed music. He was tempted to stand over the kid and take in a tune or two more. But Big Nate had already set the pace, so the two kept right on walking, a confident, flat-footed penitentiary shuffle.

"You gotta keep movin'," Big Nate warned.

Not twenty-five feet from the kid playing the guitar, Patch noticed the giant CO, Bartkowski, walking in their direction. Big Nate nodded slightly then cast his eyes toward the floor. But Patch kept right on lookin', which angered the guard.

"You eyeballin' me? Gimme your ID."

Patch whipped out his freshly laminated ID, the one with the bus-weary picture staring back slit-eyed.

Bartkowski read from the ID card. "Everett John Kinkade?"

"Jeez, boss, no blood no foul," said Big Nate, eager to move on.

"I'm talkin' to you, Kinkade," Bartkowski said, poking Patch on the chest with his flashlight. "Eyeballin' me with intent. I don't stand for that shit. Keep it up and you and me got business to tend to, hear me?"

It wasn't in Patch's nature to look away. The absurdity of the confrontation angered him. On the outside, he would have taken a poke at the guy. Inside, completely different story. The guy was a head and a half taller and outweighed Patch by about fifty pounds, and he was much bigger up close than when Patch had first noticed him at the mess hall from a distance. Here was a guy capable of squashing men like bugs.

"You boys mind your p's and q's, you hear me?" Bartkowski said, laughing, handing back to Patch his ID. "I ain't jokin'."

"Like I said," Big Nate told him. "We're on our way. Don't mind him, he's just a few days in, and he don't talk too much."

"See that little Gilligan keeps his eyeballs to himself, *comprende*?"

Bartkowski ambled away, bouncing the flashlight off his massive palm.

"I don't appreciate you apologizing or covering for me. On the outside we'd put down motherfuckers like that, if it takes ten of us," Patch said to Big Nate.

"You ain't outside and he ain't worth a week in the hole for eyeballin'."

Big Nate was right. Patch hadn't dug his way in here to piss away a week stewing in the hole.

» CHAPTER «

47

Next day after breakfast, Patch decided it was high time he walked over to check in with the bike-riding contingent. There was a quiet vibe on the main line. Almost peaceful. Kinda eerie. Patch noticed it. Big Nate immediately noticed it. Big Nate, moody and blue, elected to crawl back into his bunk, skip chow, and sleep off the rest of the day.

"Go see Warlock and Stretch. I'm sure they're expecting you."

It was 7 A.M., after chow, as inmates ambled their way to their jobs. A mini prison rush hour. Some toiled in the laundry and the kitchen for a few nickels an hour while the lucky ones worked the makeshift factories for companies who lusted after cheap convict labor, paying out just-below-minimum wage. A job relieved the boredom and it was the best way to accumulate a modest bankroll while locked up inside. Compared to the world outside, living expenses inside were pretty low. A hundred and twenty dollars a month, a fortune to some, bought you just about anything you might need inside. Chips, crackers, candy bars, junk food, an ice cream or a soda. Patch was tired of living off the Bank of Nate. So, with a phone call, he lined up a visit for the following day with Redbeard and the kid. They would dump some funds into his account. Plus, he was looking forward to an update and to swapping info.

Patch made his way over to Tower Two, a lower pod where he knew he'd find a bike-riding brother named Warlock. He was now serving a couple years stemming from an incident involving siphoning credit-card info from Web sites and porn sites. That was surprising since Warlock was an accomplished bank robber just like Big Nate and his crew. Big Benny Fratello had set up the meeting between Patch and Warlock. Though they'd never met face-to-face, each knew about the other from way back. Warlock was certified good people. If Big Benny vouched for him, that was good enough. Patch knew Warlock only vaguely on the out-side. He was an independent motorcycle rider who cherished an old knucklehead he'd bought secondhand during the late sixties and kept in unbelievable shape since. Actually, Patch remem-bered the bike more than he did the man, with its bright orange tank painted by the famous bike painter Art Himsl with a beau-tiful flame and pinstripe job. The rest of the bike was painted black as night, and was as swift as lightning.

Patch recognized Warlock immediately. He stuck out of the crowd with the same round metal-rimmed John Lennon specta-cles he'd always worn. His once-red hair, tied back, was now graying. A variety of prison tats decorated his freckled arms. Standing next to him was a tall gangly dark-haired character.

"Patch Kinkade. Well, well, well. Funny seeing you here." War-lock smiled and the two bumped shoulders.

"Big Benny sends his regards," Patch said.

"Patch, this is Stretch, buddy of mine. He's cool. We've known each other since kindygarten. He don't talk much."

"Patch Kinkade," Stretch did say. "It's an honor, brother."

"The honor is mine."

Warlock got right down to it. "What brings you inside, Kinkade? I heard wind about you and the grand jury."

"You got a place we can talk?"

"Certainly. Follow me."

The three headed over toward one of the smaller exercise

yards, where a group of blacks, half of them shirtless and bathed in sweat, were in the midst of a fierce court battle.

"So what's up?" Warlock asked.

"Big investigation into gang and terrorist activities by the cops and the feds. Four of us got whacked."

"I heard about that. The Meat Locker Murders. The news swept the yard like a grass fire. I'm surprised the cops haven't got you locked up in High-Power."

"They still might. Until then, I'm free to snoop around down here."

"So how long do you intend to stay put?"

"A) Until I decide to answer the grand jury's questions. B) Until I find what it is I'm looking for."

"And what's that? Maybe I can help, brother."

"Maybe you can, maybe you can't. You heard of an outfit called the Cartel?"

Warlock scratched his head inquisitively. "Can't say I have."

"I have," Stretch said, breaking his silence.

Warlock looked surprised.

"A Russian-gang outfit, best I can recollect. We got a few Russkies around here, mostly youngsters. But I don't think they see eye to eye with the Cartel. My guess is that the wiseguys here and this Cartel group are rivals of sorts. There are a lot of rival Russian gangs. What I hear is the dude who runs them is holed up in Englewood, up in Colorado."

"Your sources are dead on," Patch said. "Except now I hear he's being shipped in here to testify in front of the same grand jury I had to fuck with. And if I'm on the right track, which I fuckin' better be, they're bringing his ass right here on a silver platter."

"I heard the same," Stretch confirmed. "And when they do, he'll be in High-Power. Bet on it."

"You mean they're not putting him up at Mom's bed-and-breakfast?" Warlock laughed. "Tell you what, Kinkade. If they fucked with the Infidelz, that means they fucked with our people. We'll help how ever we can. The bike guys inside here stick together. We take that shit personal on the inside. We're behind you."

"I appreciate that, brother. So, how's tricks in here?" Patch asked.

"Not bad. Been readin' a lot. Writin' a little. Can you believe that? I'm keeping a journal. Not a lot of bike riders here. Half dozen at any given moment. They keep us spread out. No Delz. A couple of Red Ravens. A few 2Wheelers. Soul Sacrifice. Pretty good guys. Mostly hang-arounds. We stick together and watch it go down at a distance. I'm just tryin' to keep my head down, do my time, and ride off into the sunset. Right now it's a little tight around here. I see signs."

Big Nate, and now Warlock, was right about the aura hanging over the yard this morning.

"Signs?"

"Yep. This place is about to blow."

"Signs? Such as?"

Warlock rubbed his chin in contemplation. "There's big issues. The infirmary sucks. Guys dyin' way too often. Four in the last few months alone. The flu and all sorts of shit constantly runs through this place like a cyclone. But it's mostly the little things that surface just before a meltdown. Like a lot of food items being bought at canteen. Guys are stocking up for a big lockdown. Lotsa our guys getting cited for bullshit offenses. The hard line and the hard looks on the yard. That crap."

"I noticed. One cop practically threw me in the hole for eyeballin' him."

"Yeah, a lot of that. The complaint-and-grievance system here is completely broken down. It's pretty fucked. Guys think they have no recourse but to get down, and I s'pose they will. It'll be one race against another. It always is."

"Racial bullshit."

"Yeah, that shit goes down on any yard. It should be more us versus them. Us being the inmates, them being the cops. That much we should agree on. But we can't get outta each other's way. So I just watch it go down. There hasn't been a superstrong white presence here in a long time."

"Anywho," said Patch, standing up, "I wanted to touch base. Pay my respects. Keep in touch. If you hear anything about Russians, gimme a holler. I'm over in Tower Five, down. My cellie's a guy named Big Nate McAllister."

Warlock chuckled. "I know Big Nate. Tell him I'll have his ass next football season. I gotta win some pouches back. They're worth somethin' now that those fuckin' geniuses banned the weed."

"I'll be sure to pass the word. Take care, my brothers."

"Love and respect, Patch Kinkade," said Stretch.

Something's about to go down." Big Nate was standing around the common area, shaking his head, arms folded. "I can just feel it."

"That's exactly what Warlock said."

"Over there." Big Nate pointed toward the north block. "Notice how the blacks are keeping to themselves. And over there. They have guys stationed at four corners. Could mean nothing, but I don't like it."

No sooner had Big Nate posted his storm warning than a loud pop was heard not far from where Patch and Big Nate were standing. Suddenly, out of nowhere, a battalion of COs, clutching guns and batons, came running across the yard toward Patch and Big Nate at Tower Five. Patch could hear the jingling of their keys. Some were wearing riot gear, helmets and gas masks. And lots of guns and clubs, some dowel guns, a contraption that shot wood dowels, much more painful than rubber bullets.

"Thar she blows," came a thunderous inmate bellow from upstairs, echoing throughout the prison.

Patch saw seven black inmates jump two Mexicans. CO response was swift and decisive, a product of rigorous training. It began with a shower on the nine scuffling inmates of wood blocks and large-marble-sized pellet projectiles fired at high velocity from 37-mm gas guns. Should those projectiles fail to halt the fracas, there were always the 9- and 14- millimeter rifles from the towers. Fortunately, all the nine fighters responded with immediate physical paralysis.

More cops came running, armed with the Super Soakers full of Mace and gas. Seconds later, the air was unbreathable, filled with a smoky, sickly gray gas. A fog hung over the common area. Then, something like a huge car alarm, only ten times louder, blared out. From the looks of it, the blacks had erupted first. Patch's lungs burned as his vision became cloudy then blurred. He felt woozy. Hot tears streamed down his cheeks.

The men standing in the open area instinctively got down on their knees at the sound of the alarm and the sight of the police. There was a lot of coughing and yelling. Others swung their fists at the police. Homemade knives and razors were produced. A couple guys swung white gym socks stuffed with bars of soap, or worse, a locker padlock. But they were no match for the swarm of armed cops now taking rapid and rigid control of the yard. The cops drew pistols but didn't fire them, swung batons, and bashed skulls as a couple of well-aimed tear gas shots came from the towers. A blue inmate not far from Patch fell clutching his ribs as he hit the deck. Patch could see that he was bruised and bleeding.

» 200

"Kinkade, you fuckin' idiot! Get down and stay down!" Patch heard Big Nate scream. But it was too late. Patch's prison reflexes were far too slow. Amid the commotion he remained on his feet, dumbstruck at how the premonitions of both Big Nate and Warlock had instantaneously come true.

Patch felt a herd of cops descend on him, with Bartkowski leading the pack, his baton swinging. Then he felt a dull thud on his forehead and suddenly his blurry vision went red. Patch mopped his brow to find that his face was covered in blood. He remained standing as another cop ran over and sprayed him. Suddenly he felt a four-alarm fire erupt in his eyes, nose, mouth, and his entire face. His skin burned. He tried to suck air into his lungs. He tried rubbing the fire out of his eyes, but the pain only intensified. He felt a hand yanking on his shirttail. A familiar yank. It was Big Nate pulling him down, just as he had done at intake/reception. Only this time it was more frantic, but it was also too late. Patch felt two more thuds, one cracking the crown of his head, the other, a long hard billy club smacking him across the back of his knees.

"Down, motherfucker, down," Patch heard a cop yell. His legs collapsed beneath him as he hit the concrete yard floor headfirst. Lights-out. He went down as the noise slowly faded into silent unconsciousness. Six minutes later, complete order was restored to the yard as hundreds of men were herded back into their cells for a lockdown while Patch and a couple of dozen fighters were dragged off.

It was a matter of spontaneous combustion. There was little rhyme or reason for the crush of skulls and bones other than that's what goes down when men are categorized by race behind prison walls.

Patch awoke on a hard mattress, his head sore and throbbing. He opened one crusty eye, while the other was stuck shut. He rubbed them both open and looked around. He was in the FDC infirmary, crowded with inmates nursing broken bones and cracked skulls, coughing up the residue of Mace and tear gas.

"Kinkade," said a trusty holding a clipboard. "How you holdin' up?"

"Who the hell are you?"

"Josephson."

"How long I been out, Josephson?"

"Coupla hours or so. All hell broke loose in the yard. You got smacked pretty good, and Maced."

"That part I remember. Getting here is what I'm hazy about."

"You're in the infirmary. The doctor is making the rounds. He's got a lot to tend to right now. We're triaging, seeing to the guys who have the most serious injuries first. A couple of shank wounds. Head injuries from swingin' athletic socks loaded with a bar of soap or a padlock. Razor cuts, and I'm not talkin' Super Cuts. Other than that, nothing too serious. Yer basic routine riot."

"What happened?"

"Who knows? Shit happens round here sometimes without an explanation."

"I guess the next time I'll know better to get my ass down when the shit starts flyin'."

"Guess so. I'da figured you'da known better."

"Whattaya mean *me* knowin' better?"

"Patch Kinkade. Word travels. I had a cellie who had a friend who was your cellmate in '88."

Jesus.

"How long I gotta stay here?"

Josephson looked around. Every bed was filled. Then he shrugged.

"Beats me. You able to walk okay?"

Patch got up out of bed and tested his sea legs. Not bad. Outside of a sore noggin, he wasn't seeing double or anything. His legs felt strong, though the back of his calves were a little sore from the clubbing.

"Actually, considering, I feel dandy."

203 «

"We ruled out a concussion, but if I were you, I'd lie still and wait for the doc to release you. Relax. Take a load off. Could be a few hours."

Fuck that, Patch thought.

"What time you got?"

"Quarter to four."

"I got a visit scheduled."

"I wouldn't count on it. All visits canceled. The whole joint's locked down, at least pending an investigation."

"Investigation?"

"Yeah, to find out who started what, if one group is at war with another, or if it started as an isolated spontaneous incident. Once they determine what's what, they'll open the yard back up. It doesn't take long. A day or two, max."

"I see." Patch noticed his face and head had been crudely bandaged. "Who did this?"

"I did."

"Much obliged," Patch said, pulling off the bandages, "but I won't be needing them."

Josephson walked away as Patch sat upright on the bed and looked around the room. He spotted the doorway that led out to the hallway. Since he had his shoes laced, he headed for the door.

"Kinkade," Josephson yelled out. "I thought I told you to stay put till the doc released you."

"I'm outta here." Patch waved and saluted. "Back to my cell."

Josephson looked over at the sole doctor across the room, deluged with groaning patients. He shrugged again.

"Suit yourself, Kinkade. Nobody's gonna exactly miss your ass."

Patch stepped out into the wide hallway. If the infirmary was chaotic, with the lone doctor bouncing around, at least the hallways were spotlessly scrubbed and empty. Just then, Patch heard what sounded like a small army rounding the hallway bend. A

CO armed with an assault rifle. Followed by another. Then a pair of guys in suits. They looked like G-men, federal agents. One of them babbled in a language Patch wasn't familiar with. A young, dark-haired twentysomething prisoner wearing an orange short-sleeved shirt signifying "fish in reception" rounded the corner, trudging slowly behind the suits and the gunmen, who were followed by yet another pair of armed guards. The newly processed prisoner was chained around his waist, but not the way Patch had been when he was admitted. This guy had double, triple the hardware. And cuffs. And shackles on his feet. On both arms was an amazing work of slung-ink artwork, a leopard on both arms, stalking his prey. One of the rear gunman guards caught Patch's eye.

"Look away. Look away," he ordered. Patch looked away, but then burned a look back at the prisoner. The young man shot Patch a vicious look. Twisted. Insane. Bitter. Resolute. Patch nodded ominously. His opponent's eyes narrowed.

One of the suits in the entourage conversed with the prisoner in a guttural language. At first Patch thought it might be German. But the prisoner uttered one word.

"*Nyet.*"

Patch shot a laser glare at the young man. *If looks could kill, I'd be home tomorrow.*

The prisoner and one of the suits turned around and threw Patch a stern look. The prisoner growled.

"On your way, inmate." shouted the rear guard. "You heard me. Back to your cell." Then the group stepped up their pace as the prisoner craned his neck back toward Patch. The jingle and clang of rattling chains and shackles disappeared around the next corner.

Patch instinctively knew who he had just seen. *We'll meet again soon, motherfucker.*

After they were gone, Patch's heart pounded harder. He hurried his step back to Tower Five, walking fast, just short of running. *You don't run in a federal lockdown unless you feel like getting shot dead.* He couldn't believe his luck. Or his eyes. Could this be the same guy who headed up the Cartel? The same guy who masterminded those bank jobs that everyone, even seasoned robbers, were starry-eyed impressed over. *The same fucking guy who killed my brothers.* Patch's blood boiled. He was within spitting distance of the very guy he'd burrowed deep into the federal detention center to get next to. It had to be him.

Back at Tower Five, the cell doors were open, but the main line and breezeways were empty, as everyone remained confined to their cells. Patch spoke to no one as he climbed to the top bunk. Big Nate was fast asleep, snoring loudly. Patch's climb didn't stir him.

Sleep didn't come easily that night again. Patch felt the burn of revenge in his belly. He kept seeing the face of the kid, looking back. And the massive three-color big cat tattoos on his arms. Patch lay awake the entire night seething, wondering how he was going to get next to this character. Who was he? How would Patch gain his revenge, then check out of this joint? Suddenly it didn't seem so easy.

First thing tomorrow he'd hit the telephone, dial collect, and make damn sure that Redbeard and Hollister gathered more information based on what he'd uncovered just minutes ago. All Patch had to go on was a bunch of ink on skin and a look in the eyes of a maniac who seemed like he'd been to hell and back.

The next morning Patch hit the pay-phone bank outside the pod. He dialed his home phone collect. Hollister picked up on the third ring.

"I have a collect call from an inmate at the federal detention center," the operator said. "Do you accept the charges?"

"Yeah, yeah," Hollister said, then he shouted away from the receiver, "Redbeard, quick! Patch on the horn."

Redbeard picked up the extension.

"How you holding up, kiddo?" Patch asked Hollister, trying to play it cool.

"Patch! We tried to visit you, but they held us up at the gate. Wouldn't let us in."

"What in hell's bells is going on in there anyway?" Redbeard chimed in.

"Lockdown, baby, but they let me use the phone early for—get this—medical reasons."

"Medical reasons?"

"We hadda shakedown, a riot of sorts."

"You okay?"

"Oh, yeah. I took one for the team, a rap behind the knees. But yeah, I'm sweet. Man, we need to meet." Patch figured the feds might be listening in.

"Where you at now?"

"GP, general population. More important, when can we connect?"

"We're set for tomorrow. Three on the dot."

"Great. Lots to hash over. I'm gainin' ground."

"Good," said Redbeard, "Because the grand jury is gainin' on us, too. Seen today's paper? My guess is they'll be issuing another subpoena demanding your testimony. Patience wears thin. Have you been served?"

"Not yet, but they know where to find me."

"When you gettin' out, Patch?" Hollister asked. "This stuff bums me out."

"Stay strong with both eyes open. By the way, I've suddenly developed a keen interest in leopards."

"Leopards?" Redbeard asked, puzzled. "As in cats?"

"Yeah," Patch answered emphatically. "You know, leopards. Big cats with spots. See what you can find out about leopards."

"Leopards," Redbeard repeated, stumped. "I'll see what we can dig up."

"Talk tomorrow."

"Watch your back in there, Patch," Hollister shouted into the receiver. The call suddenly disconnected. Patch's voice was replaced by a dial tone.

"Leopards? Shit." Redbeard asked Hollister as he put the phone down, "Is that some kinda code word between you two?"

"Beats the hell out of me."

"Boot up the computer, kid. We may have our first big break. Looks like we gotta start readin' up on Russian big cats."

Patch memorized the vivid markings of the leopard tattoos he saw on the mysterious HP inmate's arms. It had to mean something. He looked at his own arms, biceps, and shoulders. Underneath his shirt on his chest over his heart was his Infidelz club tattoo. There were plenty other symbols and slogans. A Sharpfinger knife dripping blood. CHERISH FREE-DOM. LEAD, FOLLOW, OR GET OUT OF THE WAY in psychedelic lettering. A grinning devil danced on Patch's left biceps with the flex of his muscle. Elsewhere on his arms and chest were the names of past women in his life. Nancy. Jane. Ramona was the freshest image. She'd left Patch and Hollister to take a bartending job at the Kickstand back in Palm Desert. Ex-wife Eve was intact, though the lettering of her name was noticeably fading. There were prison-made tattoos, drastically faded. Many a drunken night Patch had considered having one of the Nomads resurrect them with fresh quality ink, like restoring the paintings on the ceiling of the Sistine Chapel.

Body art behind bars was like contraband. Technically, like drugs, food, and tobacco, access to tattoos was taboo, against the rules, but they were commonly done on the sly. But like a lot of stuff on the inside, prison tats were tolerated so long as the design didn't aggravate the other races or spill blood out into the yard. It wasn't unusual for a bloody skirmish to erupt on the yard over a gang tattoo or a racist message, simple or elaborate. Patch remembered one skinhead who'd paraded around the yard shirtless sporting a scroll of white supremacist and Norse imagery inked all over his body. Outraged black inmates demanded his removal from the yard one way or another. The white factions searched for a solution, without appearing to kowtow or back down. Soon the assistant warden transferred the kid. Patch learned many times, both in prison and on the streets, that tattoos and body art were an extremely volatile and indelible way to spread a message.

Up to now, Patch had chosen to focus only on the good parts of doing time, the therapeutic solitude and the camaraderie. But now that he'd been back in the joint for a while, the unglamorous aspects of doing time were seeping in: the starchy food that dragged on his body and sapped his energy. The constant clatter that gave way to severe migraines. A prison mattress's unrelenting toll on an inmate's back. The inching of the minutes and hours that drove everyone bananas. It was starting to come back to him. No matter how easy or hard it was, Patch made it a point to "mark his time" permanently. In remembrance. That meant tattooing his body.

"Big Nate?"

"Yeah, boss."

"Who's the chief ink slinger around here?"

"That would be Gogol, a Russian dude. He's hell on wheels with a sketch pad and a prison tat gun. An artist. He's over in Tower Three, otherwise known as Tower Tres, because of the dominant Mexican population. But Gogol and his Eastern Euro pals, they drive their own car. He and his boys are constantly playing cards, but I'm not sure who's dealing from a full deck."

"You mean as in crazy?"

"I mean literally, they play this Russian game, but not with a full deck. Thirty-two cards."

"How will I know this Gogol character?"

Big Nate laughed. "Oh, you'll know him when you see him. Hard to miss. I worked with the dude for a while on trash detail. He's scary-lookin', but he's stand-up. Tell him I sent you. He owed me, but I wiped his debt clean. He was into me for several dozen pouches. Then he did me a favor, or should I say, provided me with some key merchandise. Being the magnanimous guy that I am, I forgave his debt. He's been a homey since."

Patch jumped down from his bunk.

"Then I'm gonna look up this Gogol dude. I could use the stink blowed offa me. I'll catch you later, amigo."

"Tell Gogol I said hey, and give him these." Big Nate handed Patch a half pint of ink stored inside a plastic soy-sauce container and a couple packets of guitar strings.

As Patch approached Tower Three, there *was* a wild card game of some sort brewing. Patch approached the table. Four guys seated. One of the players, who was munching on a bean burrito, spotted Patch first and stood up, throwing out an anxious and cautious look.

"I'm lookin' for Gogol," Patch said, holding his hands up in plain sight. "I come in peace."

"Who wants to know?" the standing Russian asked. He was tall with closely cropped blond hair and lightning bolts on the side of his neck.

"Patch Kinkade. Friend of Big Nate McAllister. He sent me. Wanted me to give Gogol these." Patch showed him the ink. "I'm lookin' to have a little ink slung. I need to know where I can find Gogol."

One of the four men seated at the card game, with his back to Patch, stood up and turned around. "Yeah. I'm Gogol." Patch noted an accent similar to the Rachkovs'.

Patch held out his hand and gave him the pint container of ink and the guitar strings. "Patch Kinkade."

"Gogol," he replied with a thick foreign accent.

Gogol was short and prematurely bald, not too old, late thirties, early forties max. Hairy back. Tattoo city. Full multihued body art wrapped around a well-defined musculature. Short, stout, but round and strong. Built low to the ground like an NFL tailback. A fearsome sight. What was astounding was the tattoo on his face. Not only did this guy wear the mileage of a hard life in his eyes, looking older than his years, but across his forehead was a vivid reproduction of black barbed wire punctuated by vibrant drops of bloodred ink. His chest revealed the drawing of an ornate crucifix hanging from an elaborate chain. Gogol pointed to the cross on the tattooed chain.

"You seem curious. It is the mark of an assassin." He winked unabashedly.

"Look, you guys are in the middle of a game. I don't wanna interrupt. I can come back."

"Nonsense. You are just in time because I am getting my tail whipped. I'm done for the day." Gogol moaned, throwing down his cards. "Plus you come bearing gifts."

"Big Nate was tellin' me about this game. Some kind of Russian bridge?"

"Preference. We play Russian style. Sometimes Croatian. We use a standard deck of cards and take out the suits from two to six."

Patch cleared his throat. "I'm here to ask about a tat, and judging from the looks of it, I came to the right guy."

Gogol's smile faded. He eyeballed Patch suspiciously.

"Like I said, Big Nate sends his regards," Patch said, palming him a few Pall Malls.

Gogol blinked and then his smile returned after he pocketed the smokes. "You speak the language, my friend." Then he threw his arm around Patch. "Come with me, friend of Big Nate McAllister."

Gogol walked Patch back into his cell, which was decorated with postcards from the motherland, Russia, as well as drawings of religious icons and the holy Madonna. But the wall was mostly papered with elaborate drawings of dark faces, all of them men, sketched in pencil and ink and ripped from a notepad. There were also drawings of various symbols and figures, pointed stars, churches, mosques, or were they cathedrals? Patch wasn't sure. Gleaming spires and towering towers. Castles. Fortresses. Animals. A few naked women. Skulls. Dollar signs, bullets, and knives. Numerals. Felines. And there it was. A growling leopard, perched to attack. Indeed, Patch had come to the right place. Patch wondered what else Gogol might have hidden in his cell, besides a virtual museum of tat images. There was something about it that spelled "operation," besides being a makeshift prison tattoo parlor.

"Tell me, how did you get into this line of work?" Patch asked.

"I was conscripted into the Russian army, after which I—how should I put this?—chose the dark side. I was a master pickpocket at first. Then I took up drawing. I escaped prison and came here as a persecuted Jew." Gogol pointed to a Star of David on his wrist. "I was supposed to serve a life sentence in Russian prison for murder, but even they could not hold me."

How did Gogol end up back inside an American federal lockup? Reverting back to a life of crime? Patch elected not to ask, nor did he bring up the barbed wire that spanned Gogol's weathered forehead. When Gogol blinked his eyes, Patch noticed his eyelids: tatted with the Xs of death.

"Inside Russian prison, we made our own ink. Making soot by burning and scraping the heel of our boots, then mixing the soot with our own urine and blood. Not so here. I have the deluxe setup."

What a relief. Nobody's piss was getting under Patch's skin today.

Gogol pointed to his Wall of Fame. "Pick one. Not all I can do for you. Some you need to earn the right to wear."

"What I had in mind was . . . that one." Patch pointed to the big cat stuck on Gogol's wall with toothpaste. "The leopard. Right there. It's perfect. I dig the full body. And the spots. Can

I get a stalking big cat crawling up my arm. Can you do it?" Patch said.

"A leopard?"

"A guy in my club owned one once. We called him Kitty Kitty. Fed him live chickens every day at noon. Can you draw the leopard?"

"I can draw anything!" Gogol hollered boastfully and with irritation. Then he lowered his voice and his eyes. "Except for that. No leopard. Sorry."

"Did I choose some kind of sacred religious symbol or something? Is that why you can't ink me?"

"Something like that. Like I tell you, some of these marks, a man must earn. Some of these marks, they symbolize grave evil. Like that one. It used to be a great piece of art, but then it was corrupted by a group of men, men without character. The leopard, to my people, is now a very dark symbol indeed. In fact, I don't even know why I keep it in sight." With that, Gogol tore the leopard down, crumpling the drawing and throwing it on the floor.

215 «

"What's more powerful than a leopard?" Patch asked.

"What do you mean?"

"What kills leopards?"

Gogol thought for a moment. "Only man. With guns, traps, things like that. The pelt is highly prized."

"Then give me a snare or a trap—something that kills leopards. If the leopard is such a bad symbol, then something that kills them has to be a righteously good one, right?"

Patch raised his shirt, revealing acreage of red, black, and blue ink drawings, notably his club tattoo. "I don't have much available space left these days. Why don't you put it on my forearm."

"This I can do. In my country, the leopard has, how you say, deep political meaning. The spilled blood of innocent people. The handiwork of cowards. To me, a leopard tattoo would be the equivalent to wearing swastikas on your arms."

"You've sold me, Gogol. Give me a snare, like a bear trap for leopards. It will keep the evil away."

Gogol's setup was crude but ingenious. He opened the soy-sauce container then unraveled one of the guitar strings, clipping the end off with a pair of cutters he had hidden under the commode. The barrel of Gogol's tat gun (which held the ink) had been a 0.7 mechanical pencil in its former life. Using a metal pen pocket clip to mount the "ink barrel" onto a motor, Gogol drove the tat gun with a round motor commonly found inside a Walkman cassette player. The circular motion of the Sony cassette motor drove the "needle" up and down as the ink traveled through the barrel and beneath Patch's skin. Fortunately Gogol used the new G "sterile" guitar string Patch had brought with him. It was rudimentary but highly operational. Ingenious. Without the tell-tale buzz of a traditional high-speed gun, the Walkman motor was effective in inking clandestine designs behind bars. As for the pain threshold, the problem here wasn't so much the pain as it was the risk of infection afterward. Guitar strings were far from sterilized. But, fortunately, knock on wood, prison tats still healed quickly onto Patch's body. They always did.

"You know, you mention politics. Seems I have heard about some kind of organization having to do with leopards. I think they're Russians. Bank robbers. Some kind of beef with the government. Is that what you're referring to with this?"

"Yes."

"Some kind of cartel?"

"Not some kind of cartel, *the* Cartel. Enemy of the Russian state. Please hold still, Mr. Kinkade."

"I wasn't aware. I thought the guy who runs them is locked up here in the States."

Talking always helped dull the pain of a prison tattoo. Patch could see a savage-looking steel-toothed trap appearing on the tender part of his forearm. He continued pumping Gogol for more info.

"He is. But they are still an organization run by lunatics," Gogol replied. "Do you remember that bank job a few weeks ago?"

"Hell yeah, it's the talk of the mess hall."

Gogol nodded knowingly and whispered: "The work of the Cartel."

"No shit."

"No shit," said Gogol, not looking up from his needlework, but adding under his breath: "Fucking dogs."

"I don't get it, Gogol," Patch said. "What loyalty do you have to the Russian state anyway? Haven't they done enough to you? Locked you away? What do you care if someone takes them on?"

"And imprisoned my family! Still, I am Russian. And I always will be Russian. I will die a Russian. What's happened to me in my life is of my own doing. I take the full responsibility for my actions. But my heart will always belong to my mother country."

A couple of the cardplayers listened in until Gogol sent a wry gaze their way, then they looked away. Gogol was clearly the man driving this car.

"All this conversation is very interesting, Mr. Patch Kinkade." Gogol's eyes narrowed. "Let me ask you this. What do you care about all this leopard stuff?"

"I just do," Patch responded.

"Don't tell me this Cartel boss is a friend of yours, or that you admire his cause."

"No friend of mine," Patch answered sternly. Gogol could sense the hate in Patch's reply.

"Right answer, Kinkade. I hope not." The cold look in Gogol's eyes told Patch to end the conversation there. They finished the rest of the procedure in silence.

Finally, when the detailed outline of the killing machine fully appeared, instead of a gauze pad, Gogol ripped a small page of tracing paper from one of his tablets and placed the sheet on top of the trap that now covered the tender side of Patch's left forearm. Patch saw the image of the trap emerge onto the paper from a mixture of his own blood and sweat, seeping through the thin sheet. The detail was superb for a first run. Though the drawing was monochromatic, it was nonetheless detailed. The teeth of the trap resembled those of a wild animal as it strained to deliver the killing blow. No doubt about it, Gogol was an artist.

"You are finished. Maybe later we can fill in more detail."

"Don't think so. I don't plan on stayin' much longer. But I'm much obliged, Gogol." Patch shook the Russian's hand firmly. "It's been a pleasure. How can I pay you?"

Gogol grabbed Patch's hand and shook it hard.

"You already pay. For Big Nate, I do this for you. He had me over a barrel, but then he gave me a big break. That I don't forget."

"And I appreciate the art and the info on such short notice, brother. Your work definitely leaves a permanent impression on me."

Gogol shook his head and laughed as he led Patch out of his parlor cell and re-joined his game of Preference. Patch waved farewell and melted back into GP, holding the tracing paper over his arm, making his way back home in Tower Five. He now had something in common with his adversary, something that might bring them together. But how? Patch needed to work that part out, somehow get upstairs into High-Power. But tomorrow he had a visit from Redbeard and Hollister lined up. Barring any more spontaneous uprisings on the yard, they would come bearing the greatest gift, more information.

A boring day in the FDC. The minutes and hours c-c-r-r-a-a-w-w-l-l-e-e-d-d as the hands snail-paced their way around the clock toward the three and the twelve, Patch's designated visiting hour. Big Nate was out and about. What Patch wouldn't give for a little Waylon Jennings to listen to. Or some Pearl Jam to kill the time. Anything loud. Or anything peaceful, for that matter. Something to divert the empty boredom of his cell. He examined his latest markings. Seemed to be healing fast.

Finally. After an eternity.

"Kinkade. You got a visit scheduled."

Patch was ushered into a private room, an interrogation room located between the visiting center and law library. Most visits took place in the noisy crowded visitors' lounge, a large open room with a series of tables and chairs, placed too close together for comfort and privacy. A friendly gesture to get him to cooperate and testify?

"Since this is your attorney you're meeting with," the guard said on the way, "you've got one hour."

My attorney? Redbeard had scammed his way again.

Redbeard and Hollister were already seated at the table when Patch arrived. The white walls and the fluorescent lights were blinding. Headache inducing. When Patch walked into the room wearing his prison blues, Hollister cracked up, then scowled, then smiled.

"Look at you, Mr. Fashion Plate. I've never seen you in jail, in prison blues, before."

"Listen, kid, just because I'm inside doesn't mean I can't bust your chops. That'd be worth spending a week in the hole for. Gimme a hug."

Patch hugged Hollister, to the irritation of the guard outside, who rapped loudly on the window with his flashlight. Redbeard was already set up, files open and organized.

"We only got an hour," said Redbeard, "so let's get right down to it."

"Check this out," Patch said, rolling up his shirtsleeve, revealing the new tattoo on his arm.

"Wow!" Hollister gushed.

Redbeard frowned at first. "You got this inside?"

"Yesterday," Patch said. "It's the sort of thing that kills leopards. And get this, I saw our guy. Ran into him in the hallway outside the infirmary. Surrounded by G-men. Had to be him. A little guy. Not what I would expect of a guy running a Mob. He's got two elaborate tats running up both forearms, gigantic leopards."

"Which explains your curiosity about big cats," said Hollister. "And it looks like we might have a few pieces of the puzzle."

"What do we hear from the Rachkovs?"

"Layin' low. Doin' their wheeling and dealing," said Redbeard. "They're keeping tabs on the grand jury. No progress. Deadlock.

"Hollister and I did some research on the Cartel and this leopard thing. We were chasing our tails for a while, until you called about the big cats. Then it got interesting. Real interesting. There's a guy who goes by the name of Leopold Amur. Gangster type. Interesting alias. We think he runs the Cartel. He's sorta the Eastern European version of Gerry Adams, the Sein Fein guy in Northern Ireland, except he's much more hands-on in the covert-operations department. Amur's got an interesting past. First thing, he's not Russian."

"Whattaya mean he's not Russian? I heard him myself. 'Nyet. Nyet.' Ain't that Russian?"

"He may walk like a Russian and quack like a Russian, but he ain't no fuckin' Russian duck. Farthest thing from it. Trust me. The government here has kept the curtain of secrecy on him as far as American media coverage is concerned. But in the international press, the German political magazines, some British journals, and particularly in the Eastern European press, he's written about. Technically our guy is Grozistani."

"What's that?"

"Lemme see," said Redbeard, flipping through printouts of translated news items and maps from the Internet. "According to this, Grozistan is a former Soviet province. Now they're in the middle of a messy confrontation with President Putin and the Russians over the issue of Grozistani independence. After the fall of the USSR, Grozistan, which happens to be small but chock-full of oil, declared their independence. The catch is that the rest of the world fell in line with the Russians by refusing to recognize Grozistan's sovereignty."

221 «

"So this is about oil?"

"Partly. Oil and independence. Take your pick. It says here, 'To convince the Russians to grant them independence, Grozistani rebels have been waging a very conspicuous war on the streets of Moscow and the outlying areas.' "

"Are these those assholes who killed those schoolkids in Russia?"

"No. That's the Chechen rebels. But similar. These guys liken themselves to freedom fighters. They're demanding a larger share of oil revenues to build up their nation. They've been hammering Moscow, trading gunfire and bombs with the FSB, the Russian

Federal Security Service, a part of the former KGB, and police for a couple years.

"There's more," said Redbeard, shuffling through his pile of articles. "Robbing banks. Soliciting political support from other former Soviet states. They haven't killed many Russian civilians, only government bigwigs. They're a real political thorn in Putin's side."

"So if this Amur guy is an Eastern European freedom fighter, what's he doing in Colorado and Arizona?"

"History lesson, Patch," continued Hollister. "Most of the members of the Eastern European Mob got their foothold here by settling in the Eastern United States, mostly in Brighton Beach, outside New York City."

"Yeah, kid. That's the name of the Rachkov gym."

"A lot of mobsters had a tiny speck of Jewish blood, enough to get them inside the country through the United States' policy with Israel, claiming they were persecuted Jews in the hands of the Kremlin.

"Pre-9/11, it was easier to get into the USA," said Redbeard. "Once they landed, over the past couple decades they gained a foothold in a lot of organized-crime cells. For instance, they kicked ass on the Italians. They crossed the lines of honor that families and crews would not cross. Like killing family members, wives, and kids. Waging all-out war. They're into computer fraud, identity theft, smuggling drugs, women, and cigarettes. Before that, a lot of Eastern European mobsters started out grifting the U.S. government out of Medicare checks, fraud, stuff like that.

"As the Mobs grew, so did the Eastern European crime land-scape in the United States. According to one article, 'Subsects sprouted up. Next came the rivalries. Pretty soon Russians were defending turf against other Eastern Euro Mobs comin' over to the U.S. for the easy money. Now they're worldwide.' The United States was the Promised Land, a virtual free pass for raising cash and starting up enterprises. But now it ain't so virgin anymore, with different Mob factions fighting over control."

"Are Amur's guys mobsters?"

"Not really. The Cartel mostly does their stuff to raise money for their homeland cause. None of their capos are living high off the hog. Overseas, they got a lot of working- and lower-class revolutionary appeal, people buying into their rhetoric. They're completely unafraid of what any government, especially the U. S., can do to them," continued Redbeard. "If it was the Cartel that pulled off that bank job, that means millions of laundered dollars, nearly a hundred percent of the take, made it back to the motherland to fund more guerrilla activities against the Russian government in Moscow, or else it was put back into the economy here to grow legitimate businesses to feed the operations for years, to provide a cash flow for operations inside and outside of Grozistan. Granted, after 9/11, it's harder to filter money in and out of the States, but that doesn't mean it's impossible. That's why they're here, going in and out of the southwestern U.S. through Mexico and Cuba. There's talk they might have alliances going with the Cuban government."

"That explains why they're robbing banks in Arizona. Big balls."

"Our guess," said Hollister, "is that Boris and the Nomads unwittingly got caught up with these Cartel characters. Then Amur's boys came in and took 'em out. Boris mighta been dealing on their turf with that gun haul. That's the only thing I can figure out that makes sense."

"Was Boris aware of who these guys were?"

"Hard to tell," replied Redbeard. "That's something we're trying to look into. All the club guys we've talked to didn't know half of what Boris was up to. He operated in a vacuum, for sure."

Patch felt the heat fluttering around his face and his heart begin to race. That's what happened when he got angry. Soon, he was beet red with rage. Mad at the Cartel for killin' his guys. Angry at Boris for being a careless, oblivious target.

"All the more reason to shank this motherfucker. Kill the root, everything else dies."

"You need to get next to this guy," said Redbeard, "and find out what's going on."

"Has this guy testified in front of the grand jury yet?"

"Not that we know of," replied Hollister. "The Rachkov brothers promised to give us the word, so we're clear there."

"Man, you should see this leopard motherfucker," said Patch. "He can't be much older than Hollister here."

"I read where the average age of a resistance rebel in Grozistan is twenty-three," said Redbeard. "A whole new Pepsi generation hating the fuckin' Russians. It's hard to tell who's more unpopular in the world today, the Russians or us. But—we have more. Hollister, tell Patch what you came up with on the leopard front."

Hollister pulled his chair in closer to the table.

"Check this out. He goes by the name Leo Amur, alias Leopard. Nobody knows his real name. The snow, or Amur, leopard is one of the most endangered big cats in the world. It's currently on the Critically Endangered Red List. Eighty percent of them were slaughtered between the years 1970 and 1983, about the time this guy must have been born. Specifically, the Amur big cats are on the verge of extinction throughout Asia, in Korea, and in China and Russia. There's only about thirty to fifty adult cats left in Russia, making them as rare as the Siberian tiger. When the Russian empire was broken up, there was widespread illegal trade of tiger and leopard products, whatever those are, throughout Asia, which pissed off the Russians. The Russians are now breeding these cats by importing the remaining adult specimens from European zoos shipped in from Berlin and Helsinki."

"Leopold Amur. So this guy took on the leopard name as a symbol."

"Something the Russian people might relate to," interjected Redbeard. "Or at least understand. The whole concept of class extinction. Genocide. He's very clever."

"A PR-minded murderer, a punk, and someone who made the fatal mistake of fucking with us," said Patch, rubbing his chin in contemplation. "Amur is our man and he's goin' down. He's the one I saw for sure. I need to get into High-Power so's I can get closer to this guy before he makes it in front of the grand jury. And when I do, I won't hesitate to do what needs to be done, even if I gotta sit in this shithole for the rest of my life."

"Patch," said Redbeard "We need you to stay cool with your head screwed on straight."

"This whole thing sucks," said Hollister, frowning, and slumped in his chair.

"Don't you worry, kid." Patch brought his voice down to a whisper. "The only guy who should be worried is this Eastern European motherfucker. Once I get finished with him, the grand jury's investigation is going to be in a shambles and I'll be long gone on the next Grey Goose outta here."

After the visit, Patch walked back to his cell. Big Nate was slumped over the desk scribbling a letter.

"Lemme ask you, Big Nate. Suppose I was to hit you up for another huge favor, as if you haven't done enough already. Would you kick my ass?"

"Depends, Kinkade, depends."

"I'm lookin' to take care of someone."

"Are you asking me what I think you're asking?"

"Yeah. You got any weapons of individual destruction, somethin' I could use to take care of someone important?"

"That's a serious request, Mr. Kinkade," Big Nate said, looking up from his letter.

"I've never been nothing but serious with you. Well, do ya?"

"I might."

"Might or might not? I'll pay you back on the outside. Rest assured."

"I just might. But if you get pinched, dude, that automatically means I'm goin' in the hole with you. And I hate the fuckin' hole. Drives me loony. I spent a month in the hole one week. Man, if they bust *you*, they could add a couple of years to *my* sentence, too. You'll be in here eighteen months, no sweat, most of it in the hole. I'm tellin' you so you know what you're getting into. You've just crossed a serious line, brother."

"I ain't in here for my health, poncho. I'm on a mission of no mercy."

"I figured as much with you." Big Nate put his pencil down. "Just so you know, there ain't no turnin' back once you walk down that long dark lonesome road. You get caught with that shit and you'll be in a fuckuva lot more trouble than just pissin' off a rich housewife sitting on the grand jury."

"I hear ya."

"Tell ya what . . ."

Big Nate took out a small hand mirror and held it out the open cell door. When he was satisfied there was no coppers coming, he walked to the back of the cell.

"I'm gonna have to ask you to shut your eyes," Big Nate told Patch.

"Shut my eyes? What is this, *I've Got a Secret*? Christ, don't be fuckin' ridiculous."

"Ain't bein' ridiculous, Patch. I'm serious as a case of scabies. Sometimes the less your friends know about certain shit, the better. Shut your fuckin' eyes and hold out your hand."

Seconds later, Patch felt Big Nate drop something in his palm. It seemed pretty light and harmless. Not a metal blade, that was for sure.

Patch opened his eyes.

"Trick or treat, big guy," said Big Nate. "Now be cool."

It was a long triangular shiv. Made of plastic. Patch turned his back toward the cell door and ran his thumb along one of the sharpened edges. The short cut drew blood.

"Jesus Christ, this motherfucker's a sharpie. You could kill somebody with this thing."

"Ain't that the general idea, Kinkade? If you don't wanna shank 'em, shave 'em."

"Where the hell'd you get this?"

"One of my clients got behind in his financial obligations."

"Our tattoo friend?"

"As a matter of fact, yeah. I got it from Gogol. My guess is that he made it out of a plastic bucket lid he smuggled out of the kitchen. I kept it in case of dire emergency. I assume we're talking dire emergency here, right, Kinkade?"

"Precisely."

"Well, it's yours now, and to tell the truth, I'm relieved to be fuckin' rid of it. I had it hid real good, but every time the cops tore apart my house, it freaked me. She's yours now, and if I were you, I'd think about stashing it right now. At least it won't show up on a metal detector."

"How can I repay?"

"I was hoping you'd ask that. Once you get out, you can be my tobacco mule. My supplier. I'll put one of your guys on my visitors' list."

» 228

"No problem. I'll put a member on it immediately."

Patch held the razor-sharp plastic shiv in his hand, then shoved it into his pants pocket.

Just then the cell door opened. It was Sarge, the CO who ran the night shift. Big Nate jumped to his feet. Patch stayed cool, seated on Big Nate's bunk.

"Kinkade?"

"Yes, sir, that's me."

Sarge looked around the cell. "What are you guys up to? I smell trouble."

"Nothin' much. Writin' home," said Big Nate. "That's it. When are you guys lookin' to lift the lockdown?"

"When we're damned good and ready."

"Jesus, Sarge, just askin'."

Sarge shuffled a piece of paper. "Kinkade. I got orders to ship you out."

"Ship me out where?"

"Upstairs. High-Power. Congratulations. You've been promoted."

Patch's heart jumped. *Merry Christmas!* "What happened?"

Sarge held up a section of the *Arizona Republic.* The headline: GRAND JURY EXPANDS INVESTIGATION.

"Yeah, yeah, Kinkade. You're a big celebrity."

"Will you look at that," Big Nate chimed in as he and Patch scanned the newspaper article. "It says here somebody from the grand jury told the press that you could be ordered to testify again."

"You're famous, Kinkade," Sarge said. "You got an hour to get your stuff together."

"Mind if I have a look at that paper, Sarge?"

"Keep it," he said, tossing Patch the newspaper. "Just be ready to roll. If you're late, it just makes my job harder. You don't wanna make my job harder, do ya, Kinkade?"

"Absolutely not, Sarge. Wouldn't think of it."

229 «

MOTORCYCLE GANG QUESTIONED BY GRAND JURY. Another story. Patch reread that section of the newspaper, an "insider" article mentioning the grand jury. While such proceedings were supposed to be confidential, details were leaked out to the press all the time. Both articles hinted at organized crime and bike gangs falling under further scrutiny. That meant both the Cartel and the Infidelz were under the grinder. Four bodies, a stash of counterfeit loot, and millions of real dollars heisted in broad daylight. It was enough fodder to continue the GJ's interest in organized crime and the Infidelz MC. No wonder Patch was goin' upstairs.

An hour later, the CO arrived. "Sarge is here," Patch said.

"Well, dude," said Big Nate, standing up. "It was fun while it lasted. I guess I'll see you in church."

"Yeah, guess so."

While Patch gathered his property, Big Nate tossed him a going-away gift. A shiny red crisp apple. *An actual piece of fruit!* Patch smiled at the gesture and carefully placed the apple in his net sack so as not to bruise it in transit to High-Power. He and Big Nate embraced.

"All right already," Sarge complained. "You guys are breaking my heart *and* my balls."

Sarge cuffed Patch and gently pushed him out the cell toward the elevator, which rose past the first two floors of GP, past the third, where protective custody was located, right up to the fourth floor, bringing Patch's status up to the highest federal level. Patch stepped out of the elevator and toward a sign reading CELL BLOCK.

"Not so fast, Kinkade. We got one final stop to make."

"What stop is that?"

"I promise you"—Sarge snickered—"it won't take long."

"Listen, if you wanna beat me to a pulp, why don't you do it right here? All I ask is a sportin' chance. Uncuff me."

"Relax, Kinkade. I've got orders to drop you by admin. You need to see Francine. I understand it's an emergency."

Francine? What emergency? Patch shook his head in uncertainty.

"Like I said, Kinkade, you'll be thanking me."

Sarge led Patch into the admin office with his hands cuffed in front of him.

Francine's administrative domain was a large air-conditioned office with rows of filing cabinets and a couple of computers on a single desk. FRANCINE BANKS, the nameplate on the desk read. *Head of Administration.* Adorning her clean stark desk were fresh-cut flowers and a couple of framed family photos. Two toothy and gangly preteen kids in one. In the other, a husband in uniform. Upon closer inspection, hubby appeared to be some kind of cop.

"I guess I'll leave you both to it," Sarge said, winking to Patch. "Be back in a few." He closed and locked the door behind him.

What the . . . ?

Francine couldn't have been much taller than five feet. She wore her dark hair piled on top of her head, revealing a pretty, round face with dark and appealing eyes. Italian descent. Thin lips. Red nail polish. Francine wore a cream-colored blouse and a dark miniskirt and black stockings over her short legs. As she walked toward the front of the office where Patch stood, he could hear the click and clack of her flat-soled shoes on the hard tile floor.

"We don't have much time," Francine said, leading Patch toward the rear of the office through a green door. Behind the green door was a smaller back room filled with boxes brimming with files and records. There was a desk with a lamp and a candy dish.

"Like I said," Francine uttered, quickly unbuttoning her blouse. "We don't have much time."

"Much time for what?"

Francine dropped her blouse, revealing a pair of small breasts, and then stepped out of her short skirt. No panties underneath. Stockings. Garter belt. *Lookin' good.* She lifted Patch's attached wrists and wiggled her tiny frame into his arms between his cuffed hands and his body. She immediately began kissing him, smearing red lipstick all over his face. Patch wanted to speak, but with Francine's tongue lodged in his mouth, he couldn't say much of anything, so he decided to go along with the program. With Francine's assistance, his denim pants dropped to the floor, followed by his white shorts. With his cuffed wrists encircling her body, Francine then sat back on the small desk and opened her legs. Down below, Patch required no additional consideration. Francine had his firm attention.

233 «

"So?" Patch got a word in, ripping his mouth away from Francine's. "What about the latex portion of the show?"

"That's okay. We ride bareback here."

"You might, but I don't."

Francine looked at him and smiled devilishly, shaking her head.

"Suit yourself," she said as she reached into the candy jar and pulled out a foiled rubber. After slipping it over his unit, Patch did a most awkward dance of love. Bumping and grinding in captivity. Amid the bizarre circumstances with the handcuffs, sex he hadn't expected, a continuously ringing telephone, and Francine's persistent moaning, Patch did his job, trying not to pop too soon. With each thrust he could feel the desk move an inch closer to the back wall. Fortunately the concrete walls absorbed

Francine's howls. After Patch popped, she slipped her blouse back on and hiked up her skirt, pulling Patch's pants back up with the condom still dangling from his cock. Then Francine led him back to the front office, unlocking the door just as Sarge lightly knocked.

Perfect timing.

Francine smiled at Sarge, ignored Patch, and returned to her daily routine, answering the telephone as if nothing extraordinary had happened. Both men left.

Outside the admin office, Sarge suggested to Patch, "You might wanna wipe your face, son."

"So," Patch asked, wiping the lipstick from his face with his cuffed hands, "you mind telling me what the hell *that* was about?"

"Last year, Francine found out her husband was cheatin' on her with his female partner. Ever since then, to even the score, we been feedin' her a steady supply of studs. You were just her type."

"We?"

"Yeah, me and a couple of the guys."

"So, if you don't mind me askin', what's in it for you to be pimpin' federal prisoners to the head of admin?"

"We ain't pimpin' nobody. This is a free service, mutually beneficial to everybody. Nympho Francine's a friend, her husband has it comin', and, I figured, so do you."

Patch laughed as Sarge led him down the hall toward his new home, a block of High-Power cells.

Welcome to the elite, Kinkade. Population one hundred and twenty lucky inmates." It was a voice from the sky, coming through the speaker built into the ceiling.

Unlike the cacophonous GP, High-Power was quiet. It was a world unto itself. Serious business. A collection of glass-doored cells, no bars, watched over from above by the man in the bubble. During daylight hours, the cell doors remained open; otherwise there was little difference between High-Power confinement and the dog pound. Everyone had a cell, a cage, to himself. While Patch appreciated the increased privacy (except for the eye in the sky), he immediately felt a dark sense of isolation. *How do guys live in here for months, years?*

Cops watched the cells from above, using "high-tech supervision." That meant TV monitors and very little physical contact with the inmates. Fortunes spent on design and technology were supposed to reduce staffing costs.

The way Sarge explained it: three meals would be served from a food cart wheeled past the cell. Canteen orders would be filled once a week from a provided checklist. Patch was free to watch the tube from his cell all day. *Room service and TV.* The exercise yard, situated on the roof, was open for one hour each night, from

6 to 7 P.M. No basketball or volleyball. But Patch wasn't here to shoot hoops or spike the ball. High-Power inmates would only intersect with the rest of the general population during chapel.

That was what Big Nate musta meant by his "see you in church" comment.

Patch situated his few belongings on his metal desk, the cage's lone piece of "furniture" besides a bunk and footlocker. Underwear, socks, toiletries, shoes, and blue denim jacket barely fit into the small footlocker. The stainless-steel sink hung loosely off the wall. *A piss-poor job of mounting it.* Patch placed the red apple center stage on the cold metal desk. It was a rose in Spanish Harlem, a beautiful still life. He'd save it for his first nighttime treat. Just then he heard a squeaking outside his cell door. It was the food cart, which was being pushed by a man with a familiar face.

"Kinkade." It was Josephson, from the infirmary. "New digs?"

"S'pose so."

"Can I get you anything?"

"Has my account gone through the bureaucracy yet?"

Josephson checked his clipboard. "Kinkade, Kinkade, yeah, here we go. Looks like you got a hundred on the books. What'll it be?" *A cold beer and a whiskey chaser would hit the spot,* but Patch settled for some OJ, a packet of vanilla wafers, a bottle of Prell shampoo, potato chips, and ten packages of cheese crackers. Not much else to choose from.

"Lemme ask you, Josephson. That guy they brought in the day I got sent to infirmary? The guy in chains in the hallway. Escorted by a slew of armed cops. Little guy. Did you see him?"

"Yeah. That fish made quite the entrance. What of it?"

"Who was he?"

"Not sure," said Josephson. "But I can sure as hell poke around and find out." The trusty beamed with pride, then whispered: "If it's going down on this block, I'll know about it sooner or later, usually sooner."

"Whatever you find out, I'd be much obliged, and glad to return the favor." Patch cringed right after he said the words. Hopefully Josephson wasn't queer, a peter puffer, taking his comment the wrong way.

"Let's see what I can come up with." Then the trusty was gone, rolling his cart onto the next cell.

Patch was ready to test his bunk mattress. Firm. That was good. He seized the apple off the desk. It had been an eventful few days. Meeting Big Nate and his crew; Warlock and Stretch. Getting inked by Gogol. Getting the shit knocked out of him during a prison riot. Getting laid. Best of all, he'd "spotted" the Leopard. Progress. Patch lay back and scrutinized the apple. Ruby red, like a woman's blush. Skin was firm, not mushy, but soft and shiny. His tryst with Francine had bordered on the creepy, though she kept herself in good shape, a more than decent piece of ass, though not exactly the apple of his eye. How many guys had the guards paraded through admin as Francine practiced hardcore revenge on her unfaithful husband? Precisely why Patch had passed on the bareback ride.

237 ◄◄

Patch closed his eyes and again recalled the beautiful girls at his farewell shindig at the No Name. Then he remembered Wrangler's old lady on the back of his bike. The smell of her hair. He took a bite out of the apple. It tasted just as sweet as she had smelled. In the right state of mind, an apple inside jail was the equivalent to the finest banquet anywhere. Patch took the next crunchy, juicy bite. With his newfound solitude, he not only missed real food, fresh fruit, and eating right, but the touch of a woman. After the third bite, he heard a voice whispering his name. And it wasn't a woman's voice.

"Kinkade. Kinkade." It was Josephson, at the door of his cell, not yet locked up for the night.

Patch carefully set the precious apple aside and approached the cell door.

"Got the 411, Kinkade."

"That was quick. What's up?"

Josephson looked both ways before answering. "Name is Amur. *A-m-u-r.* First name Leopold. Leopold Amur. He's in from out of state, New Mexico or Colorado, someplace in the West. He's here for a week."

"Short dark-haired guy?"

"Yeah."

"Young, early twenties?"

"Yeah."

"Russian."

"I left him an apple juice and a stash of Fritos and Oreos with nothing on his account. That means he's got pull."

"That's gotta be the same guy. Man, I appreciate—"

"Listen, Kinkade. Don't trip about it. Anything for the Infidelz. You guys are all right in my book. Them guys gettin' killed, that shit's not right. I'm just glad to be of service," he said with a wink. "Just lemme know when I can do my part."

» 238   After Josephson left, Patch lay back on the bunk and returned to his apple. If Josephson was able to gather information that quickly, it meant one thing. This Leo Amur was within spitting distance, within Patch's grasp. Tomorrow morning he'd check out the rooftop during yard time. He'd use the newfound ink on his arm to get to the guy. Either gain his trust or his wrath. Not only could Patch feel the Leopard's presence, he was beginning to taste the sweetness of revenge mixed in with the crunch of his apple. This was the type of blood sport that kept Patch from going crazy in the insane human zoo he was locked inside of.

Patch lay in his cell for the 5 P.M. count. There were two counts a day, the first at eight in the morning, mainly a bed check to see if an inmate was alive and breathing. While the correctional officers counted, Patch thumbed through a dog-eared year-old copy of *American Iron* magazine, courtesy of Josephson the trusty. Also on Josephson's cart was a package from admin. Cookies. Chocolate bars. A pack of smokes, currency now considered contraband. Playing stud for admin had its privileges.

Then came the six o'clock slow yard stroll. By law and in accordance with the Geneva Convention, POWs and prison inmates in isolation were entitled to minimum yard time for exercise. Once the rooftop yard was opened to the guys in High-Power, it was time for a stretch, time to breathe outside air, Patch's first breath since he'd boarded the Grey Goose . . . how many days or weeks ago? He'd already lost track of time; its passage was now confused and disoriented.

Down the hall, Patch could hear the slammin' of the bones. Somebody was racking up a noisy game of dominoes. After a quick birdbath, he tightened up the laces of his trainers. He checked the eye in the sky, the guards from above, then quickly extracted the shiv that Big Nate had passed on to him down in

GP, which he'd stashed in the handy gap behind the sink of his new cell. He slipped it into the pocket of his denim jacket and headed out of his cell toward a single set of metal stairs that led up to the rooftop yard.

Once Patch hit the roof, he scanned the hundred or so men milling about aimlessly, a gaze of hopelessness or sheer boredom in their eyes. They reminded him of *Night of the Living Dead* zombies. Up here, High-Power didn't seem so exclusive. A hundred guys walking the rooftop with only two guards overlooking the scene. That put the prisoner-guard ratio at about sixty to one. Looking around at the camera angles, he noted that the rooftop had its share of blind spots, too. *Sloppy setup for a federal detention center.* Now all Patch had to do was score some quality time with Amur, wherever he might be.

It felt good to be out in the open and stretch the leg muscles. Although the rooftop asphalt burned through the soles of his sneakers, the weather had turned mild, high seventies, low eighties. Breathing the dry urban air sure beat the smell of disinfectant and body odor.

The blacks had already commandeered one far corner. The Mexicans had taken another. Patch picked a spot near some white guys and ran through a quick regimen of stretches and burpees. A card game on the opposite corner was dominated by a group of peckerwoods. There were a few millionaires roaming this yard, Patch figured, while the underworld kingpins kept to themselves. They did their time low-pro, not calling much attention to themselves, waiting for their Gucci-loafered lawyers to spring them on appeal or on a technicality. Was Leo Amur one of these elite kingpins? Off by himself and catered to? Patch wondered. According to Redbeard's profile, members of the Cartel weren't catered to. If Amur wasn't locked down, hunkered in his cell like a pampered don or a scared rabbit, he had to be up here.

Patch didn't recognize a soul in the entire yard. Considering his mission of no mercy, that was a good thing. An older-inmate crowd. Noticeably absent were the young gangbangers flashing their bling-bling gold teeth and chains, talking loud and getting into one another's faces. Conversely, not a lot of skinhead surf-punk crowd were around. They were downstairs sporting their racist tats and shaved heads.

Walking anonymously among the High-Power inmates were the shot callers. Each race had one, and that person wasn't nec-essarily the meanest-looking hulk on the yard. What a shot caller says goes, both on the rooftop yard and beyond, and their de-crees rippled throughout the entire multitiered institution. If someone needed straightening out, it got settled privately at first among the shot callers. Turf issues or arguments could be re-solved with a warning. If a "removal" was in order, a hit could be set up. Regardless of whose race was involved, if a man had to die to settle a larger score, then *qué sera*.

But that wasn't going to be the case with Patch and his beef with the Leopard. Patch didn't want or need anybody's blessing for what he was about to do. No heads-up. No suspicion. No ru-mor. No warning. He called his own shots. He kept to himself, a lone wolf, for that reason. Outside, he was used to the club look-ing out for his larger interests. Inside, he was flying solo.

Patch felt a shudder of loneliness, which had its advantages. He knew his risks. The Leopard was going down in the quickest and cleanest way possible. His Cartel comrades couldn't cover Leo Amur's back up here. Up here and inside, the playing field was level.

Then Patch saw a nondescript figure.

Off in a lone corner of the rooftop, not far from the cardplay-ers, at a sheet-metal table with a couple of empty chairs, sitting alone reading a book . . . the sight shook Patch as he felt the air blast out of his chest. He quietly ambled over, past the black guys rapping, past the northern Mexicans strumming guitars and singing their lonesome folk songs, past the tattooed white boys giving one another high fives, laughing loudly and playing dice. Past a couple of the "others," two Asians sneaking a smoke together. Patch walked until he was just a few feet from the young man who looked no older than Hollister.

Leo Amur was reading a ragged paperback copy of *The Count of Monte Cristo*. As he looked up from his Alexandre Dumas tale, Patch saw that his thick dark hair was tossed and oily. He had a pair of black bushy eyebrows and a dense layer of dark stubble across his olive-complected face.

Patch approached Amur and stood behind him. "You know, *The Count of Monte Cristo* was Mike Tyson's favorite book when he did prison time in Indiana."

Amur looked up, squinting in the sun. "Do I know you?" His English was clear and proper. His eyes caught the fresh tattoo on Patch's arm. "Interesting mark on your arm, comrade."

"Yeah, it is. Goes well with yours, I think."

"How do you mean?"

"Well, your tattoo is of a leopard, right?"

Amur considered the question for a moment. "Yes."

"Mine's a trap. It kills leopards. It's a good match, I think."

"Who are you?"

"I know who you are. It's Amur, right?" Patch asked, pulling up an empty chair.

"How do you know my name?"

Patch ignored his query and pointed to the young man's arms. He couldn't have been any older than most of the Infidelz's prospects.

"Who are you?" Amur asked again.

"They bused your ass clear down from Englewood?"

"What?" Amur said.

"And that bank job your crews pulled off. Man."

Leopard's ego couldn't allow him to hide the slightest trace of a smile.

"It was magnificent."

The Leopard put down his book and looked up.

"Who are you? A cop or a snitch?" he asked with a perplexed but smug look on his face.

Ordinarily, Patch would have flattened him for the snitch remark, but he put up his hands playfully and grinned.

"Hey, look, I'm just doing my time here. There's word on the yard that you called the shots."

"Look, I don't know what you're talking about."

"Helluva deal. A takeover job. And then those four biker dudes in the freezer. Big balls."

"What?"

Patch pointed at his Infidelz MC tattoos.

A blank look crossed Leo Amur's face. "What are you talking about?"

Patch found his indifference odd. *Either this guy is clueless or a supercool customer.*

"Four men on motorcycles. A gun deal gone bad."

Amur shook his head blankly again.

243 «

The Leopard eyed Patch suspiciously. "Look, now that you've had your say, leave me alone. We have nothing to talk about." His dark weary eyes returned to his book.

"I think we do." Patch's hands shook with rage as he reached down into his jacket pocket.

At that moment a struggle broke out between two dice-throwing peckerwoods on the opposite corner of the rooftop.

"Punk-ass cheatin' motherfucker," one white kid shouted to the other. Patch and Amur both heard it.

"Who you callin' a punk ass?" Those were fightin' words. A slap was followed by a swift kick, followed by a combination of well-placed punches that sent both white bodies slamming to the ground.

An earsplitting alarm sounded out as both guards on duty sprinted toward the incident, clutching their pistols, hands on their clubs. Seconds later, a half-dozen reinforcements streamed into the yard, clutching their wooden clubs and Mace guns. Patch had seen this movie before. This time he fell to his knees.

"Get down," he yelled to Amur. "On the ground. Now!"

The young man remained calmly seated, detached, casually flipping the pages of his book. A couple of COs glanced over toward Patch and Amur.

"I said get on your knees, motherfucker, before they come over and beat us both senseless."

Patch reached up and pulled Amur down off his chair by his shirt. The Leopard tumbled to his knees. Patch dug his face into the asphalt, then reached inside his denim jacket pocket and clutched the sharpened plastic shiv. He grabbed Amur by the hair, jerked his head back up, and stuck the shiv next to his jugular artery. He leaned in close and spoke tersely above the shrieking alarm.

"That Phoenix bank job was a work of art. Killing those guys in the meat locker was ingenious. But you fucked up. Those were my brothers you left in that meat locker."

The smug smile had long since left the Leopard's face.

"Stop. I'm telling you. What meat locker?"

"The four bikers your Cartel killed and left in the freezer, their throats slit, and your disgusting funny money spread all over the place. They rode for my club. You didn't think you were going to get away with that, did you?"

Patch tightened his grip on Amur's throat. The Leopard sputtered his defense, slobbering and choking for air.

"You talk nonsense. We have no quarrel with any men on motorcycles. I don't know what you're talking about. I was in prison."

The bleeding peckerwoods continued to trade punches and swipes on the ground while the COs pried them apart.

Amid the raucous distraction of the yard, Patch kept his death grip on the Leopard.

"You ordered their deaths, Amur. My men are gone. Now you're done. Kiss your ass good-bye."

"I—" Leo Amur could only let out a pitiful gurgling sound as Patch's grasp cut off his air supply.

"I'll see your lying ass in hell," Patch snarled as he held the triangular blade close to Leopold Amur's throat, drawing the first trickle of blood.

Amur flailed to struggle free, puffing breathlessly, on the edge of suffocation, on the verge of blacking out as his face turned from hot crimson to pallid blue. Then Patch loosened his grip.

"We killed no one in no meat locker." Amur gasped desperately for air. "You're talking shit."

Patch retained his grip around Leo Amur's throat, raising a pulsating jugular vein to slash. He pressed the shiv to the vein. The Leopard, unable to break free of Patch's grip, suddenly offered no resistance.

"Cutthroat," Amur croaked as he gasped for his last breath. "Cut-rate assassin."

Patch braced himself for the final, fatal slash.

"Go ahead. Kill me," said Amur, resigned, "but *you'll* never live to spend a penny of the bounty."

245 **«**

Bounty?

"What fuckin' bounty?" Patch asked, pulling the weapon away from the young man's throat. He loosened his grip again as Amur panted for precious oxygen.

Across the yard, the brawl was nearly contained. Patch used the diversion to pick up Leo and forcibly drag him by his neck into a shaded blind spot against a wall.

"What fucking bounty?" Patch repeated.

The Leopard spit out his reply.

"Three million euros. On my head. Which is why you're here."

"Bullshit."

Amur coughed and sputtered. "The Russians, the FSB. They put up the bounty. It's been on my head for months."

"You're a liar," growled Patch. He pressed his face closer to Amur's.

"And you're a fool." Amur squirmed in Patch's clutches.

Amur's revelation was strangely congruent with Redbeard and Hollister's latest findings.

"You're tellin' me you're worth a few million dead?" Patch asked. "To whom?"

"I told you! FSB. Russian government. Putin himself. Whoever hired *you*! You tell me."

The alarm stopped ringing. The rooftop yard grew quiet. Patch pushed the Leopard to the ground and stood over him. Amur got up and dusted himself off, coughing and struggling to catch his breath, so dizzy he could barely stagger to his feet. Patch was just as dizzy with conflicting facts.

"You mind-fucking me, Leo? 'Cause if you are, I won't stop at your throat. I'll cut your fuckin' balls off. Tell me the truth."

"I am." Amur was still gasping for air. "I'm telling you the truth."

Patch slid the plastic shiv back into his jacket pocket. He took two steps back and pointed an accusing finger at Amur, who looked at once baffled and relieved: baffled that he hadn't been sliced open like a Fourth of July watermelon; and relieved that he was still alive to be baffled.

"You, I'll deal with later," Patch muttered as he blended into the rooftop crowd. The young whites who had been fighting were both handcuffed and Patch was already heading down the stairs, back to his cell to try to figure out exactly who was mind-fucking whom.

One thing about High-Power. The dead quiet pitch-black nights spent sealed inside his cell after lights-out gave Patch plenty of time to ponder what had gone down on the roof. He needed to clear his head. Sort it out. The Grand Plan that he and Redbeard had hatched with help from the Rachkovs was unraveling. It made even more sense why the Rachkovs might want Amur and his Cartel out of their way. As Patch mulled his situation over in the darkness of his cage, he asked himself, was Amur a bald-faced liar or was Patch the blindsided chump? He feared the latter.

Those Rachkov bastards, Patch thought.

How could I be so stupid? Why would two Russian hustlers with political connections hook up with a motorcycle club like the Infidelz? Patch was devastated by how foolishly he'd played into their hands. The trap was so cleverly set, it was he who ultimately sprung it on himself, finalizing the deal with an egotistical willingness to go inside and do the job himself. He'd been beautifully set up and played. Like the Cartel's bank job, it was a magnificent plan. Perfect execution. Unfortunately, Patch now faced his own demise. If the Rachkovs were truly in bed with the Russian government and the FSB, what would stop them from ratting Patch out to the feds after he'd efficiently knocked off

Amur and they collected a bounty worth millions? If Patch wasn't in such deep shit, he would have been duly impressed.

Suddenly the walls of High-Power were closing in on him. The Rachkovs had outfoxed the Infidelz into bumping off the Cartel, with a massive three million euro payday to boot. And the Rachkovs got the job done while keeping their hands clean. Dead brilliant. Once the Leopard was eliminated, they could collect their seven-figure bounty and continue their shady business dealings unimpeded. No wonder the G-men were protecting Amur. The price on his head explained the gaggle of feds that Patch had seen accompanying Amur in the hallway. But leave it to the U.S. government to do a half-assed job. They figured that High-Power was the absolute safest place for Amur to be. They figured wrong. Nobody had counted on a guy like Patch to enter the mix, dupe-turned-hit-man, to assassinate the poor bastard. His head was swimming. He needed to think this through.

Patch could only imagine what the grand jury was investigating now, and why a chained Amur was surrounded not only by guns, but by suits and deep-cover State Department personnel. Maybe they were manipulating the anxiety between the United States and the Russian governments over the Grozistan rebels. Maybe on one side, the State Department was eager to keep Amur locked up and alive to piss off Putin. Remnants of a cold war that had never thawed? Who knew?

Patch laughed at the absurdity of his dire situation. Only a few weeks before, he'd been just a regular Joe riding his motorcycle, trying to stay off the federal law enforcement's radar screen. Now here he was, a guy suddenly embroiled in the midst of some geopolitical fiasco.

Patch was stuck in a deep hole, locked in a cage—a pawn in an international chess game with both political and underworld implications. He looked out of his electronically sealed cell-door window. As the walls stared back at him, and as the steel door with high-tech electronic latches separated him from the outside world, he felt like a stooge, deceived by a couple of fast-playing international sharks. The perfect plan. The Rachkovs eliminate their underworld nemesis; trick the Infidelz into doing their dirty work; and walk off with a three-million-euro reward.

Patch was dead meat.

Or was he?

A dead Leo Amur might be worth three million euros to the Rachkovs while the Russian government and the FSB benefited from his assassination. But what if Leopold Amur lived? What if the havoc that Amur and his men had been wreaking on the Russians, not to mention the Rachkovs and their posse, continued? Maybe Patch had more cards to play after all.

You've got one hour."

The attending CO shut the door to the private visiting room. Redbeard sat on the opposite side of the table, his hands folded, looking solemn. Patch and Redbeard had one hour to pull this debacle out of the fire.

"Let's start from the beginning," Redbeard said. "What happened exactly?"

"I was ready to turn out the lights on this motherfucker Amur so I could get the hell outta here. Then he brings up this three-million-euro bounty on his head, supposedly put on him by the Russian government and the FSB. That's more than three million Yankee bucks."

"Three million euros? Holy Christ."

"Unfortunately I believe the scrawny bastard. I've run this over and over in my brain and here's what I've come up with."

Redbeard was attentive. "Tell me."

"The Cartel is a major liability to the Rachkovs' empire. Assuming that the Rachkovs and the Cartel are fighting over the same turf, the bottom line is this: the Cartel is bad for business. So what if this is ultimately about money, and our guys got caught in the middle? The Rachkovs want the Cartel out of the picture. Their cause is bad for biz. The Russian government wants them out. So they both use us to do their dirty work by having me come inside here and knock out the other team's quarterback.

"My biggest concern is that if I don't kill Amur, someone else will, for a piece of the bounty. And there's little doubt who'll catch the blame no matter who kills him. Me. God only knows what conspiracy conversations the Rachkovs have on tape between all of us. With a few million dollars at stake, they could hire anybody else inside here to do the job as backup, whether I do it or not.

"The payoff for the Rachkovs is twofold. First, with Amur out of the way, they can run their operations without any aggro from the Cartel. Number two: they pick up a paycheck while keeping their hands impeccably clean."

A thought popped into Redbeard's head.

"What if the Cartel *didn't* kill your boys and my brother?" Redbeard asked. "What if the Rachkovs killed them? Maybe they ran a bogus gun deal behind Boris's back and whacked the Four in silence, knowing we'd come roaring out to settle the score against the Cartel? Maybe the Rachkovs were the ones that carved those claw marks into Boris's arm, hoping we'd know it was a Cartel calling card and go after them?"

251 «

Patch nodded slowly.

"The Rachkovs have effectively pulled the wool over all our fucking eyes. The Infidelz. The Cartel. The grand jury. We've been caught with our pants below our knees. The Rachkovs conned us."

Patch shivered at the thought.

"Something tells me I'm Leo Amur's new guardian angel."

"Yeah, and we need a new plan," said Redbeard.

"And how, and fast," said Patch.

"Hmmm. Maybe we can horse-trade some information," said Redbeard, nervously running his hands through his hair and stroking a stubbly chin. "I have a source that might do the trick."

61

A car pulled up to a strip-mall sandwich shop. The driver recognized Redbeard's ride parked out front and walked inside the food establishment. Redbeard was at the counter ordering a meatball sandwich and a Diet Coke. The man tapped Redbeard on the shoulder and then flashed a twenty at the girl behind the counter.

"Excuse me, I'll take care of his order, and give me another Diet Coke, please."

"Proctor? How the hell are you? Look, we gotta talk."

The two picked out a booth in the back of the shop.

"Redbeard, my man," Proctor said, after taking a sip of his soda, "you still sneaking through the back-alley Dumpsters and going through those dusty city-hall files?"

"You could say that." Redbeard smiled. "How are things goin' down at the paper since they moved you from city hall to the police beat?"

"Less bore and more gore. I'm always looking for a few angles."

"Well, I might have one for you. Regarding that grand-jury investigation."

"The one about the biker murders?" Proctor asked.

"Yeah, and there's a little more to it than that."

"You got something for me?"

"Maybe. That is, if you have something for me."

"Shoot," said Proctor. "You show me yours and I'll show you mine."

"Fair enough," responded Redbeard. "I need to know if you have anything on the Infidelz murder-counterfeit thing. This is personal for me."

"I might," said Proctor, smiling but cautious. "Sounds like you're cruising for the heavy stuff."

Redbeard got to the point. "I stumbled onto something regarding the hat-trick Bank of Arizona robberies that you might find pertinent. Apparently, the grand jury is trying to tie the Infidelz bike club to an Eastern European Mob crew that pulled off those heists."

"No shit?" Proctor smiled. "This could be good." He pulled out a small pad.

"I have word that the feds have brought down a kingpin with a group that calls themselves the Cartel from Englewood penitentiary, where they had him in federal custody. The jury is sniffing around about them being in cahoots with the Infidelz, but I can tell you that they're barking up the wrong tree. There's no connection."

"The Cartel? Sounds like something out of a thriller. Hmmm, that's interesting. Do you have a name?"

"Amur. Leopold *A-m-u-r*. He's the prisoner that's coming down to testify. A Grozistan rebel. In fact, they got him in Phoenix right now under deep cover behind bars."

"So this is an organized-crime thing, after all?"

"You bet, Proctor."

Redbeard took a bite from his sandwich. "Now, tell me what you know about the Infidelz murder and funny-money investigation. C'mon, dude, you're the king of the loose lips down at the cop shop."

Proctor looked around. "I heard something from law enforcement familiar with the case. I won't say which. The Secret Service is investigating a guy named Karpov as being a source of the counterfeit bills. Gaspar Karpov, some player from the Ukraine."

"What do you know about the hat-trick robberies?" asked Redbeard.

"Just one small tidbit. According to an eyewitness in the police reports, one of the Scottsdale gunmen had a cat tattoo or something on his right hand. A tiger, a panther, or something."

"It's most likely a leopard. You might want to check that out further on your end. Anything else you might have?"

"That's it, partner."

Redbeard was ready to split. "Say, one more thing. What do you know about Vladimir and Nicholai Rachkov?"

"The ex-boxers? A couple of political glad-handers. Heavy contributors. Manna for the local pols."

"You might want to keep an eye on them, too, Proctor. Could be some political scandal from those guys in the near future."

Hollister walked through the screen door at the Kinkade Kompound and tossed his helmet on a chair in the living room. Redbeard sat on the sofa and motioned him over to sit down.

"I saw Patch today." His frown was not a good sign.

"So," Hollister asked nervously, "what's the deal?"

"Things are getting . . . well . . . kinda . . . complicated, kid," allowed Redbeard, deep in thought and digesting the latest developments of his visit. He rose from the couch, walked over and shut the front door, then sat back down on the sofa. It was force of habit: what's said here stays here.

"Okay. Here's the story so far."

"Good news or bad?" Hollister interjected.

"A little of both, I'm afraid."

A jolt of disappointment shot through Hollister's chest like an electrical shock. He managed a deep breath.

"Damn. What's up?"

"This you know. Patch has located Leopold Amur, a.k.a. the Leopard," replied Redbeard. "That's the good news. He's made contact. But now we find out that apparently there's been a three-million-euro bounty handed down to get Amur whacked, with Patch inside doing the dirty work for free."

"What?" Hollister was dumbfounded. "A bounty? Like a contract? Three million euros?"

"Apparently by the Russian government. FSB. Who knows?"

"Russian spies? Are you kidding me?"

"Patch isn't a hundred percent sure it's true," said Redbeard. "I just wish there was a way we could confirm it on our end."

"Where'd you find this out?"

"Amur blurted it out."

"How come we haven't heard about this stuff before?"

"Damn good question, Hollister. And that's where the bad news comes in. It appears to Patch, and to me, too, that the Rachkov brothers haven't been altogether straight up with us."

"As in lying assholes?"

"Precisely."

"As in they're using Patch to get inside that jail facility to score the money once he kills that guy?"

"Right again."

"Shit, I coulda figured that out." Now Hollister was frowning. "Jesus, Redbeard. I shoulda put my foot down. I knew Patch shouldn't—"

"Now look, Hollister. Don't freak on us. It's important we keep our heads straight. Make the right moves. Patch specifically told me to tell you not to get freaked out. Look, it's important at this critical juncture that we take advantage of the fact that the Rachkovs are unaware that we now know about the bounty. In the meantime, I'm closing in on a lead on a possible counterfeiter. Somebody called Gaspar Karpov."

Suddenly Hollister popped up from the couch, reached over, and grabbed his helmet. "I think I might have an in to find out what the Rachkovs are up to. It's a stretch, but a chance worth taking."

"Where you going, kid?" asked Redbeard.

"Out. On the prowl."

"Just play it cool. That's all I ask."

Hollister rolled up to the No Name and cut his engine right at the front door. A bouncer stood outside on a cigarette break. He nodded in Hollister's direction.

"Nice bike, kid." A Yank, not a Russki. Hollister was relieved.

"Thanks," Hollister replied as he approached the brawny door-man. "Excuse me, sir," he asked the bouncer politely, behavior the guy was not accustomed to. "Is a girl named Valentina on shift tonight?"

"Who wants to know?"

"Oh, no, listen, it's not what you think." Hollister laughed in mock embarrassment. "It's just that I'm supposed to deliver a message from a friend of hers. He rides with the Infidelz. You know Rotten Rick?"

"From the Infidelz?"

"Rick's the president of one of the Arizona chapters. He told me to come down here. I need to see Valentina."

"Wait out here." The guy flicked the last of his cigarette toward the curb. It was after seven o'clock. "Lemme check to see if she's working now, or if she's due in for the night shift." The bouncer disappeared inside the club. Hollister walked back and took a seat on his chopper.

Five minutes later the bouncer came back outside. He gave

Hollister the thumbs-up sign. Dropping Rick's name had worked. A minute later, Valentina emerged from the front entrance wearing a satin robe over her lingerie costume. Hollister swallowed hard, taking in the brunette's milky-white skin and long thin legs. He met her halfway. Valentina wore spiked heels and now stood an inch taller than him.

"Valentina . . ." Hollister turned on the charm. "Hollister Timmons. You remember me from a couple weeks back at the party?"

"The motorcycle ride. How could I have forgotten that?"

"I figured I'd see how you were doing."

"I'm nearly done. Off at seven-thirty. How about another ride and a bite?"

Hollister grinned at the opportunity. A date? It had better be cheap, considering he had little cash and no plastic. He thought of the lone twenty spot in his front pocket, enough for a couple of slices of pizza and enough gas money home. "Nothin' too

fancy, okay?"

"Money no problem." Valentina opened her clutch bag. It was overstuffed with ones and fives and tens and twenties. "Wait for me, okay? I'll be out in twenty minutes."

"Take your sweet time," Hollister said, pointing at the beefy doorman. "I'll just kick back and shoot the shit with Rambo over there."

"Shoot the shit? Who is Rambo?"

"A joke, Valentina. Lost in translation. I'll be here. Waiting."

She shook her head, half understanding the joke.

Twenty minutes later, Hollister and Valentina were motoring out to a small Italian pizzeria, a hangout of Patch's and not far from the Nomad Delz clubhouse. As they picked out a booth, every mulleted male head turned and followed the girl. Although she was dressed down in a pair of tight jeans and a tiny New York Dolls T-shirt, Hollister's hormones were raging at high velocity. The two nursed Diet Pepsis while waiting for their pizza.

"So tell me." Hollister leaned in. "How's Arizona treating you since moving here?"

"Fine, I think," she said. "I work so much. I have so little time to—how do you say?—adjust. I'm doing many shifts at the club until I get on my feet."

"You have an apartment nearby?"

Valentina looked down. "I have place to stay."

"Where's home? Originally, that is." Hollister recalled asking that question before.

"I'm, uh, from Europe."

"Valentina, exactly where do you come from?"

The girl fiddled with the straw in her drink and wrinkled her nose. "You Americans put so much ice in your drinks, no?"

This wasn't going to be easy. Hollister pressed on gently. "Lemme put it this way. Where does your family live?"

"I come from Bosnia," she replied, relenting.

Hollister swallowed hard. The name conjured up cruel images of the war and carnage he'd seen on the tube. Hollister put two and two together. She was no cute little exchange student. The Rachkovs were pimping Eastern European beauties who were strutting their stuff around the No Name.

259 «

"Don't you miss your folks, being so far away?"

"My parents are both dead," she said without emotion. "I have one aunt and a grandmother left. They're in Bosnia."

"Sarajevo?" Hollister ventured a guess, the only Bosnian city he knew.

"Not far from there."

"What made you want to become a dancer and visit America?" As he asked the question, he hoped that Valentina only danced, hoped she wasn't doing anything more . . . hospitable.

Valentina fidgeted in her chair, staring down at the table as she spoke. "I'm here. I work. Sometimes it's hard." Then she looked up and raised a smile. "Let us talk about you and your nice yellow bike outside. No?"

Just then the food arrived. Hollister, sitting in the booth across from Valentina, divvied up the pizza and salad onto two large plates. The conversation shifted to the two of them, exchanging tales of younger and more innocent days, devoid of the hard times and tough breaks both had experienced. Although separated by many thousands of miles of land and sea, the two swapped cheerful stories of picnics, rides to the country, and carefree summer days. Hollister spoke fondly of his late father, Angelo Timmons, a flawed hulk of a bike-riding man, who'd tried his best to raise his son without a mother. Valentina listened with empathy. Hollister left out the gory details of his life, the hard times, no money, his father's wasted demise, and focused only on the pleasant memories. Valentina did the same. They spoke nonstop until they left the eatery.

Outside, next to his bike, Hollister took the opportunity to press Valentina close to him and kiss her. She was easy. While the two held each other out in front of the pizzeria, Valentina started to weep. Hollister held the girl tighter and stroked her hair.

"Just hold me," she said sadly. "I'm lonely and so homesick."

Hollister handed over his red bandanna and Valentina dried her eyes and blew her nose. Even in her distress, she was a looker.

Valentina wiped her eyes with the red handkerchief. "Can I keep this?"

"Go ahead."

Valentina stashed the handkerchief in her bag.

"Valentina. The Rachkov brothers. How are they treating you? Do they have an arrangement with you?"

"Arrangement?"

"Is everything on the level with you at that club?"

"I work hard there," she said, "and one day I hope to be free to walk away. That's the deal we made." She looked down at the ground.

"Look, Valentina, we barely know each other. But I feel like there's a connection. Do you feel it?"

The young girl nodded.

"I could use your help. I need to know if Nicholai and Vladimir are on the up-and-up."

"Up-and-up?" she asked.

"Are they treating you, with, uh, respect? Look, I need to be straight with you. If these dudes are bad guys, we need to get you away from them. Valentina, can you keep a secret?"

"Yes, Hollister." She sensed his resolve.

"Do you trust me?"

"Yes."

"Do you want to help me help you?"

"Yes." Hollister had her attention.

Just past 9 P.M., Redbeard was feeling useless. Since Patch's incarceration, most of what he'd contributed had been dull research, paper shuffling, digging, digging, and more digging. That was the dirty little secret about being a lawyer. And a PI. It was 90 percent grunt work. Shuffling paper. Ten percent drama. If you were lucky.

Redbeard leaned over and switched off Hollister's computer. Grabbing the keys to his chopper, he walked outside and started up. Engine sounding fit and tuned. Nice night for a putt. An even better night lookin' for adventure. The black knucklehead camouflaged into the night, and as Redbeard blasted his way out of Patch's long dirt drive toward the highway, he kicked up a thick cloud of dust on his way to the No Name.

Across the street from the Rachkovs' bar, Redbeard glided to a quiet full stop. Leaning over his peanut tank, he reached into his leather jacket, flicked open his Zippo, and lit up a cig. On his second puff, a long Town Car pulled up in front of the No Name.

The door of the No Name popped open. Out came Vlad and Nicky, laughing and jiving, slinging a magnum of champagne. It was obviously them. The profiles they cut in the night were identical. In tow were four lovely young ladies. Even from across the street, hidden in the darkness, Redbeard could tell these girls were tens. Stone-cold foxes for sure. These Rachkovs didn't settle for second best on anything.

Redbeard coughed as he took another drag. The acrid effects of the smoke made him wish he could quit. If only. But bad habits died hard in his family; Redbeard would die a lifelong smoker. He was hooked way beyond patches and gum.

As the pimp-daddy-mobile Town Car headed out of the No Name parking lot, Redbeard noticed another vehicle following it. It was a compact but sporty sedan. Some guy in a Beemer coupé, two doors. Like the Town Car, the Beemer was coal black. It looked sleek. After a hundred-yard head start, Redbeard revved the motor, flicked his smoke, and followed both vehicles down Bell Avenue.

Then came the boring part of PI-ing once again. The Rachkovs stopped at a couple of go-go clubs, not staying too long at either one, but long enough for Redbeard to go through most of a pack of Marlboro filters while waiting outside, camped on his bike. What was interesting was that the Beemer's driver, like Redbeard, was maintaining the exact tail on the Rachkovs. Redbeard laughed to himself at the absurdity of following someone who was following someone. A minicaravan and conga line. These boys were in demand. Redbeard kept a careful distance from both cars. Now, who was driving the dark Beemer? Cops or feds?

Just before midnight, Redbeard followed the Rachkovs and the Beemer to what had to be the final stop, a condo situated next to a country-club golf course. The Rachkovs got out of the Town Car, laughing and frolicking with the girls. Whatever the Russians and the four girls were celebrating for the next couple of hours inside the condo probably would be of no relevance to Patch's situation.

It was the perfect time to call it a day. Or a night. But then, Redbeard thought, why not shadow the Beemer?

Redbeard saw the Beemer blast off in a skid. He followed in pursuit. The Beemer driver seemed to realize he was being tailed just as Redbeard realized the Beemer's occupant probably wasn't a cop. As the Beemer headed out of the city limits, Redbeard's knucklehead roared faster and faster, reaching over eighty miles an hour, straining to keep up. Redbeard tightly squeezed the handlebars of his Harley, his knuckles white, steering it through top speeds he hadn't attempted in years. It actually felt good.

With the deafening roar of his engine, he looked nervously down at his fuel gauge. What he saw disappointed him. How could he have been so careless? Less than a quarter of a tank left. What would happen if he had to travel at this speed for another twenty, thirty miles? He cursed his stylish, retro, teeny-tiny peanut tank. Would he make it or would the knucklehead give out and sputter to a premature stop in the middle of nowhere in the middle of the night at precisely the wrong moment? Goddamn. He hoped not.

As the Beemer drove farther and farther north toward desolate isolation, Redbeard maintained close contact. He felt the knucklehead surging with power. Either he was now riding Super Knuckle or the Beemer had slowed down enough and was curious to see who it was who was putting up such a relentless pursuit.

What the hell. Redbeard decided to catch up, ride by the black Beemer, try peering through its windows, and then pass him, taking off the rest of the way back toward the Kinkade Kompound. Call it a night. Redbeard was confident he had enough gas and glide to at least make it to the station at the bottom of the hill from Patch's pad.

Redbeard estimated another few minutes before he hit Observatory Road, Patch's turnoff. The road arced slightly to the left. Then to the right. Redbeard was at one with the highway ahead of the Beemer. Kicking ass. Suddenly the Beemer surged again, causing Redbeard to whiz past the last sign signaling the Observatory Road cutoff less than a mile away. That was his turn to make it back to Patch's. The Beemer accelerated harder, coming much too close to Redbeard's rear tire. Twice the Beemer's front fender neared his rear wheel. Twice he adeptly kept the knucklehead upright.

As his turnoff came up, Redbeard let loose on the throttle, jerked the bike to the right, and made an abrupt maneuver, speeding off the road onto the shoulder, then onto the turnoff and toward the Kompound.

The Beemer missed the turn completely and accelerated down the straightaway just as Redbeard made *his* exit on Observatory Road. Then, suddenly, the Beemer slammed on the brakes, leaving behind yards of skid. The dark car executed an all-wheel-drive 180-degree swerve and scooted back south toward the exit.

Redbeard already had a mile or so lead. The road led one way, directly to Patch's. As the Beemer picked up speed, Redbeard saw his lead shrink smaller and smaller. He gnashed his teeth in frustation. He shouted aloud for the knucklehead to pick up the pace. But the presence of the Beemer behind him was growing louder and louder, halogen lights brighter and brighter. Redbeard was no match for its velocity and power. Now he wondered: Would he catch a bullet in the back?

265 «

Redbeard took a quick look behind to judge how close his pursuer was. Two-tenths of a mile at best, and closing in fast. Then, for the fraction of a second he took his eyes off the road, Redbeard's wheel began to jolt back and forth. He steadied the handlebars as best he could.

The knucklehead veered into a sideways skid until it careened off the road and onto hardened roadside desert dirt. Redbeard hung on and let out an ear-piercing scream. Everything went into slow motion. Redbeard was speeding on the side of the road. Pulling over, and with little time to downshift, he skidded and let off on the throttle. Redbeard kept the Harley up on two wheels for as long as he could, jackknifing back and forth. Finally bringing the bike down to 25 mph, he laid the knucklehead down sideways at the last possible moment in the darkness and the dust, sliding to a stop.

Redbeard heard the sound of skidding tires a few yards behind and the slam of a car door right behind him. He was still a few miles from Patch's. With no gun or knife of his own to pull, he saw the approaching man in a black stocking hat draw a gun. As Redbeard tried to get up on his feet, he was looking up into the bore of a Makarov semiautomatic pistol.

Who are you?" Redbeard and the Beemer driver asked each other in unison.

"You first," dared Redbeard. "And why are you following the Rachkovs?"

"Do you work for them?" the man asked.

"Who the hell are you?" It dawned on Redbeard that this was no cop. He saw a small leopard tattoo between the stranger's right thumb and forefinger. "Do you work for Amur?"

The man kept aim at Redbeard's forehead.

"Leo Amur is locked down in the FDC," Redbeard said, not knowing if his words hit home. "I know all about him. I have a friend inside the prison with him."

The gunman motioned with the barrel for Redbeard to stand up. Redbeard groaned as he struggled to his feet.

"I know about the bounty," said Redbeard. "Three million euros. The Rachkovs are after the money and are trying to kill your leader. I need answers. My friend is locked up inside the same federal detention center. His name is Patch Kinkade. He told me the Leopard is going to testify in front of the grand jury. Has he? Is Amur still alive? Dammit. Am I making any sense?" Redbeard started to crack. "Jeez, man, put that fucking gun down, will ya? I'm on your side, asshole!"

The man lowered his weapon and walked toward his car. He opened the passenger door and motioned with the gun toward the passenger seat. Redbeard picked up his bike and leaned it against a fence post. He walked over and hopped into the car. The Beemer started back up and screeched onto the highway, heading back toward the city.

As the sleek sedan snaked through the night roads, Redbeard looked over at the taciturn driver. He pointed at the man's right hand, which was guiding the steering wheel.

"I know who you are," he said under his breath, even though there was only the pair of them in the car. "You're one of the Scottsdale bank robbers."

The man looked straight ahead and kept on driving.

"But look, man," Redbeard continued, "it's none of my business. But what is my business is a guy named Karpov. Gaspar Karpov. Is the name familiar?"

The driver looked straight ahead.

"Look, whoever you are, I just need to be pointed in the right direction. I'm looking for the people responsible for my brother's murder. I'll see to it that Amur is safe behind bars. I promise you. I'll do what I can. But I need to know if Karpov has done any counterfeiting for the Cartel."

The driver stared straight ahead. Redbeard peered over at him until he broke his silence.

"Karpov is not one of us. He's Ukrainian. A hired hand."

"Who did he work for? Our mutual friends the Rachkovs?"

The driver nodded.

"How do you know?"

"We've had the Rachkovs under surveillance for several weeks."

The Beemer pulled into the gravel lot next to the Nomads clubhouse. It was pitch-black with no streetlights. Redbeard climbed out of the car, which rolled back onto the street and disappeared into the night.

Redbeard rang Hollister on his cell. It was just after midnight.

"Where you at, kid?"

"I'm in the city."

"Good. So am I."

"I'm with that girl, Valentina, the one I met at the No Name."

"That's perfect. Now listen. I tracked down a source from the Cartel."

"How did you do that?"

"It's a long story, Hollister, but he corroborated some valuable info for me. Dig it. He confirmed the name of the counterfeiter. It is Gaspar Karpov."

"Whoa."

"Look, Hollister, we still need to link the counterfeiter with Vlad and Nicky, if there's any connection there. Can your friend from the No Name get us any information on that front?"

"She's here with me now."

"Great. I need you to see if you can get any information linking the Rachkovs with that guy named Gaspar Karpov. He's the printer of the cash."

"I'm on the case." Hollister jotted the name on his hand. "I'll be in touch. It's better if I call you. Later. Out."

Okay, here's the deal," Hollister said to Valentina. "I need to figure out what the Rachkov brothers are up to and gain access to their office at the club. Any chance you could get me up there for a few minutes while they're gone?"

"Vlad and Nicky aren't at the bar tonight. Conrad, the night manager, closes up around three."

Hollister jumped on the yellow chopper and kicked over the still-hot engine and fired it up on the first go.

Hollister revved his bike. "Jump on. You got a place where we can hang for a little while?"

"We'll go by my place," said Valentina, "and kill some time. Then I take you back to club later on."

Hollister reached back and grabbed his helmet and handed it to the girl. "Put this on. Where we headed?"

"Do you know where the Belladonna Motel is?" she yelled over the rumble of the idling Harley. "It's a few blocks past the club."

Hollister scooted his chopper into the traffic and followed the broken white lines past the No Name and into the nearby Belladonna parking lot. The motel was a run-down hovel. A buzzing pink neon sign perpetually flashed VACANCY. ROOMS AVAILABLE. No wonder Valentina had been hiding where her "home" was.

"I'll go get my key," she said as she jumped off the bike and ran toward the office. Hollister scoped the grounds. He hoped she had a room on the lower floor. He wanted to keep an eye on his bike parked right outside. A yellow chopper stuck out like a sore thumb here. As he waited a few more minutes, he observed a squirrelly-looking white guy in a three-piece suit leave one of the rooms and jump into a silver Lexus. Slipping on his wristwatch, he started up the car and hightailed it out of the parking lot. Not a long-term guest at the Motel Belladonna.

Valentina returned. "Leave your bike, my room is right here." She pointed to a faded pink door with blistered paint about twenty feet away on the lower level. The "3" on room 31 was missing a screw and had flopped over. Inside the room Valentina had a few books and knickknacks stacked in the corner. It was a pathetic motel squat, nothing more. She was oblivious to the squalor of her tiny quarters, which centered around one double bed. Hollister hid his pity and displeasure. The Belladonna, a seedy dump for hos and crackheads.

271 **«**

"Maybe we can leave the drapes open a little so I can keep an eye on my ride?" Hollister tried to hide his apprehension.

Valentina kicked off her high heels then walked over and turned on the tiny television. She kept the sound mute as a black-and-white western lent the small room a dim radiance. Then she lit a small scented candle next to the nightstand. The bare walls flickered and flashed in the TV/candlelight glow.

Standing by the bed, Valentina unzipped Hollister's leather jacket, slipped it off, and let it fall to the floor. Then she pulled off her T-shirt, facing Hollister forehead to forehead, wearing nothing but tight jeans and a mischievous smile. Sans her high heels, the girl dropped a few inches in stature, to the perfect height. Hollister grabbed her in his arms and caressed her soft skin. He ran his hand down the small curve of her back. She had a small, but perfectly shaped apple-bottomed ass. He ran his hands up to her breasts. He felt her beating heart as she quivered under her breath, then glided his hand down to her warm, wet pussy. It was the most erotic sight he'd laid eyes on. Valentina pulled his face to hers and gave him a deep kiss. The two collapsed on the bed together. Valentina jumped on top and unbuttoned Hollister's shirt, which he willingly shed as the two half-naked teens explored each other's bodies. It was exhilarating for Hollister, far beyond the schoolboy games he'd played with girls so far. It was as if the blood was rushing straight from his brain to below the belt. Valentina continued to kiss and fondle him, taking charge.

"Whoa, girl," he exclaimed after a few minutes of making out. Valentina was now a raging nymphet.

"What's the matter? You don't like my body?"

"Quite the opposite. I like your body. Very much. It's just that we need a little protection, a little common sense."

Valentina reached past the burning candle to the nightstand, opened a drawer, and pulled out a couple of condoms. She handed one to Hollister as his eyes widened.

Hollister awoke from a short snooze. For a few seconds he couldn't remember where he was. Then he looked over at Valentina. Now he remembered. It was almost three in the morning. Valentina lay awake next to him, giving him the eye.

"Hollister, you need to visit the club tonight?"

"Jesus, what time is it?"

Hollister bolted up from the bed, reached down, and grabbed his shirt and pants. He'd just had the romp of his short life. In a panic, he peered out the window. Whew. The bike was there. Maybe the large Infidelz support sticker had helped ward away bike thieves—but then again, in this neighborhood, maybe he just got lucky, as lucky as he had gotten with this Bosnian beauty.

"Here's the deal, Valentina," said Hollister. "You need to figure out a way to get us access to the club so I can snoop around the Rachkovs' office."

Valentina borrowed Hollister's cell phone and called the No Name. The crew was hustling to get out the door; it was past closing time. If she needed to come down and pick up something, she had better hurry.

"Conrad, the night manager," she told Hollister, "he likes me. Don't worry. I'll get you inside the office."

The two raced up the street toward the No Name. Hollister waited on his bike just down the road as Valentina entered the nightclub. The place was empty. The chairs were off the carpets and floorboards and up onto the tables. The bar had been re-stocked for the next day. The club crew was eager to hit the road as the night manager stood by restlessly, waiting to deposit the evening's takings.

"I just need to pick up something in the dressing room," Valentina said to the night manager. "I won't be a minute."

"Make it snappy, V baby. It's been a long night." Conrad stared unabashedly, ogling Valentina's round ass. She made her move.

"Why are you in such a hurry, baby?" she cooed as she brushed her hand slowly across Conrad's crotch. She headed toward the dressing room.

Conrad gripped the deposit bag filled with cash and checks. A few minutes ticked by. Valentina reappeared.

"Sorry, Conrad. I took a while." She sidled up to the horny night manager and moved her hands across his body again. This time he reciprocated and grabbed her behind.

"I've been waiting for this time to happen," she said to Con-rad. "Why don't we have some fun right here, right now?" Valen-tina squatted down and attempted to unbuckle Conrad's belt. The night manager fidgeted at her purring invitation.

"Listen," he said eagerly as he fumbled with the deposit bag. "The night drop at the bank is only a few miles down the road. Just wait here for me. I'll get rid of this and we can come back and play. Okay, V?"

"Don't be too long, Conrad." Valentina pouted her lips. "I've wanted you for so long. Please hurry."

After Conrad's Camaro sped off, laying significant patches of rubber, Hollister scampered into the No Name. He pointed toward the Rachkovs' office door.

"Hurry," Valentina said excitedly, jumping up and down like a scared kid. "Let's get started before Conrad comes back."

"So, how do I get into the Rachkovs' office?"

Valentina cracked a wry smile as she extracted a ring of keys from her bag. "With these." She dangled and jingled half a dozen bones on a brass ring. She liked her newfound role as Hollister's sidekick sleuth. "There was an extra set in the strongbox, which Conrad left open."

Valentina tried a few keys on the office door until the lock clicked. She pushed open the door marked STAFF, which led up-stairs to the Rachkovs' office.

"Wait down here by the door," Hollister instructed, "and just in case somebody comes in, knock twice lightly. Understand?"

"Okay, but hurry." Valentina was scared and intrigued at the same time.

Hollister dashed up the stairs. He fired up a small desk light and searched the Rachkovs' office quarters. There was no time to rifle through file cabinets. He scanned the desktop for anything that might resemble appointment reminders or personal records.

"Karpov, Karpov," Hollister muttered under his breath. "I need to find some dirt on Gaspar Karpov."

Then he spied a leather-bound book. He flipped through the pages. It was Vladimir's—or Nicholai's, who knew?—appointment book, filled with notes jotted down in a nearly illegible scrawl.

Unlike the handwriting, everything on the desk and around the office was neat and organized. Hollister figured his best bet would be to just steal the black book. But then someone would notice it missing. Careful not to move any more objects around, he noticed a copy machine situated by the office doorway. He crept over to the machine, switched it on, and took a short crash course on illicit photocopying.

Then he heard a hushed voice from downstairs.

"Hurry!" It was Valentina. "Are you almost done? We must leave soon. I'm frightened."

"I'll be down in a minute. I think I found something. Hang in there a few more seconds," he whispered loudly.

He picked out a chunk of the diary to copy and went to work. The flashing lights bounced around the darkened office. A few minutes later, he dutifully placed the diary exactly where he'd found it and grabbed the stack of warm photocopies from the tray. He scurried lightly down the stairs. Nobody should suspect a thing. He couldn't picture the Rachkovs keeping track of a copy count on their Xerox machine. For the second time that night, his heart was beating wildly with exhilaration.

Hollister grabbed Valentina by the hand and the two rushed out the No Name exit, closing the locked door behind them. Hollister guided his Harley onto the road out of town, heading back to Patch's ranch house.

275 «

"Where we going?" Valentina screamed over the din of the rumble, wind, and torque.

"You're coming with me, back to my place," Hollister yelled to the young woman he was packing. "You're gonna get a couple more days away from that dump, girl. The change will do you good."

With that, Hollister threw the chopper into high gear and blew through the darkest part of the night just before the dawn. Barreling down Interstate 17, fresh from adventure, he wore a satisfied smirk on his face, one he couldn't wipe off if he tried.

» CHAPTER «

67

After his meltdown on the rooftop with Amur, Patch saw neither hide nor hair of the guy. After a one-day lockdown, the residents of High-Power were allowed back outside for their one-hour evening stretch. By 6 P.M., the Arizona sky was arid and smoggy and gray. Once he hit the roof, Patch noticed that the yardscape hadn't changed one iota. The same races grouped in the same spots. *Prison is about routine. Day after day after miserable day.*

Out of the corner of his eye, Patch saw his first familiar face on the rooftop yard. Gogol. *Musta been transferred to High-Power.* At first it seemed like a good omen to see a recognizable mug. But Gogol was stone-faced, walking with a determined stride across the yard. Patch grinned and waved his hand in a half salute. But Gogol didn't return the greeting, nor did he smile back. This was no relaxed take-your-sweet-time FDC yard stroll. It was an aggressive gait, and Patch had done enough time to instantly know the difference between someone simply walking versus someone spearheaded on a focused mission.

Gogol was advancing toward a specific target. Patch turned the other way and, for the first time, saw Gogol's target. It was Amur, his head once again buried in a book. When he looked up, for the first time Patch saw terror in Amur's eyes. Amur immediately jumped up and took a couple of steps back, but there was nowhere to run. He was boxed in. His back was up against a wall.

Patch's reaction was automatic. His gut told him to intercede. With Gogol now only a few steps away from Amur, he ran across the yard, risking a bullet in the back from one of the sharpshooters stationed up in the tower. As Patch reached the pair, he saw Gogol pull a black metal shank, a weapon purposely dulled and darkened so as not to throw any reflection of light in the direction of the towers. Amur didn't yell, didn't run, but instead sank into a defensive crouch, ready to defend himself with his bare hands.

Patch positioned himself between the two men and reached inside his pocket, pulled out his bucket shiv, and stood his ground against Gogol. Gogol swung his metal from side to side. It was now Patch and Gogol, one-on-one, hand to hand. The first swipe was in Patch's favor, a slicing cut to Gogol's right biceps. But Gogol responded like a mad bull, brandishing his weapon, undeterred by the blood spurting through his shirt and dripping onto the hot-tarred rooftop. Clenching the triangular plastic blade, Patch swiped again, and then a third time, each time nicking the top of Gogol's hand and wrist. He hoped Gogol would drop the metal blade and run away. But Gogol's barbed-wired forehead was furrowed and determined. Patch needed much more than a makeshift plastic blade to bring this assassin down.

Patch turned slightly to see if Amur was standing there. But as he turned, he felt Gogol's metal blade pierce his side. He felt his skin tear. Patch dropped his weapon in pain. A millisecond passed. Patch's bucket shiv hit the ground. Then Amur made *his* move, tackling Gogol, the two landing in a ball, rolling around the burning rooftop yard, ensnarled and exchanging blows to the face. Patch held his bleeding side. He could see the arc of Gogol's hand with the knife, coming closer and closer toward Amur's back. One or two good plunges of Gogol's blade, he surmised, and Amur could be bloody meat. Then Gogol's mission would be accomplished. So, without a second thought for his own safety, Patch jumped into the fray, and now three men rolled around furiously on the rooftop, a tangled mass of thrusting arms and legs.

It seemed like minutes, but it was only a few seconds. Live ammo from the gun towers bounced around the combatants. Yet the three men whaled away on one another. One CO came armed with a Super Soaker–type weapon. But instead of water, Patch felt the stream of wet aerosol Mace burning his face and the membranes of his eyes and nose. Rubbing his eyes only made it worse. He went momentarily blind, but could hear the taunts and shouts of the inmates, some calling for help and reinforcements, others egging on the three to continue the slugfest.

Then another wave of COs arrived. Clubs were unsheathed and free-swinging. One blow after another to Patch's head. To his kidneys. The same merciless punishment was meted out to Amur and Gogol. Blinded, bleeding, burned and scraped from the hot rooftop tar, Patch lost consciousness after suffering one last baton strike. When the brawl was over, Gogol, Amur, and Patch were loaded onto stretchers and strapped in tightly. They were carried three floors down to the infirmary. Amur's body was surrounded by a horde of worried and troubled federal agents.

Patch came to and opened his leaded eyes slowly. His vision was hazy. He felt a burning sensation at his side. Miles of bandages were wrapped tightly around his midsection, which he suspected was the only thing keeping his guts from spilling out onto the infirmary floor. His very first sight was Bartkowski towering over him, holding his club, his pistol dangling from his hip.

"Kinkade, you awake?"

Patch could only weakly nod his head.

"Can you hear me? Can you hear me?" Bartkowski asked persistently, now shouting.

I can hear you; I can hear you, ferchristsakes.

"Okay, Kinkade, now hear this. You've been nothing but trouble since you got here. Once they stitch you up, I'm taking you to the hole myself. You belong to me, personal property of A. W. Bartkowski." Before stalking out of the room, he gave Patch a sharp and painful nudge with the end of his hardwood club. Patch unleashed a painful groan. His lungs ached and burned. Short of breath, he felt like an army of flamenco dancers had danced on his entire body.

None of the hospital staff would speak to him or untie his arms from the side of the bed. And after Patch had spent a couple days locked up in a solitary hospital cell, Bartkowski made good on his promise. It was good-bye infirmary, hello solitary in the hole. Patch hadn't a clue as to what had happened to Gogol or Amur.

Patch now sat in the penalty box. The cooler. The hole. In complete darkness, he could talk to guys in other solitary cells, but he couldn't see them. Clad in a pair of boxer shorts and his chest tightly bandaged and throbbing with pain, his only creature comforts were a bar of soap, a tube of toothpaste, and a stubby toothbrush.

"Kinkade. That you?"

It was a familiar voice. Good God. Big Nate.

"Christ, Nate, is that you?"

"Sure is."

"What the hell are *you* doing in here?"

"Dunno. They musta traced the shiv back to me. Either that, or somebody, maybe it was Gogol, ratted me out. I know you didn't."

"Anyone else in here?"

"No. I suspect it's just you and me. They shipped the rest out yesterday."

"How long have I been in here?"

"Goin' on about two days. I had no idea it was you in there. All I could hear for the first day was groaning. You okay?"

"I can't say for sure, but I feel like homemade shit. I'm sore. I'm sliced open and drawn and quartered and diced. Did you get an ear as to what went down?"

"The rumors are flying, brother. Gogol got shipped out yesterday to some SHU"—solitary housing unit—"out of state. The other guy, I understand, didn't make it. According to your buddy Josephson, he left in a body bag."

"Are you sure?" Patch asked.

"Yeah, sure. Josephson said that it's even on some sick Web site. Pictures. Fuckin' COs, man. Anything for a buck. Why were you involved, anyway?"

"I was trying to save him. The little guy."

"Really? Because it looks like you were trying to kill him. They're never going to let you out of here, man. They're going to nail you and Gogol both for murder, brother. The little guy was a prize fish. From what I hear from Josephson, a whole bunch of government guys converged on the infirmary right after it happened. He came in bleeding, left in a body bag, escorted out by about two dozen feds. Dude's fuckin' deader than Dillinger."

"You going to catch heat for any of this?" Patch asked.

"Hopefully they'll let me out soon," said Big Nate. "I'm already getting wiggy in here, startin' to feel bugs and shit crawling on me. Creeps me out. I warned you about this. Since that guy's dead, I suspect you're in some deep shit."

"Listen, Nate, I'm gonna make sure you don't get nailed on any of this. I accept this shit one hundred percent."

"I suspect in a couple of days, they're gonna wanna interrogate you for their investigation. You can tell 'em what you want."

"Investigation of what?"

"Of how the fight, the stabbings, how it all started. Was it an ordered hit? Was it a racial thing? Was it an isolated incident, or was it called for from above? All that. They're gonna wanna know."

Patch nodded to himself. *I seriously doubt there will be any such investigation.*

Just as Patch had anticipated, a few days later there was still no prison investigation into the stabbings. No interrogation. No third degree. It just went away. One big federal cover-up. Instead, just a voice in the dark coming for both Patch and Big Nate. Patch was going back to High-Power, Big Nate down to general population.

"Kinkade," Big Nate said. "Honestly, I ain't gonna miss you that much. You've done nothing but bring me heartache and grief. But you're okay. I dig your spirit."

"And I owe you big-time, big guy," said Patch. "I'll make good, I swear. When you get out, you need to look me up so I can at least try to—"

"Don't trip about it, Kinkade. God knows where they'll ship me next. I just wanna finish out my time. I'm done with prison. Finito. But let's hope our paths don't cross too soon. I need a period of recovery from you, brother." And with that, Big Nate headed out of the hole. Poor Nate McAllister, he couldn't get out of there fast enough.

"Big Nate."

"Yeah?" he answered.

"Have a good life."

"You, too, bro."

Patch was smiling faintly as he was escorted back to High-Power. Or at least, that's where he thought they were escorting him. Instead, the CO led him a different way.

"Where are we going?"

"You've got a visitor."

Patch nodded. Redbeard, he figured. If Amur's stabbing had already reached the Internet, and the news, then Redbeard had probably come to help fight the good fight. If Patch was going to be accused of murder, then he was going to need some help. Redbeard's visit was well timed.

Patch sat down at the visitors' station, but the man sitting across from him wasn't the man he was expecting.

"What the fuck do you want?" Patch asked.

The man sitting across from him sported a cruel grin surrounding a silver toothpick. It was one of the Rachkovs' muscle, their right-hand man. He was the same guy who'd worked Patch over when he first walked into the No Name bar.

"Is that any way to greet a coworker?" the silver toothpick asked.   283 **◀◀**

"We don't work together, asshole."

"That's where you're wrong. I work for the Rachkovs. You work for the Rachkovs. You just don't know it. Man, they fucked you up real good."

"I don't know what you're talkin' about."

"They sent you in here to do a job, man. They sent you in here to take out the Leopard. Mission accomplished."

"You think I killed the Leopard?"

"That's what the news says. They reported that an organized-crime figure—that's Amur—was killed by a biker gang member and a Russian mobster. That's you and Gogol. And my boss, he gets three and a half million bucks. And all for playing your ass like a goddamn acoustic guitar."

"You're pinning this on me?"

"Hey, it's sure not going to come down on Vlad and Nicky.

They're free and clear. Hell, what better alibi can you think of? The hit happened in prison! Thanks, Kinkade. You realize, they're going to make you fry for this."

"Why come here to tell me this? Aren't you afraid I'll tell your little secret to the feds?"

"We're not too worried about that, Kinkade. Who are they going to believe? A couple of immigrant success stories, or a guy who was found at the scene, with a homemade knife in his hands, blood everywhere? You did a good job, I'll give you that. But the brothers just wanted me to come down and let you know who was really calling the shots. Nicky, especially, he has an ego. He pulls off something this sweet, he wants people to know how it worked."

"You piece of shit. You think a couple of COs are going to stop me from ripping you apart?" Patch surveyed the room, the veins popping from his neck.

"I wouldn't, Kinkade. It's just another nail in your coffin. History of violence, you know? Not that it matters—how many more years can they add to a life sentence?"

"One question, you fucking tool. Don't they need a body to push a murder charge?"

"We've seen the body, Kinkade. It was on the Internet. The press covered it. We have confirmation."

"Yeah, confirmation—you got information from a con, is what you got. Maybe you don't want to believe everything you see."

"What are you talking about, Kinkade?"

"The brothers, they got lots of spies, don't they?"

"They got ears everywhere."

"They got anyone with ears on the grand jury?"

"What are you getting at?"

"What I'm getting at is I ain't done playing this hand."

"It ain't going to work, Kinkade. It doesn't matter what you tell the grand jury. No one believes testimony from a convict."

"Don't worry. It won't be me they'll be listening to," Patch said, turning his back on the goon and walking away.

C *link.*

The next day, it was the sound of a fine crystal glass soon to be filled amply with a Château Pichon-Longueville-Comtesse 1986 Pauillac. A strong and expensive French Bordeaux.

The Rachkov brothers, now a few million richer after converting three million euros to dollars, decided to have lunch in. They could afford it. The money came in free and clear, no kickbacks, no taxes, no commission, and with very little overhead.

So let the food and wine flow. Pickled herring and boiled potatoes with dill, an assorted fish platter including sturgeon, sable, and lox, *baklazhannaya ikra* (an eggplant spread), stuffed tomatoes, and potato pancakes. Enough food to feed an army. The works.

All to celebrate the death of Leo Amur and the Rachkovs' collection of the bounty. The bounty, wrapped inside a small package, was delivered via a messenger, all in cash. Vlad and Nicky's young assistant, a beautiful Serbian girl, hadn't a clue what was inside the package when she brought it upstairs. Had she known, she might have headed out the back door permanently, package in tow, never to be seen again.

"To us, brother," said Vladimir.

"And to Patch Kinkade, the Infidelz, Gogol, Leo the Leopard, and the federal grand jury." Nicky cackled wildly, toasting the Rachkovs' sucker list.

"Eat, brother, eat," Vlad said, shaking his head in approval at the two-hundred-dollar bottle of wine. "Who knows what tomorrow may bring?"

"Amen," said Nicky. "To us."

Clink.

While the Rachkovs sipped Bordeaux for lunch, a dark unmarked sedan containing a secret grand-jury witness pulled up to the rear of the federal courthouse. There were no cameras to dodge and no crowds to confront. Escorted by one lone, armed federal marshal, the small unshaven handcuffed man dressed in an orange jumpsuit was swiftly led through a back entrance.

The U.S. attorney paced nervously before the grand jury as the witness was ushered to a chair at the front of the hearing room, before the presiding federal magistrate. The secret witness was sworn in.

"Will you please state your name for the record?" the U.S. attorney asked.

"I'm best known as Leopold Amur," the witness answered, with only the slightest accent.

"And where are you currently residing, Mr. Amur?"

"At the federal penitentiary in Englewood, Colorado, though for the past week or so I have been living inside the federal detention center outside of Phoenix, Arizona."

After barely an hour of testimony, sporting a limp and looking scruffy and unshaven, he was ushered back out through a rear hearing-room door, where he then disappeared into the bowels of the federal building. He was then shoved into the backseat of a fed's patrol car, en route back to Colorado to serve the remaining years of his sentence.

Hollister, packing Valentina, roared into the South-west railway yard and headed straight toward Benny Fratello's trucking-company headquarters.

"Is Benny here?" Hollister asked Gail at the front desk. "And I need to see Gus Hatch. I don't have an appointment, but could you tell them it's an emergency?"

Gus and Benny ushered Hollister and Valentina into an empty conference room. As the four sat down, Hollister rose from his chair and pulled the blinds shut. Benny took his spectacles off and cleaned them with his handkerchief. He sensed the urgency.

"Damn, kid. This must be important. What's on your mind?"

"First off," Hollister said, "thanks to you and Gus for sitting with us. I'm in crisis mode. Patch is rotting in prison right now. He's in trouble, and I need your help to get him out."

Hollister pushed a stack of photocopied datebook entries across the table for Gus and Benny to peruse.

"What are these?" Gus asked.

"Some private notes from the Rachkov brothers. Vladimir and Nicholai Rachkov have double-crossed Patch," explained Hollister, "and if we don't do something, Patch is looking at serious time. The Rachkovs are up to some weird stuff."

Benny and Gus looked at each other, then at Hollister and Valentina. "You mean to say the Rachkovs are involved?"

"I need to know if there are any incriminating names in those papers that you may recognize in regards to anybody that might have killed the Infidelz Nomads."

"Can you leave these, and we'll get back to you?"

"I can't. There's no time. Can you look through them now? I know it's a lot to ask." Hollister wiped his brow. "It's kinda heavy out there, and I need names now. Anything you can tell me would help Patch."

Gus and Big Benny looked at each other, nodded, and shuffled through the pile of papers.

"There's one name that particularly interests us," said Hollister. "A character marked in there named Gaspar K. That's Gaspar Karpov, who's been known to pass phony notes. He is our counterfeit connection in the Nomads murders."

"Who's the broad?" Gus quizzed, eschewing diplomacy.

"My friend Valentina here worked at the Rachkovs' nightclub. She knows firsthand what they're up to, and just to let you know in confidence, Valentina is prepared to go to the press with details about the Rachkovs running an international girl-for-hire ring."

"Do you think that's a good idea, Hollister? Is it safe for her to come forward?" Benny looked over at Valentina. "Young lady, do realize what you're doing?"

"Yes," she answered quietly.

"I spoke to Patch's partner about this, a guy named Redbeard," said Hollister. "He's gonna set her up with a crack immigration attorney. She's going to turn herself in to the immigration authorities, seeking refugee status. She'll be under the personal protection of the Infidelz, so nobody's going to mess with her. Rotten Rick, the president of the Phoenix chapter, has assured me of that."

Gus looked up from the stack of documents.

"Just running through these quickly, I can tell you there's more than a few heavy aliases entered into this diary, some heavy hitters in the murder-for-hire game. Listen, you kids be fuckin' careful with this stuff. These fellas are big-time hit men in the Brighton Beach, Eastern Euro scene. I recognize some names from Staten Island. They got these guys coming in and out of town right about the time of the Nomads murders."

Gus sighed. "Yeah, this is some pretty major stuff. Let me copy these papers and I'll mark the names in yellow." He rose from his chair.

"Valentina." Hollister patted her hand. "Go with Gus and give him a hand." The two exited the conference room. Benny's eyes followed Valentina out of the room.

"She's nice." Benny smiled.

"I know," Hollister replied. "But she's in some deep trouble, and I'm going to see her through this."

Benny took a slip of paper and scrawled a phone number on it. He handed it to Hollister. "That's my personal number, kid. Keep me posted if anybody fucks with you. You got guts, kiddo."

Patch dialed the next available High-Power pay phone. Collect call.

"I have a collect call from an inmate at a federal facility," the operator said. "Do you accept the charges?"

"I do," replied a stunned Vladimir Rachkov.

"Greetings from the inside," Patch told Vlad. "I'll bet you never thought you'd ever hear from me again."

"Where are you calling from, Kinkade?"

"You heard the lady. From inside a federal facility. Remember? It was part of our plan."

"I don't know what you're talking about," Vlad said.

"Very smart, Vlad. You know the calls are monitored. Don't worry—I'm not trying to trick you into confessing anything. But one good turn deserves another. You sent your man to tell me you played me, that you were the puppet masters. Well news flash, asshole—I've been pulling your strings for days."

"What are you talking about?"

"You guys tried to fuck me. But it didn't work. I know it was you who killed the Nomads."

Silence on the line. "I'm listening," said Vladimir. "Go on with your nonsense."

"You guys are up to your eyeballs in bullshit. You set up Boris with the gun deal, I figure to start arming yourselves for a war with the Cartel. But you paid him in counterfeit cash. When he came back to complain, you killed him, and the other Nomads. Then you saw an opportunity. You thought you could avoid the war yourselves, and have someone do your fighting for you. So you tried to put it all on the Cartel by leaving a little calling card behind—the leopard claw mark. But we didn't bite on that. So when I came to you to find out about who's calling the shots with funny money, you do the next best thing. You pointed me toward your enemy's leader."

"It sounds very clever, Mr. Patch," Vlad said. "But it is merely a fiction you've devised. My brother and I are legitimate businessmen."

But Patch wasn't done. "But you didn't figure that I was more than just a brainless thug. I made some inquiries. I found out about the bounty. And that's when I knew I was getting set up."

"And that's why you killed Amur? Brilliant, Mr. Patch."

"No, that's when I started talking to Amur. I've got a friend, he acts as a kind of telephone. Lets me communicate with my friend Leopold. Amazing what a little tobacco can buy you here. Amur and me—we struck a little deal. If I didn't get you, then someone else would. But if we could take you out, maybe even fuck up this bounty, then there's some currency I can trade with Amur. So here was our little deal—if I help him out, then he would testify to get the law off the Infidelz's backs."

"You're a liar."

"It wasn't easy. Then I went to Gogol. I knew that he hated Amur. I told him about where he could find the Leopard, and when. I would have done it myself, but too much could go wrong. I needed an out. I needed to be the hero. So when Gogol makes his move, I make mine. I take him out, and put some holes in Amur that look real convincing. They bleed really well. Hell, they'd probably even look like mortal wounds on the Internet."

"You did that?"

"Like I said, it's amazing what a little tobacco can buy. I've got a friend in the infirmary. He can get his hands on anything, for the right price. So he records the shots of a dead Amur. And the fuckin' COs and the feds play along so they can convince everyone to stop taking potshots at their star witness. Because, you see, now he's agreed to testify. So he fucks you, he saves me, and convinces your paymasters to pony up three million euros."

"We saw the footage . . ."

"So now the FSB or whoever it is, they got a problem. Now they're going to think that you just conned them out of their money. They're going to want it back. Are you just going to give it to them? And now that they've seen how flawed their little bounty idea is, they'll probably think twice about keeping that offer out there. No more bounty. No more grand jury. And pretty soon, no more Vlad and Nicky."

"It sounds to me, Mr. Patch, like prison is making you soft in the brain. Such stories. Perhaps it's the food."

"Yeah, the food here is pretty bad. But what's the food going to be like on the run? You can't stay in Arizona anymore. You guys are marked men. Stick around, and you'll probably get capped by some friends from the old country, if the feds don't lock you up here. You can sample the food then, if you like. So you pieces of shit better grow eyes in the back of your head, because there are a lot of people out there pissed off and out to get you. Have a nice day."

Patch hung up the phone. Vladimir Rachkov, speechless and pale, swallowed hard as he lightly put the receiver down.

In less than an hour, under a late-afternoon Arizona sky, a motorcade led by the FBI and Alcohol, Tobacco and Firearms, rolled into the No Name's parking lot leading a virtual army of LE that included Secret Service and reps from Internal Revenue. Sheriff's deputies and federal agents with guns drawn are one thing, but one IRS agent along for the ride is the scariest sight of all. Rounding out the circus was a couple of local-news camera crews and a team from the TV show *Cops,* tipped off in advance and invited to join in on a PR effort to help John Law sell their latest bust to the viewing public. What better video op could they ask for than busting a genuine roadside strip joint?

To enhance the reality-TV experience, the parade of agents filed into the club wearing their traditional loud-colored wind-breaker jackets with FBI and ATF in large block yellow letters em-blazoned on their backs. Their arrival instigated a full-scale exodus of clients "lounging" inside the air-conditioned No Name lounge. The never-ending card game in the back abruptly came to an unceremonious halt. Players bagged their winnings and scur-ried off.

A naked table dancer stopped in her tracks at the sight of the agents advancing toward the bar. In seconds, the "gentlemen's club" was cleared of its remaining "gentlemen." The agents took instant command of the building, sealing off the exits and post-ing guards. Once the respectable gentlemen skittered out like mice, it was nobody in, nobody out.

293 **«**

"We're looking for Vladimir and Nicholai Rachkov," announced Inspector Rance Kelly, waving a warrant at one of the bartenders.

"Never heard of 'em," muttered the mulleted barman, not looking up from the cocktail he was mixing.

"Kelly," yelled another agent from across the bar. "Upstairs. Offices."

The lawmen tramped up the stairs and burst through the door of the large upstairs office. The cops tore the place apart, and soon the feds were dollying out file cabinets, computer hard drives, ledgers, boxes of paperwork, plaques and pictures off the wall, which were smashed and damaged as they were tagged, carried out, and loaded into a van. In a few hours, the Rachkovs' orderly domicile looked like an LE tornado had hit it.

Inspector Kelly stood in front of the hot lights of the cameras. "Padlock this joint," he blustered, "and put a warrant out for the arrest of the brothers Vladimir and Nicholai Rachkov."

Kelly, a savvy lawman with media experience, paused, then asked the TV crew: "Was that good enough? Do you want another take from a different angle?"

The Rachkovs, after receiving a last minute tip-off call from city hall, were officially wanted and on the lam.

Indeed, who knew what tomorrow might bring? Overnight, the Rachkov empire was crumbling and under siege from all sides. The whole world was now after them: the cops, the FBI, the IRS, the ATF, Secret Service—not to mention the Infidelz MC, and shortly, the unlucky Russian agents who'd paid the brothers three million euros in cold cash to eliminate a man who was not only still alive, but lucid enough to be smuggled in and out of state by the U.S. government to testify before a grand jury.

And if things hadn't caved in badly enough for Vlad and Nicky, across town another federal dragnet had been ordered at the same time as the No Name was being rousted. Officials raided Gaspar Karpov's operations and found the definitive set of currency-printing plates, garnering distinctive reproductions of the twenty- and fifty-dollar bills that had been found on the dead Nomads.

The Infidelz MC never cooperated with the cops. They didn't have to. Not only were Vlad and Nicky accused of pimping, pandering, and laundering money gained from prostitution, but the feds received additional evidence linking their whole operation to the murder of the Infidelz Four.

At the same time, an unidentified attractive young brunette woman walked into Phil Proctor's cubicle at the *Phoenix Gazette* and anonymously dropped off a fat manila envelope that had RACHKOV scrawled on the front. Inside was a full set of photocopied datebook entries detailing the Rachkov brothers' meetings with Karpov the counterfeiter. Also included was a handwritten account of Vlad and Nicky's call-girl operations.

3:30 P.M. Patch's doze in his High-Power bunk was interrupted by a hard nudge to his rib cage.

"Either that's a flashlight, hoss, or you're real happy to see me," Patch said.

It was Bartkowski.

"Wake your ass up, cowboy."

"Bartkowski, what are you doin' up here with the bad boys?"

"Double shift, overtime, getting rich off your sorry criminal asses."

"No, seriously."

"Seriously, Kinkade," Bartkowski said, pointing at the cell door, "you are to report directly to admin. At once."

"What about my property?"

"You heard me, Kinkade. At once."

Patch put on his pants, shirt, and trusty trainer shoes and made his way toward admin. Or rather was escorted. *By another pimp?* He had mixed feelings about seeing Francine again. But once he made it to admin, Francine was nowhere to be seen.

"Where's Francine?" Patch asked the Mexican guard/clerk.

"You're the third guy to ask that today. Popular gal. Francine's on administrative leave."

"Vacation?"

"Did I say vacation? Administrative leave. State your name, FDC number, and your business, inmate."

"Kinkade." Patch read his FDC number off his ID card and then added, "They told me to come here pronto."

The clerk smiled and nodded. "Oh, yeah, Kinkade."

Oh, shit, now what? Am I gonna hafta fuck this guy, too?

"It says here you're a free bird."

Patch grinned.

"It's stamped here, 'assigned release.'"

"Meaning I hafta testify in front of the grand jury?"

"It says nothing about the grand jury. All I see here is an order for your release. Unconditional. Kinkade, you care to argue with that?"

"No siree."

"Then return to your cell, Kinkade, and once the paperwork clears, a CO will retrieve you. You should be out by tomorrow morning."

"Don't I get a phone call?"

"Nope. Part of the condition of this release is that it's done on the down-low. Sounds like somebody's trying to avoid the press. Would that be the case, Kinkade?"

"I wouldn't know." Patch chose not to look a gift horse in the mouth.

Patch stuck around long enough for his Last Supper, a bag lunch, PB&J minus the J, one small packet of dried-out carrots, and some broken Lorna Doones. The next morning Sarge came around and he and another CO escorted Patch to the property room and then back to admin to turn in his ID and sign his paperwork in exchange for his street clothes. As his property was being handed over the counter in a clear sack, he was nearly choked up to see his funky pair of black jeans, T-shirt, and ancient cowboy boots.

Patch hadn't been able to make contact with Hollister or Red-beard. The phone was off-limits.

According to Amur's testimony, there was no association be-tween the Cartel and the Infidelz. There was no war between the Cartel and the Infidelz. No indictments were returned against Patch's club.

Y ou're free to go," a female cop in uniform said to Patch at the FDC gate. Dusk had set in when he walked out a free man.

Then came the cheers, whoops, catcalls, and a few firecrackers. To Patch's surprise, he was met by a regiment of fifty Infidelz Harleys gunning their engines in tribute to his release.

"Kinkade!"

It was Rancid, at the front of the pack, in from Palm Desert.

"How'd you know I got out? The feds were trying to keep it mum."

"A guy named McAllister. Know him?"

"Yeah, I know him well."

Behind Rancid were the Nomads. Big Head led the rest of the remaining members—Greek, Tommy, Gorgeous George, and Caesar. Big Head approached Patch.

"Patch," muttered Big Head, "it's good to see you out." He extended a hand in peace. "Help us recruit a few more members. It was a drag not having you around."

Patch gave Big Head and the rest of the Nomads a long hard stare. A lot of thoughts jumped into his head. Like, *how dare you second-guess me and question my loyalty to the club*. But the thought of those hours alone in High-Power made his animosity toward his fellow Nomads evaporate. Instead he felt a grin cross his face. He wanted to join this army of bike riders now and find those fucking Rachkovs. Not a single willing man's efforts would be wasted or taken for granted. Patch beat on his breast Tarzan style and hugged Big Head.

"I'm FREEEEEEEEEEEE!" he screamed to the darkened sky.

He fell to his knees, causing a passing CO coming on shift to shake his head and smile. Patch couldn't remember a sweeter release in all of his jail-sitting days.

"Check it out," Rancid said, pointing to a club pickup truck. Perched in the truck bed was Patch's sweet, sweet baby, Mean Machine. After wheeling it down off a wooden ramp, Patch stood for a minute and drank in the sight of his precious friend and most cherished possession, whose two wheels had never fucked him over, lied to him, or let him down. Mean Machine was a dazzlingly welcome sight. He plain wanted to kiss her. 299 **«**

"We had her serviced while you were inside," said Big Head. "Brakes, oil, new tires, tuned to a tee. She rides like a song. Then we had her hand-washed by a bikini-clad beauty. For good measure, we had her straddle the seat and leave her scent of approval for you."

Patch ceremoniously fell back down to his knees, sniffing MM's glistening saddle.

"Better than drugs, boys, much better than drugs," he said, sniffing the seat. "I need to get me some of that right away."

Patch joyfully jumped on his bike. MM started up in a heartbeat.

"Where are Hollister and Redbeard?"

Rancid looked around the parking lot. "They should be here by now. But I ain't seen 'em yet."

Patch gathered the troops and throttled his bike loudly. She was responding better than he'd remembered. Rancid and the Nomads followed Patch, followed by Rotten Rick and the rest of the Phoenix Infidelz pack, who, like a massive herd of buffalo, gained rumbling speed until the horde hit the highway in sync. Within minutes they were tiny dots on the horizon, headed back to Patch's spread way off Interstate 17.

Patch and the fifty cycles tore a dust-storm path straight up the long driveway through Patch's spread. They were on a crusade to rejoice the rest of the night, celebrating their leader's release. Before vengeance they'd party a little. A truck was on the way, loaded down with eats, kegs of beer, and a case of whiskey and champagne. Patch couldn't wait to personally thank the two who had worked the hardest to beat the cops and the grand jury at their own game. But the house was dark: no sign of Hollister or Redbeard. Patch anxiously slid the key into the front-door lock. Twisting the knob, he was eager to see, smell, and feel home sweet home again. But when he opened the door, what he saw was far from a welcoming sight.

He saw his home ransacked and vandalized. The furniture had been slit and broken, his things were strewn throughout the house. Bottles and dishes were smashed against the walls. Ornaments and club plaques torn from the walls. Lamps broken. His home had been turned upside down. Was this the work of disappointed cops? Where were Hollister and Redbeard?

A sense of anger circulated throughout the members as more and more riders entered the front room's mess. They'd come to party. The brazen burglary and ransacking infuriated them.

"What the fuck?" Rancid asked, spitting mad at the audacity of such an assault.

"Some burglary," declared Rotten Rick.

"More like a sign of struggle," Patch said. He stood in the kitchen. There was blood splattered on the floor. Crimson footprints.

Patch's anger increased as he stomped around the rest of the house, irritably kicking around the debris. No need to preserve the scene. No cops were going to be called anyway. His face was flushed with rage as the veins popped out on his forehead and temples. His first thought was the hidden gun safe under the front steps of the house. When he checked it, he found it locked and fully stocked. He handed out two pistols, an S&W .44 and .357 revolvers with shoulder holsters to a couple of the Nomads who weren't already armed. Then he looped one Sharpfinger knife onto his belt and hid the other inside his boot. As he surveyed the room, the other Infidelz pulled out their pistols. The club was locked and loaded, strapped and furious. There would be no victory party until final victory was achieved. The troops were assembled and ready to rumble.

When respect isn't given, it's taken.

Patch looked around at the disarray in the room. *I know who is behind this.*

Big Head burst into the house. "From what I can make out, it looks like a lot of tread marks outside in the dust, and none of them are ours. Trucks or a couple of vans."

"Any idea what this is?" Big Head asked.

"I know exactly what this is," growled Patch. "It's a declaration of war."

If these motherfuckers grabbed Hollister and Redbeard, there had to have been a lot of them, Patch thought. Surely Redbeard wouldn't have gone down without a struggle. Then he feared the worst. Redbeard was probably dead. *That mighta been his blood in the kitchen, or else . . .* Hollister. As for Hollister's safety, he didn't want to go there. Especially after what had happened to the kid's father.

If those bastards split one fucking hair on his head . . .

He couldn't bear losing the kid. No matter what it took, he had to save him. He'd risk going right back to prison. Hollister was his most important responsibility. Nothing was gonna happen to the kid on his watch. No fucking way.

The plan was to send out a squad of Infidelz to the Rachkovs' possible hangouts, including the No Name, now padlocked, and their gymnasium. Another battery of riders would patrol the small Russian district near the Brighton Beach gym and the No Name.

The command post was set up at Patch's place. It was best to keep things low-key in case the house was under surveillance. Although it was excruciating to admit, while the Delz cruised the streets, the best thing for Patch was to watch and wait at the Kompound. In case Redbeard and Hollister resurfaced. If any contact was made or if any info came in, Patch and his posse could take off on a second's notice, mobilizing the rest of the Delz club members throughout the territory.

The landline rang just before midnight. It was the voice of an Eastern European who refused to identify himself.

"I would like to talk with Kinkade."

"This is Patch Kinkade."

"We need to speak concerning some mutual friends."

"We can speak here and now." Patch was in no mood for any more cloak-and-dagger. "I don't give a fuck if these lines are tapped or not. Talk to me. What is this about? The Rachkov brothers? Where the fuck are they?"

"I am an associate of Leopold Amur," the emotionless voice said coolly.

"Did the Rachkov brothers do this? They may have kidnapped my boy and I need to find them now. The clock is ticking, and I have no time to play games. Whoever you are, if you have any information, cough it up."

The caller remained icy and detached. "Take down this address and meet me there in twenty minutes." It was a well-known, busy intersection. "When you arrive, I will phone you again with another location nearby. Do not bring an army with you. Trust me. The more discreet the better."

"Listen, pal, let's drop the games," insisted Patch. "Just tell me where to meet you . . . Hello? Hello?" The line was dead.

"Shit," Patch shouted. "Rick! Big Head! We're heading out. Follow me. The rest of you stay here."

The trio burst out the front door, hopped on their cycles, and blasted into the city. It was a blazing three-bike motorcade, ram-rodding its way through nighttime intersections, main drags, and open roads. When they arrived at the appointed intersection, a nearby pay phone rang. It was the same man.

"Patch Kinkade."

"Yes!"

"Do you see the warehouse rental building directly southeast from where you're standing?"

"Yes, I see it."

"Do you see a window on the second floor covered with a white towel?"

"Yes, yes, I see it." Patch, usually the cool customer, was growing frantic.

"Come up to that location, and I will tell you what I know."

Big Head, Rotten Rick, and Patch skidded across the intersection, jumped off their bikes in front of the storage warehouse, ran through the front doors, bolted up two flights of stairs, and burst through the door of the abandoned storage room. A man in a beige shirt and a pair of white Docker pants stood calmly waiting for them. It was the driver of the Beemer that Redbeard had followed. No introductions.

"I need answers," huffed Patch. "And information and especially the whereabouts of the Rachkov brothers. I think they've abducted my godson and may have killed my friend. I'm gonna skin the bastard personally. Time is ticking. What do you know?"

The man held up his hand. "We've had both of them under close watch for days. When they were tipped off before their impending arrest, the two brothers separated. Their original plan was to meet at the Mexican border, then, in disguise, flee the country. The police and the FSB are both looking for them as we speak. But at this moment we have the lead. Nicholai is firmly in our sights. So don't worry about him."

"Did Nicky grab my godson?"

"No." The man handed Big Head an address. "But this is where you'll find Vladimir."

"Where? I'm not here to play games," Patch demanded.

"Do you know where the No Name is?"

"Yeah," said Big Head.

"Behind is a warehouse. That is where you'll find Vladimir. He has a trio of hostages. Two men and a girl."

"What fucking girl?" Patch asked.

"Never mind," the envoy said. "You must leave now."

"Patch!" said Big Head as he reached for his cell. "I know exactly where they are. Lemme lead the way. I'll call ahead to the guys and tell them to head over to the No Name on the north end. But we need to go easy. No guns blazing. There's a lot in the back. That's where the warehouse is. Patch, let's move it!"

"You lead, I follow," Patch said.

"No time to waste, boys. Let's roll!" echoed Rotten Rick.

Patch, Rotten Rick, and Big Head hurried out the door, scurried down the stairs, and raced out onto the street. The thunderous departing roar of three screaming Harleys set off every car alarm within a two-block radius.

Inside a large warehouse behind the empty No Name bar, Vladimir Rachkov paced the floor. The warehouse held the Rachkovs' liquid reserves, the center of a lucrative liquor distribution biz in which the Rachkovs' strong-armed local tavern owners to buy their booze at inflated prices. Or else.

A dozen or so Rachkov henchmen were surrounding Vlad, armed with semiautomatic pistols and AK-47s, as Redbeard, tied to a silver metal chair, began to come to. He had a nasty gash on the back of his head. His ribs were sore. His shoulders ached as his arms were stretched back to excruciating limits, hands painfully and tightly tied behind his back. He'd taken a sound beating and kicking from Vlad Rachkov and his posse back at the Kinkade Kompound. He now barely recalled being thrown into a van with Hollister and Valentina and driven away. He had no idea where the fuck he was.

Redbeard looked over at Hollister, who was tied securely in his chair, conscious, his mouth gagged, struggling unsuccessfully to twist his hands free. Valentina was tied up next to him, her face drained pale white, her eyes darting above her gag with terror and fear-fueled anxiety. The three formed a triangle facing one another as Vlad circled them, clutching a bottle of whiskey in one hand and a silver-plated engraved .38 revolver in the other. He was raving and babbling partly in Russian, partly in English, stalking the room like a desperate animal.

Redbeard glanced around the place and out the large windows. He surmised they were being held captive inside a warehouse with rows of boxes, cases, and stray bottles on shelves. A familiar giant man hovered over him, his dark overcoat draped over him like a tent. He didn't speak or move a muscle. He wore dark wraparound shades. It was the bearded man with the silver toothpick. He held a semiautomatic weapon, stationed at the door, posted like a cold-war sentry. Nobody was leaving alive, at least not if this giant hulkster had any say in the matter.

Redbeard thought about trying to talk his way out of this. Was it fruitless trying to get into Vladimir's head in a last-ditch attempt to mind-fuck him? More questions popped into Redbeard's head as his eyes darted worriedly around the room. Vlad was in a desperate state, stalking the room and waving his six-shooter. And where was his brother, Nicky? Redbeard had never seen them apart.

309 «

Redbeard felt another dull blow to his skull. He looked up to see Vladimir drunkenly looming over him, shouting, and bashing at him with the butt of his silver pistol. Redbeard felt a booze-smelling spray of spit scatter over him. Vladimir prattled on and on under his breath. He had obviously gone mental. He put down the half-empty bottle and picked up what looked like a set of tin shears. In one hand, he snip-snip-snipped the cutters threateningly, inches from Redbeard's nose. In his other hand, Vlad gripped the shiny pistol, ejecting the empty chamber and spinning it around and around with insane amusement. Redbeard didn't need a translator to know what was next. He dreaded the tin shears, but the empty, spinning pistol chamber was more foreboding.

Vlad looked deviously at the shears, then glanced at the empty pistol, as if he was trying to make a tough decision, staring recklessly down the gun barrel and empty chambers with one eye closed. Then he burst out laughing like a hyena. Vlad tossed the shears aside, turning his attention to the silver revolver. He dug his left hand into the front pocket of his pants and pulled out a fistful of silver coins. Amid the loose change was a half-dozen .38 bullets, their casings as shiny as the pistol.

"*You* executed the Infidelz. One of them was my younger brother," Redbeard said. "You set up a gun deal with Boris. Then you killed the Nomads after trying to pay them in counterfeit notes."

"In this very room. They threatened us after the gun deal. Like we're scared of a fucking group of motorcycle riders. They had to go."

Redbeard realized he was speaking to Vlad's psychotic side.

"You know," Vlad slurred, shaking his finger wildly at Redbeard, "I am just as American as you are, my friend." He laughed at his own remark. "Yet you see me as just another cold-war commie. But we Rachkovs are good, strong, proud people. My father toiled like a slave in his country. Folks laugh at us about Russian roulette. Well, I'll show you."

Laughing boisterously, Vlad loaded one sole round into the empty chamber, then let the five stray bullets fall to the floor. He walked over toward Hollister, securely gagged and tied to the chair. Vlad ceremoniously spun the chamber with his thumb and with his palm clicked the cylinder back into the pistol frame.

A layer of sweat drenched Redbeard's brow as he struggled to jump out of the chair. His ascent was blocked by two of Vladimir's large minions, who held him sadistically in place, forcing him to witness the insane contest that was about to unfold.

"So, are you a gambler, Mr. Beard?" Vlad asked. "Because I have a little game. We call it six chambers, one bullet. One spin only."

"Vladimir. Wait. Let's talk."

"Fuck talk. Let's play."

ollister now had some severe problems. His fate had already been randomly decided by the single spin of the chamber of Vlad's silver pistol. One errant round lurked in the once-empty chamber of the six-shooter. Vladimir pressed the barrel snugly against Hollister's temple and pulled back the hammer, safety off, finger twitching on the trigger.

"No! No! Vladimir!" Redbeard screamed. He closed his eyes and actually prayed. *There is no God, I know. But if there's any goodness or a sliver of justice in this cruel, demented world, someone please stop this crazed lunatic from murdering this boy.* Luck was Hollister's only ally now.

Valentina screamed through her gag as tears of fear streamed down her face. She had seen similar atrocities before. During the Bosnian civil war. Hollister remained stoic, as if he had already accepted his unmerciful fate. As Vladimir grasped the pistol grip, his finger danced around the trigger dramatically. Then he squeezed the trigger.

Click.

Hollister heaved a breath of life.

Next Vlad walked over to Valentina and pressed the barrel against her temple.

"Valentina, why did you betray me to these low-life bastards? I brought you here for a better life. Now you destroy me?"

He pulled the trigger a second time. Valentina screamed and struggled in her chair.

Click.

Valentina, like Hollister, had dodged a certain death.

Next, Vladimir stuck the barrel to Redbeard's head. Redbeard kept his eyes wide open, staring boldly into the face of his executioner. Vlad pulled the trigger for the third time.

Click.

In a bizarre twist, Vladimir put the pistol to his own head, then quickly pulled the trigger.

Click.

Then in an act of pure self-hatred, he put the gun to his own head again and pulled the trigger.

Click.

Redbeard's face was caked in dried blood and sweat as Vladimir's laughter filled the room. Valentina passed out in fright, slumped over in her chair, as limp as a rag doll.

» 312

"One shot left," Vladimir taunted. "And we know what's next, don't we?"

"Vladimir. Let these kids go!" Redbeard screamed. "Kill me. But hear this. I'll die knowing the Infidelz will track you down, cut you into little pieces, and feed you to the buzzards."

"Fair enough," Vlad snorted. "You shall have your wish."

Vlad walked over to Redbeard and pressed the revolver to his sweaty forehead for the sixth and final shot. Redbeard's heart sank as he closed his eyes. His mind took him far away. He was racing on an open scenic highway, riding the very first Harley chopper he owned. He relived the initial joy and freedom, the wind in his face and the sun in his eyes. He heard and could feel the rumble of the Harley engine between his legs.

The next sound was a loud explosion.

Only it wasn't a bullet dispatched from Vladimir's engraved pistol.

It was the sound of the front door being blown apart with a single shotgun blast, then being kicked open. The giant jumped back and sprang into attack mode, pointing his weapon at Patch Kinkade, who burst through the doorway.

Patch aimed a sawed-off shotgun directly at the giant's head, whose face then exploded into a stew of red membrane and ooze as his brains flew out the other end of his shattered cranium. Patch then tossed the shotgun to Big Head.

An army of Infidelz gunmen streamed in after Patch and Big Head, like Apache warriors. They downed a dozen of Vladimir's bodyguards in a fist-swinging, knife-wielding, pistol-whipping free-for-all. Then the two largest windows were smashed open from the outside. More Infidelz reinforcements jumped through, toting clubs, knives, and pipes.

Rachkov stood, mouth agape, holding his pistol containing the last round. He could only look on in horror and disbelief as his ranks were quickly neutralized. Vladimir's next reaction was to pocket the silver-plated revolver, turn around, and run for his life. He dashed toward the rear of the building to the warehouse area, filled ceiling-high with shelves containing boxes and crates of liquor, wine, and beer. Vladimir disappeared instantly into the vast storage space, now a defensive maze. Patch followed in pursuit.

313 **«**

Rachkov!" yelled Patch. "C'mon out. You're a fucking dead man!"

His threat was met with silence. Then defiance.

"To kill me, you must find me first."

Patch pulled one of his Sharpfinger knives, the one on his belt, from its sheath and squeezed the handle. His knuckles were white with rage.

"Rachkov. There's no escape. I'm gonna cut your gizzards out and serve them for Russian tea."

Patch felt something whiz by his head and shatter. Drops of dark purple liquid splashed onto his face. He glanced at the broken bottle on the concrete floor.

Patch had taken another couple of steps farther down the aisle when another bottle flew by him, missing his head by inches.

Patch was no wine connoisseur, but it looked to him as if Rachkov was throwing down some pretty expensive booze.

He took a look around him.

A second later, another bottle came flying from above. Patch looked up.

Vladimir was breathing hard, looking down, out of Patch's line of sight, struggling to catch his breath, scouring the shelf he'd climbed up on, looking for another bottle to fling down Patch's way. He could keep tossing bottles until he had a clearer shot at Patch's head with the last bullet from his silver pistol. Or he could attempt Plan B.

Vlad reached for a bottle of ninety-proof tequila. He pulled a handkerchief from his back pocket, unscrewed the cap, soaked the handkerchief, and poked it back into the bottle's wide mouth. Then he pulled out a lighter from his breast pocket, ignited the cloth fuse that was doused with the flammable liquid, and lofted it down in Patch's direction.

Patch saw the flaming bottle sail toward him. It landed and shattered across the concrete floor next to a large pile of packing material and cardboard boxes. The flaming liquor ignited the pile with a small explosion. Soon the warehouse was bathed in suffocating white billows of smoke. The flames quickly spread. Patch coughed and hacked as the inferno soaked up the room's oxygen supply. The fumes overcame him. He tried breathing through his black handkerchief, gasping through the thick cloud of rising heat and smoke. He was dazed, walking a smoky maze, clutching Sharpfinger. He couldn't give Rachkov a chance to escape the blaze. Just then, another flaming bottle came hurling from above, spreading more fire and smoke through another section of the wooden warehouse. The building's interior was now completely alight. Patch half expected a rain of sprinklers to kick in and douse the fire, but nothing came. Flames only shot higher and got hotter as the smoke thickened.

315 «

Patch held his black handkerchief tight to his mouth. His breathing strained, he stalked slowly up and down the aisles, counting the minutes before he would have to evacuate and allow Vladimir to escape. But rather than hunt, he'd wait. Let Vlad's frantic act of arson smoke out the real loser.

As seconds passed, it became nearly impossible to draw a full breath. Vladimir would have to come out or he would die. Patch heard heavy coughing in the near distance. Then he saw a figure running full speed his way. It was Vladimir, dashing feverishly toward a door, clutching his pistol. Crouching behind some beer cases and squeezing his knife, Patch stuck his foot out into the aisle, tripping the sprinting Vladimir, sending him tumbling to the floor facedown. Patch heard the Russian's pistol drop and slide down the concrete aisle.

Patch ran out and made a flying leap toward Vladimir. As the two rose to their feet, Vlad kicked the knife out of Patch's hand and into the flaming inferno. Both men stood up for a face-off, fists drawn.

Patch struck first and landed a hard, swift left to Rachkov's face, momentarily stunning his opponent.

He now realized with dread who the trained professional boxer was and who rode motorcycles and mixed it up in bars after too many beers and tequilas.

Patch looked up at Vladimir Rachkov, who towered over him, six inches taller and at least fifty pounds heavier. The two combatants clearly belonged in separate weight classes.

"C'mon, Kinkade." Vladimir was hyperventilating, egging him forward. "Now we're on my turf. Gimme your best shot."

Patch threw a hard right and completely missed the Russian target, punching air and exposing his right side. For that misstep, he paid dearly as he took a hard roundhouse combination, sending him into a pile of bottles.

Patch was a street fighter; he counted on the first-punch surprise to daze his opponent in order to get him through a scrape. As a boxer, though, he never had much stamina. Now he was pitted against a professionally trained pugilist. Barely able to breathe from the smoke and exhaustion, he became Vlad's punching bag.

Patch took a battery of savage blows to the face. *The motherfucker's a lefty.* Then an ambidextrous right came. *Okay, maybe a righty.* Then a few body shots. Patch found it harder and harder to absorb the blows. Rachkov had fists like canned hams, and as each wallop landed flush, Patch could feel his bones and the cartilage in his face crunching and bending, molding to the punches. His nose was gushing torrents of blood and mucus. He was no match for this Russian tornado. Crimson ooze streamed from Patch's ears, eyes, and lips.

Then came the most painful strike, a solid blow to the liver. The same punch Patch and Redbeard first witnessed at the gym.

Patch reeled, and then fell backward.

As Vlad stood over him, ready to deliver the coup de grâce, Patch desperately reached down, pulled out his spare Sharpfinger from his boot, and with his remaining energy jumped to his feet. He lunged forward, etching a scarlet path across Vladimir Rachkov's throat, slashing a fat vein, sending a geyser of blood that sprayed both men. Rachkov grabbed his neck, screaming in a vain effort to stop the flow, but it only increased. In moments he convulsed, fell to his knees, and slumped facedown on the concrete. Patch looked down and watched as a ruby lake spread beneath the body.

"Now we're on my turf, motherfucker."

317 «

Patch staggered back down the long warehouse aisle, confused whether to go right, left, or backward to exit the burning building. Dizzy, disoriented, and barely on his feet, he stumbled aimlessly, trying to find his way out of the incinerating building.

Suddenly he felt a hand grab him by the collar and drag him in one direction. It was Redbeard. Patch's body went limp as Redbeard guided him out of the blazing warehouse.

Out in the open air, Patch fell down on his hands and knees, coughing furiously to catch his breath. Heaving, spitting blood, and hacking the smoke out of his lungs, he looked over at the welcome sight of Hollister and his young female companion.

"Somebody grab Patch's bike and ride it back," Redbeard yelled above the crackling of flames. "If everyone's accounted for, start up the truck and the bikes, load up, and let's get our asses the hell outta here before the PFD and the cops show up."

One truck and a battalion of motorcycles started up one by

one, crescendoing into a single deafening roar. Like a swarm of hornets, the Infidelz pack made their escape into the night through the dark, unlit backstreets. A couple blocks away, the riders heard an approaching brigade of sound-piercing sirens converging in the direction of the burning warehouse.

Nicholai Rachkov paced anxiously on the corner of Walk and Don't Walk holding a canvas gym bag full of cash and a small suitcase. Soon a spit-shined navy-blue Town Car with dark-tinted windows pulled up. The driver wore a dark velour bucket hat pulled low over his face. He leaped out of the car, grabbed Nicholai's suitcase, and hastily slung it into the trunk while Nicky took a seat in the back. Nicky held on fast to the gym bag. He and Vlad had spoken only a few hours ago. Both men were confident that they were misleading the bumbling feds, the Delz, and the FSB by implementing a quick escape out of the country through Mexico.

The plan called for Nicky to meet up with Vladimir at a predetermined location near the border. Nicky's idea was to scoot south from Phoenix and meet Vladimir in Tombstone. The two would continue south to the eastern tip of Arizona, where they would cross the Mexican border into Agua Prieta. The brothers would disguise themselves as tourists from Texas. Ten-gallon hats. Turquoise gaucho ties. Fake passports and phony IDs. Friends would wire money once they reached Mexico City.

Nicholai's Town Car was soon cruising smoothly down Highway 10 toward Tucson as Nicky stretched his legs and lit up a Cohiba Churchill. The driver put on some soft music and turned up the A/C. After the brothers made it across the border, they would leave Mexico City and fly to either Brazil or Costa Rica on a hired jet. Once settled, they would transfer cash from Caribbean accounts to buy land and a couple of villas.

A few hours after passing through Tucson, the Town Car stopped to gas up in Benson, a tiny town off the highway. From Benson, it was a straight half-hour shot to Tombstone. Once there, Nicky would check into a motel, contact Vlad, and check up on his whereabouts. The next morning, the two would hook up and head into Mexico together. Their timing was excellent; it was a college-break weekend and plenty of Texas and Arizona *estudiantes* were clamoring toward the border, ready for cheapo beer and some down-and-dirty Mexican partying.

As the Town Car rolled into a well-lit filling station in Benson, Nicholai extracted three crisp twenty-dollar bills and handed them to his chauffeur. The driver stepped outside, filled the large gas tank, settled the bill, and returned behind the wheel. He held up Nicky's change, a ten, a five, and some ones, which Nicholai took and put back into his money clip.

As the driver started up the car, Nicholai rolled down the back window. It was almost dinnertime. The weather outside was a dry eighty degrees. Next to the large gas station was a road sign proclaiming TOMBSTONE 23 MILES. An arid desert wind blew into the back of the car, mixing a balmy gale with the Town Car's chilled air-conditioning.

"Driver," said Nicky as he yawned and settled in for the rest of his short journey. "Keep an eye out for a place we can have a meal. Mexican food or a thick steak; you choose."

The driver shrugged and grunted as the Town Car rolled out of the filling station. Before rolling up the window, Nicholai spied another vehicle and a large man in shirtsleeves with the identical build as his driver being shoved at gunpoint into another car's backseat. Then Nicky's Town Car jerked and swerved back onto the highway. A minute later the driver—who was clearly not the same man who'd driven here and gassed up—pulled the car over, turned around, and gave a shocked Nicholai a crooked smile. He extracted a large pistol and sprayed the backseat with nine point-blank shots. Then he got back onto the highway and headed north toward Tucson. There would be no brotherly reunion at the Mexican border for Nicholai and Vladimir Rachkov. Cops would later find Nicholai's body dumped in the desert outside of Tombstone, his remains half-eaten by coyotes.

Patch's eyes popped open to the smell of drifting smoke and a dull pounding in his head. He heard the racket of people moving around. He sprang up from the mattress on the floor. *Damn, I gotta get me a bed.* Patch winced. His back ached. Again, his muscles twinged involuntarily. His joints were sprained and inflamed. He lifted up his shirt to find his bandaged torso scarred, purple, and swollen, covered in bruises.

He was back home. The Kinkade Kompound.

As it turned out, the pounding he heard wasn't in his head. Gorgeous George and Greek and a collection of Infidelz had converged on Patch's front room and were restoring the house to livability.

The smoke—not to mention the organized confusion and commotion—was coming from the kitchen. Hollister was behind the stove with Valentina, waving a spatula and whipping up eggs, attempting to cook Patch and the crew a country-fried breakfast. Patch slowly ambled toward the kitchen.

"Morning, Patch. Just in time. I'm teaching my friend Valentina how to cook up an old-fashioned country fry-up. Care for some?" He held out a plate of what looked like the severely charred and blackened remains of sausage and bacon.

"Gawd. It's the blind leading the blind," Patch muttered as he ran his fingers through his hair, a jailhouse fish cut that was just starting to grow out civilized.

"Coffee, quick," he pleaded. "Oh hell, never mind." Patch opened the fridge and cracked open a cold can of lager.

While George and Greek saw to the hammering, spackling, and painting, seated at the large oak table was Redbeard, engrossed in his morning paper, sipping from a gigantic mug of steaming-hot coffee. Seated across from him was Big Head. He was hunkered over the comics section, chuckling and giggling.

"Sit down, Patch," Redbeard said without looking up from his paper. Patch set his beer down and grabbed the chair next to his friend.

"A little service over here, please, madam," Redbeard called out. "Pour the man of the house a cup of joe. Like they say, coffee is for closers. And this case is closed."

Valentina bounced around the dining room, barefoot and in short shorts, wearing Hollister's blue work shirt tied at her midriff. Her hair was piled up high with one of those plastic sticks that resembled a chopstick stuck in the back. She scampered over toward Patch with a steaming coffeepot and a mug. She poured a cup, hovering over his shoulder as he took his first caffeinated sip of the morning. Patch looked up at Hollister's new squeeze. He had to admit, she looked damned cute. He wished he could feel the same about her morning brew.

"So?" she asked anxiously.

"So?"

"My first pot of coffee. I made it! You like?"

"Mmm, not bad." It was terrible, actually, and tasted worse than battery acid.

Valentina ran back to the kitchen, giggling.

"Now that we've mastered coffee, sausage, and bacon, we move on to biscuits, eggs, and home fries. How do you guys want your eggs?" asked Hollister.

"Cooked," Patch said drily. He looked over at Redbeard and grimaced.

Hollister was grinning. "A few more lessons, Valentina, and maybe we can get you a job at Luke's, my fave diner down the road. We eat there a lot, don't we, Patch?"

Patch cringed. "So far."

"Gee." Redbeard chuckled, feigning innocence, and then holding up the newspaper. "It says here that there was a four-alarm warehouse fire adjacent to the No Name bar. The police are stumped. They suspect arson. Anybody here know anything?"

"I know nothing," said Valentina. Then she smiled and turned around and gave Hollister a hug. "Nothing."

Patch pointed his coffee cup at a stuffed canvas bag sitting in the corner of the room. "Where did this come from?" He looked inside. "Holy shit!"

"It appeared on the front porch. I found it this morning," Hollister said. "Check it out. I was waiting for you to notice it."

The bag was filled with American greenbacks, every denomination. It could have been a couple hundred gees. And a bottle of vodka. According to the label, Grozistan's finest.

"I think I can figure out what to do with that," said Redbeard. "I got a few friends who can launder this dough for us."

"Us?"

"Okay, you."

"Take a few grand for yourself, Redbeard. PI fees. Then I wanna get some of this money over to Ski and Kemp, who acquired the lost guns," said Patch. "To cover their asses. The Infidelz don't need anyone burned. No reason why they should be hanging out there any longer than they already have. Just be careful, Mr. Beard. Don't get busted changing that stuff. I got debts to pay."

"Amen," Hollister added. "And we don't need any more family members sitting in jail."

"Speaking of debts, Redbeard," said Patch. "I owe you big-time. The Infidelz could use a mind like yours to join the

Nomads chapter. Hell, I'll stand for you personally. Can you picture yourself as a prospect for a while?"

"I could live with that."

"Then I'll drink to it," Patch said, raising up his coffee mug. "To the family." The rest of the room, including the Nomad workmen, chimed in and raised their cans, bottles, glasses, and cups.

"To the family."

"So whaddaya say," Patch asked, "we go out for a ride and tear up a little desert countryside this morning? Everybody. You guys put your tools down; you're coming, too."

"Sounds like a plan," Redbeard said.

Everybody rose from the table.

"Oh, and one more thing, partner." Patch turned to Redbeard. "You never did tell us how you got yer nickname, since you don't have a lick of red hair on your head or chin."

"Funny you should put it that way," Redbeard said sheepishly. "My given name is actually Herbert Howard Victor Rice the Third."

325 «

"So how the hell do you get Redbeard out of Herbert Howard Victor whatever?"

"Welllll, both of my ex-wives were redheads. I got the nickname because of a fondness for a certain fine part of their female anatomy. It sorta stuck. Hence the nickname Redbeard."

The room broke into laughter.

"Say no more," Patch announced to the room. "Just toss me a biscuit, will ya, Herbert? Now let's get out and fire up those bikes and hit the dusty trails."